PENGUIN CANADA

THE UNFORTUNATE MARRIAGE
OF AZEB YITADES

NEGA MEZLEKIA was born in Ethiopia. A professional engineer with degrees from Addis Ababa University, the Wageningen University in the Netherlands, the University of Waterloo, and McGill University, he now lives in Toronto. His memoir, *Notes from the Hyena's Belly*, received international praise and won the Governor General's Award for Non-fiction. His writing has received international acclaim and has been compared by critics to that of Gabriel García Márquez, Ben Okri, Wole Soyinka, and Isabel Allende.

ALSO BY NEGA MEZLEKIA

Notes from the Hyena's Belly

The God Who Begat a Jackal

To Janet

Nega Mezlekia (signature)

The Unfortunate Marriage of Azeb Yitades

NEGA MEZLEKIA

PENGUIN
CANADA

PENGUIN CANADA

Published by the Penguin Group

Penguin Group (Canada), 90 Eglinton Avenue East, Suite 700, Toronto, Ontario, Canada
M4P 2Y3 (a division of Pearson Canada Inc.)

Penguin Group (USA) Inc., 375 Hudson Street, New York, New York 10014, U.S.A.
Penguin Books Ltd, 80 Strand, London WC2R 0RL, England
Penguin Ireland, 25 St Stephen's Green, Dublin 2, Ireland (a division of Penguin Books Ltd)
Penguin Group (Australia), 250 Camberwell Road, Camberwell, Victoria 3124, Australia
(a division of Pearson Australia Group Pty Ltd)
Penguin Books India Pvt Ltd, 11 Community Centre, Panchsheel Park, New Delhi – 110 017,
India
Penguin Group (NZ), cnr Airborne and Rosedale Roads, Albany, Auckland 1310, New Zealand
(a division of Pearson New Zealand Ltd)
Penguin Books (South Africa) (Pty) Ltd, 24 Sturdee Avenue, Rosebank, Johannesburg 2196,
South Africa

Penguin Books Ltd, Registered Offices: 80 Strand, London WC2R 0RL, England

First published 2006

1 2 3 4 5 6 7 8 9 10 (WEB)

Copyright © Nega Mezlekia, 2006

Manufactured in Canada.

LIBRARY AND ARCHIVES CANADA CATALOGUING IN PUBLICATION

Mezlekia, Nega, 1958–
The unfortunate marriage of Azeb Yitades / Nega Mezlekia.

ISBN-13: 978-0-14-305306-4
ISBN-10: 0-14-305306-X

1. Ethiopia—Fiction. I. Title.

PS8576.E97U54   2006   C813'.6   C2005-907769-7

Visit the Penguin Group (Canada) website at **www.penguin.ca**

Special and corporate bulk purchase rates available; please see
www.penguin.ca/corporatesales or call 1-800-399-6858, ext. 477 or 474

ሳይደግስ አይጣላም፡፡

CONTENTS

AUTHOR'S NOTE

*A*s a young boy, I spent some of my school breaks visiting my mother's cousins in the eastern highlands of Ethiopia, hundreds of kilometres away from my dusty hometown, Jijiga. The parish priest in this Christian enclave was reverently addressed as *Yeneta,* a derivative of "My Lord." What I learned from him and his extended family, coupled with my own research, has formed the basis for this work. I hasten to add, however, that none of the characters in this book bear any resemblance to either Yeneta or the good people of Kuni, the village in which he lived.

The historical figures, however, are real; the events, verifiable. The setting of this work, the village of Mechara, does exist and is described here from memory undermined by twenty-year-old nostalgia. I had the privilege of visiting Mechara before the all-season highway brought unwanted outsiders in droves, and before the locals began to lose their unique identity along with the pristine beauty of their homeland.

FOREIGNERS OFTEN REFER to the Ethiopian Orthodox Church as Coptic. However, that term correctly refers to the Christian church of Egypt. The Ethiopian Orthodox Church differs in its rites and practices not only from its Egyptian counterpart but also from other so-called Oriental churches—the Greek Orthodox Church and the eastern and central European churches.

Though Christianity got a foothold in Ethiopia (formerly known as Abyssinia) as early as the fourth century AD, it did not find a squeaky clean home. As with all new faiths, it had to adopt some of the existing rituals. For instance, the ceremonies surrounding childbirth and the practice of circumcision in the guise of baptism, both described in detail in this narrative, are a legacy of the heathen past. The way Ethiopians celebrate Christmas may also appear baffling. It should be noted, however, that the Christmas tree adorning many Western homes was also borrowed from pagan practices, in this case those of early Germanic peoples.

The Ethiopian Orthodox Church, like its Coptic counterpart, employs the Julian calendar, as opposed to the Gregorian calendar used by Western countries, making it difficult to draw parallels between corresponding liturgical festivals. Orthodox Christians, for instance, usher in Christmas a full two weeks after their Western cousins. The dates cited in this work are in the Gregorian calendar.

ETHIOPIA WAS REFERRED to as Abyssinia, mostly by Westerners, until approximately the Second World War. As both names are used interchangeably in available references, I have deemed it prudent to do the same.

No attempt has been made to find the English equivalent of some of the local terms, partly because to do so would have stripped the narrative of its native qualities. Also, in most cases, it would have been a very difficult task. When a parish priest is addressed as *Abatae,* for instance, it means "My Father," but when abbreviated as the title *Aba,* it has a less intimate meaning. Women are often referred to as *Etiye,* which means "sister," but not with the same sentiment as when the word is used to address a nun.

The pervasive sex trade may be jarring to Western sensibilities. However, it is part of the social fabric of Ethiopia, and I have tried to present it without undue sentimentality.

PROLOGUE

*I*solated from the rest of the country by a formidable mountain fastness, a dense tropical forest, and the absence of modern transportation, the village of Mechara was, in 1961, home to Aba Yitades, the parish priest; his three daughters, Genet, Beletu, and Azeb; his likeable and often wistful wife, Werknesh; and his five thousand parishioners. They were all descendants of the early Christian settlers who, the century before, had fanned out from their ancestral homeland in the central and northern highlands, following their conquering emperor.

Azeb, Aba Yitades' youngest daughter, turned nine in 1961. Birthdays were seldom celebrated in Mechara, but that year a mysterious illness had descended on the community, causing tufts of wool to fall off the sheeps' backs. Since the markets had shunned the ghostly flock entirely, and no form of herbal potion or prayer was of help, mutton came to supplement the daily fare; birthday celebrations became a consolation for slaughtering a treasured beast.

Azeb believed her birthday entitled her to special treatment. She edged towards her oldest sister, Genet, who sat in the shade of a *zegba* tree in the family compound, cooking parts of the animal that couldn't be saved for another day. In a large pot simmered the sheep stomach and tongue; hanging above the open flame were the animal's testicles.

"May I have a 'forbidden fruit' today?" Azeb pleaded.

"You know very well the 'forbidden fruit' are for men," replied Genet, not without a pang of guilt for denying her baby sister her one birthday request.

Testicles of sheep and goats were believed to have aphrodisiac qualities and were to be consumed by men only. On women, the balloon-like organ had the most undesirable effects. Genet could think of no fewer than three women—two of them right there in Mechara—who, having eaten the "forbidden fruit" in their formative years, had adopted the mannerisms of men, talking and brawling like them.

Azeb watched the mysterious organs sweat under the searing heat. Tiny bubbles crusted on the white skin and rolled into the fire below, where they were greeted with mild applause. When Genet turned away momentarily to fetch a piece of firewood, Azeb snatched the organs and darted out of the compound, crying, "Testicles, I've got myself testicles." She dropped them when her skin began to singe, then picked them up. "Testicles," she continued to cry. "I've got myself testicles."

Azeb took her acquisition to a hideout by the river. With a twig, she poked eagerly at her spoil. Tiny flakes of meat peeled off, and she slid them into her mouth. "It is not ripe," she pronounced. Realizing that she wasn't talking about a green mango, she corrected herself: "It is watery." Her curiosity sated, she tossed the half-eaten morsel away. Then the gravity of her mistake dawned on her, and she began to cry.

Dusk settled over the river, and the rhythmic flow of the water gave way to a chorus of rival birds. Azeb heard her name called in the distance and raised her head to investigate. Shuffling through the waters in her direction were her two older sisters and a visiting deacon. Azeb was spared a well-deserved reunion with her father's belt that day because of her birthday. But the memory continued to haunt her.

BOOK I

*Passing of
the Neck-Cord*

1

A REBELLIOUS CHILD

Werknesh had been in labour for two days and two nights when she finally conceded defeat and sought the assistance of a midwife. Having given birth to two children on her own before, she had been lulled into believing that midwives were for weaklings. Perhaps the baby inside her had grown accustomed to the warmth of her womb, or maybe the six fallow years since her last travail had narrowed her birth canal. Whatever the reason, this child couldn't be persuaded to emerge.

"This may be the baby boy you dreamt of," the midwife told Aba Yitades, the baby's father, as he chanted prayers at the doorstep.

"May your predictions come true!" he said, bowing his head a little.

"The last time a childbirth took so long, it was because they were twin boys," she went on, encouraged. Her mind raced to invent a remote village where she might have participated in such a childbirth before curiosity overcame the would-be father of a son and he asked for difficult details.

"Bless you. That would certainly make up for my past disappointments," was all Aba Yitades said, however. His eyes moistened in anticipation.

"I've heard it said in foreign countries that when a baby takes so long to emerge, it is considered a sure sign of his future rise to eminence." She was now unstoppable.

"May your spit turn into honey!"

"Such a boy is sure to grow up to be a famed conqueror or valiant warrior."

"May you eat butter all your life!"

"At the very least, he could become an abbot."

"I wouldn't call that unsuccessful, but this is no time for a debate."

The midwife was saved from her restless tongue by the heart-rending cries of the newborn. She dashed inside to join a small group of women who had gathered by the new mother's bedside, while Aba Yitades, along with a few of his male friends, waited outside as tradition required, his breath in check, until the gender of the newborn was announced by the cry of joy emanating from the birth chamber. Five ululates indicated the birth of a baby boy; three, a baby girl.

"One, two, three," the men counted in unison. They collectively gasped in hope, but no more cries were heard.

LIKE ALL BABIES, Azeb was a bundle of joy. Werknesh had taken the appropriate care when she placed a touch of butter in the baby's mouth before an hour had passed after the birth. The young mother had also followed the proper Christian practices when, exactly a week after the birth, she emerged at dawn with the baby in one arm and a knife in the other. She sat and gazed upon the sun, and showed the sun to the baby, before retreating indoors. A piece of iron had never left her bedside during all those days. The iron—which might be a knife, a sickle, a chain, or simply the broken handle of a frying pan—warded off evil spirits and kept Satan at bay. Aba Yitades had done his duties as father of the newborn and confessor of the family when, seven days after the birth, he aspersed the house and the birth chamber with holy water. Things didn't go awry at the priest's household until the circumcision.

Boys are circumcised on precisely the seventh day, girls on the fifth day. Azeb, however, didn't see the blessed knife until two weeks had elapsed; the midwife had been either too busy assisting childbirths or too consumed by alcohol to attend to the unglamorous task of removing a piece of living flesh.

Azeb wasn't baptized according to the Books, either. A male child is raised up to Christianity on his fortieth day, a female on her eightieth. Azeb was brought to church on the exact date, it is true. Her mother had taken pains to plait for her a neck-cord from three coloured strings—symbolic of the Trinity. In much of Ethiopia the practice of wearing a neck-cord had been abandoned after the last protracted battle against Muslim crusaders had been won the century before, and it was no longer necessary to identify one's friends and foes by a visual symbol; but the tradition lingered in Mechara, saved by the village's insularity.

Before the birds twittered at dawn, Azeb was brought to church by her mother—with her godmother in tow—and was taken to the Door of Salutation, where they all waited in line. There were eight other children to be raised up that day, five boys and three girls. The assistant priest placed the neck-cords of all those to be baptized in the Book of Christening, from which he read throughout the sermon. Azeb's turn soon arrived, and she was brought to the officiating priest, her father.

Aba Yitades hung the neck-cord over the crucifix that he clutched in his right hand. Raising the cross over the basin of holy water, he blessed the neck-cord before slipping it over Azeb's head. Confirmation followed immediately after, as Azeb was anointed on the forehead, ears, lips, soles of her feet, and shoulders. The incident that troubled Aba Yitades years later didn't take place until after the Eucharist service. Instead of taking the baptized girl through the south exit, which was reserved for women and girls, Werknesh committed the indefensible mistake of exiting through the north door—the one meant for men!

AZEB HAD FEW CLOSE FRIENDS before the age of nine. The daughter of a priest was seldom a playmate of choice for many families, because words that slipped out of the mouths of the innocent often found their way to the ears of grown-ups, and the neighbours didn't wish their guarded secrets and sins to be known to Aba Yitades without their consent.

When she was not gathering firewood or dashing to the supply store to purchase salt and cooking oil, Azeb would be seen tagging behind her sisters. At the age of six, she learned to collect water from the stream, balancing on the crown of her head a bucket half her size. The metal container had become an extension of herself, and she often stopped on the way home to snatch a piece of gossip, to scratch an itch, or to remove a twig that had stung her bare foot, all without spilling a drop of water.

Saturday was laundry day at the preacher's home, as in much of Mechara, and at an early age Azeb carried her own load to the river. On the way, she would pause to inquire if any elderly neighbours had a piece of cloth that required an urgent rinse. "Etiye [Sister] Zewditu," she would call out over the racket of guard dogs, "I'm headed for the river. Do you have laundry to be done?"

"No, thank you," the neighbour would reply, adding, "What a fine girl that priest is raising."

Sometimes a neighbour might have a soiled head scarf, a stained tablecloth, or an everyday *netela* that required immediate attention. "Make sure you stay upstream from Ato Bereket's women," whispered a cautious widow. "The family might be coming down with syphilis, and I don't want to share their lot." Azeb's reward for being helpful was a simple "Bless you."

Azeb wasn't fond of kitchen chores, but Werknesh made sure that her youngest daughter learned the culinary skills without which she could not mature into proper womanhood. Even though only 180 fast days were observed in Aba Yitades' household (there were 250 fast days, but only 180 were binding), a feast day marking the end of a fast held a special significance. All over Mechara, family kitchens were moved outdoors on a feast day. Not only was it necessary to have proper ventilation for the unusually large number of fires lit for the occasion, it was also imperative that neighbours knew who could afford to eat meat.

Chicken feathers were strewn around, and animal hides laid out, attracting not only clouds of annoying flies but also the attention of passersby. Those households that could not afford a daily meal, much less a lamb or chicken, were especially active on feast days. Their pots were the largest and the last to come off the fire. "She is boiling empty water again," snickered those women who spied through the fence-gaps and failed to detect evidence of a slaughtered animal.

Aba Yitades had never been reduced to boiling empty water, bless Saint George. With his outdoor kitchen set close to the fence, the aroma of clarified butter and sizzling meat drifted through the village. If a passerby pretended not to have noticed the feast, Aba Yitades would think nothing of prodding him. "Wish you good health," he would greet the insulting fellow. "A meal is to be shared with God's children—would you like to come over for dinner later today?" Such an invitation was taken as a sugar-coated slight.

AZEB'S GRASP of cooking was put to the test at the Easter banquet. The fifty-four-day fast—during which all good Christians abstained from eating animal products—was winding down. Werknesh selected a good rooster from the family flock—the traditional sacrifice for the occasion. On Easter Saturday, smoke rose high in Aba Yitades' front yard, as in much of Mechara, as preparation of the Reception meal got under way in earnest.

Azeb watched with rapt attention as her mother defeathered the slaughtered rooster, washed it in lemon-scented water, and dusted it with *shiro* powder before breaking the bird into small pieces. A clay pot full of onions simmered over a fire. After adding a generous amount of powdered red pepper and some choice spices to the pot, Werknesh handed the stirring stick to Azeb.

"Make sure that it doesn't stick to the bottom," she cautioned, "or else I'll skin you alive."

Azeb's true trial of the day didn't begin until salt was added to the mixture. Since sampling the buttered stew was out of the question because of the ongoing fast, and adding salt at the dinner table was proof of the cook's incompetence, the only way of verifying the meal's readiness was to sniff the aroma. Werknesh didn't take the unnecessary risk of asking her trainee to salt the family cauldron. Instead, she ladled a serving of the mixture into a small pot and handed it to Azeb, telling her to salt her own portion.

At the first rooster's crow on Easter Sunday, families all over Mechara got out of bed eager to break the long fast. Gunfire erupted as anxious villagers made sure that no one overslept. (In the nation's capital, a cannon announced the event.) The Easter banquet was one of the rare occasions when a family sat at a dinner table together and shared the feast without regard to age or gender. In Aba Yitades' home, however, there was a slight change to the tradition. While the rest of the family members shared the stew from the main pot, Azeb was made to eat her own cooking.

Her face twitched at the overpowering taste of the salt. She reached for the carafe, but Werknesh slapped her hand, since drinking water at the dinner table was unacceptable for a child. Genet shifted in her seat, feeling her baby sister's agony, but catching her father's reproving gaze, she quickly simmered down.

"I'm not hungry," was Azeb's predictable excuse, but Werknesh, who had already raised two daughters, was too experienced to fall for it. And so Azeb was momentarily poisoned by her own cooking.

At first Azeb didn't fare any better at baking *injera*—pancake-like, coarsely textured bread made from sorghum or *teff* flour. A well-made *injera* is half a metre in diameter and has tiny pores—or "eyes"—evenly distributed over its surface. Azeb's, however, came out with its eyes almost closed, or its edges burnt and curled up. "I won't allow you to be the first woman in this household to garner ridicule," Werknesh lamented. "A family's name is only as good as the *injera* it bakes." When Azeb's *injera* came out "blind" once too often, her mother tossed it into the ash and ordered Azeb to eat it.

"I don't want to," Azeb protested childishly.

"Someone has to," was Werknesh's curt response. "The batter isn't made of dirt."

"Please, leave her alone," Genet pleaded. "She's only a child."

"She is not child enough not to eat *injera*," Werknesh snapped back.

Azeb weighed her options very carefully and decided to do the most appropriate thing: she sprang out of her seat and darted out of the kitchen, out of the compound, and into the bush. At nightfall, when she came home escorted by her godmother, Etiye Hiywet, she faced not the wrath of her mother, as she had expected, but the solemn face of Aba Yitades. The family bible lay open before him.

"What does Deuteronomy teach us about a rebellious child?" he said, with a faraway look in his eyes. His slender fingers kneaded his long beard. Though Aba Yitades didn't address anyone specifically, everyone knew that it was Azeb he expected to field his question. She sat still between Etiye Hiywet and Genet, eyes wide open, terrified to hazard a guess since she was sure that, should her answer prove wrong, it might eclipse her earlier sin.

"It teaches us," Aba Yitades answered for the family, "that 'If a man has a stubborn and rebellious child who disobeys its parents, then ... the townsmen shall stone the child to death.'"

Azeb gulped. Genet shifted in her seat; she slipped her hand behind her baby sister to steady her. Etiye Hiywet remained unruffled; the Scriptures held few surprises for her.

"What does the Fifth Commandment say?" Aba Yitades continued.

"Honour your father and mother," responded all three girls in perfect unison.

"What does Hebrews chapter 12, verse 8 tell us about child discipline?" he quickly followed up. Before anyone had a chance to digest the question, he provided the answer: "It tells us, 'If you are not disciplined, then you are illegitimate children.'" He proceeded to draw out his belt. "'No discipline seems pleasant at the time, but painful. Later on, however, it produces a harvest of righteousness and peace for those who have been trained by it.'"

"Aba Yitades," Etiye Hiywet finally spoke, "this is throwing dirt in my eyes. Not only am I an elder, but I practically raised you, as well."

"This is a matter of the Scriptures," Aba Yitades retorted.

"I will carry a billet of wood upon my shoulder if I must, and beg for your forgiveness, but you are not going to touch this child before my eyes." Symbolic of the Cross that Christ carried to the execution ground, a billet of wood was sometimes used by intercessors to elicit sympathy. The godmother knew that Aba Yitades frowned upon the practice.

"No one tells me what to do in my own household."

"Well, I beg of you in the name of Saint George of Mechara."

"Leave Saint George out of this."

Aba Yitades closed the door behind the snubbed godmother before introducing his youngest daughter to the fiery truth of his faith. Azeb was christened as a grown-up at the age of eight; she no longer answered to her mother for her infractions, but to her father. She came to recognize the Scriptures, chapters and verses, not for the lofty promises they espoused, but for the wrathful retributions they unleashed.

AZEB BECAME EVEN MORE FAMILIAR with her father's brand of discipline when he singled her out to be his personal attendant. Each morning, she got up at dawn to start the kitchen fire. The aroma of roasting coffee drifted through the room—which served as kitchen, storehouse, and the family's sleeping quarters—and stirred members of the household back to life. She took the roasted coffee outside to grind. With all her might she lifted the wooden pestle high above her head and landed it squarely in the mortar. The rhythmic thud reverberated through the still morning and awakened the neighbours.

While her father greeted the new day with rolling prayers from the warmth of his bed, she heated up water for him to wash. With a metal basin in one hand and a jar of lukewarm water in the other, she helped him clean his face. She served him breakfast in bed before formally inviting the neighbours for the early morning coffee ceremony—the first of the day's three.

Mild greetings were exchanged between the neighbours. Some told their dreams of the night before as they nibbled at the snack from the side basket, while others sat visibly anxious until the first round of coffee was served and someone read the fortunes of the new day from the coffee dregs in their cup.

"Expect a visitor," read one of the coffee cups on a Saturday morning.

"A winding road lies ahead of you," read another.

"Good fortune is in your stars," pronounced a newly purchased cup, cheering up a one-eyed hawker who had sat on the edge of her stool. Her usual cup had been broken and she was uncertain of what the replacement held.

Aba Yitades looked on, his contempt for his neighbours' superstitions clearly written on his face. He had long since forbidden his wife to indulge in coffee-cup reading, but could do nothing to discourage his neighbours from the practice. He had removed all vestiges of the heathen past by methodically uprooting suspicious seedlings from his front yard before they matured into sacred trees, demanding prayers and sacrifices. Even spirits of the family ancestors were not spared the axe. Werknesh never consulted her grandmother's ever-protective spirits in cases of pressing feminine matters—at least not within earshot of her husband.

After the third round of coffee was served and the neighbours went their separate ways, Azeb cleaned up the coffee mugs, and after a quick breakfast she followed her father to church. The priest seldom returned home for lunch, so she carried a small basket of snacks for him—usually leftovers from his breakfast—and a bottle of home-brewed *tella*. The bottle, tightly wrapped in rings of string, had been left standing in moist sand throughout the night so that the water-soaked wrapping kept the bottle's contents refreshingly chilled.

Seldom did father and daughter exchange a word during the twenty-minute walk to church. When they did, it was because the priest was suddenly inspired to impart a piece of wisdom. One fine Sunday morning, as the two plodded quietly along, Aba Yitades spied a pyjama-clad woman in a doorway. Father and daughter had just turned down a bushy trail, a shortcut to church, and it was by sheer chance that he caught sight of the woman. Since the only people up at such harsh hours were beggars and churchmen—and the occasional burglar—the priest paused to see what was going to happen next.

The woman, a dashing divorcee, had made a name for herself by violating all but one of the Ten Commandments. Seeing her in her provocative garb awakened a raw emotion in the priest. As he fought to keep his feelings under control, it dawned on him that she was inspecting the deserted street for prying eyes. She was clearly satisfied that there were none, for she had no sooner gone back inside than a man, and a married man at that, emerged from behind her and dashed towards the bushes across the road.

The enraged priest devoted the balance of the journey to the Book of Ezekiel—the "Two Adulterous Sisters."

AT THE CHURCH ENTRANCE, father and daughter were greeted by a platoon of beggars. As the gates to the compound were locked and fortified from the inside, the priest had to wait for the resident monk to open them. Ever since he had taken total control of the church activities, Aba Yitades had introduced gradual but lasting amendments to its routines and practices. The most notable one forbade the homeless from camping on holy ground.

"Good morning, Aba Yitades," each beggar said as he passed. The priest curtly nodded his reply. He reserved a few kind words for those men and women he recognized from his student days.

"It has been six months since Ato Girma's funeral," announced a blind old man that Sunday morning. "I hear that his children have prepared a grand commemoration."

"Oh, I almost forgot about him," lied Aba Yitades. "Is that why the crowd is so large today?"

While all families remembered their dead on the third and fortieth days following committal, those with means observed the seventh, twelfth, and eightieth days as well. And the sixth month, the first year, and even the seventh year. The third day was marked by the removal of the mourning tent, when the family of the departed brought to church three baskets of bread, three pots of home-brewed *tella* or *tej,* three dishes of sauce, a load of fire-wood for the Bethlehem—the church kitchen—and absolution money for the officiating priest. The food and drink were divided up so that the poor, the head of the church, and the chamberlain each received one-sixth; the remainder went to the lesser clergy—the deacons and scribes.

Ato Girma's six-month commemoration was anticipated with great excitement at Aba Yitades' household, as it was in the ranks of the beggars. Aba Yitades had made Azeb pack an extra food basket before they left home. Earlier in the week he had alerted two young deacons to the occasion, advising them that he might need their assistance with his share of the donated food.

Around nine o'clock, the family of the remembered arrived, carrying heavy food baskets on their heads and full jugs on their backs. As the sixth month was one of the main commemorations, the one at which the women discarded their black mourning dress, a live bull was also brought along as a sacrifice and "for the drying of tears."

The deceased's chattering kin stood surrounding the church building, while inside, preparations were under way. Relief was apparent on their faces because they knew that Aba Yitades had been a personal acquaintance of the departed, and thus they were confident the sermon would be long and fitting. Many an officiating priest had been accused of glossing over an absolution. The family of the deceased had sometimes gone to the head of the church—in bigger dioceses, to the governor—to lodge their complaints. The day Aba Yitades neglected to mention the dead by name, he was summoned by the then head, Aba Berhanu. "Kin of the deceased didn't stint with the absolution money," admonished Aba Berhanu. "Why did you err against the ritual?" The family demanded a partial refund of the absolution money, but were only given a promise of a better service at the next commemoration.

Ato Girma's absolution didn't anger the kin. Azeb didn't leave the church grounds until the day had mellowed, the drawn-out ritual was finally over, and the food was divided up. The bull was slaughtered, the sacristan receiving the hide, tongue, head, and stomach; the servitor, the heart; the chamberlain, the ribs; and the head of the church, the breastbone with its meat. That was what Leviticus had ordered.

Aba Yitades didn't defile his holy person by carrying any of the donated victuals home. Instead, he arranged for the two young deacons to help his daughter. With the assistance of her two sisters and her mother, Azeb sorted out the vegetarian food and set it aside for fast days. It would be spread out in the sun until the *injera* had completely dried, so that it could be ground into pieces and packed in leak-proof bags. In lean times, when his neighbours lamented the absent rains and the creeping famine, the priest and his family would feast on porridge of dried *injera*.

The priest's home registered a suspiciously large number of visitors on commemoration days. Few of them left empty-handed.

Werknesh divided the beef in two. Keeping one half for her family, she carved up the rest to give away to deserving neighbours. Blocks of meat lay on the table, each tagged with the name of a valued friend.

"Did I forget anyone?" she thought out loud.

"Yes," remembered Genet, "Etiye Wubalesh."

"No, I don't think she will get any," Werknesh replied bitterly. "You remember, she ate a whole sheep by herself?"

Azeb distributed the banquet to the neighbours while Werknesh and her two older daughters painstakingly sliced the family's share of meat into long strips, sprinkled the pile with salt and chili pepper, and hung it to dry above the fireplace. Soon it would be packed in a number of food baskets and set aside for hard times.

Aba Yitades monitored the women's activities with the look of someone who had delivered the moon to his family. A plate of raw meat was on his lap, a glass of purchased *arake* next to his chair. After dicing the beef into cubes, he dipped each morsel in a sauce of chili pepper and *arake* before slipping it into his mouth. He followed each bite with a sip of the alcohol. The price of such indulgence was often felt in a week or two, when the parasites from the uncooked meat had grown inside one's body and stirred the intestines. The roots of the *cosso* tree were always at hand, but sometimes it required modern medicine to purge the parasites. Fortunately, Aba Yitades had the foresight to keep a supply of *Yommesan* tablets, purchased from a faraway pharmacy.

DUSK SETTLED over the village, and the villagers moved indoors.

In whispers Azeb told her mother she was hungry.

"Be quiet," Werknesh scolded her. "You are old enough to know that a woman never reveals her hunger."

"Let her have a snack," Genet intervened. "She has been outside all day."

"You have plenty of time to spoil your own children," Werknesh shot back. "As long as I live, my girls will not misbehave."

"She is only eight," argued Genet.

"Saint Libanos was eight when he delivered his first miracle!"

The priest's face was flushed from all the alcohol he had consumed. Throwing a bedsheet around his waist, he removed his trousers and turned them inside out. Using the flickering candlelight, he peered under the seams of his pants for live parasites. The moment he saw a louse, he tossed it into the flame. The insect hissed as it returned to ashes; the candlelight dimmed as it consumed each sacrifice. As the number of burning insects mounted, the smell of the melting wax turned foul. It didn't help matters that the priest belched each time he shifted in his seat.

"Dinner is ready," announced Werknesh.

The children beamed at the sight of a stack of *injera* on a large *messob,* a woven food table with a tight-fitting lid. They chattered and shoved one another to get a better position around the table.

Ato Girma's six-month commemoration coincided with Genet's birthday, and Werknesh had hoped that the head of the family would join them at the dinner table. She served her husband the wash water herself, lest an excited child spill it on his holy person, triggering his unsteady temper.

The priest was exceptionally animated that Sunday evening; his prayers lasted into the wee hours. The anxiety around the dinner table reached a pitch. Once the *injera* touched her father's lips, Azeb knew, it would be a sign to start eating, a sign that her long and arduous day was finally over, and that her stomach could cease its noisy murmur. All eyes were fixed on him when Aba Yitades rose to his feet, reached for the lid of the *messob,* and firmly shut the woven table.

"Reflect on the spiritual value of disappointment," he concluded, before heading back to his stool.

Azeb burst into tears. Werknesh pleaded with her husband to show mercy, at least to the youngest of them, but she succeeded only in kindling his pent-up anger.

"Enduring physical hardship is a prerequisite for spiritual development," the priest pronounced, wagging an accusing finger at his wife. "Unfortunately, you haven't been trained by it, so one can't expect you to teach by example."

Genet exhibited great resourcefulness when she proceeded to send Azeb to their godmother, who could be depended on to come to the aid of a disciplined child.

"Oh dear," she chimed, "I completely forgot that Etiye Hiywet asked for a loan of coffee beans." She doled out a fistful of green beans from the storage bin, tied the bunch to the end of an old *netela,* draped the cloth around Azeb's shoulders, and escorted her out of the room.

It was dark outside. More by instinct than sight, Genet found the wooden gate of the compound and heaved it out of her way. Tree branches rustled in a gentle breeze. A stray cat emerged from the leaden shadows and sauntered towards an abandoned barn. Genet waited until her eyes could make out the road ahead before letting go of Azeb's arm. Her ears straining for signs of man-eating beasts, she watched her baby sister sprint down the hundred-metre trail and disappear from view. Moments later, urgent knocks were heard and a shaft of light sliced the oppressive darkness.

Genet went back inside, assured that Etiye Hiywet would escort her godchild back home.

2

A DOTING GODMOTHER

*L*iving in a village that was tucked away behind a dense tropical forest and girdled by a chain of mountains and a cavernous valley, the people of Mechara led an isolated existence, little affected by the changes that had swept the rest of the country for three generations. Life revolved around the Holy Church. And in the absence of police and courts, the parish priest held sway over the day-to-day affairs of his flock as much as over their spiritual well-being.

The village had been founded by a small band of men and women following their conquering emperor. He opened up the entire region, which had originally been inhabited by unbelievers, to Christian settlers. The land the incomers had left was ravaged by a recurring drought, famine, and pestilence, and they held on to their new-found home with the tenacity of a drowning sailor clinging to a life jacket. In the eyes of many, Mechara was the Garden of Eden that their Good Book had so vividly spoken of, and they were not about to part with it (or share it) if they could help it.

And what a Garden of Eden it was that they found: a land blessed with dependable rainfall, wild fruit trees, and soil amenable to most cultivable crops. Citrus trees flourished, protected by inaccessible terrain, and at the riverbank, banana plants heaved under their rich pickings. Coffee was never cultivated until a motor highway (and the speculators it brought) generated an appetite for the beans on a scale that the wild shrubs could no longer sustain.

THE EARLY SETTLERS of Mechara couldn't have foreseen the number and diversity of people who would one day want to call the village they founded home. The first herbalists arrived to attend to the sick and dying, it is true, and no one raised objections when they chose to stay. The toothless tailor, the barber, the teahouse owner, and even the proprietor of the rowdy alehouse were all considered welcome additions to the growing community. But when a potter and his nephew, a blacksmith, wanted to set up shop, the community drew a line.

As everybody knows, potters have evil eyes, and the devil congregates around the anvil. A local potter wasn't considered necessary until the price of everyday clayware escalated to such a dizzy height that breaking a coffee pot became a second-degree felony. If the community finally gave its permission for a foundry, it was on the understanding that the artisans would stay out of the locals' way. They were to find their own source of water, potable or otherwise, and to refrain from casting bad spells on their noble neighbours, as their kind was known to do from time to time. Even in the hereafter they were to steer clear of good Christians; they were told to chart their own burial ground.

Trading in goods had always been part of the farming tradition, but calling a farmer "merchant" was a slight that wouldn't go unanswered. When young Hiywet, who would later become Azeb's godmother, announced that she had found a suitor in a young vendor, a man who had breezed into the village from a place no one had ever heard of, the first question she was asked was, "What did he touch you with?"

"His heart," was her unabashed reply.

Her proud ancestors will turn in their graves, the community concurred.

At first, the young couple lived in and operated their business from a single hovel. On market days, they loaded their trinkets on the backs of mules and donkeys and set out for distant places. At the beginning, the return on their financial investment wasn't much, but, they argued, the poor seldom charged for their labour. As long as a fifty-cent bag of incense was sold for a cent more, the transaction was deemed a success.

The business grew. In addition to everyday items such as sugar, tea leaves, salt, cooking oil, candles, and incense, they stocked perfumes, sweets, exotic fabrics, and ready-made cloth. The one-room hovel was dismantled and in its place was erected a large store with a corrugated metal roof—the first of its kind in Mechara. A decade and a half later, their business would diversify to include a small hotel-and-restaurant establishment in the nearby town of Gelemso.

Four years after their wedding, when neighbours thought the community's curse had finally taken hold and that the couple would remain childless, a baby boy was born to young Hiywet and her husband. A year later, one more baby boy was added. The young father dreamt of the day when his sons would be able to take over the family business; his wife thought otherwise.

"I don't want this life for my children," she declared one Saturday evening as the two of them returned from yet another arduous journey.

"What is wrong with our life?" her husband demanded, stung by her unexpected anger.

"We work like mules," young Hiywet replied.

"But see what we can afford to buy!"

"We still eat three times a day, and we don't wear more than a pair of shoes at a time," she argued.

"What else is there to want?"

"Salvation."

What Hiywet planned for her children—priesthood—caused a rift between husband and wife. Weeks went by before the couple reached a tentative agreement: the boys would pursue their seminary training while at the same time looking after the family business.

Whether the boys would end up serving their Father in Heaven or the one on earth was never established. For, two years after the memorable dispute, long before the boys were to complete their education, father and sons, on their way home from a faraway market, were ambushed and murdered.

No SOONER had she sold the family-owned grocery store and retreated into her private shell than Etiye Hiywet began to receive the community's help and support. It was as though the intervening two decades of hostility, the cold shoulders and name-calling, had never taken place. As invitations to attend the daily coffee ceremonies began to mount, she abandoned the habit altogether.

"But why?" her own mother demanded.

"The coffee had begun to weigh on my heart," Etiye Hiywet lied.

"This is no time to offend the *rekebot* spirit," her mother argued.

"There is nothing the spirits can do to me that Saint George hasn't already done," was Etiye Hiywet's bitter reply.

No sooner had she stemmed the tide of coffee invitations than a different crowd began to darken her doorway: mothers petitioned her to be godmother to their newborns. And as news spread of a rich and childless widow living in seclusion, such requests began to arrive from hamlets and settlements that few had heard of before.

"It won't kill you to say yes to one or two of them," her mother pleaded.

"I don't want children to run around my house. I want my peace and quiet," retorted Etiye Hiywet.

"No one said you have to babysit them. All you have to do is buy the kids a shirt or a blouse every now and then," her mother argued, to no avail.

Etiye Hiywet soon slipped out of the villagers' everyday thoughts. A resigned acceptance enveloped her. The friends she had cultivated during her sequestered years continued their regular visits. Werknesh was her most talked-about company because of the age difference, but the one person who would assume a major role in her isolated existence was her soul-father—the man who had come into her life on the day of her marriage.

A SOUL-FATHER is a confessor, family counsellor, confidant, and will executor all rolled into one. Young couples chose their family soul-father long before they formalized their wedding. Considerable thought went into the decision, as the individual they picked would remain a lifelong tagalong. The potential candidate must hold a rank of the holy orders, but the weighing factor was often integrity.

The most routine task of a soul-father was looking after the spiritual well-being of his charges. Someone who had violated one of the numerous tenets would seek out his or her soul-father to clear up his or her conscience. The parish priest held regular sessions, it is true, but few could live with their guilt for a week. Instead, they would go to their soul-father's home or send for him for a private session. Before granting his final absolution, the soul-father always demanded a sum of money to distribute among the church poor.

The church poor kept tabs on the soul-fathers of the rich as diligently as they logged upcoming commemorations. If they hadn't heard from a soul-father for an extended period of time, they would deduce that he spent the absolution money on himself. They revealed this violation of trust to his charge in a roundabout way. "Etiye Hiywet," said an old man who led a troop of beggars on a Tuesday morning, "Etiye Hiywet, your three *birr* absolution money got to us, bless you. Incidentally, is everything all right with Ato Abraha, your neighbour? It has been almost six months since we heard from his soul-father, you know."

Soul-fathers received a small but steady inducement for their services. Some people gave them a *netela* or a blanket on major holidays. Others pressed a few *birr* notes into their palm following an absolution. Etiye Hiywet kept her soul-father on a regular payroll. Ever since the death of her husband and two sons, she had come to rely on him for much more than his regular duties. He read her letters for her and wrote replies that she dictated, but most importantly, he handled the financial books.

After she lost her family, Etiye Hiywet seldom needed absolution, for her regimen of fasting and prayers had steadily increased until she was living the straitened life of a devout monk. Her soul-father was particularly troubled by her rigid observation of *Gahad*, which, unlike a fast that required abstinence from animal products for a fixed duration, necessitated the absolute rejection of food and drink for a period of nine sunlight hours—from sunrise until mid-afternoon.

Etiye Hiywet observed the Lenten Fast, the Fast of the Apostles, the Assumption, the Fast of *Nanawei*, the Christmas Fast, the *Gahad* of Christmas, and the *Gahad* of Epiphany. And there were fasts and *Gahads* formally unrecognized by the Church and therefore missing from *The Dooms of the Kings* that she managed to locate and observe. The *Tsegi* fast, which ran from October 5 until November 14; the Fast of Heraclius, which fell on February 24; and the *Gahad* of the Revelation of Mary, which was observed on January 28, were only a few of them. Altogether, Etiye Hiywet observed 253 fast days and no fewer than 55 days of *Gahad*.

Her unusual regimen of fasting and *Gahad* had earned Etiye Hiywet the hostility of the clergy, who felt shamed by her unparalleled dedication, for many of them observed no more than the compulsory 180 fast days. She was elevated in the eyes of the villagers, however. Parishioners who had lost track of their fasts came to regard Etiye Hiywet as a reliable reference. Neighbours often sent children to her home to inquire about the beginning of a fast that crossed from month to month—the Lenten Fast, say, which, according to Ethiopia's thirteen-month calendar, might begin in a different month from the year before.

WHEN SHE WASN'T with her soul-father or tending to the graves of her loved ones, Etiye Hiywet found time for her diminishing circle of friends. When Werknesh was still single, she had managed to snatch a few hours of quiet reflection each day with the woman who was old enough to be her mother yet was destined to remain her closest friend and ally for many, many years. Werknesh was troubled by her fast-advancing years, by the distinct prospect of spinsterhood, and she often broke down in tears.

When Werknesh finally found her man, Aba Yitades, and was about to bear a child, Etiye Hiywet was beside herself with joy. "I hope it will be a baby girl so that I will have my first godchild," she declared, as a boy would have a godfather. Etiye Hiywet would go on to be godmother not only to Genet but to her two sisters as well. Her strongest attachment, however, was to the youngest, Azeb.

AZEB WAS STILL CRAWLING when she slipped out of bed at dawn and attempted to find her way to her godmother's home. She scratched at the locked door and moaned and groaned until her exasperated mother finally ordered one of the girls to take her away. Her sisters were never pleased at losing a good hour of sleep on behalf of the little one, and they made their displeasure known. On days when their father had already left for church and therefore wouldn't be aggravated, their squabble turned into a small drama.

"It is Genet's turn," Beletu, the middle child, noted one drizzly morning.

"No, it is your turn," protested Genet.

"I took her once too often last week," Beletu remembered.

"That was because I was baking *injera*," Genet responded angrily.

"Mam, why can't you let Azeb sleep over at Etiye Hiywet's home, instead?" said Beletu, hoping for a lasting solution.

"We have been through this before. Now get up and take her," Werknesh ordered.

"But I am fearful for my health." Beletu was unrelenting.

"What are you afraid of?"

"That I might come upon a road curse and fall sick once again." Beletu had once stepped on a headless rooster concealed under a mat of weeds on a busy trail. A week later she developed a harsh fever and unsightly blisters, the infections of the patient for whom the chicken had been sacrificed. "I haven't completely recovered, you know," she lied.

"I told you children to make a wide berth when turning a corner, lest you stumble upon an ominous object," reminded Werknesh. "I told you, too, not to touch a road sacrifice, much less eat from it." Such vigilance is especially necessary early in the morning and during holidays, when the roads and trails are known to be mined with deadly objects. "Now, get up and take her away."

From her doorway halfway up a bluff, Etiye Hiywet watched the lone figure of a small girl, with an even smaller one strapped on her back, plod through the mist. The old woman had endured another night of tortured thoughts, as she had done since the death of her two sons and her husband. At her feet was a bag of alms for the poor. In her right hand was a string of rosaries, and each time the eleventh bead (the paternoster) slipped between her fingers, she mumbled the Lord's Prayer.

At the sight of her youngest godchild, the tension in her face began to relax; she tucked the string of beads inside her woven waistband. Azeb chuckled and struggled to get off her mount. Etiye Hiywet helped her down and kissed her on both cheeks, as she would do a hundred more times during the day. After a brief "Bless you" to the deliverer, she took her bundle inside.

After feeding Azeb a warm breakfast, she tucked her in bed before attending to the troop of beggars who made their rounds, singing. As she doled out food from the specially prepared bag,

Etiye Hiywet beseeched the poor to remember to say their prayers for her departed ones. She gave an old dress, a *netela,* and a used head scarf to a woman with a young child. Before accepting the alms, the beggars bowed until their heads almost touched the ground, and said, "Bless you." By the time Etiye Hiywet had finished attending to the poor, Azeb had fallen asleep.

Azeb treasured the mornings she spent cuddled in her godmother's bed, with its fluffy mattress and downy comforter. At her own home she knew little more than the dappled cowhide and threadbare blanket that she shared with her mother and two siblings. The uneven dirt floor, felt through the thin bedding, made the few moments before sleep agonizing for everyone.

Werknesh attempted to ease the nightly pains for her youngest daughter by forming a cushion out of the family's dirty laundry. The assembled clothes weren't always without their discomforts, though. When a button or zipper stung her soft skin, Azeb burst into tears, testing her father's patience. On Saturdays, when the family did its laundry, even that measure of luxury was lost.

Aba Yitades had the only thing that passed for a bed in the household. In the far end of the hut lay a mud-dais, on which was a straw-filled mattress. The family members stayed clear of the bed, unless they were sick and rolling out the cowhide bedding would interfere with the daily activities.

FEASTING ON A DIET of buttered eggs and sweet yoghurt at her godmother's home, Azeb grew bigger and faster. She became the envy of mothers who could ill afford to nourish a weaned child. Some of them passed judgment on Azeb's size within Etiye Hiywet's hearing. A stranger who remarked on Azeb's well-fed look was stopped in her tracks by the irate godmother, who demanded that the stranger spit on the baby. "Spit on her!" repeated Etiye Hiywet, determined not to give the evil eye a moment's chance to get a hold on the baby. The woman was upset at being suspected of such a vile act, but to avoid potential blame—in case the baby came down with a mysterious illness within the week, say—she steeped the tip of her tongue and, wishing the baby good health, spat on her twice.

No matter how protective Etiye Hiywet had been of her favourite godchild, Azeb was assailed by a variety of ailments. Often the old woman was able to relieve the child's suffering by sifting through the family medicine chest. For hiccups and indigestion, for instance, she had distilled dill water; for frequent intestinal gas, she gave Azeb droplets of allspice oil; and for fever and nasal congestion, she doused the patient with fumes of eucalyptus leaves. Sometimes, however, even her rich medicine cabinet wasn't enough to cure an affliction.

Following a persistent body rash and dry cough, Azeb received a professionally made talisman in a sealed leather pouch that hung from her neck-cord. Although a not uncommon sight on others, the amulet irked the baby's father, who had grown weary of all practices that were not clearly sanctioned by the Good Book. He let his daughter wear the talisman out of a lingering respect for her godmother, but his relationship with the old woman was never the same.

ONCE A MONTH, Etiye Hiywet left the village to attend to business matters. She had retained the family-owned hotel-and-restaurant establishment in the nearby town of Gelemso. The business thrived as the bustling town, with the region's only bank and post office, became a gathering place for merchants and farmers within a radius of two hundred kilometres.

During the ten-hour horse ride, she was accompanied by two armed men and her soul-father. While the paid guards ensured her safety, her soul-father handled her written matters. Etiye Hiywet had the foresight to keep her small fortune in the state bank, removing all temptations to raid her residence in her absence.

Before returning home, she visited the post office to see if there was any mail for her neighbours. The man who operated the state-owned agency did so with a uniquely personal touch. The townspeople had learned not to look for him at his desk. If it was the beginning of the month and he had received his erratically arriving paycheque, he could be found in the alehouse. Other times he roamed the open markets looking for handouts, or simply hung out in one of the local stores.

Etiye Hiywet sent local children to locate the postman. But before she could find out whether there was any mail for her, she had to soothe his prickly temper with a bottle of cold beer from her bar. She sat and listened while he ranted about how little rewarded his tireless services were, and how ungrateful the townspeople had been.

"Did you know that if I were to die today, there would no longer be mail delivery?" he confidently predicted.

"Hush," she upbraided him in a motherly way. "Don't let Satan in on that."

His job frustrations finally allayed by the cold beer, and with Etiye Hiywet's reassuring words ringing in his ears, the mailman rushed to his office to bring her pieces of mail for her good neighbours.

Her homecoming was greeted with elation. Neighbours flocked to her door to hear the latest news. Impressionable young people asked her about recent innovations. Many came to know the larger world through her colourful descriptions: a car is a small house on wheels operated by a balding man with a dreadful temper; a telephone is not unlike the toys of Ato Tamirat's boys— two tin cans connected with a string—only the string is longer.

Her godchildren had come to expect more from such trips. Etiye Hiywet brought Genet and Beletu satin head scarves, imported underwear, colourful hairpins, and balls of knitting wool. Werknesh received kitchenware and bagged groceries. Occasionally the godmother brought along allegorical renderings, mostly framed pictures of Saint Michael, wings spread wide, and Saint George, on horseback spearing the serpent that was commonly believed to be threatening Etiye Brutawit. She distributed the pictures among the village's bedridden and bereaved. New mothers invariably received a painting of the Virgin with baby Jesus in her arms.

ABA YITADES was never the champion of material acquisition. Long after he had risen through the ranks of the clergy, he continued to live in a one-room hovel. His wardrobe comprised one pair each of trousers, shorts, and shoes (made of rubber), a khaki jacket, and two linen shirts. He wore long pants on the Sabbath, on holidays, and during rare official services such as weddings and commemorations. He shunned laundry on the grounds that frequent washing wore down a good garment. When Etiye Hiywet bought Azeb a dress for her first birthday, the priest was overcome with rage.

"It is her money," Werknesh attempted to reason with him.

"If the Lord had meant for a one-year-old to be clothed," he argued, "He wouldn't have delivered her bare naked."

The priest wasn't alone on the issue. In tradition-steeped Mechara, dressing a baby bordered on an obscene display of extravagance. Many got their first clothes when they were old enough to run errands, usually at the New Year. Children might get a replacement, but only once a year. Footwear was a luxury that few households could afford. The day Etiye Hiywet bought six-year-old Azeb a pair of shoes (and leather ones at that), even Werknesh couldn't conceal her disapproval. "What a waste of money," she noted wistfully, "leather shoes for growing feet!"

That day, the priest's home saw a record number of rowdy visitors. Girls came from far and wide to witness the imported footwear. As they tried the shoes on, some of them heaved a long sigh of despair. A barefoot teenager who took a sniff of the polished leather gleefully noted its pungent smell. Aba Yitades watched the goings-on from the vantage of his mud-dais, kneading his overgrown beard. His face betrayed little of his emotions.

That evening, following a late dinner, he gathered members of the household for a moment of shared reflection. While leafing through the family bible, Aba Yitades caught sight of his youngest daughter admiring her shoes, which she had carefully placed so they would catch the flickering candlelight. Mercifully, he passed no judgment.

Finally, he located the appropriate passage to close the hectic day and he cleared his throat. "'And the Lord said,'" he began tentatively, "'do not store up for yourselves treasure on earth … store up for yourselves treasure in heaven. For where your treasure is, there your heart will be also. No one can serve two masters. You cannot serve both God and material acquisition.'"

Aba Yitades reached over and picked up Azeb's treasured shoes. Pulling a sharp cleaver from the overhead rack, he proceeded to work on them, with only a muted sob heard from the assembled women. First he bisected one of the pair, then the other. He removed the brass buckles with a swift movement of the knife. The heels flew with a sudden jerk; the decorated tips followed. The thick leather soles lodged their complaint, but only for a brief moment. When the priest's pent-up anger was finally spent, a mere five minutes later, only thumb-sized pieces of the shoes remained.

The priest was appalled by the godmother and her corrupting influences on his children. His appearance of restraint in not restricting her access to Azeb was not because of a shared bloodline, which the two of them could trace all the way back to the early settlers, but because Etiye Hiywet was the one person who had come to the priest's aid during the darkest hours of his youth.

3

FATHER IN THE MAKING

*T*he dawning century was exceptionally promising to Azeb's great-grandparents. They packed up their meagre possessions and left their ancestral homes in the northern highlands to start afresh in the newly opened territories—a land where no one spoke their language or shared their imported faith. Mechara was uninhabited then. Neighbouring natives were hostile to the newcomers, as any conquered people would be. Since vital state institutions such as the police and the courts had not yet reached this remote district, it fell upon the settlers not only to administer their day-to-day affairs but to defend themselves as well.

Men were trained to bear arms at an early age. A lot of weight was attached to courage and tenacity. Aba Yitades was only ten when, as an initiation rite, his father brought him along on a hunting expedition. Seven other boys took part in the event. The adventure took the young men away from their familiar settings and into the lowlands, where they would spend a week honing their survival skills. For many of the participants this was a moment to treasure. The simple rite spawned many fables. Legends sprang up of the week-long adventure. Years later, when memories had faded and witnesses succumbed, the exploits of a participant assumed monumental proportions; his accomplishments would be told and retold by his proud offspring for generations to come. Aba Yitades' father never tired of recounting how his sire had wrestled a full-grown lion to the ground, slit the beast's throat with a swift movement of his side dagger, and, for good measure, plucked a strand of its flowing mane and flossed his teeth with it.

The moment arrived for young Yitades to leave his own mark on local history, to weave his own fable, so to speak. Unlike his illustrious grandfather, however, his duel wasn't with the king of the beasts but with a pint-sized warthog, which the troop had located in an underground burrow.

"Thrust your spear into the hole," the men shouted at the bewildered young man. "Show no fear," they urged. "Wild animals smell weakness."

"You are carrying your grandfather's weapon," his own father reminded Yitades. "The spear will kill the beast without you."

Yitades blindly poked his spear into the hole, secretly hoping that he would miss his target. Instead, the beast's ear-splitting cries shattered the still morning. Nesting birds took to the air in droves. Terrified, the boy took a few cautious steps backwards—against the advice of his father—his eyes riveted on the mouth of the den.

Moments later, the beast emerged, dripping blood from its wound. Far from running for its life, as most animals would do in such a position, the angry hog readied itself for mortal combat. Although it weighed less than a hundred kilograms and stood only half a metre in height, its giant tusks made the wild pig a most fearsome prey. Big cats show a healthy respect for the ill-tempered beast. Warthogs are known to have unzipped rookie lionesses with a swift movement of their tusks. Yitades remembered only too late the animal's reputation for combativeness.

At the sight of the bloodied pig, Yitades lost what little reserve of courage he had. He could neither raise his spear nor dash for cover. The confused animal darted left and right, drawing some more jabs from other trainees. Even though one of the trainees broke his spear in the warthog's hind leg, and the thrust of another exposed the contents of the animal's stomach, the beast rapidly regained its feet. Noticing Yitades, the only one of the boys who hadn't sought shelter behind a tree, frozen in his tracks, the warthog headed his way, quickly closing the ten-metre gap. The grown-ups hurled conflicting advice at the wild-eyed boy. "Don't show fear. Stand your ground with your spear thrust," some urged. "The warthog is gasping for its last breath."

"Throw your spear and dash for cover," hollered those men who had come to their senses. "There is nothing more dangerous than a wounded warthog."

"Move an inch and I'll disown you," his own father admonished. "You will never set foot in my home again."

Yitades stared breathlessly as the animal sprinted the last few metres, groaning and grunting, its sabre-like tusks clearly aimed at him. Then a shot rang out and the beast's legs gave way under its dense weight. Blood splashed the face and body of the unmoving boy. Yitades had been saved by a cousin's intervention.

YITADES REMAINED BEDRIDDEN for the days that followed. Although his father hadn't carried out his threat and thrown his only child out of his home, the two didn't exchange another word for almost two weeks. What few messages passed between father and son were relayed by the woman of the house. Yitades' cowardice was immortalized in a proverb, which was told and retold to growing men as a cautionary tale. "You do that and you will become another Yitades" became a common refrain.

Few were surprised when, a year and a half later, long before the family's good name and heroic heritage were fully restored with the birth of Aba Yitades' twin grandsons some three decades later, his father passed away. Although neighbours knew the man had suffered from tuberculosis, which had ravaged his body for many years, they were all convinced that his son's cowardly act had played a decisive part in weakening his constitution. Not that Yitades' mother was spared the community's wrath either. She was made to endure scoffs and name-calling for raising such an unworthy son. "I have got two daughters," said a malicious neighbour to her once. "You have one."

Soon after celebrating the fortieth-day commemoration of her husband's death, Yitades' mother left the colony for good. She was destined never to see her son again, as she chose to remain in her ancestral homeland, a day's journey away on horseback.

YITADES SECRETLY RELISHED his freedom. With no one to dictate his future, he was now master of his destiny. He enrolled in the local seminary.

Three generations after its founding, the village had but a single house of worship, the Church of St. George. Attending to the church's affairs were a head priest, who was dying of old age, a left master, a right master, four priests, a chamberlain, a head deacon, nine deacons, a sacristan, and eight *dabtaras*. In the northern and central highlands, where ecclesiastical training had reached its apogee, a seminary student had the choice of three learning houses: the House of Music, the House of Poetry, or the House of Reading. One could spend as long as twenty years pursuing higher learning. In Mechara, there was no guiding master to handle the music program, so the deacons gave the required lessons in singing, time-beating, and dancing before students were sent to bigger seminaries. Poetry and reading were combined in one program and offered from a single room.

The schoolhouse was the tomb-hut of one of the village founders, after whom the seminary was named. As there were no priests to assume the additional task of teaching, a *dabtara* took over. Like most people of position in Mechara, the old man boasted a direct lineage to one of the early settlers. The *dabtara* didn't belong to the circle of the ordained, but his training permitted him to read the lessons as well as take care of the church music and small scribal duties.

The schoolhouse offered Yitades not only a career opportunity but living quarters as well. He wasn't thrown out of the old colony, but the animosity, even two years after the event, was simply too hard to bear. When they saw him approaching, many villagers looked the other way; some changed direction. The most unkind were women who threw dirty water after him, and boys who spat on the ground that he walked on while looking him in the eye. His father's kin may have made a name for themselves as brave adventurers, but nursing a grudge, even when it involved a helpless child, was never beneath them.

YITADES ADJUSTED QUICKLY to the routine at the schoolhouse. After the daily sessions had ended and the six other students had gone home to their families, he unrolled the dappled cowhide that had been tucked away in the corner and began organizing his "home." The rawhide served him as both mattress and lounging mat, as it would do for Azeb and her siblings many years later. A factory-made blanket, donation of Etiye Hiywet, and a thread-bare *netela,* legacy of a family that had been giving away the effects of a departed one, were his only other accessories.

As soon as the class finished for the day and the church grounds were abandoned, he removed his shorts and shirt and wrapped himself in the *netela*. Since they were his only clothes, the boy could ill afford to wear them while alone. Then he fetched the food basket that he had hidden in a shrub across from the schoolhouse. For much of the day he had kept one eye on the shrub, making sure that no student or beast got too close. Now he untied the leather straps holding the lid in place. His mouth watered at the aroma of the sun-baked food, his major meal of the day. He dipped his fingers into the basket, at the same time listening for approaching footsteps. At the slightest indication of a broken twig or rattling gravel, he removed the basket from sight. Yitades was ashamed for not sharing his meal with visitors, but there simply was never enough food to go around. Like the blanket on his bed and the cloth on his back, his daily food was another donation. Often it came from Etiye Hiywet's kitchen.

After dinner, Yitades brewed the day's third round of coffee (the first round was served in the morning, as in all households; the second, at midday). Still guardian of tradition, he kept six cups on the coffee tray. The mandatory snack basket was placed to the left of the tray, the coffee pot to the right. He sprinkled the first cup of coffee at the doorstep of his lodge for the *rekebot* spirit. He next served his invisible companion from the snack basket, tossing pieces of bread or roasted legumes at the doorway, before helping himself. There were few moments in his daily routine that reminded Yitades of the loneliness that shrouded him; the traditional coffee ceremony was one.

After the evening coffee, Yitades washed his bare feet. By the dying glow of the sun, he peered between his toes for signs of hatching jiggers. He removed the jiggers with a needle that he had sanitized in the fire. Sometimes he made the rounds to see if all the doors and windows of the buildings inside the church precincts were locked. Other than himself, only one soul called the church grounds home: a blind monk who had long since lost his reason. From time to time Yitades brought him food. He made sure that the door and windows of the monk's shelter were locked before he fortified his own quarters for the night. Years later, Azeb would voluntarily assist the dying monk, who had by then receded from the memory of everyone, including her father.

In just seven and a half years, Yitades had mastered the 260-character long syllabary, the first seven verses of the Epistle of Saint John, the Miracles of Mary, the Gospel, his psalter, and the Qalam Sis of John. He rattled off any Biblical exegesis that his teacher asked of him with the utmost ease, often drawing envious glances from his classmates. His handsome handwriting drew the attention of the head priest, Aba Berhanu, who assigned him to transcribe a book on the exploits of Saint George in his spare time. Yitades was paid a princely sum of thirty-five *birr* for his services when he finally completed the task a year and a half later. At the age of twenty, Yitades received the deaconate. His scholastic excellence was further recognized when Aba Berhanu assigned him to assist the *dabtara* in teaching the young lads.

The village of Mechara began to take stock of its new deacon on Palm Sunday that first year after his graduation. The event drew over two thousand parishioners in Mechara—almost two-thirds of the inhabitants. The church precincts, which usually seemed a vast expanse of untamed land, became a sea of faces for a day.

Yitades was the choirboy for the event. Dressed in a white long-sleeved tunic secured in place with a woven girdle, and on his head a mozzetta-like cape that matched the tunic in colour and design, he was a sight to behold. He held a lit censer in his right hand, which he swung from side to side throughout the sermon. Aromatic plumes rose from the incense burner and hung low in the cramped nave of the church, where the officiating clergy conducted the service hidden from view. For a few moments that day, all traces of his vagabond appearance were erased.

Yitades raised his voice a note above the drumbeat and sistrum rattle that punctuated the hymn, and delivered a heart-warming performance. Parishioners quietly congregated outside the temple walls, wrapped up in heavy *netela* against the morning cold, stirred back to life. "*Egzio-o-o-o* [The Redeemer]," said one out loud, and others repeated after. Each time Yitades sang an ode, the excitement rose. His type of tenor had never been heard before in the confines of St. George of Mechara, and the parishioners didn't know what to make of it.

Palm Sunday celebrations usually lasted until mid-morning, by which time half the parishioners would have slipped away unnoticed, but that day the curious filled the church precincts. Like the sermon itself, the hymns and psalms were written in the ancient liturgical language of *Geez,* which few commoners could fathom, but that Sunday the Scriptures could have been written in the local tongue. Mouths wide open, the faithful had the look of those who have finally grasped what has eluded them all their lives.

As the identity of the new choirboy didn't come to light until a week later, speculations began to swirl.

"He is a eunuch," said a respectable-looking woman. "No one else could sing so beautifully."

"No, I heard he flew here on the back of a winged horse," contradicted her lady friend, who was known for her imaginative mind. "He was found at the church gate one morning, with the horse dead at his feet from exhaustion."

"They said he was the Emperor's performer," speculated a young lass. "He fled the capital fearing for his life. They said women of the palace slept at his door."

The choirboy's identity was revealed during the Eucharist service the following Sunday, but it did little to clear up the mystery. "His father must have been admitted to heaven" was the most common explanation for his uncommon talent. "Why else would the Almighty bestow such a startling gift on the son?"

Yitades' worth to the Church of St. George of Mechara became unmistakable when parishioners attending Sunday Mass doubled in number, then tripled, until three months later there was no more room to accommodate the faithful. Many crossed mountains and rivers to hear the sweet voice of the new talent. Miracles multiplied. A middle-aged woman came forward to announce her recovery, after hearing the young deacon sing the Songs of Lent, from the rheumatism that had plagued her adult life. Another woman gave birth to a baby boy long after she had given up hope, following a performance of a cycle of songs composed in honour of the ancient church of St. Paul of Sion at Aksum, which Yitades had delivered exceptionally well.

No paved roads connected Mechara to other parts of the district, but that didn't deter recruiters from knocking on his door. Bigger and more famous churches wanted him on their payroll. With this kind of popular attraction, any price he named would have been considered a bargain; his employers could easily recoup their investment from donations and sacrifices. Yitades, however, was not easily tempted.

ALTHOUGH HE HAD EARNED the adulation of complete strangers and the recognition of the people who mattered most to his career, Yitades had yet to change his blood relations' opinions of him. They avoided him entirely. Even when they attended the baptism of a newborn or the weekly Eucharist, they ignored his presence at the church service.

His late father's homestead was a mere half hour's walk from the church, but Yitades hadn't been back since he had unceremoniously left home some ten years earlier. In Mechara, as in much of the country, death bound the living more than life ever could. A community was never more united than at the funeral of a neighbour or a commemoration of the dead. Yitades defied all norms and manners when he failed to pay his last respects to the family of a deceased niece.

YITADES FOUND HIMSELF in demand outside the church confines as well. There were the usual requests facing a learned deacon. Illiterate villagers hovered around seminaries in search of someone who would read their letters for them, or compose a reply. Unlike professional letter-writers, who demanded cash payments, a deacon expected nothing more than a warm meal and a homebrew. Yitades was asked to perform prayers and blessings as well. Women waited for him outside the church gates at all hours of the day with minor petitions. "Yitades, my boy has come down with a fever. Would you please say prayers over him?" a desperate mother asked. "Yitades, my husband is away on a court trial," came another typical request. "This sacrificial rooster is to help him win the case. Would you please say a fitting prayer and slaughter the bird for me?" As an appreciative gesture, he was asked to show up later in the day and partake of the meal, but he seldom did.

Indeed, many of the requests that came Yitades' way were for prayers to be said over a sacrificial animal. A professional butcher usually stood by to slaughter the creature, but sometimes Yitades was asked to complete that task too. Unlike hired help, who demanded the skin of a butchered sheep or goat as payment, a deacon expected little for his services. Yitades dreaded such requests; after all these years, he still couldn't stand the sight of blood.

In many ways Yitades never shed the image of the ten-year-old boy who froze at the sight of a wounded warthog. He seldom looked people in the eye; he was tongue-tied in the presence of strangers. While most men's shyness towards women mellowed with age, his seemed to deepen. Unwed women found amusement in making him blush. "I'll make him talk to me," said a young lass to a friend, and she blocked his exit, her back towards him. Yitades had to mumble his pleas three times before she made way for him.

"I'll make him look me in the eye," wagered another girl, and she blew on the back of his neck until a smile creased his face.

An attractive divorcee—a woman whom Azeb would forever associate with the Two Adulterous Sisters of the Book of Ezekiel—almost gave him a heart attack when she interrupted his daydreaming.

"Yitades," she said, straining over the wooden fence of her compound, where she had been waiting for him. "May God have mercy on your late father. I have always been a friend of your family, you know. Would you find it in your heart to come inside and bless the Assumption bread for me?"

Slicing bread was bloodless, and Yitades gladly obliged. Although they had met before, it was the first time he had been inside the home of the woman he would remember for the rest of his life. His face lit up at the sight of her rare and luxurious furnishings. Like all village women, she dressed in a traditional white skirt and matching *netela* for social events; at less sombre occasions, she indulged in a floral dress, though no less conservative.

The colourful skirt she wore at home hugged her well-contoured silhouette snugly, terminating on the wrong side of her knees. Her high-heeled shoes were unlike anything the young deacon had seen before. He couldn't make up his mind whether it was her rosebud heels, her fiery toenails, or her exotic shoes that left him warm and itching under the collar. He found sensuousness in the stretch lines on the soft side of her thighs, and each time her dress shifted, his heart skipped a beat.

As tradition required, the guest was offered, and he accepted, a slice of the sacrificial bread and a beverage. The drink was a brew of *tej,* and the honey-laced alcohol went down his parched throat easily. The heat of the day magnified the effect of the alcohol, and soon he began to slur his words.

Yitades felt the velvety mass of the woman press against him. He dreamt that her sensuous fingers raced down his thighs and explored the place he had always thought of as a sanctuary with a private altar. He felt an explosion go off in his head. Thus far he had managed to keep all temptation at bay through the powers of prayer and sacrifice, but now he wondered if it wasn't something he had always wanted and dreaded at the same time.

It was pitch-dark outside when Yitades finally opened his eyes. He was surprised to find himself naked. Lying next to him on the bed, her bare thigh straddling him, shamelessly displaying her most secret body parts, was the gorgeous divorcee.

"Jesus the Redeemer," Yitades managed to cry before darting off the bed. "What have you done? What have you done?"

"Oh, shut up," she scolded him. "You are not a monk, you know."

Half dragging himself and half floating through the air, Yitades emerged from the room into the starless night. He chanted choice prayers on the way home. In his eyes he had been subjected to the temptation of Eve, and he had failed. What is more, his dreams of ever assuming the post of *Qomos* were dashed in a blink. For the prerequisite to becoming a *Qomos* (loosely translated, "canon") was cleanliness in flesh and soul.

By the time he reached his shelter, what seemed to him like ages later, his vision had blurred and his head was spinning with conflicting thoughts. Blood oozed from his toes. A person walking through pitch darkness usually lifted his foot high above the ground and landed it squarely on solid earth, avoiding bumps and bruises, but that night the care of his bare feet was the last thing on Yitades' mind.

Yitades went into a self-imposed exile from which he refused to return.

FOUR DAYS LATER, when Yitades skipped Sunday Mass without prior notice, Aba Berhanu could no longer feign indifference. Parishioners had already begun inquiring about the star performer. Another few Sabbaths without the popular choirboy and the Church of St. George of Mechara would slip down the popularity charts and, God forbid, into its former obscurity.

Yitades had never been the most popular boy in his class. He had been snubbed by those who came from decent homes and enjoyed a balanced family life. He had been derided for his vagabond looks. Those who had learned to expect career advancement and social acceptance based on name recognition alone were especially mean to him. His meteoric rise in the profession deepened his unpopularity. As a student, he sometimes found his cowhide bed smeared with human excrement, his coffee pot spiked with urine. Following his career advances, the attacks became vocal.

"He is fake," said one. "He recites his lessons without grasping their true meaning."

"He is a parrot," embellished another.

"His type won't go far."

"He killed his father."

"Come his eighteenth birthday, he won't sing as well," predicted his classmates, who had detected his talent long before the public did. When his voice failed to change pitch with age, these men were confirmed in their earlier suspicion that he was, after all, a eunuch.

Yitades' mysterious withdrawal following his awkward encounter with the infamous divorcee opened up new avenues for speculation.

"The popularity has gone to his head," said one.

"Now that he no longer eats other people's leftovers, he thinks himself a lord," pitched in another.

"The goon."

"The imbecile."

"The coward."

Sometimes such derision was voiced within earshot of the head priest, but Aba Berhanu wasn't beyond reproach himself. Although he had been ostentatiously well disposed towards the humble deacon in earlier days, contributing to his education and maintenance in front of a roomful of students, the priest had of late become a changed person. As with all men of feeble character, his sense of charity was geared towards maintaining a perpetual donor-and-receiver relationship. As a result, the moment his beneficiary improved his station in life, Aba Berhanu felt threatened and set out to destroy him. "Is it my eyes, or is Yitades' nose higher in the air?" he was heard to say on more than one occasion.

Now that Yitades had come down with a mysterious illness, one that distracted him from his church duties and obligations, the head priest had to take action. After all, the extra parishioners the young deacon had drawn, and the funds they infused into the church's coffers in the form of offerings and contributions, had allowed the head priest to lead a pampered life. Since Yitades had assumed the position of head deacon eighteen months ago, and money had begun to pour like a spring flood, Aba Berhanu had replaced his daub-and-wattle house, with its leaky thatched roofing, with a two-bedroom timber structure topped with corrugated metal sheets. He had even begun to contemplate paving his dirt floor with a concrete slab.

ABA BERHANU seldom paid a social visit to a subordinate. Since Yitades had moved to his newly built stud-and-mud hut a year and a half ago, the head priest had dropped in on him only once—for the housewarming. Yitades remembered that while the other guests sat on the mat that he had laid on the floor, forming a wide perimeter that ran the full length of the hut, Aba Berhanu insisted on standing, declining the special chair reserved for him. He had also slipped out long before the others did.

When he finally decided to visit his ailing deacon, the head priest didn't expect to linger a moment longer than necessary.

"Anybody home?" he yelled, pounding at the closed door. Surveying the dark shadows of the nearby woods, he was surprised at how secluded his protégé's house was. "Anybody home?" he repeated as he forced his way in. The wooden door squeaked, scraping the uneven dirt floor. The interior was no brighter than the outdoors. Only a dying fire in the corner betrayed the fact that the hut was occupied. Aba Berhanu had to call Yitades by name before the young man realized he wasn't dreaming.

"Do come in, Father," he managed to mumble. "But don't get too close—I must have contracted the flu," he lied. Yitades lit a candle and sat up, bundled and covering half his face. "I think I have the flu," he repeated.

The head priest had already got wind of what had happened. The young divorcee was not known to hold her tongue in check. She had bragged to women she had met—whether at the butcher's shop, the tailor's, the alehouse, or the market—that she had slept with the superstar.

Aba Berhanu loudly cleared his throat, and shifted his weight from one leg to the other. "Son," he began, "I've heard what that evil woman has done to you. It is nothing for you to be ashamed of." Aba Berhanu was surprised by his own utterance, his compassion and heartfelt forgiveness.

"I was drunk," Yitades mumbled between sobs. "Father, you have my word: I will not touch alcohol again."

"Son," Aba Berhanu intoned, finding another opportunity to impart his favourite quote, "remember that 'not that which goeth into the mouth defileth a man; but that which cometh out of the mouth, this defileth a man.'"

"Oh, Father, absolve me against the evil sin that woman made me commit!" Yitades was inconsolable.

"Son," Aba Berhanu droned, "the flesh might be weak, but it is nothing that the sacrament of marriage cannot easily redeem."

Indeed, Aba Berhanu had given considerable thought to the weakness of the flesh. His own daughter, Werknesh, was an old maid at the age of twenty-eight, waiting for an eligible man who never showed up. Yitades had the makings of a good and providing husband, if one was willing to overlook his few flaws. And Aba Berhanu had already demonstrated his forgiveness. The biggest beneficiary from the union of the two young people, the head priest reasoned, would be the Church of St. George of Mechara. Weighed down with a wife and, hopefully, a few children, Yitades would never be tempted to leave his home church for a bigger and better diocese; and Aba Berhanu would meet his Maker secure in the knowledge that the temple he had nurtured with love and tenderness was in capable hands.

"Tomorrow is the Birthday of the Virgin," Aba Berhanu reminded Yitades, ending his brief visit. "You will celebrate with us."

4

A BINDING COMMUNION

Werknesh's past was a painful subject to her, something she rarely talked about. Long after she had adjusted to her new home and surroundings, she was tormented by sudden flashbacks to what she had left behind in a place she no longer recalled the name of, and to a time that she couldn't pinpoint with any degree of certainty. "I must have been six or seven," she ruminated reluctantly when Azeb pestered her about her childhood. "It was the dead of night when I was bundled out of bed and ferried out of the village, leaving all I had known behind."

It had been a full two months before her family finally found their way to Mechara. She and her parents had survived a cholera outbreak that had wiped out half the population of her birthplace, claiming the lives of all five of her siblings. With a new village to call home, and his dreadful past safely behind him, Aba Berhanu, her father, set out to open a fresh chapter for his family. He renamed his surviving daughter: "You are gold—Werknesh."

But Werknesh's past never left her. Surviving an epidemic that decimated her family made her a target for her new neighbours' suspicions. Like her daughter Azeb three decades later, young Werknesh found herself with few friends, though for a different set of reasons. She was often seen alone at liturgical festivals, which in Mechara, as in the rest of the country, were celebrated with cherished friends. When girls summoned each other to fetch drinking water together, to do the weekly laundry, or to collect firewood, she was seldom invited.

Etiye Hiywet had been moved by the sight of the lone and drifting girl, and she took her under her wing, allowing her to lounge in her shop. At that time, her own family was still intact. Her two boys and husband were busy with the family business, spending days on the road, catering to markets in the surrounding villages. Etiye Hiywet found the company of the skinny girl a welcome diversion from tending to her brisk customers.

With no school to attend, and with little of her time claimed by domestic chores, owing to her family's small size, Werknesh found ample opportunity to while away the hours at the grocery store. At the peak business times of mid-morning and late afternoon, she sprang to her feet to offer assistance. Etiye Hiywet left to her care the boy who walked in with two empty bottles in hand and asked for five cents' worth of cooking oil in one bottle and ten cents' worth of lamp kerosene in the other. A child who asked for three cents' worth of sugar in a paper cone with two cents' worth of tea leaves sprinkled on top was also looked after by Werknesh, who not only was adept at building a leak-proof cone from a piece of old newspaper, but could also identify the right measuring weight, even though she, like her mentor, was unable to read the labels.

When business ebbed at midday, the woman and the girl disappeared behind the high counter, where they spent the lazy hours sipping sweet tea and sharing village gossip. For a few moments each day Etiye Hiywet left the care of the store to her young friend, and went out to visit an ailing neighbour or to burn incense at the church door. Hovering outside the store doorway, waiting for such an interlude, were children who, when they thought the coast was clear, marched inside to pester Werknesh for a treat of sweets.

Like all storeowners in Mechara, Etiye Hiywet kept bits and pieces of candy from depleted containers in a glass jar. When her young customers asked her to "bless" their purchase (a euphemism—they were looking for a free sweet), she would reach inside the glass jar and hand them scraps of candies. A storeowner who refused to bless a purchase once too often would lose the errand runner, and the business he or she brought, to the competition next door.

With few exceptions, the crowd that pestered Werknesh was made up of older boys. Standing out in the group was a tall, lanky lad, son of the local tailor, a recent arrival with a yellow set of teeth, which he attributed, depending on his mood, to excess or insufficient fluoride in his drinking water. (At the time, few people in Mechara knew what fluoride was, though it occurred naturally in the drinking water of nearby villages.) His name was Endale, but people called him Endale Fluoride. If those brief interludes when she was in charge of the store brought Werknesh a lasting memory, it was Endale Fluoride. The rest of the faces would soon fade from her memory, to be replaced by a fresh and younger crowd. And as the girls she had known settled down to raise families, she found herself gradually sticking out more, like a stalk of reed in receding waters.

"I will never find a husband," she tearfully admitted to Etiye Hiywet the day she turned twenty-five.

"Hush," chided the older woman, "a beautiful girl like you would be a catch for any man." Etiye Hiywet had a few eligible men in mind for her, not least of them Yitades.

Werknesh had known Yitades for as long as she could remember. He was a ghostlike presence in the bustling church grounds, but the two seldom exchanged more than customary greetings. When her father told her that he had invited the young deacon to celebrate the Birthday of the Virgin with the family, she didn't read much into it. After all, Yitades had been steadily ascending the clerical ladder; it was just a matter of time before he shared a table with the head of the church.

YITADES WOULD LONG REMEMBER that first visit to his future in-laws' residence, and the vulgar display of wealth that greeted him as soon as the door was opened. Standing against the white-washed wall of the family room was a towering armoire with a full-length mirror on one of its swinging doors. Instead of the traditional woven food table, the *messob,* which in many house-holds was brought out of storage as needed, there was a real wooden table, permanently situated in the sprawling dining room, with enough chairs for a small congregation. As the kitchen was detached from the dwelling, the rooms were smokeless.

The fact that there were two bedrooms in the head's residence was already known in the parish, but to witness this marvel was quite an experience for Yitades. In each room was a bed large enough for a small family. Imported coverlets were draped over the stuffed mattresses. Matching chests of drawers and bed stands testified to an attention to detail.

If the young deacon had had any respect for the head of the church before, it existed no more. "How can a man remain true to his faith with so many worldly possessions?" he asked himself. Yitades was gazing at a lone incandescent bulb dangling from the dining-room rafters—an affectation in electricity-free Mechara—when it dawned on him where he had seen such ostentation before: at the home of the infamous divorcee, of course!

The young man was witnessing a holy man embarking on the road of sinners.

DESPITE HIS DISAPPOINTMENT, Yitades maintained his compo-sure throughout the evening. Dinner was soon announced. The priest's wife brought a stack of *injera* on a moon-sized plate, placing the freshly baked bread between the men. Not far behind her was Werknesh with a pot of steaming stew. Small servings of chicken stew, lamb stew, vegetables, lentil stew, split peas, and *shiro* formed a bracelet around the *injera.* More out of tradition than a need to prove the food wasn't poisoned, the lady of the house nibbled a sample before retreating to the far corner, where she shared a small plate with her daughter. From time to time the women got up to refresh the men's drinks or the stew that was favoured most.

Each time Werknesh turned her back, Yitades was briefly distracted. Her well-rounded behind was the talk of the neighbourhood. Even the anonymity of the traditional white dress and the *netela* that draped her shoulders couldn't hide her proverbial hourglass figure and pronounced hips. Every now and then she caught him assessing her, and he quickly averted his eyes. Werknesh spoke little throughout the evening. In fact, the only audible conversation came from the men's table. It was poor form for women to be heard from in the presence of male visitors, and Aba Berhanu's women were in truly fine form.

"I hear the bishop is coming our way," Aba Berhanu announced.

"That would be a miracle," replied Yitades, almost choking on his meal. "When do you suppose that will happen?"

"I shouldn't be surprised if His Eminence arrived before the harvest," the head priest answered. He paused a moment before adding: "I passed your name as a candidate for priesthood. You are one of the reasons for the visit. The other reason is the miracles of St. George of Mechara, which everyone talks about."

For the rest of the evening Yitades thought of little other than the bishop's visit. Affixing the title *Aba,* derivative of *Father,* to his name was the dream of a lifetime. But he was also aware that a deacon couldn't be invested with the powers of a priest before he had taken a spouse. Long after he had given up hope of ever becoming a *Qomos,* Yitades hadn't come to terms with the idea of raising a family.

IF WERKNESH HAD BEEN EXPECTING an unpleasant surprise that evening, she must have been relieved when the guest finally took his leave. The Virgin's Birthday passed uneventfully. Days later, when the young deacon had finally receded from her memory once more, she was jolted by an impertinent question.

"What do you think of Yitades?" her mother casually asked her.

"I don't think of him at all," was Werknesh's response.

"I mean, would you consider him fit for a husband?"

Werknesh paused a moment before giving her unequivocal answer: "No."

A quarter of a century later, when her youngest daughter announced her plans to marry a man of whom Werknesh disapproved, and sought her godmother's blessing in place of her father's missing consent, Werknesh attempted to dissuade her. She explained the reason why she, Werknesh, had got yoked to the wrong man: "I married your father because I was naïve enough to take Etiye Hiywet's advice," she told Azeb heatedly. "I don't want you to make the same mistake."

Indeed, Etiye Hiywet had been the most vocal advocate of the marriage of the two young people. "The quiet types make good husbands," she told Werknesh, citing her late husband as an example. She eased Yitades' concerns about his suitor's pampered upbringing, and the difficulties it might create in his straitened life, by referring to the touch of butter that all babies receive at birth. "Some of us get to enjoy the butter a tad longer than the rest," she said. "It is not a character flaw."

If the marriage ceremony was any indication of the life that awaited the bride, it was not promising. At the groom's insistence, no celebration tents were pitched or carpets spread. No parading attendants, either. There was no exchange of gifts between the affianced, and no confirmation of surety. On the wedding day, a Sunday, a large crowd gathered at the church, largely out of curiosity. The marriage ceremony lasted only two hours. The holy matrimony was formalized, and the nuptial tie pronounced binding, when the bridegroom attached a silver ring to his wife's neck-cord.

Forty days later, the couple reappeared in church to receive the Eucharist together. Eucharist weddings were rare because, unlike civil marriages, they bound couples for life, with no earthly recourse should the union go sour. In Mechara, Yitades was only the fourth man to take Communion with his wife. He was encouraged in his decision by Aba Berhanu, who wished to remove any possibility of a future breakup. For nothing but death can separate a couple who take Communion together.

BOOK II

A Game
Called Gena

5

THE FAMILY QUEEN

*A*zeb caught fire. She had been experimenting with an unproven method of relaxing hair when the accident took place. The night before, she had coated her skull with a thick layer of scented butter. Early the next day, she lit a pile of charcoal, and when it turned glowing red, she tossed in a scoop of sugar and bent down to straighten her hair. No one had told her that sugar could catch fire.

"Whatever gave you the idea?" Genet demanded as she trimmed the charred ends of Azeb's hair and attended to her singed skin.

"Beletu," Azeb replied.

"One of these days, she will get you killed," her sister cautioned.

Beletu, the middle child, was the beauty of the family. Some believed she was the goddess of the village. And as far as Beletu knew, there was not a soul in the country who could hold a candle to her. But that was only as far as she knew. What she didn't know, but clearly suspected, was that without her, there might not have been such an adjective as *beletu,* meaning "triumphant."

"I want to change my name," she had told her mother at the age of eight.

"But why?" demanded Werknesh.

"I don't think 'Beletu' is *me.*"

"What is that supposed to mean?"

"I want to be called *Tsehai*—The Sun."

"That name brings nothing but trouble," said Werknesh, citing two compelling examples: a young woman by the same name who had lost her vocal cords after she swallowed a splintered fishbone, and a mother of two who had drowned while attempting to cross a raging river on the back of a lame mule.

Beletu had come to recognize her beauty at an even earlier age. While she was still in her mother's arms, women stopped to admire her looks. "What a pretty child," they said. *"Tif-tif,"* they spat on her, adding, "May He protect her from the evil eye."

Beletu was four years of age—or maybe five—when a stranger doubled back to get a better look at her. "That kid …" the woman began, then decided not to complete her sentence.

"Mama," said Beletu, "did you know what that woman was about to say?"

"No, what was she going to say?" Werknesh asked, grinning.

"She was going to say, 'That kid is beautiful.'"

BELETU HAD Mediterranean features: a long, pointed nose and tiny lips, which she liked to equate with those of the angels (paintings of which she had grown up admiring). Her hair was straight and fell to the small of her back. She was darker than the rest. Genet had the fairest skin. Beletu proudly noted that she, Beletu, was "grey like a fish." Her teeth were well formed, though that might have more to do with her mother's hard work than a simple gift of nature. The moment her children lost their milk teeth, Werknesh massaged their gums with wood ash each morning, so the replacements would grow in straight. That Beletu's teeth were strikingly white, however, had a lot to do with her own tireless efforts.

BELETU RESENTED nothing more than domestic chores. The moment she detected a piece of work heading her way, she came down with the most unclassifiable diseases. Often she was able to diagnose her own afflictions. "Yesterday, I was laughing in public when I felt a piercing jab in my side," she once said. "I am still unable to lift anything"—the inference being that she had been stung by the evil eye.

There were times when Werknesh grew tired of Beletu's endless excuses, and ordered her, say, to pick up a bucket and follow her sisters to the river. At these times Beletu might leave the house with the bucket, but she wouldn't go farther than the nearest bush. Instead, she sent neighbourhood boys, who were ever anxious to do her bidding, to fetch the water for her. She was disdainful of her compliant sisters. "They have no use for their heads," she said, "so they may as well carry something on them." When her exasperated mother ordered Beletu to do the weekly laundry, she conceived a way out.

"Azeb," she said, taking her worshipping sister aside, "if you do the washing for me, I'll show you how to get your hair straight like mine." As a reward for a job well done, she advised the naïve one to smoke her hair with fumes of sugar.

Beletu wasn't entirely opposed to doing daily chores, if the task was something that no one else could do as well. She spent countless hours admiring her reflection in the mirror, for instance, because it was a job that no other person was qualified to do better. She brushed her teeth five or six times a day. At the time, tubes of toothpaste and bristle brushes were not stocked in local stores, but that didn't deter Beletu; she devised a homemade substitute—a mixture of ground charcoal and salt—which she carried on her person at all times. If she happened to have a moment's respite from the domestic chore she was busy avoiding, she would take out a brushing twig and the vial containing her unique tooth powder and work at her teeth.

Beletu was permanently in the market for a good brushing twig. The moment she got a whiff of the whitening properties of a certain weed stalk or plant root, she gathered a small army of boys and set out to harvest the field in earnest. In her bag were carefully trimmed, pencil-sized stalks, bunched together accord-

ing to their hygienic potential. Azeb might pilfer one or two to
sate her curiosity, but the theft was discovered immediately.
Beletu wasn't unreasonable; she simply reminded her younger
sister what services might be expected of her in return for the
stolen goods. For example, if shortly afterwards Werknesh asked
the family beauty to take a borrowed pot back to its owner, Beletu
would delegate the task to Azeb, mentally ticking off a payment
she was owed.

"One of these days she will put something in her mouth that
will seal her lips for good," Werknesh once predicted, aggravated
by Beletu's obsession with her teeth. But what her daughter put
in her mouth next had the opposite effect. As her teeth couldn't
be whiter than white itself, Beletu figured, the only way of
enhancing their radiance was by darkening the background. One
afternoon she came home having had her gums tattooed with
lamp soot. When they healed, her gums turned decidedly green,
achieving the desired effect. And after that, it took a funeral
procession to force Beletu to close her mouth, if only for a fleeting moment.

Beletu elevated personal hygiene to a higher level, her dedication to cleanliness rivalling her father's commitment to the soul,
when she decided her weekly bath was entirely inadequate.
Already it was the talk of the village that the preacher's daughter
dived in the river more often than a nesting fish-eagle. When she
began frequenting the waters even more, questions began to be
raised.

"What is she trying to wash off?" many puzzled.

"It is a curse," observed a passing merchant one Wednesday
afternoon.

"What curse?"

"There is a shop owner in Gelemso who was cursed at an early
age," he expounded. "Even locking his door has become a tiring
chore for him, as he has to check it again, and again, and again,
and …"

Most villagers bathe once every few months. Such infrequent washing doesn't result in a foul body odour, as one might expect, but in itchiness of the skin. In Mechara, good Christians take a bath on major holidays, such as the Festival of Epiphany, the Feast of the Finding of the Cross *(Meskel)*, Christmas, Easter, and the New Year. On the morning of September 11, Ethiopia's New Year, the rivers of Mechara contained bare humans who surpassed in number the schools of fish that visited the shores during the spawning season.

Beletu defied tradition once more when she took her dip in broad daylight, as opposed to under cover of dusk or dawn. Her naked presence in the waters set off a heightened activity behind the adjacent bushes. And by the time she had dried herself and put her dress on, the dark basalt rocks where the boys lay hidden looked as if they had been harbouring pigeons.

BELETU WAS THE FIRST in her family to discover the existence of a much bigger and more vibrant world beyond the mountains girdling her native village. A glimpse of this other reality—which she instinctively felt to be her own—came into her view quite by accident. One day as she was lounging at one of her favourite hangouts, a dry goods store, donkeys arrived from nearby Gelemso, delivering a stack of old newspapers, among other goods. Leafing through the papers, she came across torn pages of a European fashion magazine, a rare insert.

Colourful pictures of bleached men and women dressed in odd-looking garments marched out of the frames. Some of the men wore boxers only, and a few of the women were bikini-clad. The storeowner was, predictably, aghast at the lewdness of these images, but Beletu was less horrified. As she continued browsing through the pages, a long-dormant passion awakened. There were photos of large sedans with pronounced tail fins, and pictures of television sets and electrical utensils, the purpose of which neither Beletu nor the storeowner could make out. This was long before a paved highway connected Mechara with the rest of the world, bringing with it an awareness of such modern amenities as automobiles, fridges, ice cream, and motion pictures.

"May I keep these?" Beletu asked, holding the clippings in a deathlike grip. It was the beginning of a love affair with the enticing world that would last for the rest of her life.

This other world acquired a voice each Sunday afternoon when the national radio broadcast *Listeners' Choice,* a program of popular music, which beckoned to Beletu even more strongly than the mute pictures. As in many towns and villages, only a few households in Mechara owned radio receivers in the 1960s. The only time people recognized a need for the suspicious invention was when the Emperor was scheduled to speak, at which time they congregated at one of their neighbours' homes, or at the public teahouse, where for the price of a cup of tea, a mere five cents, they could enjoy the much-anticipated broadcast to their heart's content. The teahouse radio, activated by stacks of batteries mounted on a side table, not only was the biggest in the village but could also receive the clearest signal.

And it was the teahouse radio that Beletu favoured. On Sunday afternoon, when the pace of life in the village slackened somewhat and families found a moment to bring comfort to their bedridden neighbours, when her own baby sister, Azeb, took it upon herself to aid the old and frail at the church grounds, the priest's middle child slipped undetected to the teahouse, where she camped out for the balance of the day with her equally wayward teenaged friends, savouring the music that beamed through a loudspeaker mounted at the doorway. Beletu knew all the popular lyrics by heart, and the particulars of the vocalists never escaped her attention. She had fallen in love with many of the singers, many times over. At five o'clock, when the radio station concluded its three-hour weekly broadcast and the teahouse owner finally managed to turn the machine off without risking his glass windows, tears gathered in her eyes. She took the longest route home, avoiding all human contact.

Genet was the first to recognize the trouble brewing inside her younger sister.

"Young lady," she once said to her, "you should watch yourself."

"What is that supposed to mean?" Beletu demanded angrily.

"You should think of what people might say about you."

"Why should I care about what anybody says?"

"Because you don't live on an island, that's why."

"I would rather live on a lonely island than in this godforsaken place."

"You don't really mean that!"

"I do, with all my heart," was Beletu's bitter retort.

If Beletu hadn't yet found her island, it was because Mechara was still in the grip of the previous century, rooted in uncharted wilderness, totally isolated from the bigger and more promising world. None of her immediate family members had strayed farther than nearby hamlets, a few hours' ride by horse, half a day's journey on foot. Not until the advent of the modern highway and the automobile it brought with it did Beletu finally find her bearings and her promised land.

IF BELETU WAS THE FAMILY LOVEBIRD, and Azeb the quintessential rebel, Genet was the mainstay that kept the household women anchored to solid ground. Neighbours readily admitted her level-headedness. Aba Yitades frequently proclaimed that a name and a person had come into a perfect fit when he (or was it her mother?) picked *Genet,* which means "heaven." In his less guarded moments the priest was even heard admitting that she was a blessing in feminine disguise. However, Genet's most vocal admirer was Werknesh, who had detected her first daughter's insight at an early age.

Genet was barely six when she decoded a cryptic language her parents used to communicate their love life. The practice involved a set of bedsheets, a wedding present from Etiye Hiywet, which, uniquely for bedding, were a red-and-blue plaid on a white background. The set was kept under twin padlocks in a large wooden trunk among the family's scant valuables until it was removed on rare occasions to be spread on her father's mud-dais. "Do you want me to lay out the plaid bedsheet?" Werknesh sometimes asked Aba Yitades as she made his bed. "No, I don't think it will be necessary," he often replied.

The days her father gave his consent for the plaid bedsheet to be produced from its storage, Genet noticed that in the dead of the night, when her mother thought her children were sound asleep, she slipped out of the bed she shared with her daughters, reappearing among them before the rooster crowed. At times Aba Yitades himself broached the subject, though very rarely. Following Azeb's birth, the plaid bedsheet was never removed from its trunk again, and a different routine evolved.

At the heart of this later practice was a middle-aged *dabtara* who lived by himself and whom Werknesh had known for much of her adult life. "Go ask him if he wants his *netela* washed," she would say to one of her daughters, usually on a Saturday. "If he says yes, see if he wants it rushed." Sometimes these instructions were given in the presence of Aba Yitades, but the message, pregnant with illicit longing, aroused no suspicion as it was not uncommon for families to come to the aid of the needy. The afternoons the *dabtara* wanted his *netela* washed—and he often responded in the affirmative and with a note of urgency— Werknesh left home when the coast was clear, returning in time for the third coffee ceremony, which at the priest's home was performed at sunset.

After months of agonizing complicity, Genet finally mustered the courage to confront her mother.

"Mam, I don't think what you are doing is fair," she said to her one Saturday morning, her eyes filled with tears. "Dad may not suspect the affair, but Our Father in Heaven has his eyes on you."

"How long have you known?" was Werknesh's surprised response.

"Longer than you think."

It was the last the *dabtara* had his *netela* washed.

IF WERKNESH WAS SOCIALLY AWKWARD in her youth, with depressingly few friends, her oldest daughter turned out to be her exact opposite, with many of the village girls calling her their true confidante. Even at the Wednesday market, where outsiders often outnumbered the locals, many addressed Genet by name while they only nodded at her mother. "How did you come to know all these people?" Werknesh never tired of asking.

Genet was so finely tuned to the pulse of the community that her mother seldom questioned her judgment. "Mam, you should consider visiting that new mother, even if she is a tanner's wife," was a suggestion Werknesh readily complied with. "Mam, are you still going to charge the blacksmith for the grindstone that he inadvertently chipped?" was a question that prompted her mother to quietly abandon her plans.

Genet managed to bridge the chasm that had opened between her father and his family when, as a ten-year-old, he froze at the sight of a wounded warthog. It all began when she unexpectedly showed up with Azeb in tow at a favourite cousin's wedding preparations. Although she had long been on speaking terms with many of her relations, and although those who had come to know her had nothing but good things to say about her, her sudden appearance at her father's cousins' compound raised a few eyebrows.

"I thought you might need a few extra pairs of hands," was all that she said to her wide-eyed hosts before getting down to work. It was the beginning of a healing process, one that she would struggle to maintain through thick and thin.

6

A VIGILANT SHEPHERD

g enet may have done her part in bridging the chasm between her father and his cousins, but her work came undone on Good Fridays when the priest handed out penance.

On Good Friday, parishioners of St. George of Mechara, like their good cousins in much of the country, lined up before their parish priest to confess their sins and receive their penance so that they could celebrate Easter with consciences as clean as their garments. The solemn event was conducted in a specially erected tent, designed to accommodate the large turnout. Aba Yitades cut a remarkable figure during the service. He stood with his chin held high at the front of the tent, clutching in his right hand a wand of wild olive, symbol of sin purged, and in his left the inevitable accessories of all priests: a small brass cross, a prayer stick, and a fly-switch.

One by one, the parishioners were ushered in to face their confessor.

"Father, since Passion Week, I have ploughed my land," revealed a farmer on a typical Good Friday.

The priest stroked the man's shoulder lightly with the wand before passing his judgment. "Prostrate yourself ten times!"

"Father, I have cut my wood," said the next one in line.

"Ten prostrations!"

"Father, I have washed my laundry," confessed a fidgety woman.

"Ten!"

"Father," said a man Aba Yitades recognized as being from the old compound, a loathed cousin, who stood kneading his fingers, "Father, I've cut my wood."

"Fifty!"

With the exception of a few who chose to make their reparations at home, the rest performed their assigned prostrations in the same tent, under the watchful gaze of their exacting shepherd. With a friend counting for them, they bent down until their forehead touched the ground and kissed the bare earth under their nose while asking the Almighty's forgiveness, before raising themselves up. An exceptionally heavy-set man or woman might not be able to complete the required number of prostrations without running a serious health risk. Aba Yitades recognized the problem, allowing them to complete their penance in instalments.

The priest's cousins, those who considered themselves unfairly targeted by him, resorted to a more crafty method: they assigned a servant to complete their penance. Soon there sprang up a small industry of professional penitents who, for a lump sum, would do the whole set of prostrations for the wealthy. Business was brisk and the waiting line long, until word reached Aba Yitades and the bottom fell out of the market.

ON WEDNESDAYS, Aba Yitades took his mission on the road. Wednesdays were market days, when neighbouring farmers and merchants descended on Mechara in droves. The women strapped their merchandise on their backs, or, if they happened to be nursing babies, balanced the bundle on top of their heads, while the men led mules and donkeys with loads rising high into the heavens.

By midday, downtown Mechara was buzzing louder than a beehive, as sellers and buyers haggled over the price of produce or traded insults over an attempted deceit. Roosters crowed. Goats and sheep fought over a banana peel. A donkey mounting a receptive female triggered a commotion among the young crowd. The boys rowdily cheered the copulation, while the girls covered their heads with the ends of their *netela* and feigned unawareness of the wild sex act.

Azeb was by his side when the priest left home around midday. Along the way, he received homage from villagers who tipped their hats or removed their *netela* and bowed their bared heads in veneration. Some of them approached him for a blessing. While mumbling his benediction, Aba Yitades touched their foreheads with his cross and permitted them to kiss the revered icon before hushing them out of his way. Children knelt down to buss the tip of his shoe before they kissed the cross.

The same children sprinted ahead of him to report his impending arrival to merchants, who gave the youngsters sweets and pennies for their invaluable services. By the time the priest's turban-wrapped head emerged from the distant crowd, the ruckus in the market had died down by a few decibels, and some of the produce had been tucked out of sight.

One Ash Wednesday, Aba Yitades asked a young lady, mother of three, who hadn't seen him coming, "Why are you buying eggs on a fast day?"

"It is, er, for my child," she replied.

"Which one?"

"The youngest one, of course."

"Is she not five or six?"

"She is barely four, Father."

"Well, even then, she is old enough to observe the fast," he ruled. The chastised woman quickly shuffled out of the market, leaving the eggs behind.

"Who is your parish priest?" Aba Yitades asked the guilty merchant, while at the same time extending his open hand to Azeb. Without being told what it was her father wanted, Azeb reached inside the carpet bag that she carried on her back and handed him a worn notebook, which the villagers had aptly labelled the Black Ledger, not only because of its appearance but also its incriminating content. The priest entered the following details in the ledger: *On Ash Wednesday, the year of our Lord 1959, a young merchant by worldly name of Aster Kebede and Christian name of Daughter of St. Michael has brought to market a small basket of eggs in direct violation of the Lenten Fast. The said woman is from St. Peter's parish of Boke Gudo (not much of a parish). Her soul-father is Aba Shimeles.*

A little farther ahead were grain merchants. Piles of sorghum, barley, chickpeas, lentils, soybeans, and safflower seeds lay on a mat, with a cup full of the grain on top of each pyramidal mound. Each type of grain was sold according to its own tin measuring cup so that customers could compare prices without resorting to confusing mathematics.

Aba Yitades picked up a measuring cup from one of the heaps, emptied it, and examined the bottom to make sure that it wasn't hammered in, thus reducing the measurements. With his prayer stick, he tapped a sack that he found lying next to each merchant. The moment he detected the jingling sound of an empty tin cup, he ordered the merchant to open the sack. Often he found tampered measuring cups hidden in the sack's belly, ready to be used on unsuspecting customers.

In earlier days, Aba Yitades used to order the guilty merchant not to set foot in Mechara again. After all, it was a village founded by his ancestors, and the settlers set the rules. But as the practice of tampering with measuring cups became widespread, he found the most practical solution was to dispose of the confiscated cups. In a village where there was no police force, no manned jails, no state-appointed court, or any discernible government, Aba Yitades was plaintiff, prosecutor, witness, judge, and jury.

The fact that the market day in Mechara was Wednesday may have placed an additional burden on Aba Yitades, as Wednesdays and Fridays are often fast days. Even when it was not a fast day, the priest found wickedness where he least expected it. One Wednesday afternoon as he roamed the open market with his daughter in tow, Aba Yitades was drawn towards the butcher shop. Smoke bellowed through the rusted corrugated metal roof, and the sweet smell of sizzling beef slithered through the gaps in the timber enclosure, beckoning even the blind from miles away. The patrons who overflowed the small building were—with the exception of a few shy women who slunk in and out of the shop with wrapped packages in hand—adult men. And they were mostly outsiders, visiting farmers and merchants who, once they had successfully conducted their weekly transactions, stopped by for a well-deserved treat. They ordered a slab of meat that on an ordinary day they could ill afford. Some of them devoured their brisket raw, congregating around the busy counter, while most wanted theirs barbecued. In the corner was a giant frying pan fashioned from the bottom of an oil drum. It had been baking on the open fire since the shop opened at dawn.

The butcher diced a piece of meat the size of a small fist, sprinkled the pile with salt and cayenne powder, and tossed it on the frying pan. Then the patron took over. With a long wooden stick, dripping with grease from long use, he stirred the beef until it was roasted to his liking. When Aba Yitades walked in, with his Black Ledger not far behind, the frying pan had just been emptied onto a serving board, and the customers had begun to dig in.

"Aba Yitades," the men shouted, almost in unison, "do join us."

"He who arrives when a meal is served has been kissed on his rear," observed a sage. Indeed, kissing babies on the rear was thought to bring them good luck in later life; many of them arrive when food is on the table.

"Oh, I don't think I can eat any, I just had my—" Aba Yitades began to say, when he was drowned by loud protestations.

"Father, may I remind you of the old adage," continued the same sage, "that 'Those who don't share a plate are destined to be enemies.'"

"Well, a mouthful won't kill anyone."

The butcher suspected the real reason for the priest's rare visit, but he didn't wish to engage his confessor within earshot of the guests, so he beckoned him towards the open backyard, momentarily leaving the store in the care of an assistant. Azeb remained where she stood, by the door, her back pressed against the uneven frame, her eyes downcast—not so much out of politeness as to avoid unwanted attention from tipsy customers.

"It has been almost three weeks since I last saw you in church," Aba Yitades reminded the butcher, the moment they were a safe distance away.

"You know how it is in this business, Father," the butcher began, nervously rubbing his hands on his soiled apron. "I travel a lot. The price of a bull has gone up around here because of the approaching highway."

"Who slaughters the bulls for you these days?" Aba Yitades quickly demanded.

"My assistant, of course. I no longer have the youthful energy to trip a five-hundred-kilo bull." The butcher tapped at his pot-belly as he spoke, as though his bulging waistline held the clue to the burdens of creeping old age.

"That won't do!" Aba Yitades was all business. "That young man might as well give up his neck-cord. I no longer see him in church, not even on Easter Sunday. What that man slaughters can't be called Christian."

The butcher realized the ramifications of such an accusation: If word of his selling "unchristian meat" leaked out, it would mean not only the end of his business but also relocation of his entire family. He and the members of his household would be instant outcasts. Beads of sweat gathered around the butcher's eyes and upper lip. His hands began to tremble. He secured the priest's reprieve only after offering a heartfelt promise to make instant amends.

"I will alert his soul-father to the fact," the butcher swore, "and I will see to it that this Christmas he donates the *Demera* [the centre pole around which the festival fireworks were built]."

Before returning to his post, the butcher obtained further concessions from his confessor. "For the moment, this conversation will stay between the two of us," Aba Yitades assured him.

Over the priest's ringing protests, the butcher carved up a sizable slice of prime beef, rolled it in old newspaper, the customary wrapper, and handed it to Azeb to take home to her mother. Such a windfall wasn't entirely unwelcome, since the last commemoration observed in Mechara had been almost three months ago. Thus, the busy day would have ended on a pleasant note for the diligent shepherd and his mute tagalong had it not been for a minor incident at the exit.

A teenaged girl was emerging from the shop, not far behind Azeb, when a playful local boy pinched her on the rear.

"Son of a whore," she said to him.

The crowd burst out laughing. They were used to her predilection for foul language and enjoyed provoking her. Aba Yitades, however, couldn't afford to be seen walking away from such gross indecency.

"Young lady," he admonished her, "with such a sharp tongue, your place in hell is assured."

"You will get there first," she told the priest.

No one laughed this time.

Aba Yitades could only take the matter up with her guardians. Secretly, he hoped that her father, Abebe the Bandit, was away from home, running from the law as usual.

ABEBE THE BANDIT had only attained the tender age of five when he first ran afoul of the law: he was caught pilfering a banana from a fruit stand. His father, a respected *dabtara,* had done everything in his power to reform his son, baptizing him twice and renaming him as often. He drew out his belt so frequently that in the end he decided to wear the piece of leather not around his waist but around his neck, so that he could easily reach it when the occasion called for instant discipline.

The community had done its fair share of collective child rearing; men and women alike boxed the boy's ears the moment they caught his hands where they didn't belong. Far from being reformed, however, the boy thrived on the attention. His wickedness deepened. Abebe the Bandit had broken into homes, shops, barns, the church Bethlehem, and the storage place for sacred vessels; he had dug up tombs of famous people in the hope of finding hidden treasure; and he sold the personal effects of his dying grandmother, his one true sympathizer. In the end, though, he realized that his fortune lay elsewhere. He decided to ambush merchants on their way home from distant markets.

Every other year or so, he came back home following a Crown pardon. "Two things I am never accused of," he bragged. "I have never robbed people of my home village or taken another person's life." Etiye Hiywet, who never ceased to wonder about the fate of the men she lost, quietly differed on both counts. During his visits home, Abebe the Bandit was rarely seen outside his fortified lair, but the villagers took no chances. Doors were barred, and the locksmith worked overtime. In the end the community discovered, with a sigh of relief, that the storm had passed over: Abebe the Bandit had flown the coop once more.

THE DAY ABA YITADES DECIDED to drop in on the family of the girl who had publicly insulted him, he had every reason to believe that the homegrown bandit was on the run yet again.

"Anybody home?" he yelled over the high wooden fence and over the barking of the guard dogs. He called out twice more, with no human response. He was about to take his leave when he spied an eye assessing him through a crack in the gate.

"Well, well, well, if it is not the holy man himself," Abebe the Bandit announced, breaking into a wide grin. "What a pleasure it is to see you, Father," he added, extending a hand. Aba Yitades wasn't quite sure if the feeling was mutual, but he took the hand all the same. "Do come in," Abebe the Bandit offered, moving out of the way. Before latching the gate, he took one more look outside, making sure that his august guest hadn't brought hostile company.

Aba Yitades was surprised by the number of children the bandit had fathered, seven in all. As many dogs ran around. There seemed to be scarcely a year's difference between one child and the next. And they were attired in increasingly ragged clothes, each younger one worse dressed than the ones before. Handing down was strictly enforced at the bandit's home, the priest quietly noted. He noted, too, that many of the children couldn't find their way around on account of the flies that had permanently camped on their eyes.

The priest couldn't recall baptizing all of the children, but however hard he strained his neck, he was unable to tell, from where he stood a mere five paces away, if they wore their identifying neck-cords.

Their mother was exceptionally hostile. A lit cigarette was in her mouth, and one of her breasts dangled in the breeze. The baby in her arms was asleep, but she seemed to be either too distracted or too worn out to tuck her breast back inside her dress.

Five chairs were laid out, willy-nilly, around a giant *zegba* tree. A bottle of imported ouzo was visible from a distance, but the number of glasses, with various amounts of alcohol in them, couldn't be accounted for by the number of adults.

"Take a seat," Abebe the Bandit said, pointing at one of the chairs. He poured a generous amount of the alcohol into a not-so-clean glass and handed it to his guest. The enigmatic smile hadn't left his face.

It soon became apparent to the priest why there were so many glasses. While he watched in horror, Abebe the Bandit poured a shot of the alcohol into a glass, tossed some water in with it, and, when the mixture turned chalk white, handed it to his four-year-old son.

"The price of cow's milk is sky-high, so I raise my children on Mary's milk," he explained, the silly smile still plastered on his face.

The priest wasn't amused by the crude reference to the Virgin.

"Would you mind if I asked you a personal question?" Aba Yitades tentatively began, his face drawn closer to his host.

"Not at all," Abebe the Bandit assured his guest, all smiles.

"Have you ever thought of your soul?"

"Well, there's a question for you, Father!" Abebe the Bandit roared boisterously. "And do you know what? It deserves an answer." He refreshed his glass of ouzo before picking up the thread of his discourse: "My late father was a man of God—"

"That he was, may the Lord have mercy on his soul," Aba Yitades interrupted.

"Every night, he used to make us read from the Holy Bible," continued Abebe the Bandit, without missing a beat. "The *dabtara* was especially hard on my older brother and me, his sons. We dutifully memorized our catechism, and could recite the Ten Commandments backwards and forwards. And then one day I had a revelation."

"A revelation?"

"Yes. Suppose Moses made a mistake transcribing the Ten Commandments."

"That is some revelation!"

"With the exception of observing the Sabbath," continued Abebe the Bandit, paying no attention to the priest's sarcastic remark, "the Good Lord couldn't have dictated what Moses wrote down."

"Where did you get that idea?"

"The evidence is in the Old Testament."

"Enlighten me."

"Take, for instance, the Sixth Commandment: Thou shall not kill. The fact that the Good Lord had recommended a capital punishment for infractions for which no sensible judge today would hand down more than a suspended sentence is proof that He thought nothing of taking someone's life. Condemned to death are, for instance, the child who cursed his mother or father,

and the man who slept with his daughter-in-law or his neighbour's loose spouse (which, incidentally, means half the men in
this village). And if we were to believe Leviticus, mercy is not to
be shown, either, to the young boy who has lost his virginity to a
dumb sheep—which, by the way, is still a popular pastime among
shepherd boys."

"But He had long since amended those laws," Aba Yitades
corrected.

"What about the Fifth Commandment?" Abebe the Bandit
continued, ignoring the priest's protest.

"What about it?"

"The fact that the Good Lord had never known His Father is
proof enough for me that He couldn't have conceived the idea of
honouring parents. And as for the Seventh Commandment, can
you imagine Joseph passing up a loose wench?"

"This is the alcohol talking," the priest exclaimed.

"The Good Lord has a soft spot for the Sabbath, I grant you
that," continued Abebe the Bandit, once again ignoring the
priest's impertinence, "and that was His big mistake. If He had
only taken that extra day to refine his creations, I can assure you
the world would be a much better place today."

"For a son of a *dabtara,* you are a disgrace," Aba Yitades spewed.

"I take that as a compliment." Abebe the Bandit bowed almost
to the level of his knee accepting the praise. "Father, have you ever
heard of the Agñwak tribe?"

"Yes, I have. Why?"

"A while ago, someone told me how they practised their
religion."

"But I thought they were pagans."

"You may call them pagans, Father, but those naked people
might be on to something big. From what I was able to put
together, they build their god from the ground up by forming a
mound from trinkets they have gathered. (After all, who created
whom is almost secondary—as humans, what we need most is

something we can worship.) Both men and women of the tribe take equal part in the activity. (Naked men tend to be less prejudiced towards similarly nude women, you know.) In the mound they have built you might find a broken mug, an old teakettle, the rim of eyeglasses they had found in some trash, or someone's missing sock. In the days and weeks that follow, they gather before their homegrown deity to make their petitions and offer sacrifices.

"Not all their prayers are answered, and these people appreciate the limitations of their deity. But if the god they have built with their sweat and labour proves insensitive to their needs, they don't shy away from expressing their displeasure. They shout at it, hurl stones at it, and in the end, if it proves entirely worthless, they tear it down, discard the old pieces, and set out to build a new god from a different bunch of materials."

"I see. What you are saying is that we should start looking for a new Jehovah," interjected Aba Yitades, his sarcasm written on his face.

"Father, I am afraid you missed the point. What interests me, what I am trying to bring to your attention, is the *communication* part. The idea that you can give your god a piece of your mind without fear of wrathful retribution is first-rate thinking. Also, the fact that you can custom-tailor your deity to suit your individual needs and temperament is a groundbreaking achievement."

Aba Yitades rose to his feet. He stretched and reached for his prayer stick.

"You are not leaving so soon, are you?" Abebe the Host was arm-twisting.

"I have had enough blasphemy for one day," Aba Yitades curtly replied.

"But I thought you were here on business. Surely you didn't come all the way here looking for the one sheep you lost." Abebe the Bandit was all teeth as he said this.

Recalling what had brought him so far out of his way, Aba
Yitades broke into a smile. Compared to her father, the girl
seemed meeker than an altar boy.

The bandit fired a parting piece of news. "Aba Yitades, this
time I have come to stay. I have decided to be a good father to my
children, and a better citizen. Don't be surprised to see me at one
of your Sunday Masses."

BEFORE HE RAN into Abebe the Bandit that memorable afternoon, if someone had asked Aba Yitades who the black sheep of
his flock was, he would have readily answered: "Endale Fluoride."

Indeed, Endale Fluoride had come a long way from the days
when he hovered with kids half his height around the grocery
store that Werknesh tended, pestering her for scraps of candies.
Besides his intimidating bulk and persona, he had developed an
insatiable lust. At any given time, he was thought to keep two or
more concubines.

"He is such a rogue," said a respectable-looking woman at a
festive gathering. "What do women find so attractive about him?"

"His size," replied a homely lass, who admired his two-metre
height and his solid build—which were rare in the region.

"And don't forget his stamina," pitched in the infamous
divorcee, who could only think of a different type of size.

At a very early age, Azeb had developed a strong aversion to
Endale Fluoride, not because of his physical attributes—she knew
he was handsome, and Werknesh openly admired his looks—but
because of his rough and abrasive manner. The moment she saw
him head her way, she either changed direction or made herself
scarce by slipping behind an open door or walking in the shadow
of an adult until he passed out of sight. Often he managed to run
her down or surprise her. He relished inflicting pain on her.
Whether it was his viselike bear hug or his nipple-pinching fetish,
Endale Fluoride never let go of his victim until she dropped a
few convincing tears.

"I'll marry you when you grow up," he told her, with a parting laugh.

"I wouldn't marry you if you were the last man on earth," Azeb replied, her face drenched in tears.

Onlookers found his antics amusing, and no one interfered. After all, what could a man in his thirties want from a preteen girl, if not childish distraction?

Like Abebe the Bandit, Endale Fluoride never held an honest job, though for a different set of reasons: he lived off his romantic conquests. Since the age of twenty he had cohabited with a woman who was twelve years his senior, but who, as the owner of the village's only tavern and two rental houses, was considered by many to be a worthy catch. She not only covered Endale's living expenses and padded his wallet, but turned a blind eye to his philandering as well. This unorthodox living arrangement and the sad example it set in the community angered Aba Yitades more than the abuse sustained by his daughter.

No less angered by Endale's domestic setup was Abebe the Bandit, who maintained that a man shouldn't lay claim to other people's money until he had been tested under fire (preferably by .44-calibre, 250-grain Black Talon ammo), as he most certainly had been when holding up better-armed merchants. And he didn't shy away from expressing his views within hearing of his arch-enemy, which led to frequent scuffles. Many came to regret Abebe the Bandit's decision to stay home and become a good father to his children and a better citizen, for it soon become apparent that the village of Mechara was big enough for Abebe the Bandit or Endale Fluoride, but not both.

Any night out in the village could turn into a circus, with the two misfits trading insults and sometimes fisticuffs. Abebe the Bandit may have been a head shorter than Endale Fluoride, but no one bet against him. One exceptionally charged night, as the two misfits left the tavern with the clear intention of letting blood, an elder intervened. "Why don't you settle your differences on Christmas?" he said. "It is only a month away."

The old man, like most villagers, was haunted by a similar incident that had taken place some five years before. Two young men had been at each other's throats for quite some time, when they finally decided to settle their differences once and for all. As they were almost the same height and build, the fist fight dragged on for over an hour. Finally, out of sheer frustration, one of them produced a knife and thrust it into his opponent's heart, ending the contest—for the moment.

But only for the moment, because he was soon ambushed by his victim's nephews, who left an identical knife in his chest. In all, four people died, two from each side, before the village elders finally managed to bring order. It was the one and only case of multiple homicide in Mechara, and no one wanted a repeat.

"Okay, Christmas," Abebe the Bandit agreed.

Endale Fluoride delivered a parting jab: "Don't turn tail."

In MECHARA, as in the rest of the country, Christmas was a community affair, celebrated with one's neighbours and friends out in the open. Every town and village had a field designated for the occasion, commonly called the *Meskel* Square, after the Feast of the Finding of the Cross, by far the biggest liturgical festival in the nation. In Mechara, the *Meskel* Square was the Wednesday market, the only open space large enough to accommodate the anticipated crowd.

On Christmas Eve, the village elders left their homes with select groups of people to erect in the middle of the field a giant wooden pole—the *Demera,* which that year was donated by the butcher's remorseful assistant. Around this centre post, the community would build its pyramid of torches and celebrate the festival together.

Christmas preparations had begun weeks before, when boys left for the woods in search of suitable material for their torches. They cut willow switches by the bundle, which they then fastened together to form a *chibbo,* which looked like a stiff broom. Since the one who built the largest and most impressive *chibbo* was held in high regard, the project was completed in secret. Although only one *chibbo* per family was expected, it wasn't unusual to see each boy shouldering his own handiwork when the time arrived.

Not every household had a male member who was fit for such a grand undertaking, but the community saw to it that no one was left behind. Boys were encouraged to visit the elderly, the widowed, or families such as Aba Yitades' own that could use their assistance.

"Etiye Selamawit," a boy asked a woman who had recently lost her only son, "do you have someone to build a torch for you this Christmas?"

"Yes, Ato Bereket's boys have promised to," she graciously replied, "but you could carry it to the field for me."

An elderly couple whose married children had moved to another district were in the hands of the community. "Everyone has deserted us," the woman told a boy who had come to offer assistance. "What is the world coming to when elders are so thoughtlessly abandoned?" she carried on. "I shouldn't be surprised if we are smitten with a plague any day now."

"Don't worry," the boy assured her, "from now on I will look after you." In return for such charitable acts, boys received a good reputation.

Although the men were responsible for building the most recognized symbol of the event, the women didn't sit idly by. They fetched green grass and wildflowers—symbolic of great things the event would usher in. The grass was spread on the living-room floor, becoming a mat for the following three days, while the cut flowers were arranged in water-filled vases. The women also brewed jugs of *tella* and baked festival bread for the multitude of guests who would arrive during and after the event.

From an early age, children were told whose birthday they were observing during the Nativity, so they came to expect no personal windfalls. Unlike the New Year celebrations, when they received new clothes and spending money, they wore their old Sunday outfits at the Nativity. In Aba Yitades' home, only Beletu expressed displeasure. "What sort of a birthday is it where you don't even get to drink a bottle of soda?" she often said.

ABA YITADES reserved his longest sermon for the Nativity. By the time the drawn-out service came to an end and the parishioners headed for the *Meskel* Square, it was mid-afternoon.

The marketplace, which on an ordinary day drew all sorts of unsavoury characters, was transformed on Christmas, becoming what Aba Yitades had always wanted it to be, a holy ground. Not only were the attendees properly attired in their Sunday outfits, but they put their best faces forward as well, greeting each other in the most cordial manner.

Azeb had fond memories of the Christmas of 1960. It was the one and only time she wore a crinoline, one bought for her by Etiye Hiywet, unusual even for the godmother, in celebration of Christmas. Azeb wasn't the only one who found the piece of clothing captivating. For much of the day the village girls stood by cheering while she put on a show, spinning around and around before abruptly sitting down, so that the skirt she wore on top belled out like a tent around her. However, like her first pair of leather shoes, the undergarment didn't last long; Aba Yitades put the cleaver to it a few days later when he discovered its existence.

BUT THAT FESTIVE AFTERNOON, the exacting cleaver was the last thing on the priest's mind. He was in a joyful mood.

Standing at the approach to the square, he greeted each passing adult, "Thank the Lord who let you survive for this."

"Thanks to Him we have both survived for this," came the answer.

Each family placed their *chibbo* around the expanding base of the centre post, the *Demera,* before taking their position behind the growing ring of celebrants. A tense period ensued, as they all waited anxiously for their tardy neighbours to show up. And the instant someone emerged from the distance to add his family's contribution, the crowd broke into wild applause, followed by uncomfortable laughter. The moment everyone had been waiting for finally arrived when Aba Yitades doused the pyramid of torches with gasoline and, after a brief prayer, threw a lit match at it. It was not until the pile of *chibbo* was reduced to charred remains, with only the smouldering post left standing, that the crowd made way for the second phase of the festival: the *Gena*— the Christmas game.

The *Gena* had actually begun the week before, with young boys as participants. On its final day the boys gave way to the adults. Heading the opposing teams were, as expected, Abebe the Bandit and Endale Fluoride. The players had been carefully chosen days and weeks before to ensure that no love was lost between the two sides. The ball and the play-sticks were both fashioned out of sturdy wood. The ball was the size of a ripe orange, and the head of the play-stick was set at an obtuse angle to the handle (thus resembling an ice hockey stick).

In a hole dug in the middle of the field (called the house), the referee placed the ball. He then gave a signal to start the game, the object of which was to score goals by hitting the ball across the opposing team's end line. The game started harmlessly enough, with only minor scuffles between the two teams. But as it gathered momentum, and the number of goals mounted, the shoving and jostling gave way to punches and elbowing. Soon, play-sticks were flying, catching the unwary in the torso. Some spectators were revolted by the degenerating game, but others offered words of advice.

"Break his legs," yelled one man.

"Aim for his balls," advised another.

"Show him that *Gena* is not like lifting a woman's skirt," shouted a man who clearly despised Endale Fluoride.

"I don't mind lifting my skirt for that one," the gorgeous divorcee chimed in.

"Coward, go back inside."

"Referee, get out of their way!"

"Break the referee's legs!"

By the time the game was finally over, an hour and a half later, there wasn't a single player who wasn't nursing a wound. Abebe the Bandit lost a front tooth; Endale Fluoride sustained a broken nose and a fractured wrist. But that was the game of *Gena,* and the rules clearly stated that there was no compensation for lost life or limb, nor should anyone think of vengeance.

7

ENCROACHING WORLD

Although they didn't know it at the time, Abebe the Bandit and Endale Fluoride marked the end of an era that memorable Christmas. In less than a year Mechara would be part of the larger world. The highway that would ultimately link the village with the town of Gelemso and the rest of the country had been steadily encroaching over the previous three years. Mountains had been blasted, and hundred-year-old trees brought down, leaving an ugly gash in the virgin forest.

From the vantage of mountaintops, the villagers watched in awe as the man-made animal, groaning and belching columns of smoke, chewed its way towards their treasured hamlet. Bulldozers and caterpillar machines fought for space on the narrow trail. Behind them fleets of dump trucks unloaded mountains of gravel on the unpaved road. Heavy rollers pressed the gravel level.

Ever since the highway had come into view, the villagers had been preoccupied with the greater meaning of this modern invention and the ways it would affect their everyday lives. Fear of the unknown weighed heavily on the minds of many. A regular trip to the butcher or the tavern, or even the daily coffee ceremony, turned into a forum for the exchange of ideas and information. Heated debates ensued.

Mechara had never been entirely isolated from the outside world. Besides the merchants who visited weekly, there were others who regularly passed through the village. Some of them

spent a night at a local's home, graciously accepting the community's hospitality. There was a certain piety associated with
welcoming a stranger who came to your door asking in the name
of the Lord if he could stay with you for the night. The answer
almost always was, "A home is to be shared with the Lord's
children. Do come in."

Friendships grew out of such chance encounters. Fables told of
travellers who came to a village leading a mule or a donkey, often
with a load of produce, and who on their return trip brought
small gifts for the families who had earlier welcomed them. Some
of the great anecdotes, which were told and retold by the fireside,
had their roots in good deeds done for strangers. One tale
involved a lonely widow who had gone hungry when she served
her last crumb of *injera* to a pilgrim she sheltered. The next
morning when she uncovered the bundle on the mat, expecting
to find the stranger, she found in his stead a Dream Catcher, a
finely woven fabric that was endowed with magical powers of
ensnaring dreams and realizing the good ones. For years afterwards, the old woman earned her living by walking from door to
door and catching dreams with the exotic fabric that she draped
overnight on her customer's window.

And who could forget "The Resourceful Kebede," a man who
not only turned a handful of pebbles into a delicious stew—by
cooking them with diced onions, lentils, oil, and spices, and in
the end discarding all six pebbles—but also won the heart of his
young hostess. She married him two weeks later, ending her long
solitude and his roving streak in one fell swoop.

Not all good deeds were rewarded, however. There were
sinister characters among the ordinary-looking wayfarers. An
individual possessed of an evil eye might change his skin in the
dead of night and become a hyena—a ravenous, ill-disposed
Schweinehund that could turn on its kindly host. One fable,
thought to have originated in the highlands of Ethiopia, involved
a wolf that was wily enough not only to devour the soft-spoken

grandmother who took him in, but also to put on her Sunday attire and lie waiting in her bed for his next victim, her adorable grandchild. Later, ravenous, ill-disposed *Schweinehund* missionaries stole the story and, after superficial modifications, adopted it as their own.

Of course, there was always a way to unmask the wicked before they earned their infamy by committing a crime. One proven method was to burn a secret blend of dried herbs and animal parts and smoke the evil out. In Mechara, "evil-eye" repellent mixtures were much sought-after during the holiday seasons, when shady characters were known to emerge in droves.

THE MODERN HIGHWAY, with its automobiles that whisked passengers by in a blur, had yet to leave its mark on the popular mythology. One of the villagers' unspoken fears was, therefore, that this modern intrusion might affect their treasure of myth and fable. Their other worry was the unwanted interference of the state apparatus.

Glimpses of the new order appeared long before completion of the highway, when construction workers descended on the village after their daily shifts. For many of the men, the local tavern was the preferred rendezvous; some of them visited the butcher and other shops as well. On Wednesdays, the open market saw more than its usual number of customers. Aba Yitades was taking in the changing face of the crowd one busy afternoon when a giant of a man in a yellow construction hat and steel-tipped leather boots caught his attention. Despite the man's ragged looks and strange accent, the priest was able to detect the good Christian underneath.

"Why are you buying eggs on a fast day?" the priest inquired.

"It is none of your goddamn business," the stranger shot back.

Indeed, it was no longer Aba Yitades' goddamn business that the merchant sold the eggs for double the usual price; even less so that she was a complete stranger, not speaking his august language, nor dressed like anyone he could identify with. That some of the construction workers had a predilection for taking the Lord's name in vain was also none of his goddamn business. And if the priest knew what was good for him, he wouldn't look askance at the truck driver who had just cussed a young woman for snubbing his advances.

Most disturbing, however, was that neither Aba Yitades nor any of the village elders now had any say in who could and could not move into the village their ancestors had founded. All it took to claim a deed to Crown land was a piece of paper from the governor of Gelemso, whose domain now extended to the village of Mechara and the hamlets in between. A nominal processing fee was involved, because the enterprising governor saw no reason why he shouldn't wring a small profit for himself. And although the Emperor had clearly stated that preference should be given to Christians who wished to settle the newly opened territories, to the man in Gelemso the hundred-*birr* bills that went into his pocket looked the same no matter who gave them to him.

The closer Aba Yitades looked into the governor's record, the less certain he became of the future of his parish. For in only a decade the town of Gelemso had been transformed from a peaceful municipality, where people attended to their daily business without looking over their shoulder, into one where men in uniform ruled the roost. And that was because the good governor happened to have a few job-seeking nephews.

Before the governor was appointed to office, the town of Gelemso had only two policemen on its payroll, both shabbily dressed and inoffensive-looking. A small cell hastily attached to the side of the one-room police station served as the only detention centre. The crime rate was low, violent crime rare. The policemen did take turns roaming the open market, but that was mainly because they could expect handouts from sympathetic merchants. The two officers were such an integral part of daily life that they were often invited to coffee ceremonies.

The moment the governor dressed his three nephews in uniform, however, crime went through the proverbial roof. All of a sudden, upright citizens were found to be breaking laws and bylaws, ones that few of them knew existed. Four more policemen were hired (as the governor was endowed with far too many nephews), the single-cell jail was torn down, and in its place a large prison complex was erected. Alleys and telephone poles were plastered with notices of bylaws and their attendant penalties.

As in most growing towns, the bars and restaurants of Gelemso boasted but a single washroom each, which was out of commission for much of the year. So paying customers used the less-travelled alleys to relieve their bladders. Such was the condition of the back streets that at high sun, a blind man could easily find his way to a tavern by trailing the wafts of evaporating urine.

The walls of the alleys were now checkered with signs that read, *Twenty* birr *says you won't piss, Check your wallet before opening your fly,* and *Do you have a few banknotes to piss today?* Manning the alleys at night, in their own time, were the newly hired policemen, conveniently dressed in plain clothes. They had the decency to wait until the culprit had finished his business before drawing his attention to his crime. The governor's nephews were not sticklers for detail; they were willing to negotiate the amount of the penalty. The law was considered to have taken full hold, and the townspeople to have successfully completed their transition to a decent society, when the officers moved into their newly built villas.

MECHARA DIDN'T HAVE TO WAIT for the governor to appoint an enterprising nephew before it too began to suffer. With so many strangers and alien farm products already making their way to the expanding market, it was only a matter of time before the traditional way of life exhibited strains. First to fall victim were the sheep. Tufts of wool fell off the herds' backs. All known herbal potions, dosages, and blends were tried, in vain. No measure of prayers or aspersion of holy water was of any help. It was a malady that simply couldn't easily be eradicated.

As the markets shunned the ghostly flock, mutton came to supplement the daily fare. In Aba Yitades' home, Azeb's ninth birthday became a consolation for slaughtering yet another of the family's small herd. Looking back on this birthday many years later, Azeb wished that the celebration had never taken place. For without the pretense of the birthday, she wouldn't have been emboldened to pilfer the "forbidden fruit"—the roasted testicles. In her eyes, the watery morsel would forever remain—as was the apple for Eve—the single object that marked her descent at a very early age from the heights of righteousness into a pit of infamy.

BOOK III

*In Search
of a Totem*

8

EXPANDING HORIZONS

A Land Rover arrived bringing with it yet another novelty: a family of white people. Villagers abandoned their chores to have a look at the unusual cargo. Merchants and shop-keepers left their counters to snatch a glimpse of the newcomers. Only Beletu kept a cool head amidst the turmoil.

"They are humans like us," she declared, rolling her eyes in disgust, "only a bit more civilized. In their country, they drive large sedans with tail fins, and they go about their daily business in bikinis and boxers," she added, recalling some colourful images from her magazine clippings.

Small boys and girls trailed the strangers at a safe distance. The moment the man turned around to look, they broke formation and fell back in ripples. The woman smiled at them. Reaching inside her oversized shoulder bag, she produced colourfully wrapped candies, which she offered to the children. The kids were torn between a desire to snatch the sweets and a fear of being snatched. The woman made up their minds for them when she tossed the candies in the air, momentarily diverting their attention from her family.

"ጤና ይስጥልኝ" the man greeted each grown-up he met. Few of them replied; they couldn't trust their ears. Had he actually addressed them in their own language?

With no special aim or purpose, the strangers roamed about the awestruck village, pausing here and there, taking photographs of the birds in the trees, and admiring the fauna and flora. At the open market they proceeded to investigate what the region had to offer, but as it was a Tuesday, there were few merchants around. The man's attention was soon drawn towards a herd of sheep sporting the new hairdo. He set out to examine the phenomenon in earnest. With his translator as a go-between, he made inquiries about the disease and when it had taken hold.

Aba Yitades was in the church grounds, tending to everyday matters, when the white family dropped by. Not far from him, Azeb was harvesting the overgrown grass of the type that women wove baskets from. She separated the stalk from the leaves, split the stalks in two, and tied each fist-sized bundle together. In the days that followed she would spread her harvest out in the sun until it dried completely. Genet would then dye the sapless stalks various colours before putting them to use.

Spying the white family, Azeb stopped what she was doing. She stood and watched as a strange-looking girl headed her way. The ghostly apparition had fire-red hair, and her freckled face was bronzed from the sun. The girl was about the same age as Azeb, and of comparable build.

"ጤና ይስጥልኝ" said this new girl, smiling.

"That greeting is for adults," Azeb corrected her, in a not unfriendly way. "You should say ታዲያስ።"

"I am Oona. What is your name?" the girl continued, not minding the correction.

"Azeb. Where are you from, Oona?"

"America."

"Where is that?"

"Very far from here."

"Do you speak Amharic in America?"

"No, I learned my Amharic in Addis Ababa."

"I've never been to Addis Ababa," Azeb noted mournfully. "Did you wash your hair with henna?"

"No."

"Then how come it is so red?"

"In America many people have red hair."

"Oh!" was all Azeb could think of.

Oona's eyes were soon fixed on the small leather pouch dangling from Azeb's neck-cord, the talisman that Etiye Hiywet had given her many years before. "What is in the pouch?" Oona asked.

"Medicine."

"What type of medicine?"

"Inscriptions, I guess."

"Have you ever seen it?" she said, feeling the contents with her fingers.

"No, you are not supposed to see it. If you do, then the medicine will lose its potency," Azeb explained. A moment of uneasy silence elapsed before Azeb inquired, "Would you like to see a newborn monkey?"

"Yes," replied Oona with no less enthusiasm.

"Then come with me," said Azeb, grabbing Oona by the hand. With her father's instruction not to stray too far with the new girl ringing in her ears, Azeb wove her way through the knee-high grass that swallowed the church precincts and into the brush behind the schoolhouse. A grove of gigantic *zegba* trees blocked the sun's rays. In the dim light, the girls detected movements high up in the trees. Soon the silky black and white coats of a family of monkeys came into view.

"They are the most beautiful monkeys I have ever seen," admitted Oona, clearly enchanted.

"Their Amharic name is *guereza*," Azeb whispered.

"Do they eat humans?" Oona wondered, seeing that some of them looked agitated.

"Don't be silly, they *are* humans," Azeb told her. "When a *dabtara* dies, he comes back as a *guereza*. Sometimes we come here and find a new *guereza* when no one has died. In a few days we find out that a *dabtara* in another village has passed on," she elaborated. "Did you know that killing a *guereza* is a sin?"

"No," answered Oona.

"It is," emphasized Azeb. She went on to tell her a story that the villagers used as a cautionary tale:

It was a commemoration that few people would ever forget. Two well-fed bulls had been brought to church "for the drying of tears" by kin of a well-to-do merchant whose six-month interment the community was remembering. While only one of the sacrifices was divided up among the usual claimants, the clergy mostly, the other was served to those attending the event. Hanging from tree branches were choice parts of the bull. Men and women alike carved up pieces of the raw meat and devoured them standing. For many it was a rare treat.

A man had been gobbling up a morsel the size of a baby's fist when a piece of the meat blocked his airway. A ligament caught between his teeth prevented the morsel moving either in or out. No matter how hard he was hammered on the back of his neck, or how high he was tossed before dropping to the ground, the piece of meat refused to dislodge. He had just finished a second lap around the church building, his hands flailing desperately in the air, when the light finally ebbed from him. The community conducted a thorough soul-searching before establishing that, only two weeks before, he had killed a *guereza.*

"If you kill a *guereza,*" Azeb concluded, "you will die within days."

"I don't like killing animals," Oona said, "but when we lived in Vermont, Dad shot and killed a deer. We ate it."

"What is deer?"

"It is a goat-like animal with a pair of branched horns."

"But does it have split hooves?"

"I don't know."

"Well, you can eat it only if it has split hooves," Azeb stressed. "It is in the Bible!"

THAT EVENING, Aba Yitades asked Azeb to hand him the Black Ledger, and he pencilled in the following entry: *An Italian family came to visit,* he began. Like many of his generation, the priest associated all white faces with Italians, who had made the existence of their race known during a brief occupation of the country during the Second World War. *They don't appear to be warlike. The man goes by the name of Robert Harding; his wife, Vivian Harding. (What strange-sounding names!) Their children are well brought up (they smiled often and bowed at the appropriate moments). The girl's name is Oona, the boy's Jeff. The translator is a native; interestingly, he is the one who was ill behaved. They all seemed to be interested in our Faith, though none wore a neck-cord, not even the native translator!*

As SUDDENLY as they had appeared, Oona and her family departed from the village, leaving their foreign names and ghostly memory behind. For Azeb, however, the window on the larger world had just begun to open.

Etiye Hiywet continued her monthly trips to Gelemso, though now by car and with two fewer companions—she didn't deem it necessary to have armed guards. Ahead of her time, the godmother promoted the benefits of expanding children's horizons by introducing them to the bigger world. She wanted to be the one to take Azeb on her first car ride out of the village. Obtaining Aba Yitades' permission wasn't difficult at first, although later some complications arose.

For days, Azeb's family had been consumed by the planned trip. Genet was full of advice for her youngest sister. "They say electricity is a killer, so let someone else turn the light on and off. If you must dine without Etiye Hiywet, avoid meat entirely, since you can't be sure of who might have slaughtered the animal. In any case, since the Fast of the Apostles begins this week, you may not have that many days to indulge. [For forty-five days, Wednesdays and Fridays would remain fast days.] If you somehow slip up and eat buttered cookies, for instance, on one of the fast days, then make sure you see a priest immediately to receive the service of purification."

"Don't forget to chew with your lips sealed, and only on one side of your mouth at a time," Werknesh added. "And remember, you are almost grown up now, so don't eat your fill in front of strangers."

Beletu had only one thing to say. "Why does she have to be the first to get to do everything?"

ON THE EVE of the journey, Azeb was such a pack of nerves that she spent a restless afternoon and a sleep-deprived night. Hours before her scheduled departure, she kissed each member of her family on the cheeks twice, dropping tears of mixed joy and anxiety. She was at the gate of the compound, with Genet as her shadow, when Aba Yitades was suddenly reminded of the spiritual significance of disappointment and the unique opportunity the occasion offered, and called off the trip.

"Reflect on the higher value of frustration," he advised.

A month later, Etiye Hiywet made another attempt to take Azeb along with her to Gelemso. "Aba Yitades, promise me that you won't call off the trip this time around."

"You have my word," he mumbled, upset that someone should misinterpret his noble intentions.

AS WAS THE CASE with all public transport in the country, the autobus she and her godmother boarded that morning was filled to the brim. Each bench was occupied by at least twice the allotted number, and additional passengers stood in the aisle and sat on the rooftop rack and even the engine cover between the two front seats, which sported bold inscriptions that read: *Don't sit on the engine!*

The Fiat bus swayed under its enormous load, groaned, and belched sooty smoke. Midway through the journey, an oncoming bus blinked its headlights, signalling the Gelemso-bound coach to pull over. Seated only a row behind the operator, Azeb could listen in as the two drivers exchanged information: the traffic police were out in force. These uniformed men ensured the safety and comfort of the paying passengers by comparing the head count with the legal payload. To the driver, their sly presence meant a hefty fine unless he could pull the proverbial rabbit out of his glovebox.

Indeed, since the highway to Mechara had come into service four months earlier, many a rabbit had been pulled out of all sorts of strange places. The most favoured ploy was "we are coming from a funeral," where the extra passengers were persuaded, on pain of finishing their journey on foot, to wail. The women rearranged their *netela* in the mourning fashion while the men attached a piece of dark cloth to their jacket sleeves. As soon as the traffic police came into view, the cries and chest beating intensified, encouraged by the bill-collector-turned-conductor. The patrolling officer would often suspect a ruse, but he would have to be heartless to ticket a driver transporting a bus full of mourners. The bus would grudgingly be waved along.

When the funeral ploy began to wear thin, the "we are on our way to a wedding" scheme was devised and introduced. Trees lost their limbs to waving passengers, and the singing and ululates drowned out the engine noise. But unlike with a funeral crowd, there was little shame attached to inconveniencing overjoyed passengers. This latest scheme afforded the driver a mere bargaining chip. In time he would establish an understanding with the traffic policeman in charge of his route, and stop only to grease his palm.

Azeb's group sang its way to town.

ETIYE HIYWET'S ESTABLISHMENT, the Memorial Hotel, comprised sixteen rental rooms, a tavern stocked with a wide variety of modern spirits and beers, and a sprawling eatery serving not only the local menu but also choice Italian cuisine. The hotel was named in memory of the three men Etiye Hiywet had lost— her husband and two sons. Its phenomenal growth seemed to underline the resilience of the human spirit in the face of devastating loss. At a personal level, its success was a clear vindication of the owner, a refutation of those individuals who had openly doubted her business abilities.

Like all bars and restaurants in the country, the Memorial Hotel employed a platoon of prostitutes, all legal, to wait on tables and attend to the small urges of the nightly clientele. For lonely men, these young, vibrant, and graciously accommodating women helped cushion the sharp edges of solitude; whereas for the attached ones, they offered a reason to stay in a marriage—for with a good-looking wench on the side, only a fool would divorce the woman who kept his home and wardrobe in order.

The first week of the month was a busy time for hotel and restaurant owners in Gelemso. That was when teachers and other wage earners received their monthly paycheques, and they made the rounds, paying up debts they had accumulated in the intervening weeks and spending what little money was left over. A fallow week followed, in which they all whiled away the long nights with a cup of tea in hand. By the middle of the month, most of them would have filled in the "Model 10 Form," the standard government-issued application for an advance on the coming month's paycheque. It was a vicious circle made even worse by the fact that the paymaster seldom kept to his schedule.

As was her practice, Etiye Hiywet immediately got down to work balancing the books with the aid of her soul-father, who also served as her accountant, leaving Azeb to find her own way about. Before Etiye Hiywet was a bulging ledger for customers dining on credit and a smaller one for the bar clientele. She discouraged selling alcohol on credit. "Everyone can manage without a drink," she said. Her reluctance to advance credit on spirits was not as benign as it sounded, though. Experience had taught her, as it had many of her peers, that a debtor in a bind would default on his bar tab in a blink, but would be extra-careful not to skip his restaurant bill or antagonize his regular prostitute. For no eatery would advance him credit without a proper background check, and unpaid prostitutes would raise a stink at the workplace.

FOR AZEB, her godmother's nonchalant attitude towards the sex trade came as a total surprise. Astounding her even more was the fact that such a disreputable practice could be tolerated in a nation ruled by an emperor whose direct lineage to the All-Knowing was never in doubt.

"Are they really prostitutes?" she asked her godmother twice.

"Yes, honey," replied Etiye Hiywet each time. "The world is quite different from what the Scripture tells us. These are not bad women, only victims of bad times." As she headed for her backroom office with her soul-father in tow, the godmother added, "Go talk to them—they don't bite."

Since it was only midday, too early for business, the girls hadn't left their common room, which they disparagingly named the Barn. More like a pit stop than a proper residence, the Barn was sparsely furnished, with only a single bed tucked in the remote corner, to be used by all; a dresser with a full-length mirror; and pieces of luggage strewn about. In heaps in the nearby corner lay four metal buckets and as many scrub brushes, the actual use of which Azeb didn't learn until late that afternoon.

Lounging on the hastily made bed were four young women in various stages of dressing or undressing. Seated on a stool in one corner was a teenaged girl having her hair tended by a friend. Two bikini-clad women were sorting out their evening clothes on a hanger nailed to the wall. Their chatter was deafening. A delivery boy arriving with a load of freshly pressed laundry interrupted them briefly.

"Get out, you weasel," shouted one of the bikini-clad women, seeing that he had lingered to stare at her half-dressed behind. He ran away laughing.

"Who might you be?" asked the same woman, noticing Azeb for the first time.

Azeb was half hidden behind the door frame. She kept mum, as no one had yet told her how to respond to women who had lost all their inhibitions.

"Honey, where is your mother?" asked the teenaged girl.

Azeb refused to answer.

"Where did you come from?"

No comment.

"The girl is deaf," said one of them, and the rest burst out laughing.

Azeb finally spoke. "Are you really prostitutes?" This only seemed to crack them up even more.

"No, honey, we are nuns on vacation," replied one of the women on the bed, and the chorus of laughter increased.

"I think this kid is Etiye Hiywet's godchild," said one of them, and that seemed to sober them up somewhat.

"Sweetheart, this is no place for you," advised the teenaged one.

"And why not?" challenged one of the half-dressed women, grinning. "I was her age when my stepfather drafted me for this job." The others doubled up in laughter, as though it was the best joke they had heard in a long time.

Azeb left only because her godmother wanted to introduce her to the hotel manager.

"This is Fatima," said Etiye Hiywet, pointing to a stocky woman of advancing years whose uncommonly light skin reminded Azeb of the Hardings. "Fatima, meet my favourite godchild," the godmother added.

"Are you an American?" Azeb couldn't help asking.

"Whatever gave you that idea?" Fatima demanded, seething with incomprehensible anger. She calmed down only after Etiye Hiywet told her about the white family who had visited them only weeks before. The godmother further assured the manager that Azeb couldn't have been referring to the outcast tribe the townspeople commonly referred to as Americans, since few people in Mechara knew of their existence.

Calling the tribesmen Americans was a practice adopted after the Emperor spoke against the tradition of referring to craftsmen, including tanners, blacksmiths, and potters, by derogatory names. The euphemism had created confusion even for the courts. In an oft-cited murder trial, a witness was asked how many people were involved in the crime, and he replied, "Two men and four Americans."

"So, you mean six people," pressed the presiding judge.

"No, only two people, but there were four Americans as well," the man insisted.

"HONEY," said Etiye Hiywet, turning to Azeb, "Fatima is from the Adere ethnic group. Aderes tend to have fair complexions, you know. Don't you think Fatima's hair is even more beautiful than that of your sister Beletu?"

Whether they merely got off on the wrong foot or she detected a threat in the young girl, Fatima remained hostile to Azeb, although she kept her feelings under wraps in the presence of Etiye Hiywet. Some eight years later, when the two of them met again under altered circumstances, the hotel manager would exact a measure of revenge against the girl who had ruffled her feathers so many moons before.

But in those heady days there was little time for Azeb to dwell on minor irritants; the prickly manager was soon far from her mind. There was so much to see in Gelemso, so much to absorb in the week that she was scheduled to stay in town. Late afternoon was a busy time for the working girls, and that first day Azeb lurked in the shadows taking in the hectic activity that preceded the nightly trade. Viewed through her ten-year-old eyes, the atmosphere seemed festive.

Two of the girls stripped naked before her very eyes, "as though it was the most natural thing to do," in Azeb's own guarded assessment. Each carrying a bucketful of water, a sponge, and a towel, they marched towards the back of the building, where they proceeded to wash themselves without a care in the world. Azeb thought they were craving attention. Only later in the week did she learn that the girls would have preferred to use the showers in the hotel rooms, but the hotel manager demanded payment (a bribe, actually) for the privilege of using the hotel facilities.

Two days later, when she finally felt at ease in their presence, Azeb followed the teenaged girl and one of her friends to the public bathhouse. "Go see what it looks like," Etiye Hiywet had said to her. Rows of shower stalls flanked the small stone-paved courtyard. A loud diesel motor pumped water from a well situated in the middle of the property and into a wood-burning furnace. Twin brass pipes distributed the water, both hot and cold, to the twenty-two booths. The dirty suds glided down a lined channel and out of the compound. In the open gutter outside, children played in the soapy water.

Azeb's two companions took their position at the end of a long line. When the column of waiting customers showed impatience, the Arab proprietor knocked on a door and threatened to shut off the water unless the booth was vacated immediately. The moment an empty stall was found, he collected twenty-five cents from the person at the head of the line, issued a warning not to spend too much time, and waved them ahead. From time to time young lovers came forward to shower together. "Perverts," the toothless owner mumbled, but as a couple paid double the going rate, he never turned them away.

It was an adventure that would long stay with Azeb.

An hour before the bar opened for the nightly trade, Fatima lit a charcoal burner permanently installed behind the front door, tossing into it the house blend of incense and fetish—the latter to draw unsuspecting customers. As in all households, the first cup of coffee was sprinkled at the doorway, for the *rekebot* spirit, and then a handful of roasted legumes. A litany of supplications followed, which had long since lost their meaning to the regulars.

The first patron was greeted exuberantly. "I hope you are a harbinger of good luck," Fatima said to him. If business turned sour this night, he knew he would be the one blamed. To avoid such a responsibility, a wise person made sure not to be the first to march inside an empty tavern. Many preferred to arrive in a group, or would peek inside to see if there was already a fall guy in place before putting in an appearance.

Next to show up was the manager of the state-owned Electric Light and Power Authority.

"Meet my favourite godchild," Etiye Hiywet said to him.

He nodded smugly.

"Be extra civil to this man," Fatima whispered in Azeb's ear. As every pub owner in town knew, the burly man could make or break a business. Only a month before, he had turned the town's electricity off long before the scheduled time of midnight, sending bar and restaurant patrons scurrying to bed too early. The curfew lasted a full three weeks. No one, not even the all-powerful governor, was able to dissuade him. "The diesel generator runs on imported fuel," the manager answered angrily, "and we are short of supplies." Business owners had to raise five hundred *birr*—the equivalent of his yearly government wage—towards his home renovation expenses before power was finally restored.

"You don't suppose that my power line could be linked up with that of the clinic?" Etiye Hiywet asked him, not for the first time.

"I will see what I can do," was his noncommittal response. No fewer than five other businesses were already serviced by the line feeding the clinic, the police station, the police chief's residence, and the governor's villa, thus enjoying a twenty-four-hour-a-day supply of light and power.

PROTECTED FROM the raucous crowd by the high counters, Azeb watched, with a chilled bottle of Fanta in hand, as the business gathered pace. Most of the customers were patronizing to her, calling her "my little darling." Some of them offered to pay for her soda, but Etiye Hiywet wouldn't allow them to. "She is my guest," was her response.

Each time a habitué walked in, Fatima quickly consulted the ledger tucked away under the countertop to ensure that the individual had settled his accumulated tab before advancing him further credit. If the person was a prominent figure in the community, he would be introduced to Azeb.

"This is the police chief," said Etiye Hiywet, "and because of him we live in the safest town in the country."

"We are trying our best," said the chief, blushing.

"This is the governor," she continued. "Say hello to the school principal ... to the incomparable tailor ... the one and only ..."

As was his custom, the postman arrived after the usual crowd had gathered.

"Postman, do I have any mail?" some of the men asked him, mostly for a laugh. The postman was economical with his responses. If a person was concerned enough about an arriving piece of mail, he would begin by buying the postman a drink. Business etiquette required that the conversation begin with the usual niceties—inquiries about the postman's health and his family's well-being, say.

The postman wasn't as tardy as some people made him out to be. Before making his nightly rounds, he first checked the delivery bags. If an addressee could be located in a pub, there was no sense looking for him elsewhere. In most cases it was a mutually beneficial arrangement: the addressee got his delivery on time, and the mailman was instantly rewarded for his efforts. Some, however, thought the postman's methods could use some improvement.

The statement "I thought you might want to have this letter right away," whispered in the ear of the police chief, didn't elicit the expected enthusiasm.

"That is very thoughtful of you," said the chief, "but, as I said before, you might have dropped it at the office." Nevertheless, he ordered the bartender to give the postman a drink before picking up the thread of his conversation with the governor.

If the postman added a theatrical flair to the nightly routine, the director of the State Highway Authority was a pure breeze of urban sophistication. He had arrived in Gelemso from Addis Ababa, the nation's capital, bringing with him high-paying construction jobs for the locals and uncertainty for Mechara. For the nightly crowd, his European attire and unique manner of speech had become an affront to their collective sense of self-worth. Only the school principal, who was also an urbanite and comparably educated, could imitate the director's way of inflecting certain words, and could spice his Amharic with choice English words.

Long after he had made a name for himself by paying a hundred *birr*, the equivalent of a teacher's monthly wage, for the virginity of a newly arrived prostitute, the director commanded unflagging attention. His nightly arrival was preceded by a waft of imported cologne and caused a stir among the working girls. Some of them abandoned their penniless company to join his table. They laughed at his stale jokes and attempted to anticipate his wishes. He pretended to ignore them.

"You no longer bring new girls," he told Fatima as she passed his table.

"What is wrong with the ones I have?" she replied, not without rancour.

After downing his second shot of gin, the director left his table, as was his habit, with one of the girls on his arm. Through the glass window at the side of the bar, Azeb saw, as did the hotel manager, the light of the Barn flick on then turn dark again as the door closed behind them. Moments later the door opened once again and the director stumbled into the ill-lit compound. Short of breath, his face glistening with sweat, he assumed his seat.

No longer enamoured of his first choice, he waved her away, inviting someone else to fill her vacant seat. Two more shots of gin would slither down his parched throat, infusing him with renewed vigour, before he got up once more and headed for the Barn, his new choice on his arm. Azeb watched in horror as he repeated the performance with machine-like insensitivity. She attempted to gauge the feelings of his prey, but they didn't turn a hair. The director continued his scandalous debauchery until the first of two blackout warnings at 11:30 p.m., when the town's lights blinked twice, reminding the nightly crowd that they had only half an hour to find their way home.

The director's unusual bedside manner never ceased to amaze even the jaded home crowd. Etiye Hiywet quietly disapproved of his conduct. "These may be working girls," she mumbled, "but toys they certainly are not." As would any sensible restaurateur, she understood why a recent divorcee or a grieving widower might look to a working girl for comfort and consolation. And everyone sympathized with that newly arrived schoolteacher who kept a paid concubine on the side while he looked for a decent partner. What good would it do, Etiye Hiywet argued, as did many of her peers, if, in the simple search for physical satisfaction, the young man were to latch on to one of his female students, or, God forbid, the wife of a fellow worker?

There was even something to be said in favour of the out-of-town farmer who walked in this particular evening with an awkward look on his face. He was one of the growing number of entrepreneurs who made the long journey to the bustling town once every season or so. Following their busy day, some of them spent the night at one of the local hotels and headed back home early the next morning. Business must have been exceptionally brisk for this farmer, for he ordered a shot of brandy on the rocks.

"Ice cube in a brandy?" said the waitress, raising an eyebrow. It was more an accusation than a request for clarification. Despite his spotless Sunday outerwear and the swagger in his walk, she had recognized the farmer for what he was the instant he walked in. She had now found the evidence to prove to him how green he was, ordering his brandy on the rocks.

The out-of-towner produced a packet of Marlboro cigarettes from his jacket pocket and laid it face up on the table. Few people could afford imported cigarettes. At home he would have rolled his tobacco in a piece of old newspaper, if such a rare item could be found; as a rule, he would have used the dried sheaf of a cornstalk. After each drag he would have pinched the tip of his tongue in search of a tobacco flake that might have drifted with the fumes. Although he puffed on a filtered cigarette tonight, he still kept on pinching his tongue.

"Won't you join me?" he asked the waitress when she returned with his drink.

"Sure."

"What would you like to have?"

"Whiskey," she said. She collected the seventy-five cents for her drink before fetching it. If the farmer had taken a sip from her glass, however, he would have found that she was drinking tepid tea, which was meant to pass for the reddish-brown spirit.

"How much do you charge for a quickie?" he asked when she finally settled next to him. The nervous tic on his face and the uneasy shifting on his seat betrayed the fact that he was inexperienced at this sort of transaction. The waitress suspected he might even be cheating on his wife, but, as she saw it, that was none of her business.

"Two *birr*," she answered.

"We shouldn't be seen leaving together," he said, handing her the money. "You go first."

If she had had doubts about his marital status before, they existed no longer. A less than honest prostitute would have taken advantage of him, refusing to provide the service for which he had paid in advance. A man in his position wouldn't have gone to the pub owner, the manager, or the police to lodge a complaint for fear that word would reach his wife's ears. Fortunately for the farmer, he'd met a woman who remembered some of her Commandments.

THE COMMANDMENTS were also on Azeb's mind as she prepared to go back home. Her stay in Gelemso had shown her many novelties, but nothing so enduring or unsettling as the blatant sex trade and her godmother's casual attitude towards it. Azeb would never vaunt Etiye Hiywet as a saintly widow again, nor would she think of her without recalling those wretched women of the night. Indeed, not long after, when this decadent world collided with her own, she would accuse the old woman of lax morality.

9

NEIGHBOURLY THOUGHTS

*I*t was a damp Friday morning, a full three weeks after their first appearance, when two of the Hardings—father and son—reappeared. The back seats of their Land Rover had been removed, making room for six yellow plastic drums. Each drum bore a skull and crossbones and an inscription in bold foreign letters. Mr. Robert Harding, head of the family, Jeff Harding, his son, and the translator, whose name the locals would never care to remember, appeared to be on a grand mission.

While the storeowners looked on in puzzlement, the strangers unloaded the cumbersome containers in the middle of the marketplace. Leaving Jeff with the drums, the two men walked from door to door asking sheep owners to come out with their diseased flocks for free medical treatment. In his broken Amharic, Mr. Robert Harding reassured those men and women who looked askance at his translator, whose bare neck (bare of a neck-cord, that is) said everything they wanted to know about him.

Grudgingly the villagers emerged with a sheep or two, leaving their large flocks behind. It was bad form to say no to someone who had come to your door asking for a favour, even if that favour was to treat your diseased livestock for free. Also, no one wanted to risk upsetting the mysterious white man, who, for all the villagers knew, might have been dispatched from wherever it was that white people lived in order to test their faith.

If any villager had pinned his hopes on the medical expertise of the strangers, those hopes were dashed the instant one of the barrels was opened to reveal its contents—a tar-like fluid. Why, every child knew that medicine, true medicine, came in the form of either bruised herbs or a ground substance; that it was harvested from a virgin forest, as a rule, in the small hours of the morning by a man dressed in nothing more than his birthday suit. Besides, what medicine man would conduct his trade without the proper pomp and ceremony—without burning incense and chanting in a language that no one else could fathom?

More out of ingrained politeness than from any lingering hope, the villagers went along with the outlandish scheme. They watched, amused, as Mr. Robert Harding applied the sticky substance on the balding spots and peered into the eyes, ears, and mouth of each sheep, before signalling his readiness for his next victim. With no less zeal, his son and the translator herded the painted sheep out of the way to make room for the next in line. By mid-afternoon, what few sheep there were had been taken care of. At sunset, having waited in vain for any reluctant herdsmen to show up, the out-of-towners reloaded their vehicle and retraced their way out of the village. Not even one barrel had been used up.

Some of the sheep owners scrubbed the paint off their animals' hides as soon as they reached home, to stave off possible after-effects. Most of them let the promised rains do their job. A mere two weeks after, the latter group began to notice that, whereas the paint had faded on its own, wool had began to sprout in its place. A month later, no one was able to tell where the bald spots had been. The financial implications of this miracle were lost on no one, for by then the price of a sheep had almost quadrupled.

When the Hardings showed up again some six weeks later, they were received with ear-splitting ululates and warm hand-shakes. They were offered a brew of coffee and *tella,* and were invited to partake in the Festival of the Transfiguration, *Debre*

Tabor, which was slated to unfold late that afternoon. This latest gesture affirmed the genuineness of the outpouring of friendliness and gratitude, for *Debre Tabor* is considered by many to be a family affair, observed with one's close friends and relations.

"We will take a rain check," replied Mr. Robert Harding, and the community reluctantly relented.

Only Abebe the Bandit expressed displeasure. With the crop seeds already in the ground, he held, no one should think of checking the rains.

"You are dumb," interjected Endale Fluoride, his arch-adversary, who had been listening to his protest. "*Rain check* doesn't mean they will actually check the falling of the rains!"

WHEN IT WAS REVEALED that the white family planned to call Mechara their home, no one could think of better neighbours. In the years to come, Mr. Robert Harding would be asked to deliver many more miracles, including reinvigorating the balding head of the governor's nephew and accelerating the growth of Beletu's fingernails. But he was destined never to replicate his early success.

MR. ROBERT HARDING was a giant of a man, almost the same height and build as Endale Fluoride. Like his daughter, Oona, he had fire-red hair. His mane seemed to light up when his face changed colour—and he often appeared to be excited for no obvious reason. He smiled just as frequently, but no one could remember ever seeing his teeth. While his carefully groomed beard, which had greyed at the chin, and tinted glasses had come to symbolize for many the new face of the medicine man, his excitable disposition and enigmatic smile magnified the aura of mystery that continued to envelop him.

Mrs. Vivian Harding, a petite woman in a teenaged boy's frame, was the antithesis of her husband. Although she had given birth to two children, her appearance bore no trace of the fact: her bosoms had not fully developed, nor were her hips pronounced like those of the village mothers. Her brown hair was closely cropped, and she wore leg braces—both of which Beletu attributed to recent fashion trends. The fact that her son, Jeff Harding, sported a completely different head of hair—blond (or golden, as the locals call it)—and that each of them had a different eye colour made people doubt that they belonged to the same family. This scepticism persisted even though the governor, who had assumed responsibility for integrating expatriate members into his jurisdiction, repeatedly gave assurances (once over the Holy Bible) that they were indeed blood relations.

By THE TIME the Hardings decided to make Mechara their home, the village had drawn many new settlers. Much of the prime land had been carved up and allocated to storeowners, who could afford to part with a governor's ransom. A sizable area had been set aside for use by the Coffee Board, a branch of the Ministry of Agriculture and the prime instigators of the road project. With the exception of a narrow tract of land that was designated for the governor's pet project, which might come to light any day now, only the inaccessible bush and the high hills had remained untouched.

The Hardings settled for a piece of land next to the open-air abattoir—an area that was shunned by villagers for fear that the spilt blood and wandering souls of butchered animals might attract the Evil One. Their three-bedroom timber house had been erected in record time, a short five months. The construction had involved hundreds of volunteers and Aba Yitades' unflagging support.

The Hardings had been basking in the community's hospitality and goodwill when the age-old question of their bare necks was raised once again. Uncharacteristically, the inquiry was made not by Aba Yitades, as one might expect, but by Abebe the Bandit. Back after a brief stint in the bush, he was in a self-rehabilitation mood.

Aba Yitades hadn't given the matter much weight (though, it will be remembered, he had already pencilled in the observation in the Black Ledger). He swatted away the complaint with a casual swing of his fly-switch, until respectable members of his parish began to echo the Bandit. He felt obliged to deliver his answer from the church nave, where the officiating clergy conducted the service hidden from view. "We can't hold this against the Hardings," Aba Yitades declared, "because, for all we know, the Church may not have reached their distant homeland. These are intelligent people; given time, they will see the Lord's way."

There were further signs that Aba Yitades had softened his stance towards people of suspect spiritual bent. He gave Azeb free rein to mingle with the Hardings. As long as she wasn't needed by his side or at home, she could spend as much time as she wanted playing with her new friend, Oona. "But don't touch anything they cook," cautioned both Aba Yitades and Werknesh. "We still don't know what they eat."

In fact, what the Hardings ate remained the subject of intense interest for a considerable time. How they slaughtered their animals—the rituals they followed before killing their prey—was under scrutiny. After all, what distinguished the heathen from the faithful wasn't just what they considered to be clean and unclean food, but also how they went about preparing their meals. What made a piece of meat Muslim or Christian, for instance, were the few words of prayer said over the animal before it was slaughtered.

At dinnertime, the Hardings' residence became a magnet for curious villagers. To the frustration of many, however, the white family seldom cooked outdoors, and they ate out of sight. It was already accepted that the Hardings would never ask anyone to join them for dinner, even when they had seen someone hovering at their doorway for hours on end, but what came as a shock to many was what was unveiled next.

Staking out the Hardings' residence was Abebe the Bandit, whose concern for the community's welfare and spiritual well-being had yet to slacken. Dispirited by the failure of his week-long surveillance to turn up any answers, and by the sheer number of hours he had wasted in the cold and damp, he decided one evening to try his last available tactic: he burst in on the household, catching them in the act—at the dinner table.

"They are not a family," he announced, knocking on doors, waking up those who had gone to bed early. With a single daring act, he laid to rest what had weighed heavily on many minds.

"But how do you know?" he was asked.

"They don't eat together," he replied. "Each one of them has his or her own plate."

Even such a startling revelation didn't lessen Aba Yitades' empathy for the Hardings. "Maybe they are experiencing a momentary falling-out," was all he could think to say, kneading his overflowing beard in utter bewilderment. He did remember to reach for the Black Ledger, though. The priest did not feel deep concern until Abebe the Bandit revealed yet another oddity.

Mr. Robert Harding had come home with a warthog he had tracked. On its own, such an act wouldn't have aroused much interest, as it was still customary to take boys out on a hunting expedition as an initiation rite, and Mr. Harding had taken along his son, who was said to be thirteen years of age—a commendable act indeed. Custom required that the family keep the hide and tusks of the beast, carving up the meat for the family pet. What Abebe the Bandit discovered stood tradition on its head: Mr. Robert Harding kept the warthog's meat for his family's consumption, discarding the animal's hide and tusks.

Even Aba Yitades couldn't come up with an explanation. *Who would eat meat (pork!) that all three known religions—Christians, Muslims, and Jews alike—consider unclean?* he confided to his one and only true friend, the Black Ledger.

Aba Yitades wasn't prepared to give up on the Hardings just yet, however. He nurtured hopes that one day soon he would be able to baptize the entire family, drawing them into the fold of the Church. In the meantime, he couldn't help but impose further restrictions on his youngest daughter. In addition to avoiding what the Hardings ate, Azeb was instructed not to touch their drinking water either. For no one could be sure that their glasses and pitchers weren't contaminated with pork.

For her part, Azeb quickly proved herself an indispensable ally to the Hardings. On market days, Mrs. Vivian Harding seldom left home without the company of the priest's daughter. Oona spoke flawless Amharic, it is true, but she had yet to find her way through the labyrinth of intrigue and double-talk that characterized the marketplace. "You can always trust the farmers," Azeb told Mrs. Harding, "but you should be on guard with the professional merchants. The trick is to identify the latter."

The modern highway had a liberating effect on many a merchant who formerly had kept a watchful eye out for the exacting priest. Now, Aba Yitades could no more dictate how they conducted their affairs, or what produce they brought to market, than King Canute could prevent the tides from coming in. They could mark up their prices as high as the traffic would bear and fleece the unwary without looking over their shoulders. Thanks to Azeb, Mrs. Vivian Harding quickly caught on to the measuring-cup ploy and mastered the subtle art of haggling. Even months later, however, she still lacked the confidence to conclude a purchase on her own, never tiring of asking: "Azeb, do you think this is a good buy? Azeb, do you think this chicken is not sick? It seemed like a very good deal, you know. Azeb, do you think …"

Mrs. Vivian Harding met with one surprise after another. And she took them in her stride. One carefree afternoon, she had stopped to purchase a box of safety matches from a vendor who displayed his meagre wares on a tray, fashioned from a cardboard box, that dangled from his neck. "Twenty-five cents for two boxes of matches," he screamed at each passing face. A dime less than what the stores charged seemed to her like a good buy, so

Mrs. Vivian Harding reached for her wallet. Azeb asked her not to rush. She slid open one of the boxes, rearranged the sticks, and revealed to the awestruck woman that the box, which looked full at first glance, was actually half empty.

"How did he do it?" Mrs. Vivian Harding demanded, convulsing in laughter.

"Easy," said Azeb, and she showed her how it was done, by forming a bed of criss-crossed sticks on which she carefully laid the rest.

"But what would he do with the ones he removed?" Mrs. Harding wondered. "Surely he can't find new boxes to put them in to sell."

"He may use them to light up his tobacco," Azeb speculated.

Mrs. Harding surprised Azeb when she paid for the tampered boxes of matches anyway. "It will save him face," she said. "Besides, I don't think he will play the same trick on me again." She offered Azeb one of the boxes to take home to her mother.

"We don't use matches," Azeb told her.

"Why not?"

"There is always fire in our kitchen."

"How is that possible?"

"We leave a few lumps of live charcoal under a bed of ashes after we have finished cooking," Azeb explained.

"Suppose the charcoal burned itself out?"

"If that happens, Mam will send me to a neighbour for a starting fire," Azeb explained. "That is how everyone else does it." And she was telling the truth. Early in the morning and late in the afternoon, children could be seen walking from door to door with a battered plate in hand, asking if a neighbour had a few lumps of lit charcoal—a start-up fire.

"Well, this will save you a trip," said Mrs. Harding, pressing the box into Azeb's hand. But the priest's daughter remained adamant, remembering her early training that when you help someone, you don't expect rewards.

MRS. HARDING wasn't laughing when one sunny market day Endale Fluoride plucked Azeb from her side and began fondling her before Mrs. Harding's very eyes. "I was beginning to think you were avoiding me," he said between spurts of cigarette smoke. Having forgotten her basic Amharic, Mrs. Harding resorted to her native tongue, heaping on him insults that did little to deter him. When he eventually let go of his victim, it was as a result of Azeb's convincing tears. (Later that day, Mrs. Harding alerted Werknesh to the abuse, but if she had expected righteous indignation, she was disappointed. "He has yet to grow up," was the response she got.)

The same afternoon, Mrs. Harding came upon a teenaged girl selling prescription medicines. On a threadbare towel, the girl had carefully laid out her exotic merchandise: tablets and caplets, which she had arranged by size and colour, and vials of clear fluid with syringes. Some of the syringes bore signs of previous use. The metallic cap of a few of the glass vials had been tampered with, exposing the pinkish rubber stopper underneath.

The girl's father, Abebe the Bandit, lured customers with colourful promises. "Meet the future," he cried. "The future belongs to tablets and caplets. Herbal medicine as we know it is dead." Curious men and women stopped to look at the rare merchandise.

"Etiye Selamawit," Abebe the Bandit yelled at the sight of an elderly woman, "how is your backache?"

"Bless the Lord, I haven't had one in months," she lied.

"How about occasional dizziness, headaches, constipation, coughing and sneezing, or sheer tiredness?" he rattled off, gazing at her retreating back.

"I suppose I experience occasional dizziness," admitted an unsuspecting outsider, another elderly woman.

He pressed a couple of oval capsules in her palm. "And this is for what you don't yet have," he said, throwing in a tiny tablet as a bonus. "Fifty cents, please!" No sooner had he collected his money than he saw another potential customer. "Ato Abraha, what a pleasure it is to see you," he bellowed. "I was thinking of your weak heart when I purchased this import," he said, handing the man a reddish bottle of syrup. "I'll collect the seventy-five cents later."

Not only had Abebe the Bandit pioneered the first modern pharmacy in Mechara, he had removed the middleman as well. Little stood between patients and their prescriptions anymore, only his fast-talking self and a few hard-to-come-by pennies. His ill-mannered daughter, who had insulted Aba Yitades at the butcher's doorstep not long ago, found her calling too. In between dispensing the medications and counting their earnings, she adorned her father's lofty promises by detailing cases of syphilis and malaria that had been cured by their array of capsules.

"That's right," added her father. "No more trachoma or glaucoma, gonorrhea or diarrhea, herpes-simplex or simplex-complex, either." Seeing Azeb and the Harding women, he interrupted himself to make them an offer. "Azeb, ask your white friends here what their ailments are. There is ten cents in it for you."

Mrs. Harding was beside herself with rage. "Is this man mad? Tell him he can't do this."

"And why not?" was his defiant response.

"Because you might kill someone."

"Rubbish! I am selling approved prescriptions," he fired back. "I am dispensing medicine that is wholly and universally certified to cure diseases," he stressed. "You don't even have to manifest outward symptoms in order to use my medications. Prevention, more than cure, is what I am striving for."

Mrs. Harding surprised Azeb once more when she purchased the entire stock of tablets, capsules, and bottled medicine for a whopping five *birr*.

"Nice doing business with you, Mam," said Abebe the Bandit, sounding sincere for the first time. "See you next Wednesday."

ABEBE THE BANDIT got his supplies from a charity-run clinic in Gelemso. A passing merchant had told him that the foreign outfit provided the underprivileged with free medical services, including prescriptions. Always leery of such rumours, especially those that tell of someone handing over his valuable possessions without the intervention of a loaded gun, Abebe hitchhiked to Gelemso to confirm the rumour. And confirm it he did.

And so, for pocket change, Abebe the Bandit hired the town's urchins and vagabonds to procure for him the most sought-after medications. Having committed to memory symptoms and diagnoses of the most common diseases, he coached his recruits before dispatching them to the clinic. Abebe the Bandit defended his initiative on the grounds that he was doing a favour not only for the poor and homebound, by bringing to their doorsteps the medication they badly needed at a price they could afford, but also for the international aid agencies themselves, by sparing them the expense of setting up shop in Mechara. He was the unsung hero, a halo in the skies, the one and only homegrown crusader, who had shown selfless devotion to the universal cause of eradicating communicable diseases. By stealing a ride to Gelemso on the back of a loaded truck each week, thus imperilling his life, he was also doing a bit of a patriotic duty. "Come to think of it," he liked to say, "it would not be in the best interests of our country if modern medicine was controlled by white folks."

MRS. VIVIAN HARDING didn't forget Abebe the Bandit. The following Wednesday she showed up at the market accompanied by her husband, the translator, and the head of the clinic in Gelemso—another white face—who made a forceful attempt to confiscate the assorted medications. Not having anticipated the traditional unity of merchants in the face of perceived robbery, the four soon discovered themselves to be the targets of incomprehensible anger. A stick-wielding mob surrounded them, shoving and jostling, whipping up unseemly temper, until the calming voice of Aba Yitades was heard from the distance. The crowd reluctantly dispersed, and the priest ushered the rattled do-gooders to safety.

"What brought you to this predicament?" Aba Yitades finally managed to ask.

"Abebe the Bandit," replied Mr. Robert Harding.

"That man is the Devil in the flesh," sighed the priest. "For your family's sake, steer clear of him."

Mr. Robert Harding did the exact opposite: he hired Abebe the Bandit to keep watch over his property. He seemed to be saying it was better to be on the Devil's side than in his path. His compound had been subject to nocturnal raids from the start. Items left outdoors seldom saw the dawn of another day. Mrs. Harding had long since given up searching for a drinking glass or dinner plate that someone forgot to bring inside. A piece of laundry would be snatched from the clothesline unless a round-the-clock vigil was kept. However, the biggest loss to the family was the building materials they had gradually imported from abroad for a closely guarded project, and which they had left in piles outside. In question were crates of corrugated metal sheets, hand tools, and boxes of nails and fasteners—items that couldn't easily be replaced from the local markets.

Although Abebe the Bandit was never seen at his new job site, he proved to be a most effective watchman, who could be counted on to ward off nightly raids without even being present. Not a single piece of firewood was lost from the Hardings' yard ever again. What is more, Abebe the Bandit was persuaded to abandon his thriving medical practice. Until the Hardings' mysterious building project got off the ground, he could count on drawing twenty *birr* a month for his phantom guard duty. Afterwards, he could confidently expect to conclude a similar arrangement with the state-owned Coffee Board.

Like the Hardings' compound, the property of the Coffee Board had been subject to systematic nighttime raids for quite some time. Bags full of coffee beans disappeared long before they could be logged and stored. Boxes of papers sprouted wings. A weighing scale had once been carted off its stand. Partly because of the device's mammoth size and weight, and partly because the market for a platform scale hadn't fully ripened yet, it was located the following day, kilometres from the office, the village children bouncing up and down on it.

The day that fifty kilograms of prime coffee beans went missing, two of the board's full-time employees were relieved of their jobs on charges of dereliction of duty (and, some say, on suspicion of pocketing the purchase money). Abebe the Bandit secured the board's undying gratitude, and two *birr* in reward money, when he showed up three days later with the lost bag of coffee balanced on his head. "I found it hidden in the cemetery," he proudly declared.

ABEBE THE BANDIT wasn't the only person who was swept off his feet by the Hardings' easygoing attitude and unconventional manners. Werknesh seldom tired of hearing her youngest daughter prattle about her discoveries at the Hardings' home.

"Oona's mother kissed me on the mouth," Azeb told her early on, giggling.

"I am sure she meant to kiss you on the cheek," Werknesh explained.

"No," maintained Azeb, "she held my cheeks with both hands and kissed me on the lips, saying, 'Good to see you.'"

"Well, she is strange, all right."

"She kisses Oona on the mouth as well."

"How odd! Can't she see that her daughter is out of her crib?"

"Mr. Harding kisses her too."

"It is not unusual for a husband and wife to kiss," Werknesh instructed, "though it is done only behind closed doors, preferably under the cover of a blanket."

Beletu hastened to amend her mother's observation. "You can

kiss in the open, if you are good-looking," she said, remembering the miniature movie posters in her collection.

"I am not talking about Mr. and Mrs. Harding," corrected Azeb. "I am talking about father and daughter."

"That is even more bizarre," noted Werknesh. "Don't tell this to anyone."

"Jeff lets their dog lick his mouth."

"I knew there was something wrong with that boy."

"He even lets the dog lick his dinner plate."

"How disgusting!"

"He talks to his father with his hands in his pockets."

"Now, that is loose upbringing."

"And he—"

"That is enough," concluded Werknesh.

Werknesh quickly grew fond of Oona. Charmed by the girl's impeccable manners, she often said, "With a little colour in her face, that child could easily pass for a princess." Etiye Hiywet went one better. "If she had worn a neck-cord," she wistfully noted, "I would have adopted her as a godchild." For her part, Oona readily adjusted to the routines of the priest's home. At her own home, hired help—the butcher's younger daughter—handled the daily chores; and like many a servant, she was territorial. At the priest's home, on the other hand, Oona could indulge her curiosity regarding the household arts. Werknesh not only gave her free rein in the kitchen but encouraged her to hone her culinary skills. Before long, Oona mastered the subtle art of blending herbs for a variety of dishes, and she could cook all but the most demanding of stews—seasoned chicken. Her *injera* came out with its eyes wide open.

IF OONA WAS ASKED what were her most vivid memories of growing up in Mechara—her fondest recollections, but also the difficulties she faced—she would reply, "I had such a rich and rewarding experience growing up in Mechara that I can't single out a specific case without doing injustice to the rest. But my most traumatic experience, one that I will always remember, is the run-in I had with Endale Fluoride."

It was a beautiful day, Oona recalled. The sun was bright and mild, the breeze refreshing. After a night of rain, the ground was soggy and treacherous underfoot. As had become her habit, Oona accompanied Azeb to the river to fetch drinking water for the priest's household. (At her own home, the butcher's daughter took care of this difficult chore.) There were fewer adults at the water source than usual, as it was Assumption of the Virgin and the women had remained at home to prepare the celebration feast.

Girls as young as six were attempting to hoist buckets weighing as much as they did to the top of their heads. Azeb and Oona rushed to help. Like stage performers who knew their drills well, the children squatted without waiting for a cue, while the two relatively grown girls lifted the buckets high and placed them on the piece of rag cushioning each girl's head. Unable to regain her footing immediately, a girl would wobble; her neck would threaten to buckle under the strenuous weight. Oona and Azeb waited, like a couple of spotters in a modern gym, breath in check, until each one took a couple of steady steps before assisting the next.

Almost an hour passed before the two girls filled up their own receptacle. Unlike the younger girls, they didn't need to carry the bucket on one of their heads. Instead, they slipped a lifting pole through the handle and retraced their way, each holding one end of the wooden shaft. The bucket swayed and left a trail of water. From time to time they stopped to relieve their arms and to shift the load so that the weight was evenly distributed. Fetching water had become such a routine chore even to Oona, and the trail to the river so familiar, that neither she nor Azeb suspected danger might be lurking in the shadows.

It materialized halfway up the bluff. Endale Fluoride had been lying in wait for them. Azeb dropped her end of the pole and tore off at the sight of him. Oona stood looking at the empty bucket, the fruit of their labour lost to the thirsty soil.

"You're not afraid of me like your friend, are you?" Endale Fluoride teased Oona, stealthily approaching her. His breath reeked of alcohol, and his grin was wolflike, she later remembered.

"Why should I be afraid of you?" she replied defiantly.

"You are the brave one, aren't you?" he continued to taunt her, closing the gap.

"Get away from me," she cried, belatedly realizing the situation she was in.

"Let's see what you've got under that shirt of yours," he said, reaching for her chest as he was accustomed to doing with Azeb.

"Get away from me," she cried, louder than before.

Unlike her friend, who quietly shed tears, Oona fought her attacker. She bit his groping hands, kicked him in the groin, and showered him with choice insults. Like a wild beast whose killer instinct is whetted by the sight of blood, Endale Fluoride's grip and resolve were only stiffened by her angry thrashing. When he eventually let go of her, it was because a passing adult intervened and he was ashamed of his unseemly conduct.

That afternoon, Mr. Harding revealed a side that few suspected existed. Raging like a madman, he went looking for his daughter's assailant, ignoring the tearful pleas of his wife, who urged him to leave the matter to the law, and the efforts of the translator to calm him. Having misplaced his meagre Amharic, he resorted to English, confounding the villagers even more.

Shopkeepers abandoned their counters and congregated at their doorways, watching the unfolding drama in utter disbelief. Like a mass of debris in the wake of a tornado, village boys trailed the angry American at a safe distance. None of them had ever seen a white man in a fist fight, and their curiosity was vividly written on their faces. Mercifully, before Mr. Harding could locate Endale Fluoride, he ran into Aba Yitades and paused to listen to reason.

The priest was puzzled that Mr. Harding misinterpreted Endale's rough play as sexual in nature. "What sort of pervert would see sex in a ten-year-old girl?" Aba Yitades quietly mused. Endale Fluoride might be an out-and-out skirt chaser, a tireless philanderer, but surely even he wouldn't sink so low as to stalk a bed-wetter. "Endale is rough around the edges," the priest finally managed to say. "But by and large he is harmless. In any case, leave this matter to me. I will handle it our own way."

"What does the law say about sexual assault?" Mr. Harding wanted to know.

"Sexual assault? Frankly, if we have such a law, I am not aware of it."

"What would you do in situations where, say, a woman was raped?"

"As a community, there are things we do and things we don't do. We don't need a written law to tell us that rape is a serious offence," replied Aba Yitades. "In fact, we consider rape not just a violation of the individual victim, but also an indelible tarnish on her family's honour. If someone is brazen enough to commit such a heinous crime, then he will pay dearly for it."

"How exactly do you make him pay?"

Aba Yitades thought it prudent to give his answer by way of anecdote. "Did you know that the butcher had a son?" he asked.

"No, but I know he has two daughters. One of them is our housekeeper," replied Mr. Harding.

"He had a son, all right," said Aba Yitades after a drawn-out sigh. "An apology for a son, I might add." Aba Yitades was being kind, because in fact the butcher's son was an apology for many more things. He was an apology for a butcher, a weaver, a wood chopper, a charcoal maker, and a sheep dresser—all trades that he had tried his hand at, at one time or another, and invariably failed at. What he had never failed at, or apologized for, was the practice of taking to bed women who didn't belong to him.

Unlike Endale Fluoride, who restricted his conquests to unattached women, the butcher's son cast his net farther and wider, catching unlikely prey. He elevated the craft of philandering to a high-wire act when he lured to bed engaged women and celebrated virgins. The butcher's son survived many close shaves before he was caught in the act: he was found in bed with a newly wed woman. The woman lost her husband; the butcher's son, his manhood.

The butcher's son banished himself from the village. Every now and then he was sighted in one town or another. Returning merchants told gruesome stories of how the young man was seen dropping his pants for paying voyeurs, who couldn't seem to get enough of the clear plastic tube that dangled from his crotch. Against his will, the butcher's son had become a cautionary tale for young men who would otherwise consider adultery a harmless distraction.

"And that wasn't even rape," Aba Yitades concluded.

Mr. Harding stood unblinking. And when he finally spoke, it was to ask for a repeat of the highlights. As the full impact of the story hit him at last, he could no longer conceal his revulsion. "That is gruesome," he screamed. "That is utter barbarism, sheer lawlessness, vigilantism." There didn't seem to be enough words to describe his horror. His face turned ashen. For the first time since he had decided to call the picturesque village home, his eyes opened to the strong currents under the peaceful surface. It dawned on him that despite the modern highway and the steady stream of outsiders coming to Mechara, the place was still beyond the reach of the law. There was no police force or state-run court in sight.

"Surely his assailant didn't get away with his outrageous conduct," Mr. Harding finally managed to say, sounding as if he were hoping against hope.

"As a matter of fact, he did," Aba Yitades sighed. "The butcher had to let him get away with it; his mutilated son had to let him get away with it; we all had to let him get away with it. The young man hadn't done what any man with any manhood wouldn't have done in his shoes."

"Is this man still in the village?"

"He certainly is. In fact, he is the affable young fellow who came to Jeff's aid when your boy was mobbed by angry teenagers over a misunderstanding concerning street dogs." (Jeff had attempted to intervene—to his own peril, as it turned out—on behalf of coupling dogs that the village boys were pelting with well-aimed stones.)

"Aba Yitades, promise me that you will do your best to discourage such lawless behaviour. I look forward to raising my family here, and the conduct that you just told me about doesn't jibe with God-fearing people like you," Mr. Harding pleaded.

Aba Yitades set out to answer at length. "We all make choices in our lives. We harvest the rewards of good deeds and the consequences of bad ones. Whether or not one should leave the ultimate judgment to the All-Knowing above, to a state-appointed magistrate, or to the community that was wronged, it is not for me to say."

If Aba Yitades had any inkling that, with the growing number and diversity of Mechara's citizens, his outdated outlook might be a recipe for disaster, he gave no indication of it. The lesson wasn't entirely lost on Mr. Harding, however. Indeed, some six years later he would come to appreciate the full impact of the anecdote, when village justice reached into his own home.

10

THE OATH OF A MIZAE

*G*enet, the priest's first-born, would long remember the day she opened the creaky gate of the compound and let in four *netela*-wrapped elders. Two of them were from the village, and she had known them all her life, but their businesslike tone of voice said, "Girl, keep a distance."

"Is your father home?" inquired the one of the most advanced years.

"Yes, do come in," she said, bowing out of the way.

"No, please summon him for us."

Her heart racing, her mind struggling with conflicting thoughts, she rushed back inside to alert her father. Elders coming for a visit and acting in such a sombre fashion usually meant that a relative had passed away and they were about to deliver the sad tidings. But, Genet suddenly recalled, breaking bad news is done early in the morning, when the family has just got out of bed, not late in the afternoon. Also, there would have been a woman or two with them, who would assist the lady of the house with her mourning girdle.

Werknesh was the first to emerge; she was no less baffled by the assortment of elders than her daughter had been. Not far behind her was Aba Yitades. As the visitors were all men, the priest suspected that women had no business hanging around, so he herded them back inside. This was not a run-of-the-mill social call, the priest was able to tell, so he didn't invite the men in. He needed to find out the reason for the unusual call before extending his hospitality. If there was going to be a tussle over property, say, it would be better handled out in the open, where neighbours and passersby would bear witness.

"What brought you here, my brethren?" Aba Yitades finally managed to ask, his eyes darting from one inscrutable face to another.

"We have come to ask for what is dear to your heart, Aba Yitades," said one of the local men. "Do we have your permission to speak?"

"Far be it from me to deny you what the Good Lord has given you—the right to speak," the priest replied.

"We have come seeking your kinship," hinted the same elder. "We are here on behalf of Ato Abraha's son."

Aba Yitades' heart sank to his knees. At no time had he suspected that he would soon be the father of a bride. Who would have thought that the years would advance so quickly, he later mused with his wife, so deceptively fast that one minute a child is wetting her bed and the next she is ready to be married off. Was it not only yesterday that Aba Yitades himself was a mere boy—and a timid one at that—who froze at the sight of a wounded warthog and became the butt of the villagers' jokes for years afterwards? How about the two local elders standing before him—were they not some of the very young men who had taunted him for not being man enough? In fact, it was the memory of the bloody warthog and the inner wounds he had been nursing all these years that had blinded him to his children's growing maturity.

The priest chuckled to himself at his own chronic fretfulness. It shouldn't have been so difficult for him to figure out why such a distinguished number of elders would call upon him. After all, Aba Yitades himself had been an intercessor on four previous occasions, once on behalf of the nephew of one of the visiting men. "It is just that one tends to think of death and in-laws as other people's problems," he later said.

"Won't you come in?" Aba Yitades offered, remembering his manners. And the elders filed in one after the other. "Who did you say you were representing?" the priest followed up as soon as they had all assumed their seats.

"Our Abraha, of course."

"But I thought his boys were all married."

"The middle one, the one who lives in Gelemso, is divorced."

"Was he not married only two years ago?"

"More like four years," said one, and another corrected, "Three and a half."

Aba Yitades decided then and there, without bothering to consult his wife and cherished friends, that he wouldn't be seeking kinship of the unstable young man. Even by the loose moral standards of a big town, a man doesn't walk away from a holy union before the wedding debt is paid off.

If the visiting men had been ordinary folks, not pillars of the community, and if he himself had not been the head of the parish, the appropriate response would have been, "My daughter shall not seek his partnership, nor shall I give my approval." And the elders would have scuttled away. But the priest didn't have the option of being abrupt. His response would have to be carefully weighed and worded.

"Which one of my daughters does this young man have in mind?" he asked after a moment of reflection. The elders looked puzzled. Not one of them had thought of the middle child, it seemed. Barely two years younger than her older sister, and with her ravishingly good looks, Beletu should have been the one to catch the eye of any man.

"Genet, of course," the answer came finally.

"How unfortunate," Aba Yitades rejoined mournfully.

"Why so?"

"Well, it so happens that I have already accepted the neck-cord of an eligible young man," he lied.

The elders shuffled in their seats, their glances confused. It was not entirely uncommon to play hard to get; in fact, the intercessors would have expected nothing less from a respectable family such as the priest's. But the answer in such an instance would have come in the form of, "I will counsel my kin, my 'bread brothers,' and my wife, and I will give you my answer in a week or two."

"Aba Yitades," chimed in one of the local elders, "this must be the best-kept secret. May we ask who this fortunate man is?"

"Well, if we had wanted to make the news public, we would have done so by now," answered the priest, his eyes downcast from the shame of fabricating a story.

The intercessors departed glumly. But they didn't stay away for long. A week later they showed up once again, although this time adding one more elder: the soul-father of Etiye Hiywet. They seemed to be saying to the priest that if Genet had been engaged, her godmother would have been in the know; Etiye Hiywet's soul-father would have been privy to the fact, by virtue of his mandate, and he wouldn't have come along if he had thought the mission was hopeless. Most disconcerting to the priest, however, was the elder who showed up carrying a billet of wood on his back, effectively saying, "Here is my crucifix. Either give us your daughter or crucify me."

As the parish priest, Aba Yitades discouraged the practice of carrying a billet of wood in routine intercessions. The last time he had endorsed such a move was in a case of divorce, not marriage, and that was because the community had demanded that the breakup of a young family be avoided at all costs for the sake of the couple's handicapped newborn. When the usual petitions failed to yield the required result, the priest sanctioned the simulated crucifixion, and it worked. The couple stayed married.

Aba Yitades reprimanded the elder carrying the billet of wood, saying, "Why humble yourself and humiliate me before my 'bread brothers'? I may forgive your impossible conduct, but I doubt if the Good Lord will look kindly on you for making a mockery of His trial." Turning to the remaining intercessors, the priest had this to add: "My brethren, if my daughter were available, why would I deny her to you? She neither carries my thoughts for me nor guards my holy shrine."

And that was the last time anyone came on behalf of the unstable young man. More importantly, Aba Yitades didn't lose his worthy parishioners on account of the failed intercessions.

Many more elders would come seeking kinship of the priest, and seven agonizing months of indecision would elapse, before he gave his blessing. True to the promise he had made his wife early on, that he would entrust the final decision to Genet, he stood before one stunned group of elders and declared: "Genet is the one who marries the young man, so the final decision should be hers." And he promptly added, "But if I know my daughter well (and what good father doesn't?), she won't disapprove of my choice. So, my brethren, you have my blessing, and her tacit approval."

ONCE THE INTERCESSORS had done their job, responsibility passed to the *Neger Abats*—which, literally translated, means "spokesfathers"—to work out the finer and, more significantly, the thorny details of the marriage without directly involving the in-laws. One was chosen to stand for the would-be groom and one for Genet. An arbiter was selected from the village elders to judge the asseverations made by the spokesfathers and settle any disputes that might arise.

First for the spokesfathers to verify was whether the two young people could be legally married at all, the deciding factor being lineage. No two Christians could say "I do" if they shared a bloodline within the past seven "houses"—generations. The tiresome process of sorting out the houses was set in motion by the spokesfather of the would-be groom.

"Our son is the fourth child of Ato Ayele and his good wife, Weizero Wubalesh," he began. "Ato Ayele is the son of Ato Negash, who is the son of Ato Mengesha, who is the son of—"

"Which Mengesha?" interrupted Genet's spokesfather.

"Mengesha of the village Boke Gudo, of course."

"Was he not a tanner?"

"No, you are thinking of the *other* Mengesha."

"Judge, would you look into this matter?" urged Genet's spokesfather.

"I certainly will," said the arbiter, making a mental note of the mysterious Ato Mengesha, who might turn out to be the mole that brought down the entire house.

Aba Yitades, for once, could be proud of his estranged ancestors. The arbiter waived the requirement of spelling out the priest's lineage when he said: "My brethren, we all know that Aba Yitades is from good stock. There is not a drop of bad blood in him, so let us not waste our time on him." Werknesh, however, proved difficult to trace beyond the fifth house on her father's side and the sixth on her mother's. But as she was originally from a far-off district, her chances of sharing a bloodline with the would-be groom were considered slim. Also, the fact that her father, the late Aba Berhanu, was a respected local priest allayed all fears that she could be harbouring "weak" blood.

After the question of the bloodlines, the financial profile of the groom was scrutinized.

"How will your son support our daughter?" Genet's spokesfather asked.

"We all know that the young man is a hard-working farmer, and—"

"We know that much, but does he mean to stay on his father's lot, or will he be a homesteader, striking out on his own?"

"As a matter of fact, he has applied for land rights," admitted the spokesfather, settling a rumour that had been circulating that the young man contemplated moving out of the village.

"In that case," said Genet's spokesfather, "we would like to know his material worth—the portion of his family's herd and other assets that would go with him. Starting out on one's own is noble, but without the right resources it can be a daunting task. We can't remove our daughter from the comforts of her home and throw her into the wild."

"Submit your charge's assets and relevant details within a week," the arbiter instructed the spokesfather of the would-be groom.

"Before we do that," said the latter, "we would like to know the bride's position on dowry."

Dowry was a relatively new phenomenon, the introduction and growing popularity of which was attributed to enterprising merchants. In bigger cities, where this new practice had taken deep root, the groom presented the bride with suitcases full of ready-made clothing and expensive jewellery. Such was the hold of the trend that the dowry day was anticipated with no less enthusiasm than the actual wedding day.

Aba Yitades had long preached against this alien culture and its corrosive effects on the moral and spiritual fabric of his flock. The groom's spokesfather wanted to know if the priest favoured what he had so often advocated, a traditional arrangement for his daughter's wedding. According to this ancient norm, both partners contributed towards their start-up capital, the amounts varying according to the economic status of the individuals. If the bride was from a less-privileged family, for instance, her share could be as low as a quarter. Otherwise, she would match, in full, what her husband brought into the union. Contributions could be made in the form of grain, cattle, furniture, kitchen utensils, jars of butter and honey, and even cash.

Werknesh wasn't such a materialistic person, but she didn't wish for her daughter to pass up this once-in-a-lifetime opportunity to indulge. In her own words, once children and the attendant expenses came into the picture, a traditional homemaker couldn't even afford a snatch of fresh breath. But Aba Yitades held his ground.

HAVING SETTLED the financial matters and the controversy surrounding the mysterious Ato Mengesha (he was found not to possess a tanner's blood after all), the spokesfathers got together once more to choose the most suitable soul-father for the soon-to-be-wed couple. Traditionally, this was the couple's responsibility, but since neither Genet nor her future husband knew the place where they planned to settle well enough, the elders decided to lend a helping hand.

"I have Aba Taddesse in mind," the groom's spokesfather began.

Genet's representative demurred. "From what I hear, Aba Taddesse's tongue loosens when he is in his cups. I suggest Aba Teferi."

"Aba Teferi is almost eighty. A young couple need a much younger soul-father. I propose Aba Grefew," his opponent counter-offered.

"Aba Grefew has far too many clients. We need someone who can afford the couple the frequent counselling all newlyweds need."

"How about Aba Metaferia?"

"He is the one," all three agreed.

WERKNESH SELDOM TALKED about her own wedding without a sigh of anger and bitterness. "I was married off like a divorcee," she said, "without the pomp and ceremony befitting the virgin that I was." She didn't want the same to happen to her daughter. The day Aba Yitades derided the traditional wedding ceremony as extravagant and contrary to good Christian values, and cited his own simple wedding as an example to be emulated by his daughters, her response was, "Over my dead body." And he quietly relented.

Werknesh might not have complained about her own Eucharist wedding in her husband's presence, but when Aba Yitades pronounced that Holy Matrimony was neither holy nor truly matrimonial unless it was sealed and ratified by the couple taking the Holy Communion together, she raised her objections once more.

"I want nothing more than the '80 bond' marriage for my daughters," she said.

"But the '80 bond' law doesn't deter a man from taking up a mate elsewhere, nor does it stop him from throwing out his lawfully wedded wife at the drop of a hat. Surely you don't want our daughter to scuttle back here with her brood," he argued.

"A Eucharist wedding didn't prevent Ato Agafari from murdering his lawfully wedded wife just so that he would qualify to marry that wench—who, by the way, had murdered her Eucharist-wedded husband as well," she retorted.

"Now, now, that's hearsay," Aba Yitades objected. "There is no proof that Ato Agafari had a hand in the drowning of his wife in a half-filled bathtub. Nor was it conclusively shown that his second wife had poisoned her ex-husband."

"Couples stay together only because they want to," Werknesh argued. "Look at Abebe the Bandit and his wife. They are neither married by the Eucharist nor by the '80 bond' law. In fact, they aren't even legally married!"

Aba Yitades was jarred by his wife's impertinence in offering the lamentable living arrangement of Abebe the Bandit as an example of conjugal bliss. "You can't talk of good Christian values and Abebe the Bandit in the same breath," he chided.

Nonetheless, Werknesh won out once more: Genet would marry by the "80 bond" law.

THE "80 BOND" LAW entitled Genet to half of the couple's property in case of a divorce; an equal right to annul the marriage if the union turned sour (it takes only one elder to release a couple from the "80 bond"); and a surety against debts—those from gambling, for instance—that her husband might have secretly accumulated and failed to pay up. Her share of the property could never be sold to settle his debts.

Also, the "80 bond" law gave Genet priority, in the eyes of the law, over any other bond wife whom her husband might be tempted to keep elsewhere, as "well-bred" men traditionally did. Not only was Genet's share of the property protected from this other woman in case of a divorce, but so was the support money due her children.

However, the greatest advantage of the "80 bond" law was that it gave both partners an equal incentive to work hard at the marriage.

CHOOSING THE WEDDING DATE hadn't been as easy as one might suppose. The fast-approaching fifty-four days of Lent were ruled out. Besides the obvious constraints the fast imposes on the celebration menu, there was the issue of the bride's honour to think of. No virgin marries during the Lenten Fast. Period.

No virgin marries on a Saturday either, because to do so means consummating the union on the eve of the Sabbath. Good Christians do not "know" their spouses on Saturday evening. If by some mistake they do, they secretly dash to the river early the next morning to scrub themselves clean before heading to church. Aba Yitades prided himself on the sacrifices he made in honour of his Maker. He never slept in his bed, much less shared it with his wife, on the eve of the Sabbath. Instead, he curled up on the bare earth below.

AFTER RULING OUT Wednesdays and Fridays and the countless fast days, Werknesh was left with 108 days in the year to choose from. For most families that number would have provided ample choice for an event that lasted three days at most, but, unlike most townspeople, her family didn't have the luxury of being insular. She knew far too many people with a loved one or two under the sod. After crossing out the commemoration dates of people whom she considered to be friends and relations of the family (for one doesn't throw a party when a neighbour is mourning), Werknesh was left with a window—the Angel of Death co-operating—of only twenty-two days.

The period preceding the wedding was hard on the priest's family. Harder still was the effect of the impending change on Azeb. Suddenly looming before her was the prospect of life without the calming presence of her oldest sister, and it made her uncharacteristically morose.

"Can I come to live with you?" she pleaded with Genet.

"You can come visit me whenever you like, but I don't think Mam, or Dad, would allow you to live with me," Genet replied tenderly.

"You can tell Mam that you need my help."

"Mam knows that I can take care of myself."

"Etiye Zewditu took her youngest sister when she married."

"That is because she comes from a family of eleven. Their one-room house was too crowded. They slept in shifts."

Beletu felt obliged to intervene. "For the life of me, I can't see why anyone would want to live in a hamlet that is inaccessible by a paved road," she said, rolling her eyes in incomprehension. Beletu had long been baffled that her older sister, who by Beletu's rare admission wasn't all that far behind her in the intelligence quotient, would agree to move out of Mechara when the modern world was finally making its presence felt.

If Beletu was troubled by Genet's decision to settle out of reach of modernity, Oona felt her horizons expanding.

"May I come visit you?" she asked Genet.

"Sure, honey, whenever you want," came the answer.

"Are there *guereza* monkeys where you are going?"

"I wouldn't know."

"Are there any monkeys at all?"

"I should be surprised if there weren't."

"Will you be having children?" Oona had the impertinence to ask.

"God knows," Genet replied, blushing at the implication of sex.

"Can I be godmother to your kids?" Oona followed up.

Genet couldn't contain her laughter. She didn't want to tell Oona that, lacking a neck-cord, she didn't meet even the basic requirement of a godmother. "We will see," was her noncommittal response.

THE WEEK BEFORE the wedding, the priest's home welcomed a veritable parade of visitors. Men and women, young and old, arrived with a gift or two in hand. Etiye Hiywet was bearing the brunt of Genet's financial responsibility, undertaking to pay not only for the construction of her godchild's new home but for furnishing it as well. The person who stole the limelight, however, was Mrs. Vivian Harding, who showed up with brand new baby clothes, three sets of them, and nursery accessories the likes of which few had ever seen.

Even the priest's old nemeses, his estranged cousins, put in an appearance, some of them for the very first time. The girls brought the bride examples of their handiwork—knits, decorated tablecloths, quilted bedcovers, and pillowcases embroidered with inscriptions that read *Happy Dreams* and *The Lord Is My Shepherd*—while their mothers donated kitchen utensils and dining-room accessories. The men made financial contributions.

FOR AZEB, her sister's wedding day was unforgettable. Little of her old neighbourhood looked familiar to her. A sprawling tent took up much of the family compound, and those who marched briskly in and out were indifferent to her. The bride herself was nowhere to be seen. For much of the wedding day Genet had been closeted inside her family home, surrounded by bridesmaids, friends, and close family members. She was washed in scented water, dusted with baby powder, anointed with rare perfume, and when Azeb thought that any minute now her beloved sister would be rubbed with basil leaves, oregano, allspice, rosemary, and sage, and pickled in hot sauce, she heard a knock on the door. Etiye Hiywet walked in to announce the arrival of the groom's party and to escort the bride to the celebration tent.

At the sight of the bride, the celebration tent resonated with cries of joy and ululates. Genet was formally introduced to her husband-to-be, whom she had known only in secret, and was seated next to him on the carpeted floor. Both had grown up in the same village, so she felt little uneasiness. Sitting across from the affianced were the two spokesfathers and the couple's future soul-father, who had made the journey expressly to attend the ceremony. The best man remained standing. For the moment he was the centre of attention, as he took the Oath of the *Mizae.*

"Do you swear by your neck-cord to treat our daughter, Genet, no differently than your own sister?" the bride's spokesfather demanded of the best man.

"I do," he replied, nervously shifting from one leg to the other.

"Do you swear that if our daughter sends for you at night, you will come at night, if she sends for you by day, you will come by day?"

"I do."

"Do you swear that you will treat her offspring no differently than your own?"

"I do."

"We are handing you our daughter in sound body and soul. Do you promise to deliver her to us, should we ask for her return, in the same condition?"

"I do."

Two brimming horn-cups were immediately brought, one holding milk and the other honey, and the betrothed took turns drinking from the cups, while an elder made benedictions. "May the Good Lord bless you two with begetting healthy offspring."

"Amen," roared the assembled crowd.

"May your offspring turn out to be the seed that populated the earth."

"Amen."

"May the Good Lord guide you in your times of loss and distress."

"Amen."

"May He make your family kin of Abraham and Sarah, and may He render your world free of famine, war, and pestilence."

"Amen."

The groom attached the wedding ring to the neck-cord of the bride. The best man then hoisted her over his back and took her outside, where a horse stood waiting for her, girthed and saddled. Holding an open umbrella over his precious cargo, the best man proceeded to lead the way towards the honeymoon bungalow—a mere twenty minutes' walk from her childhood home.

The gathered women ululated. Werknesh dabbed her teary eyes with the end of her *netela*. Azeb was inconsolable; it took two strong men to restrain her from being trampled by the groom's troop. If there was one person who had remained calm and collected in the sea of turmoil, it was, as usual, Beletu. Her eyes were riveted on the retreating back of Genet's mount when, moments before heading back inside, she shook her head and ruefully noted: "All this for a horse's ass!"

THE PRIEST'S HOME fell eerily quiet for the first time in almost a week. With the guests gone, and the dancing and singing moved to the groom's turf, there was little for the priest and his wife to do but attend to the army of beggars who had camped outside their door since the tent was pitched three days earlier. Soon even this diversion became rare. The beggars went home, having seen with their own eyes that the jugs and pots were truly empty.

THE MOMENT OF TRUTH for any bride's family came the day after the wedding, when the best man announced publicly the brutal findings on her chastity. Such was the significance of the event that the honeymoon bungalow remained a campsite until the results were released. Some in the crowd were friends of the bride, and they might have been remembering her and her family in their daily prayers. However, many were voyeurs, nothing but scandalmongers, who sought something to talk about for weeks and months to come. There were also men and women who truly hoped that this would be a day of reckoning for the priest. After all, Aba Yitades had never shown mercy towards any young woman who had misplaced her virginity.

Many years later, Azeb would recall her father's demeanour the night of her sister's wedding, and at the urging of a friend she committed her memories to paper. "Dad removed the allegorical paintings adorning the walls of our residence," she began, "and he carefully stood them up on the bamboo table before him, face forward."

In the middle was Jesus Christ on the Cross, blood dripping from the wounds on his hands and feet. On His right stood the framed picture of Saint George on horseback, spearing the serpent that had threatened Etiye Brutawit; on His left was the celebrated Abyssinian martyr Abun Menfes Kedus, serenely allowing a bird to quench its thirst by drinking from his left eye.

Lighting three candles, Aba Yitades placed them in the middle of the table. With the bible open in his hand, he then knelt before the trio and began chanting select Psalms. "'O Lord,'" he moaned, "'consider my sighing. Listen to my cry for help, my King and my God, for to you I pray.'" An idea presented itself to him, and the beleaguered father interrupted himself to address his wife, who had sat quietly in the remote corner alongside her two wide-eyed daughters.

"Did Genet ever leave her panties unattended on the clothesline?" he asked.

"No."

"That is good." His relief was glowing brighter than the candlelight. He added, speaking to himself, "They say that Ato Abraha's daughter lost her virginity after someone touched her undergarment with an evil potion. 'In the morning, O Lord, you hear my voice. In the morning I lay my requests before you and wait in expectation, my Lord and Saviour.'"

A more electrifying theme tripped the circuit of his thought, and the priest paused to share it with his wife. "I have always said that once past the age of fifteen, girls shouldn't be allowed to lift heavy objects. No responsible farmer loads his mare with a full sack of grain for fear of miscarriage."

Werknesh once again assuaged his concerns, saying, "Genet has long ceased lifting heavy things. Azeb and Oona fetch our drinking water, and as to the rest, I do it myself mostly."

"That is good." Aba Yitades adjusted the turban on his head. He took a sip of *tella* from the horn-cup next to him before returning to his Psalm in earnest. "'Deliver me, O my God!'" he read, louder than before. "'Strike all my enemies on the jaw; break the teeth of the wicked …'"

The priest had dozed off on his knees, clutching the bible, when he found himself, his much younger self, standing before a wounded warthog. "Don't show fear," some of the gathered men advised. "Stand your ground with your spear thrust. The warthog is gasping for its last breath."

"Throw your spear and dash for cover," contradicted those who saw the danger. "There is nothing more deadly than a wounded warthog."

"Move an inch and I'll disown you," his own father admonished. "You will never set foot in my home again."

Young Yitades was staring at the animal as it sprinted the last few metres, groaning and grunting, its sabre-like tusks clearly aimed at him, when a shot rang out and the priest snapped out of his dream.

DAWN HAD ALREADY BROKEN over the horizon. Aba Yitades walked out to the front yard, where, hunkering under a giant *zegba* tree, he delivered the petitions he had promised his Maker the previous evening. Soon the entire family was by his side. Azeb brewed the first round of coffee, and at the urging of her mother she brought it outside. Little was said throughout the ritual.

In the foggy distance, Werknesh made out signs of the groom's troop. It was crawling at a snail's pace, singing the time-worn

song *"Chegulash abebual zare"*—"Your fruit has flowered today."
As the crowd drew closer, she could identify a few familiar faces,
most significantly that of the best man, who, perched high on
someone's shoulder, waved the customary handkerchief.
Werknesh's grip on her husband's arm tightened. Aba Yitades'
weight shifted steadily towards the prayer stick in his grip, until
the piece of seasoned wood was bent out of shape. Breath in
check, they all waited to see if the piece of white cloth bore the
redeeming red stains—proof of Genet's honour.

Upon a closer view of the handkerchief, Aba Yitades lost his
unsteady footing, the prayer stick having snapped in two. Only
the presence of his wife by his side kept him upright. Tears rolled
down his face. He began to say something, but the words melted
in his mouth long before they formed a complete sentence. His
daughter had reached a critical milestone that day. As everyone
could see, hers had been an honourable life.

11

A BEACON OF HOPE

*M*any years later, when her unconventional marriage turned into a harrowing ordeal and she was ostracized by family, friends, and neighbours for the choice she made, Azeb found ample time to reflect on her early life. She never wavered from her belief that her problems had begun when she ate a roasted sheep's testicle, but if Genet hadn't married and left her home village so soon after, Azeb held, she would not later have found herself in the predicament she did. She even believed that with Genet around as a level-headed presence, Beletu would not have seen her beacon of hope shining elsewhere.

Beletu saw in Genet's arranged marriage her own hopeless future, and since she didn't like what she saw, she began plotting her escape in earnest. She found a lifeline in the long, winding highway, and at the other end of the line she saw a gallant rescuer, arms extended. In her eyes, the automobile was not unlike Noah's famed Ark, only modern; the bus terminal, situated at the edge of the open-air market, mimicked the landing docks of those Biblical scenes with its colourful crowd. The closer Beletu looked at her life and surroundings, the more mind-boggling seemed the parallels with the Lord's noble plans—which Noah had executed with unparalleled perfection. That she had been unable to inter-pret the Scriptures correctly for so long was her only regret.

Once she interpreted the Scriptures correctly, however, the rest was child's play. Locating her "Ark" required some serious footwork, it is true. Though Mechara had quickly become a hotbed of new and untried innovations in the field of modern transport, finding one that suited Beletu's discriminating taste hadn't been all that easy. There were pickup trucks that appeared to have been pulled in two directions, until they were twice their original length. The owners never considered their contraptions fully loaded until the modified chassis scraped the uneven ground. Some of the vehicles looked distinctly different from behind than they did from the front, and with good reason: they had been built from two mismatched pieces.

The upsurge in automotive creativity, which had placed Mechara firmly on the map and on a collision course with such world-renowned motor towns as Detroit and Toyota City, was the brainchild of the famous governor. He had felt let down by the shortsightedness and lack of vision of the major automakers. With their vehicles' pitifully low payloads and limited seating arrangements, he reasoned, one could earn so little, so lamentably little, that in the end one could pay only for the vehicle's operating costs, the owner's small profit, and the home renovation bills of the traffic police (his nephews), with nothing left over to contribute towards the newly planned Mechara town hall. The newly planned town hall was actually intended to be an out-of-sight retreat for the good governor, but since he envisioned hosting visiting dignitaries at his new residence, he argued, the construction costs should be shouldered by the taxpayers.

The governor's brainchild was reaping him a handsome dividend, and inspiring in the transit operators a renewed enthusiasm for their chosen career, when it all came screeching to a halt one rainy Wednesday morning. One of those overstretched trucks snapped in two while negotiating a slippery corner and plummeted into a deep ravine, sending all twenty-two passengers, the driver, and his assistant to an early grave.

The shocking news brought to town a high-ranking member of the province's Department of Highways and three investigators.

Much to the chagrin of the governor, the highway official deemed the modified vehicles to constitute a public hazard, and banned them altogether. Many a transit operator wept quietly over a shared professional grief. For Beletu, however, this proved to be the dawning of a welcome new era.

Almost immediately, a fleet of stylish Peugeot taxis, Fiat autobuses, Volkswagen minivans, Land Rover and Toyota trucks replaced the outlawed ramshackle vehicles. The new arrivals clearly fit into Beletu's vision of a modern Ark, and she quickly made the acquaintance of her "Noahs." Soon her name was on the lips of every taxi and bus operator. Like the young boys who had rushed to harvest the open field for miraculous brushing twigs, the Noahs were eager to do her bidding.

The village of Mechara came to appreciate the long-stifled genius of its self-appointed queen when she introduced the miracles of the modern mill. It was a day Azeb would remember vividly. Frustrated by the idleness of her middle child, Werknesh had ordered Beletu not to leave the family compound before she ground a sackful of *teff,* which would be used for baking *injera.* Beletu slipped to the market, unnoticed, to share her grief with a taxi driver she knew.

"You people live in antiquity!" cried the young man, shaking his head in disbelief. "No one hand-grinds flour anymore. Bring it to me. Before you know it, I'll have it back here, ready to make batter."

The young driver kept his word. Returning from Gelemso, he brought back the powdered grain, hot from the milling machine. Dipping her fingers inside the sack to test the consistency of the grind, Beletu was startled. Unaccountably, her sac of *teff* had been turned into fluid! It was the sort of grind that had never been conceived of, much less achieved, in Mechara before. Later that day, Werknesh took a plateful of the flour to her neighbours to demonstrate the miracles of the modern world and the insight of her middle child.

And so, thanks to Beletu's ambition, a thriving industry sprang up in the midst of Mechara, where young boys (mill boys, as they were soon called) made the rounds early each morning and collected sacks full of grain, which they then shipped to Gelemso to be ground. For a nominal fee of twenty-five cents a kilo, the owners got their flour back, usually the same day; the mill boys secured gainful employment; the bus and truck drivers, extra income; and the mill operators, a new market.

A year and a half later, long after the priest's visionary daughter had left her home village to seek her fortune elsewhere, an old Greek man would set up the first mill in Mechara, operated on a water-powered turbine. And though Beletu had nothing to do with the launching of the mill per se, she would always be remembered as the one who brought home the concept of the modern mill.

IF BELETU HADN'T HOPPED ON the first Ark and hightailed it to high ground, it was because of developments that made her home turf seem like a hub of civilization. Behind the recent progress was Mr. Robert Harding.

It all began with the unveiling of the building project he had been keeping under wraps for almost eight months. Experts flocked to the sleepy village, bringing with them the wonders of the bigger world. There was a land surveyor with a theodolite and two levels, whom the village boys persistently followed like an army of ants trailing sugar grains, leaving him to do his work only after he gave each of them ten cents of his own money and pretended to take their photos with his unique equipment. There were soil engineers who took borehole samples and studied the rainfall catchment, and census takers, a male-and-female team, who knocked on doors and inquired about family size. Despite their charming dispositions, however, the census takers were never welcomed, because counting family members was known to be an exceptionally bad omen. Such were the wonders of those early days that the villagers went to bed exhausted by the avalanche of discoveries, and got up not knowing what the new day might bring.

One fine morning, the good residents of Mechara awoke to find a mysterious vehicle prominently stationed at the bus terminal. The two-tone van was anointed with a red cross on all four sides—the most devilish choice of colour for a sacred symbol, the villagers unanimously concurred. Peering inside the van for signs of a priest, or at the very least an itinerant *dabtara,* they were disappointed to find, instead, a smiling lass in a white uniform. The starched dress hugged her sensuous curves and terminated obscenely short of her knees. As if to complete her mockery of the ordained, she had mounted a white, angular cap on her carefully coiffed hair. Her open collar revealed a bare neck.

Accompanying the young woman was a dour-looking white man in an even whiter gown. A stethoscope dangled from his sagging neck. On a small table next to the seated doctor were vials of clear fluid, each one capped with shiny white metal. "Are these not the very same vials that Abebe the Bandit used to dispense at the Wednesday market but a short while ago?" some of the villagers puzzled. On a kerosene burner simmered a tray of injection needles, ready to be inserted into the arms of unsuspecting children.

But every attempt to vaccinate the children was met with scorn and violent threats from mothers who couldn't understand why anyone would want to treat a child who hadn't come down with any illness. The young nurse, whose well-rounded behind glued Endale Fluoride to the side of the mobile clinic, was showered with insults when she attempted to siphon blood from a mill boy she had lured with candies. "I am only trying to test his blood for signs of measles," she attempted to explain, but the villagers had been around long enough to recognize a sorcerer when they saw one.

No sooner had the mobile clinic decamped than a white Land Rover truck arrived, blaring announcements through a loud-speaker on its roof. "Come out and receive your free box of powdered milk and bars of soap," the voice declared. As he handed out the goods, the smiling young man made a point of mentioning that the supplies had been donated by the good people of the United States of America.

The bars of soap were gratefully accepted, but the dried milk produced blank faces. How the good people of the United States of America had managed to train their cows to yield powdery milk was being heatedly debated when all attention was drawn to a spectacle in the dirt. A young boy was thrashing about in agony, having swallowed a handful of the chalky substance, which had stuck in his mouth and throat.

Mrs. Vivian Harding took the opportunity to hold a session for her female neighbours. With Azeb and Oona as her brisk assistants, she demonstrated how to revive the dried milk with only a pitcher of water and methodical beating. "Always boil the mixture before giving it to your children," she stressed. Despite her untiring efforts, however, no one was convinced that the smoky mixture, with its ear-bending sugariness, came from a living udder, until Etiye Hiywet stood before the alarmed crowd and identified the foreign beverage as one more item to steer clear of during the upcoming fifty-four days of Lenten Fast.

THE SIGHTS AND SOUNDS of Mechara during these days of change were arresting, even to that least admiring of its residents, Beletu. In her unguarded moments she was heard to speculate that the deluge of antiquity, which for too long had drowned her home village, was probably ebbing. She even found reason to hope that before long her lethargic neighbours might stir from their generations of slumber to march by her side.

Beletu was not as enamoured of the foreign largesse. She thought the bars of soap gave off an offensive odour and refused to use them, lest the lardy smell draw the unwanted attentions of a street dog. The powdered milk intrigued her at first, but soon she found that her stomach didn't agree. What most lifted her hopes and expectations was the massive construction project currently under way.

From the comfort of a stationed taxicab, sometimes from the front seat of a parked bus, she watched as giant tractors removed the trees with a violent swoop and laid the terrain flat. Men in safety helmets and steel-tipped boots laboured from sunrise to sunset, laying the building's foundation. The reclaimed piece of land was soon cordoned off, so that it could be accessed only through a manned gate. Abebe the Bandit, who had long been guarding the building materials in the Hardings' yard, was relieved of his duties by the construction manager, a complete outsider, who hired two off-duty policemen to keep watch over the expensive machinery. Abebe the Bandit was not troubled by the sudden layoff. He was instantly hired by the state-owned Coffee Board to deter the nightly raids that had suddenly become a regular occurrence. As before, all it took to remedy the situation was adding Abebe to the payroll.

THE PEOPLE OF MECHARA had always reserved their deepest scorn and intensest suspicion for anyone who looked like them, spoke their language, had a local-sounding name, yet sported a bare neck—someone like the construction manager. An instant outcast, no one greeted him or answered his queries. Eventually, however, even his most outspoken adversaries couldn't help but express admiration for his work. For in a matter of months, the building complex took shape.

Rows of single-storey rooms sprang up on either side of the open ground, each room identical to the next. Between the two strips and facing the main gate of the compound was an oversized building. A flight of wide concrete stairs greeted visitors to this stately edifice. A steel flagpole, steps away from the stairs, soared into the firmament, waving the national flag—the first of its kind in Mechara.

Soon an open house was held, and the villagers were ushered into the majestic building. Rows of polished wooden benches, fixed to a linoleum-masked concrete floor, greeted the awestruck public. A small podium stood at the front, with a speaker's lectern in the centre and a drawn curtain on either side of the stage. The wall behind the podium was whitewashed, and bordered by a wide black band, which magnified the screen's radiance. "Avoid leaning on the walls," cautioned the translator, swaggering in his usual boastful manner. "The paint hasn't completely dried yet."

In between the cries of the babies and the murmured conversations of the grown-ups, Mr. Harding managed to extend his invitation.

"Tonight we will hold a special event to which you are all invited," he said through his translator. "Bring your children along."

And that was how Beletu, like everyone else in the village, was introduced to the magic of motion pictures.

AT THE TIME, motion pictures were still an alien concept in much of the country, including cosmopolitan Gelemso. So, when Beletu stepped inside the electrically lit theatre that Saturday evening, accompanied by members of her household, she hadn't the foggiest notion of what the occasion held. She was certain of one thing, though: the crowd that flocked to the back of the building to view the diesel-powered generator was made up of thick-headed bovines. "Hello!" she yelled, rolling her eyes in disgust, "hello-o-o-o! It's nothing more than a car engine without the car itself!"

Ushering in the crowd was the translator, who was unusually haughty, as though he were the centre of attention. When asked a question, he would raise an eyebrow as if to say, "What language was that?" He would then shake his head as if to awaken a bug snoozing in his ear, demand that the question be repeated, and, after a profound silence and a long-drawn-out sigh, proffer his answer: "Yes, your child too can sit on the bench."

Members of the priest's household didn't have to worry about their seats, though. They were reserved for them, right next to the Hardings.

THE OVERHEAD LIGHTS dimmed. The projector, perched high on a temporary platform at the rear of the theatre, hummed.

Fractured images of lines and prisms splashed the whitewashed wall behind the podium. Numerical figures trotted one after the other. Latin alphabets followed. A few blank frames later, coloured images of a young child filled the giant screen. And as she began walking towards the camera, some in the crowd vacated their seats, as though to make way for the monster-sized baby.

"That's me," Oona whispered in Azeb's ear. "I was only five years old."

"That is our house," Mrs. Harding told Beletu. "And that is my mother."

Mrs. Harding's mother climbed out of a large sedan, which she herself drove. She kicked the car door closed with her heel and smiled into the camera. "What sophistication!" Beletu said to herself. Mrs. Harding's mother was dressed in an ankle-length coat—which the priest's daughter only later discovered was made of animal fur—that was fully open, revealing the skirt below. The collar was upturned—like a boy's, Beletu told herself. In one of her gloved hands the woman clutched a stylish shoulder bag; in the other, a little tan dog. Beletu had never been fond of pets, but that evening she fell in love with one. She decided to get herself a little tan dog the very next day. For the moment, though, she had a question to get off her chest.

"Do women drive cars in your country?" she whispered in Mrs. Harding's ear.

"Of course, honey. Even in this country you can find women who own cars. I have seen quite a few in Addis Ababa."

"Where is your mother now?"

"She is in heaven, or some such place," Mrs. Harding sighed.

"She's dead!" Beletu couldn't quite reconcile the fact that she was gazing at a person who was alive in every sense of the word yet had gone to meet her Maker.

"Yes, she died before we left America."

"But she looks so alive!" She sounded silly.

"Well, she didn't die of any illness. She committed suicide."
Sharing her mother's tragic end brought tears to her eyes, and
Mrs. Harding retreated inwards. Beletu, on the other hand, was
tormented by yet another question: Why would someone who
could afford a car commit suicide?

WHILE BELETU WAS GRAPPLING with the incomprehensible exit
of the lady in fur, the murmur in the crowd gave way to a heated
debate. Mr. Harding stopped the reel and turned the overhead
lights on, to inquire what the problem was.

"How come your soil is so white?" asked one of the spectators.

"It's snow," said Mr. Harding, but the meaning was lost in
translation, as there was no Amharic word for snow. Many in the
crowd, however, were content to have found an answer to the one
issue that had really intrigued them since the white family moved
to their backyard: why the Hardings had such an unearthly skin
tone. The answer lay in the white soil, of course.

THAT SATURDAY EVENING, Mr. Robert Harding elevated himself
from the simple respectability of a medicine man to the fearsome
status of a conjuror. And as word of his magical feats spread across
mountains and rivers, conveyed by every conceivable mode of transport, his name came to be recognized in places where no white man
had ever set foot. A month later, when it was revealed that a new
show was in the works, many flocked to Mechara, braving hours
and even days of arduous travel, to witness the miracle. For the
villagers, the paved highway had finally begun contributing to their
wealth of myth and fable; the magic of humans leaping out of a
beam of light to walk on a whitewashed wall was something around
which they would weave tales by the fireside for many years to come.

MR. ROBERT HARDING presented a professionally produced
picture at his next engagement. "It is a cowboy-and-Indians
movie," the translator revealed before the teeming theatre. Before

the reel was even mounted, every centimetre of floor space, the windowsills, and the doorways were taken up, with half as many people lingering out in the yard, unable to get in. If the motion picture was the draw of the night, the translator vied to make himself the actual attraction.

"There will be a lot of shooting in this movie," he pronounced, standing high on the podium, "so don't be frightened."

"Moron," snapped one of the out-of-town men. "We are battle-tested braves." He raised high a Mauser rifle as though to underline his point.

The feature presentation, as compared with the Hardings' homemade picture, took up more of the screen and had a sharper image. A succession of foreign characters, accompanied by alien music, rolled by before a lone figure on horseback emerged from the distance.

"He is the cowboy," cried the translator. "In America, cowboys can afford to own horses and boots." The cowboy walked into what appeared to be an alehouse. "The bartender has just brought him a bottle of whiskey and a glass to drink from," the translator decoded. "A woman joined him."

Carried away by his own eloquence, the translator swaggered about in what little room he could find, mimicking the activities on the screen with his hands and feet; words alone seemed incapable of conveying his enthusiastic rendition. "The cowboy is still talking to the woman," he clarified. "She is taking him up a flight of stairs … She is helping him take his bath," he droned. "In America, they are so civilized that they take their baths, and even make their craps, indoors." As the activity on the screen gathered pace, and the body heat in the hall began to conjoin neighbours, many showed irritation. Mr. Harding correctly gauged the viewers' anger as being directed at his assistant. Twice he issued instructions that quieted the translator down, if only for a moment.

"They are playing cards," the translator said, finding an event worth deciphering. "As you can see, the cowboy has grabbed the disfigured man's arm, and he revealed a card the man had surreptitiously hidden under his shirt sleeve. Scar-faced people tend to be crooks even in this country." After a brief argument, the cowboy flipped the round table aside and out of his way, producing a handgun from his side holster, and before any of the viewers could say boo, he shot the scar-faced man dead.

"*Egzio-o-o-o* [The Redeemer]," cried many of the viewers.

"That should teach him," said a few of the men, who clearly despised the scar-faced crook.

After the second reel was mounted, a fierce gun battle erupted on the screen, this time involving antagonists the viewers could make out even without the translator's help. He deemed it necessary to explain all the same. "The bare-chested men with bird feathers over their painted faces and singing war songs are called Indians," he revealed, "and they don't like the cowboys. You should cheer only when the cowboys win, because they are Mr. Harding's people."

The battle intensified, becoming less fun to watch. The viewers ceased cheering altogether.

"What a strange world," said an elderly woman, speaking for many. "Don't they even pause to bury their dead?"

"You should ask: Don't they have an elder who could mediate peace?" said her neighbour, another grandmotherly figure.

"No wonder the Hardings found it hard to live with their own people."

No one remembers exactly when the gunfire on the screen began drawing answering fire from the viewers, but soon bullets were flying from both sides. The crowd panicked. Some hid under the benches; others attempted to flee. As they fought to find their way in the semi-darkness, the stampede ripped the door and windows off their hinges and tore some of the benches from their concrete anchors.

Mr. Harding stood transfixed by the mayhem, his back pressed against the whitewashed wall. Only his flickering eyelids indicated that he was still breathing. The projector was nowhere in sight. In what seemed like the blink of an eye, the human hurricane had left in its wake an altered landscape. Thankfully, there was no loss of life, only a few broken bones and one missing earlobe.

THE DAY OF RECKONING finally arrived. Gathering a few village elders, Aba Yitades set out to pay the Hardings a visit. Two days after the tragic event, Mr. Harding was still in a dour mood, and remained mournful as his wife entertained the visitors.

"We have been troubled by the contents of your show," was how the priest began his discourse. "And we wish to hear from you that this will be the end of it."

Mrs. Harding attempted to make light of the situation. "It is only entertainment."

"I have seen a few so-called entertainments in my time," said Aba Yitades. "We are not all that far removed from what one might call civilization, you know. Both knife-jugglers and fire-eaters have visited this village. What we witnessed on Saturday, on the other hand, defies all acceptable norms. Gun fighting is not entertainment."

"It is a movie that is shown in cinemas throughout this country," Mrs. Harding pressed, turning helplessly from one inscrutable face to another.

One of the visiting elders piped up, "That is why children of today easily abandon their neck-cords."

Mr. Harding finally spoke. "You have nothing to worry about. The projector is totalled."

It was a small concession, but having waited almost a year for the Hardings to embrace the locals' way of life, Aba Yitades had set for himself a much higher goal: he felt it was high time they all applied for a totemic neck-cord. And a more propitious time couldn't have presented itself to do so, because just around the corner was the Festival of Epiphany, the occasion at which the heathen were customarily baptized. Before reaching for his prayer stick and coming to his feet, Aba Yitades extended his invitation, saying, "I want you all to be my guests of honour during the festival." And he received an answer in the affirmative.

IF HER FATHER found the Hardings' lifestyle corrupt and in dire need of fixing, Beletu thought otherwise. Through them, she had caught a glimpse of the future, and she liked what she saw. There was no turning back. Having waited in vain for Mr. Harding not only to fix the damaged projector but also to introduce new and exciting innovations, she realized that the influence of antiquity, which she thought had eased significantly, was once more reaching its high-water mark. She decided to look for her rescuing Ark.

Throughout those hectic months, Beletu hadn't entirely abandoned her plan to seek her fortune elsewhere. She had kept one foot firmly on dry land while testing the waters with the other. Once or twice a week she hitched a ride out of the village with her friendly bus and taxi operators. Halfway to Gelemso she switched rides, returning home before anyone was any the wiser. Then, one day approximately five weeks after the cinema incident, she simply neglected to switch rides.

BOOK IV

Tables of
the Law

12

LEGACY OF THE ARK

*A*t the heart of the Ethiopian Orthodox Christian Church, its architecture, rites, and practices, is the Holy *Tabot*. A replica of the original Tables of the Law, the *Tabot* is fashioned out of a slab of stone or sometimes from a piece of hardwood. When, in the course of the Festival of Epiphany, Aba Yitades set out to immerse the Hardings in church history, he had to take one giant leap backwards and explain to them how the Ark of the Covenant got to ancient Abyssinia in the first place.

"Makeda was a young woman with little experience in government when she was suddenly called to the throne during the eighth century BC," he began, radiating warmth and confidence as he shared his ancestors' history.

As the priest explained at length, Makeda, who would be called the Queen of Sheba following her crowning, had felt unequal to the task assigned to her, yet was unwilling to shun her colossal responsibilities. She therefore decided to pay a visit to King Solomon in Jerusalem. "There was a divine hand in her decision," Aba Yitades noted. "The New Testament chronicles in Matthew chapter 12, verse 42, 'The Queen of the South will rise at the judgment with this generation and condemn it; for she came from the ends of the earth to listen to Solomon's wisdom, and now one greater than Solomon is here.'"

King Solomon was said to be a ladies' man, and the Queen of Sheba surrendered to his charm. She bore him a son, Menelik I.

And when the boy came of age, she sent him to his sire, accompanied by a select retinue headed by a famous merchant and adventurer named Tamrin.

"Menelik I stopped to visit Gaza first," Aba Yitades recalled. "The Apostle Luke wrote about this visit in Acts chapter 8, verse 27, 'Philip met an Ethiopian eunuch, an important official in charge of all the treasury of Candice, queen of the Ethiopians.' The eunuch," the priest felt obliged to clarify, "that Luke referred to was, of course, Tamrin, the escort, not Menelik himself. And the name Candice, like the names Hendake and Makeda, is another variation used by different cultures to describe the Queen of Sheba."

In the months that followed, King Solomon trained his son in the Jewish lore and law, and offered to make him a crown prince. Menelik I, however, couldn't conceive of life outside his African home. "The king gave in with a heavy heart," said Aba Yitades, "and assigned him additional escorts.

"The notion of stealing the Ark of the Covenant and bringing it to Abyssinia was first advanced not by Menelik himself, but by Azarayas, one of the young men Solomon assigned to accompany Menelik I, who was son of Zadok, trustee and confidant of the king," Aba Yitades emphasized.

Since Ethiopia had already been chosen to succeed Israel, the larceny was sanctioned by God.

Once it reached its African home, the Ark of the Covenant was first housed in a temple at Aksum, in northern Ethiopia. Over the centuries it was moved from one house of God to another, until sometime in the nineteenth century it finally found its present home, in a church by the Blue Nile—still in northern Ethiopia. With the exception of a few monks and scribes, no living soul had ever cast an eye on the sacred relic.

WHEN AZEB'S GREAT-GRANDPARENTS settled the village of Mechara, so far away from their Christian ancestral homeland, the greatest difficulty they faced was finding a qualified hand to

fashion a Holy *Tabot* for them. Lacking one, the church they had
built with love and care, sweat and sacrifice, was no better than
an abandoned hay barn, for it was the *Tabot* that conferred sanc-
tity and honour on a man-made edifice; the bishop consecrates
the *Tabot,* not the church building itself.

The only monks and *Qomos* who possessed the requisite
moral and spiritual authority to fashion a Holy *Tabot* were to
be found in a reputable monastery, which at the time meant
crossing six hundred kilometres of hostile territory. (Aba Yitades
had hoped to become a *Qomos,* it will be remembered, before the
infamous divorcee compromised his chastity, thus throwing his
plan off course.)

A team of two priests and three deacons was the absolute
minimum required to accompany a blessed *Tabot* to its final
home, and Azeb's great-grandparents had a great deal of difficulty
scrounging the necessary number of clerics and armed escorts
from among their small band of settlers. Generations later, Aba
Yitades ruminated with pride on the hardships endured by his
forefathers during the perilous journey. "Public transport was still
in its infancy," he reminded the Hardings, "so the men spent two
gruelling months on horseback, not only fighting hunger and
thirst, cold and desert heat, but also engaging in the occasional
tussle with the conquered natives along their route."

That St. George's *Tabot* would be made of hardwood was a
foregone conclusion. It would have been all but impossible to
carry a slab of stone atop one's head—which was the only mode
of transport for a blessed *Tabot*—over the forbidding expanse. "A
consecrated *Tabot* is never transported by a beast of burden," Aba
Yitades reiterated before his rapt pupils, "but upon a human
head, making the tasks of our great forefathers that much more
difficult." He continued, "Having the *Tabot* consecrated meant
carrying it another fifty-odd kilometres to Addis Ababa, as it was
in the nation's capital that the bishop dwelled." In those days His
Holiness hailed from Alexandria, Egypt, and he charged a

bishop's ransom for his services—"ten *birr* to bless the *Tabot,* which cost only three to fashion," Aba Yitades recalled with anger and bitterness at the thought that someone should charge any fee at all for the privilege of reproducing the Tables of the Law.

Mr. Harding had the impertinence to inquire what exactly a fashioned *Tabot* looked like. It was a question that no one dared ask, and if asked, no priest would answer. Aba Yitades, however, rose above such petty superstitions. "The design of St. George's *Tabot* was quite simple," he revealed. "Unlike the original Tables of the Law, it has a cross etched at its centre, though quite an elaborate one, and ornate decorations around its edges. An inscription that read '*Tabot* of St. George' was chiselled into the wood before it was ready for consecration."

Attendance at the consecration service was limited to the ordained few. The laity were kept at a distance, as they would be from then on. If a layman happened to touch a consecrated *Tabot,* it would be considered defiled, and a defiled *Tabot* had to be re-blessed, with all the attendant expenses. To avoid such a possibility, a blessed *Tabot* was housed in a carrying case, the *Mantara Tabot,* an imitation of the Ark itself, from the moment it left the bishop's chamber, even while safely behind the church walls.

Upon receiving St. George's consecrated *Tabot,* one of the priests spread a piece of colourful cloth on the carrying case before hoisting it onto his head. A *dabtara* held an open umbrella above the *Tabot,* not just to protect the sacred object from the elements but also as a symbol of deference. The ornate umbrella told passersby the nature of the troop, since it was considered blasphemous for any individual to be in possession of this unique umbrella.

If the journey to the monastery and then to Addis Ababa was arduous for the troop, the return to Mechara was far more gruelling; it took them almost twice as long to retrace their steps. And it was not entirely because of the extra care necessary to transport the holy object. A *Tabot* passing through a village attracted a large crowd. Men and women, young and old alike, prostrated themselves before the holy relic, kissing the ground it passed over, before they petitioned the troop to accept the village's hospitality and spend the night with them. Invariably, the troop relented. The *Tabot* was escorted to the nearest church, where it was housed for the night next to the resident one (though humbly, on a platform below). The guests were then led to one of the largest homes to be dined and taken care of. The extraordinary attention lavished on any party delivering a blessed *Tabot* was legendary, and it inspired impressionable young men, such as Aba Yitades had once been, to enter the service of the Holy Church so that one day they too could be the centre of such unbridled obeisance, if only for a fleeting moment.

"What happened to the *Tabot* when a church wasn't found?" Mrs. Vivian Harding couldn't help but ask. "Surely there can't have been that many churches along the way."

"As a matter of fact, much of the journey was through complete wilderness," the priest admitted, "and the pioneers had prepared themselves for such an eventuality, carrying with them a small tent for the *Tabot*, while they spent the night out in the open." It was the sort of personal sacrifice that set his ancestors apart, and Aba Yitades didn't shy away from expanding on the theme.

Once St. George's *Tabot* was housed permanently in Mechara, he went on, the pioneers set out to share the glory with other settlers in the region, erecting three-metre-high crosses on all four corners of the settlement so that pilgrims would know a Holy *Tabot* was in the vicinity. Many made detours to kiss the doors of the church and make urgent petitions; many more said their prayers before one of the crosses, secure in the knowledge that their pleas would be heard by Saint George of Mechara. On such occasions a wayfarer felt obliged to place a stone at the foot of the cross, marking his or her communion. "In less than a year, three of the four crosses completely disappeared under a mound of stones," Aba Yitades noted gleefully, "proving to our forefathers that their noble thoughts hadn't been entirely misplaced."

13

A LATE REVELATION

*E*ver since Beletu had run away, Azeb's home duties and responsibilities had tripled. She no longer had the time to accompany her father to church, nor could she while away endless hours with her friend Oona. The Harding children were also busy that summer, with their private tutoring; they were preparing to write exams that arrived from their far-off country. Besides receiving their lessons at home, Oona and Jeff took trips to the wilderness, accompanied by their parents, the translator, and occasionally their white friends from the clinic in Gelemso, "in order to further acquaint ourselves with the natural sciences," according to Oona.

Once a week, the Hardings left the village for Gelemso. Each time, Oona rushed to the preacher's home the day before to plead with Werknesh, yet again, to let Azeb join her family. "We will be back before sunset, Etiye Werknesh. Please let Azeb come with us, please, please, please," she pleaded. But Werknesh refused to budge; she had begun to suspect that the lure of the big town was the cause of many a young woman's downfall. Already, two other girls had followed in Beletu's footsteps and run away from home. Unlike the preacher, who not only forbade the mention of his runaway daughter by name but also refused to go in search of her, the other families had left no stone unturned in their combined efforts to locate their daughters—in vain. "It is as though the girls had vanished into thin air," Werknesh said in a desperate whisper.

The mystery surrounding her runaway daughter had become a crippling burden for Werknesh, one that she couldn't easily let go of even when fully engaged at work or sound asleep at night. "Where are you, Genet, when I need you most?" she was often heard to say. Had her eldest daughter been around, Werknesh believed, she would have found not only a sympathetic ear and a shoulder to cry on, but also a resourceful mind to tap.

"Genet would have rallied the other families to do something meaningful," she told everyone who cared to hear.

"Why don't you?" Azeb asked.

"I don't even know where to begin," Werknesh replied, dabbing her tear-filled eyes with the end of her *netela*. "When the Good Lord made me, He had a dumb sheep in mind." She looked skyward and quickly added: "Forgive me, Father, I don't even know what I'm saying."

It was under such bleak circumstances that Oona was welcomed by the priest's family to fill the void left by the two absent daughters.

ONE WEDNESDAY barely a week after Beletu's disappearance, Azeb and Oona returned home from the weekly market, carrying between them a bag of produce.

"Etiye Werknesh," said Oona as soon as all three caught their breath, "would you mind if I slept over tonight?"

"Not at all, honey," answered Werknesh, somewhat surprised, "but as you know, we don't even have a mattress."

"I don't care," was Oona's bashful reply.

After a night of agonizing pain, however, tossing and turning, she decided that not everyone was made of the same stern stuff as her hosts. The next time she came to spend a night at the preacher's home, she brought along her own bedding. Walking down a busy trail with a pillow and folded blanket balanced on her head, she drew more than curious glances. "Oona shamed my husband into buying us a mattress and pillows," Werknesh told her neighbours afterwards, laughing.

"Aba Yitades," Oona said one evening, "does the Bible forbid women to go to school?"

"No, whatever gave you that idea?"

"No one," she lied. Azeb had told her that her father didn't permit her to go to school because the Bible didn't allow it. "So you wouldn't mind if Azeb took some lessons with me, would you? It is free!"

"What good would it do her?"

"She could read the Bible!"

"There is only one bible in this house, and no one reads it but me."

"My dad can get her one."

His response was noncommittal. "I'll see."

"I know women in Addis Ababa who have office jobs. The tall secretary at the American embassy is—"

"Oona! That is enough!" said Werknesh, who could sense her husband's discomfort.

Azeb did later pick up the pen, but it was not because of her bubbly friend: her godmother intervened. "I don't want you to grow up dumb like me," Etiye Hiywet said to her. "I want you to be able to read and write your own correspondence, to choose your own Psalm and the prayers that fit your daily mood."

A young deacon assumed the task of tutoring her, and before long Azeb excelled in her schooling, turning out poems that only the best of scholars could compose, which on occasion she read to her family and family friends. Oona, on the other hand, never quite mastered the delicate art of writing odes in the language of the kings, despite her head start and intensive training.

OONA PROVOKED THE PRIEST even more when she broached a subject of higher resonance.

"Aba Yitades," she said, "is it true that the language spoken in heaven is Amharic?"

"It is."

"Does it say so in the Bible?"

"No, but you must understand that the Bible—important collection of sacred Christian teachings that it is—is far from complete. Nor is it the only such document," he elaborated.

"Etiye Hiywet said it was mentioned in the Bible," Oona said.

"If she said so, she is mistaken," the priest maintained.

"If it is not in the Bible, then where can one find the reference?"

"One should look in the *Kebre Negest,* Book of the Glory of [Ethiopian] Kings," he said. "Of course, even in the *Kebre Negest* it is only implied, not explicitly stated." Aba Yitades shifted uneasily in his seat before tossing out his own bait: "Did you know that some of the most celebrated saints were our own people?"

"No."

"Well, they are. Saint Tekle Haimanot and Saint Libna Dengel, for instance."

"I've never heard of them."

"Now you have. How do you suppose they communicate with our Lord?"

"I don't know."

"Not in the *Oromo* language, I can assure you of that."

ANOTHER EVENING, Oona was helping Azeb wind newly purchased knitting wool into a little ball. She held the skein between her open arms while Azeb drew on the loose end and wound it into a ball. Sitting not far away from the two was Werknesh, sifting split peas that she had ground earlier in the day by the light of the kitchen fire.

"Oona honey," she said, still peering at the plateful of peas on her lap, "did your family suffer much from famine while in your country?"

"No. There is no famine in America."

"That's nonsense, sweetheart. Wherever people live, there is bound to be famine. Maybe you were too young to remember."

"No, I don't think there is famine in America," Oona insisted.

"There is no shame in being the victim of famine, honey," Werknesh stressed. "It is the Lord's way of testing our faith."

"It is His way of checking our indulgences and excesses," Aba Yitades corrected.

Werknesh was not alone in thinking that the Hardings fled their country to escape drought and famine. Why else, many argued, would the family abandon the land they were permanently bound to by their buried umbilical cords, in order to live with complete strangers? And there were clues, if evidence were needed, that the Hardings had left behind a very difficult past indeed. The fact that Mrs. Vivian Harding hadn't developed the pronounced hips and fleshy thighs that would identify her as a mother of two was evidence enough that she had grown up on a very meagre diet. That the Hardings tended their backyard vegetable garden with a care and diligence that would shame even the most industrious farmer was additional proof that they hadn't quite forgotten the famine that drove them from their home country.

Werknesh thought she would be able to deduce how well the Hardings had fared in their country once she knew what tools their farmers used to plough their fields. As everybody knew, one of the reasons why the fringe provinces of Ethiopia were continuously affected by food shortages was their primitive farming method: the nomads-turned-farmers of these outlying regions used a poking stick to make holes in the ground, into which they buried their seed. In Mechara, only the Hardings lacked yoking oxen, an irony that wasn't lost on many, as they were the only family to own an automobile.

"Do your farmers use hand tools to turn the soil, as your father does here?" Werknesh inquired.

"No, in America people use farm machines, much like giant cars, to till the soil and even harvest the yield," Oona told her sceptical audience. Aba Yitades shut his bible and began massaging his beard in deep contemplation, as he often did when utterly baffled. Everybody knew that the Hardings' daughter had a vivid imagination, but no one had suspected her mental agility could propel her to such dizzying heights.

For days afterwards people talked about nothing but the miraculous machine that not only transported people but ploughed the fields as well. And as the news passed from mouth to mouth, the machine came to assume additional attributes: it produced dung that could be used to fertilize the soil; it threshed the harvest by marching on it with its four sturdy legs (or was it wheels?); and at the end of its working life the machine could be slaughtered, so that its hide could be put to domestic use. (Its meat was undoubtedly rubbery, as any oxen's would be, and it likely required tenderizing by boiling for eons.)

Oona's childish imagination soon became a source of entertainment for the priest's family, a distraction that blotted out their daily problems, if only for a foolish moment. A routine quickly emerged: Werknesh would toss at the Hardings' daughter an everyday question, but one that could trigger an outlandish answer.

"Honey," said Werknesh one evening, "do you have a king or queen in your country?"

"We have a president."

"What is that?"

"An elected leader."

"What do you mean, elected? Only head of the village council, the *eder*, is elected," corrected Werknesh. The *eder* was the co-operative that provided the tent, tables, chairs, dining sets, and industrial-capacity cooking utensils required to cater for the large crowd attending funeral ceremonies, commemorations, and weddings. The *eder* leader was elected every three or four years.

"Surely your country is not so small as to be run by an *eder* leader," Werknesh puzzled. "Or is it?"

Another time, Azeb touched on the subject of Oona's troubled uncle. The man must have been born on the wrong side of the moon, because whatever he happened to do, it triggered a police riot. According to Azeb, and confirmed by Oona, the man was arrested for public drunkenness, twice. He was also detained for urinating on a famous statue and fined a small fortune for shooting a wild deer (the goatlike animal with a pair of branched horns). He spent thirty-five days in jail for brawling in a bar, and was sent away to a chain-gang farm for—

"Oona honey," Werknesh interrupted when the list began to seem endless, "what do men in your country do to entertain themselves without risking arrest or fines?"

During those heady evenings, Oona believed she was finally winning her way into the heart of her friend's family. But it was destined to be a short-lived affair. Her sleepovers, as well as the frequent visits, would come to an abrupt end following the Festival of Epiphany, a mere six weeks later.

EPIPHANY IS BOTH a religious and a national festival in Ethiopia. Arriving just twelve days after Christmas, any other festive event would have been marred by holiday fatigue. Not Epiphany. In Mechara, preparations for the momentous occasion began soon after the ashes of the Christmas bonfires were dispersed in the fields.

Days before the event, the male members of each family left for the bush in search of suitable wands for the game of *Guks* that accompanied the festivities. They gathered sticks by the armload, ensuring that each wand measured no more than a metre and a half in length; that it had no pointed end which could harm the opposing players; and that it was not heavier than the average prayer stick. That the wand ought to be straight as an arrow was more of a convenience than a game requirement.

As with any major holiday, the women gathered green grass by the bundle and picked armfuls of wildflowers. They spread the grass on their living-room floor and front steps, and arranged the cut flowers in water-filled vases. They prepared a festival meal for their own family, and brewed *tella* by the barrel in anticipation of the large number of guests who would drop in to share the glory.

On the afternoon of January 17, Etiye Hiywet, the self-appointed spiritual vanguard, dispatched a platoon of errand boys to her good neighbours, reminding them to eat their fill before retiring to bed, as the day after, the eve of Epiphany, was a mandatory *Gahad*—nine hours of absolute rejection of food and water.

Etiye Hiywet was understanding if her female neighbours failed to remember the *Gahad* of Epiphany, making a generous allowance for the distraction of daily chores, but she wasn't so forgiving when, ten days later, some of them sent their children to inquire if the Revelation of Mary was also *Gahad*—something any woman should know. "The Revelation of the Virgin is and will always be *Gahad*," she declared with righteous indignation. "It is the *Assumption* of Mary that is *not Gahad*!"

THE MEN ALSO OBSERVED the *Gahad* of Epiphany, but that didn't deter them from clearing the field by the riverside where the yearly event was held. They brought the tents out from the *eder* storage and pitched them in a settlement-like arrangement. Five large tents for the rank-and-file celebrants circled two smaller ones. The five tents couldn't accommodate the thousands of worshippers expected for the festivity; the tents were meant merely to provide temporary shelter for the old, the sick, and the infirm—those who couldn't spend the entire night on their feet, singing and dancing. The two smaller tents were reserved for the clergy. They would conduct the night-long sermon in one, and rest and recover in the other, surrounded by friends and family members, who that year, by special invitation, included the Hardings.

Epiphany was one of the rare times when the Holy *Tabot* left its impregnable chamber in the belly of the church and spent the night out in the open. No good Christian would pass up the opportunity to bask in the aura of God's visible legacy.

THE PARISHIONERS began filing to church as soon as they broke their nine-hour *Gahad,* each dressed in Sunday attire.

"Thank the Lord who let you survive for this," one celebrant greeted another.

"Thanks to Him, we have both survived for this," came the answer.

At the church gates, the worshippers were met by armies of beggars, who, like any good ushers, remembered to greet by name the most notable members of the community. The latter had remembered to bring along a servant, who carried a bag full of home baking to distribute among the beggars.

Soon the church bells, which had begun pealing at dawn at periodic intervals, rang with even greater urgency. The singing, drumbeats, and sistrum rattles that had emanated from the church belly since daybreak picked up steam as well. And as the church precincts overflowed with buoyant worshippers, the clamour to take the celebration outdoors became vocal. Many let slip their irritation at being kept waiting; some made less guarded comments.

"If Aba Berhanu was still at the helm instead of Aba Yitades, we wouldn't be languishing as we do now," said an elderly man who had known a better past.

"Even at the Great Church of Lalibela, the congregation is not made to cool its heels for so long," noted a much-travelled merchant.

"That is what you get when you let a coward run the show," said a widow who remembered the priest's shameful past. "He misses no opportunity to show us who's in charge."

The instant the clergy began to file out, the rowdy grumbling, the unseemly name-calling, and the sheer restlessness of the gathering gave way to pure enchantment. Wild applause erupted. Women ululated. All eyes were on the three young deacons who emerged first, each wearing a black mantle, richly decorated with gold-coloured threads and trimmings, over his tunic-like vestment. All three wore silver crowns on their heads.

The deacon in the middle carried a cross made of brass, which was mounted on a polished wooden pole as tall as him. Holding the cross's cumbersome handle a finger's breadth from his face, he led the way at a snail's pace. The deacon on his right held the framed picture of Saint George on horseback spearing the serpent that had threatened Etiye Brutawit. The deacon on the left held a similarly framed picture of a dark-skinned Christ on the Cross.

Immediately behind the three deacons was a highly regarded priest, semi-retired from active church duties but very much involved in voluntary services both at home and in distant monasteries. His crowning accomplishment was the sabbatical year he had spent at the Ethiopian monastery in Jerusalem, the Holy Land. Few living clergymen had set foot in that distant place. Those who knew the priest were certain he would be canonized the instant he answered the last call. It was only fitting that it should fall to him to carry the Holy *Tabot* on festival days.

Like all priests, the old man wore a mantle over his sleeved tunic. His was also black in colour, but more richly adorned than those of the deacons. For instance, the golden tassel that hung behind his neck, running the perimeter of his cloak, was broader and more elaborate than those of his subordinates; and the lining of his cloak was embroidered with silk brocade—something a deacon could only dream of. The Holy *Tabot* on his head was draped with a shimmering piece of cloth.

Sheltering the Holy *Tabot* from the elements were two of the tallest deacons, each holding an open umbrella—one on each side. Not far behind them was Aba Yitades, the head priest, flanked on the right by the right master and on the left by the left master. Each of the three priests held a lit censer in his right hand, which he swung from side to side, engulfing the entourage in aromatic plumes of smoke. In the left hand they each clutched the obligatory prayer stick, a small brass cross, and the habitual fly-switch. A troop of priests followed immediately behind.

A choir of six *dabtaras* and four deacons was the last to emerge. Two of them had drums slung over their necks, one smaller than the other, which they beat in tune with the undulating repertoire. The rest rattled their sistra, swinging them up and down in perfect unison. Every so often a drumbeat boomed like a clap of thunder, and it was answered by a chorus of singing from the three masters—Aba Yitades and the left and right masters.

Once outside the church precincts, the professional chorus was overtaken by euphoric young men, who jumped up and down crying: *"Hi loga, hi loga shibo; yibelahal gibo,"* meaning "You [the enemy] are about to be eaten by a hyena." The war song stirred the women into a frenzy. They answered the men's call to action with an equally time-honoured lyric: *"Lalo, lao, esei lao, lalo wedaje"*—"You are my favourite lover."

Midway to the festival grounds, the dancing and singing came to a sudden and electrifying halt. The unthinkable had happened: the Holy *Tabot* refused to be moved! The silence was complete. All eyes were fixed on the priest carrying the *Tabot,* but the harder he struggled to move his foot, the more firmly the *Tabot* on his head held him pinned to the ground. Fear and confusion overcame the crowd.

"Not again," came whispers from elders who remembered the last time the Holy *Tabot* resisted moving.

THE SITUATION that had caused the Holy *Tabot* to resist moving three years earlier had begun with a barroom brawl between two hot-headed young men, which had ended when one of them produced a knife and thrust it into his opponent's chest. A family feud soon followed, resulting in the deaths of four additional men—two from each side. All attempts to bring about peace and reconciliation proved futile. Only when the Holy *Tabot* refused to move some weeks later, and the episode was correctly attributed to the bloodletting, did the two families come to their senses. Appropriate settlements were made, and the wounds began to heal.

The *Tabot*'s rare and startling response etched itself into the collective psyche of the villagers so indelibly that the date became a benchmark for events that followed. "I gave birth to my little Helen a month after the *Tabot*'s incident" had, for instance, become an acceptable answer to an everyday question. It was a lot easier to measure a birthday or funeral against the date the *Tabot* resisted moving than, say, against the big flood that had consumed Etiye Tsehai along with her lame mule.

Most significantly, however, the series of regrettable events that triggered the *Tabot*'s swift response had become such a haunting lesson for so many that a year and a half later, when Abebe the Bandit and Endale Fluoride began trading insults under similar circumstances, the village men hastily intervened. The two misfits were persuaded to settle their differences in a less violent manner—at the game of *Gena*.

HISTORY WAS BEING MADE again, although this time no one could figure out the reason for the incident. Inevitably, after what seemed like ages, the *Tabot* relented, and the procession, the singing, and the dancing resumed. More war cries were heard in defence of the holy relic, and they were immediately answered by the women with the correct promises. That evening, Aba Yitades would hinge his sermon around the event that had shaken his parishioners to the core. "Why did the *Tabot* refuse to be moved?" was the question that punctuated his lengthy prayers.

But before the sermon, much rejoicing awaited the crowd. As soon as they escorted the Holy *Tabot* to its temporary sanctuary in one of the smaller tents at the hub of the holiday camp, they flocked to watch the game of *Guks* that was slated to be played in the small meadow adjacent to the campsite.

Unlike the game of *Gena* that accompanied the Christmas festival, *Guks* was played by grown-ups only. For *Guks* is a warlike contest, involving horsemen tossing wands at each other. The wands, which they had gathered earlier in the week, were imitation spears. Some of the "combatants" carried a shield on their arm to deflect flying sticks, and they all donned what looked like a lion's mane. The team that "speared" the most opponents off their mounts won the contest.

In the pioneer days, war veterans were given preference over ordinary folks so as to lend the contest that rare touch of authenticity. In the absence of true warriors, Abebe the Bandit and Endale Fluoride were invited to form the opposing teams. Endale Fluoride was receptive to the idea, but Abebe the Bandit was unavailable. His services were urgently needed by the newly opened Office of Skins and Hides, a branch of the Ministry of Commerce responsible for regulating the export of animal pelts. Next to coffee beans, skins and hides were the nation's major exports. Abebe the Bandit provided the security detail for the fledgling office.

SOON AFTER THE GAME of *Guks* had concluded, the singing and dancing began anew. Clusters of celebrants dotted the meadow. While Aba Yitades acquainted Mr. and Mrs. Harding with the fine points of the event, including the church history, over a drink of *tella* in his private tent, their children roamed the fields. Here and there, Azeb and Oona paused to sample the music that was everywhere to be heard and to chuckle at the mischief sown by the young crowd. Apart from Christmas, Epiphany was the only time when a child's rowdiness was tolerated; unless the child was involved in a remarkably scandalous act, he or she wouldn't be reprimanded, much less flogged, for the misdeed.

Every once in a while, Azeb and Oona came upon an amorous young couple hidden behind a tent shadow or a tree trunk. Azeb was more embarrassed by the open petting than her friend was. Close to midnight, the two girls spied Endale Fluoride shuffling towards the woods with two teenaged girls on his arms. Curiosity overcame their everyday caution, and the two hastily followed.

A seasonal fog lay over the field. Illuminated by the campfires that dotted the landscape, the atmosphere glowed, resembling what distant cultures would call an aurora borealis. The woods came to life. An owl sang its nocturnal song from the safety of a high branch. Bats whizzed by, pitching up and down and from side to side—"much like a *dabtara* after a rich man's commemoration," Azeb said to Oona, and the two laughed together. In a clearing far away from the singing and dancing, Endale Fluoride and his conquests of the night set up camp, sure that they were safe from prying eyes.

Hiding behind an overgrown shrub, Azeb and Oona watched, mouths gaping wide, as Endale Fluoride peeled off his trousers, shirt, and underwear and tossed them aside. Freed of the anonymity of his everyday clothing, his physique, despite the abuse it had sustained over years of carousing, was imposing, Azeb quietly admitted to herself. She was also impressed by the size of his manhood—he was the first man she had ever seen naked—and would later compare it with that of a donkey.

Endale Fluoride proceeded to undress the girls as well. "It is not supposed to be like this," Azeb said to herself. Without any small talk, without the foreplay that even the wildest of beasts would have undertaken in his place, Endale Fluoride reached for the smaller of the two teenagers, who barely reached his chest, lifted her up to his eye level, kissed her full on the mouth, and pinned her to his brutal extension.

"Mother Mary!" the girl cried.

Oona could hardly stifle her laughter.

Azeb didn't see the humour. "I don't want to see any more of this," she said, and began to crawl away.

"But I do," said Oona, and she held her back.

"This is sick," Azeb spat.

"Still, I want to watch."

Having sated his lust for the moment, Endale Fluoride felt the need to answer the call of nature. While the ravished teenagers were dressing themselves, he ambled towards the bush where his two spectators lay hidden, his appendage firmly in his grasp. Azeb could no longer contain herself. Instinctively, she got up and ran for safety. Oona followed immediately behind. Both could hear his lustful calls as they wove their way through the endless woods. Twice they tripped over protruding roots, but both times they got up and continued on, ultimately to safety.

For both Oona and Azeb, this adventure would prove to be one of the most haunting experiences of their childhood, one that would resonate years later when its belated ramifications were there for everyone to see. Azeb experienced the repercussions first, a mere two days later, when he grabbed her from behind and demanded to know, while pinching her tiny nipples, if she enjoyed what she had seen.

BUT IN THOSE HEADY DAYS, there was little time to dwell on what had happened moments before. The climax of the Epiphany festival loomed large before the girls as they joined the night-long Mass, which hadn't stopped completely since it had begun the previous morning, except for a brief pause here and there when it became necessary for the three masters to relieve each other. The moment that both Oona and Azeb were anxiously awaiting arrived when the clergy filed out at dawn to lead the way towards the Epiphany waters, a segment of the main river that was permanently excluded from everyday use by an invisible barrier.

Men and boys lined up at the riverbank, half dressed, waiting for the clergy to bless the water before immersing themselves briefly in it. Aba Yitades sprayed water from a tin can over the women and children, as it was considered unseemly for women to bathe in public. The water-dipping ritual wasn't re-baptism of the initiated, but renewal of faith. "Much like Jesus' immersion in the

river Jordan," Aba Yitades liked to say. The only individuals to be
baptized that day were the Hardings; for the rest, it was a reaffir-
mation of their faith.

"We don't consider the water-dipping to have been a
baptism," was Mr. Harding's response when the priest
approached him two days later to extend his invitation for a
private communion, at which the family members would
receive their identifying neck-cords.

"Of course not," acknowledged Aba Yitades. "No baptism is
binding without the mandatory neck-cord."

"I am afraid you've got it all wrong," interrupted Mr. Harding,
turning beet red as he often did when presented with unpalatable
conduct. "We *were* all baptized once before. I thought you were
aware of that."

Indeed, Aba Yitades was aware, as was many a villager, that the
Hardings had of late been passing themselves off as Christians.
The priest was dismissive of the claim, however, saying that it was
their attempt to fit in. "A cow that grazes with a donkey begins to
fart like one," was his sage argument.

And he had proof, if any were needed, that the Hardings were
anything but Christians. In his Black Ledger, the notebook that
Azeb carried to market so that he could pencil in the misdeeds of
the week, he had, for instance, put down the following entries:

*May 1st, the year of Our Lord 1962: Eyewitnesses came
forward to report that Mr. Robert Harding has spent the
Consecration of Saint George tending to his backyard garden.
August 22nd, Assumption of the Virgin: When women of the
village were dutifully observing the event, Mrs. Vivian
Harding was seen trimming her boy's hair! (A scandalous act!)
September 27th, 1962, the Feast of the Finding of the Cross, a
national and religious holiday: The Hardings left the village
for a hunt! (Their most wicked conduct so far!)
September 28th: They are back with their pork!*

Even as recently as a few weeks ago, while Oona babbled about her Christian heritage during one of those sleepovers, the priest couldn't help but notice that her parents had spent the morning of January 7 (the Nativity of Our Lord!) washing their car and pruning their hedges. "Even the Muslims of Gelemso have been known to abstain from physical work on Christmas—out of simple neighbourliness," noted Aba Yitades, adding: "The Hardings may not be enemies of our faith, but Christian they are not."

IF HE MERELY SCOFFED at the Hardings' claim to Christendom, Aba Yitades could not be as dismissive when it was revealed, long before the Epiphany showers had drained from the festival ground, that the Hardings were reintroducing themselves as—lo and behold!—Christian missionaries. Nor was he alone in his feelings of anger and betrayal at this late disclosure.

"Why the secret?" was Abebe the Bandit's initial reaction. "Only a bank robber would keep his plans under wraps for so long."

Endale Fluoride, who was sharing a gourd of *tella* with Abebe at the funeral of the village's first victim of a car accident, had this to add: "A man who kisses his daughter on the mouth is capable of more than robbing a bank."

Unlike Abebe the Bandit and Endale Fluoride, however, the priest didn't have the luxury of spewing his anger to the wind so as to settle his stomach. He had both the moral and the spiritual obligation to gather all the evidence—the finer, nitty-gritty, ጥቃቅን, irksome details pertaining to this latest disclosure—before charting his next course of action. The Black Ledger alone wasn't adequate; he needed to hear from the Hardings.

As a responsible patriarch, Aba Yitades' mien was the finest when he dropped in on the Hardings that afternoon, bringing with him a basket of oranges "for the kids." No sooner had he settled in his seat, however, than he introduced the subject that weighed so heavily not only on his own mind but on that of the community at large as well.

"What is this talk of being missionaries?" he said. "I thought you were teachers building a public school."

"We have built a school," answered Mr. Harding, not without a hint of creeping hostility, "but it is not public—as you have just put it."

"If what you have built is a school, where do you propose to erect your, er, church?"

"We already have."

"You have?"

"Yes," replied Mr. Harding, squirming in his seat. It was a moment, it seemed, that he had long dreaded but had done little to prepare himself for.

Aba Yitades disrupted his host's train of thought with an abrupt question: "Well then, if you don't mind my being so inquisitive, where is your church?"

It was Mrs. Vivian Harding who delivered the answer. "It is the big hall where we showed a movie not long ago," she said, feigning a polite smile. "I can't say the show was a success, though."

Aba Yitades wasn't given to mocking the flaws of his fellow man, but no progeny of Adam could keep a straight face when presented with such a blatant display of ignorance and ineptitude, and the priest didn't apologize for bursting into laughter. Why, even a child such as Azeb knew that a church, a *Christian* church, was circular in shape—oblong at the very least. Symbolic of the Trinity, the edifice was threefold, one room built inside the other. At the hub was the sanctuary (the Holy of Holies), which housed the Holy *Tabot;* the compartment in the middle was reserved for the officiating clergy, who were hidden from view of the congregation; and the outermost chamber was open for the laity and non-officiating clergy alike.

In the same spirit of the Trinity, the building had three doors, one each for men, women, and the clergy. The men's entrance faced north; the women's, south. The clergy rose with the sun, so it was only fitting that their entrance looked eastward. This was what King Solomon's Temple in Jerusalem looked like, according to eyewitness accounts, and it stood to reason that all Christians adopted the blueprint.

Of course, a church was not an island unto itself. Consideration ought to be given to the nuns, monks, and deacons who called the sacred ground home, so the church edifice was accompanied by a string of humbler buildings. A small refuge for the itinerant *dabtara* was always a welcome indulgence. A vault-like, free-standing room was also an absolute necessity, for it was here that the sacristan kept the vestments, chalice, harp, sistra, drums, extra prayer sticks, and donations from worshippers whose prayers had been answered.

Most importantly, however, a church was far from complete without an emblematic Bethlehem (which the vulgar call a kitchen). For it was here that the Good Lord was symbolically incarnated every week in the form of wheaten bread, before His brief life on earth was consummated at the altar during the Eucharist service. Needless to say, not everyone was qualified to bake the bread. From start to finish—from sifting the grain and preparing the flour, to mixing the batter and baking the bread— it was handled exclusively by blessed hands, mostly those of deacons. (Should a nun take part in the activity, her responsibility ended short of the holy griddle.)

Above all else in Aba Yitades' mind that day was the business of the Holy *Tabot,* and he didn't dilly-dally when he broached the subject.

Mr. Harding's response sounded rehearsed. "We don't believe in icons."

"Did you just call the Tables of the Law an *icon?*" The priest almost shot out of his seat as he spat the question. His eyes darted from his host to the translator and back to his host.

The translator seemed to take delight in rubbing it in. "An icon like a nomad's neck charm," he said.

Aba Yitades sank back into his seat. Sweat bubbled out of his pores and crested around his upper lip and eyebrows. The contents of his stomach churned audibly; he felt a bitterness well up in his mouth. For a man whose one regret in life was that he had gambled away his chance of ever fashioning a Holy *Tabot* from everyday material (thanks to the infamous divorcee), having his sacred heritage dismissed as a simple *icon* was worse than blasphemy, more painful than a severed arm.

Without the customary thank-you, Aba Yitades staggered out into the bright sunlight and headed home, to herald a new chapter in his people's long struggle to preserve their faith.

14

EXTINGUISHED BEACON

*T*he night came to life with rapid gunfire. Doors opened and the able members of each household emerged, the men wielding weapons, the women their fervour. As they headed for the recently developed section of the village, they echoed the war songs that only days before they had sung at the Festival of Epiphany, although this time not for merrymaking. The men brandished machetes and breech-loading rifles high above their heads as they cried, *"Hi loga, hi loga shibo..."* and the women boosted their warriors' passion with suggestive refrains.

The Hardings' church was soon on fire, and their residence was surrounded by a crowd spewing anger and hatred, demanding that they evacuate the building so that it could be set alight. "We are not responsible if you roast inside," they cried. "This is our last warning." When the family remained closeted in their fortified home, the mob sought to vent its anger on what it found in the compound. The Land Rover went up in flames; the horse shed soon followed. Having waited in vain for the Hardings to emerge, the crowd eventually, reluctantly, dispersed.

Morning brought to the village an assortment of high-ranking government officials, accompanied by a sizable militia force and policemen in crisp uniforms. Ahead of the sombre troop were the governor and the police chief, with Mr. Harding and a few white faces, all men, a step or two behind. Their first stop was the school compound, which now resembled a Christmas bonfire gone terribly wrong. All that remained of the once-elegant complex was smouldering frame-and-masonry rubble.

At the governor's urging, the village elders were quickly rounded up and brought to the school compound. But if he had thought he could intimidate them into immediate submission, he was sorely disappointed. Their defiance was total; each of them claimed to be the ringleader. The governor couldn't march the entire village to prison, so after a quick consultation with his august entourage, he opted to reason with them.

"We are not taking the appropriate action only because Mr. Harding here doesn't wish to press charges, and because no life was lost in the fire," he said. "But you will help them rebuild the complex and mend fences."

The elders' anger finally flared up, many of them demanding immediate eviction of the foreigners.

The police chief stepped in. "We are aware that you suspect the Hardings of being non-Christians," he said with a knowing smile. "You might even think they are Muslims, but I can assure you that you are wrong. They are one of the flock, only with differently coloured feathers."

"We have nothing against Muslims," Aba Yitades felt obliged to respond. "We have Muslim neighbours. What we are up against has no name that we know of."

THE MUSLIM NEIGHBOURS that Aba Yitades referred to were an Arab storekeeper and his young family. The Arab had floated into the village weeks after the highway opened up a new market for his trade. Unlike the rest of the newcomers who had moved to Mechara following the same motorway, the young man exhibited laudable neighbourliness when he sought the acceptance of the village elders. "I am Muslim," Aba Yitades remembered him saying, "but I have lived with Christians before, and I can assure you that you won't find my lifestyle objectionable in any sense of the word. I could even be a welcome addition to your growing community." Although the village elders had long lost their say regarding who could settle in the village—that responsibility now lay solely with the governor—they couldn't fail to appreciate the man's thoughtfulness. They welcomed him with open arms.

In his Black Ledger, Aba Yitades had written only sporadically against his Muslim neighbour. *December 29th, 1962: The Arab was seen chopping firewood,* was the first and most noteworthy violation on record. "We don't do physical work on St. George's day," the priest had said to him. "We can't expect you to honour all the saint days we observe, as there are far too many of them even for us to abide by, but I shall ask you to respect the resident *Tabot.*" And that was the last time the Arab and his family were accused of violating St. George's day, which—unlike the May 1 Consecration, which was observed only once a year—recurs on the same day each month.

"That is more than can be said of the Hardings," Aba Yitades noted.

FOLLOWING THE RIOT, a small police force was permanently stationed in Mechara, and village life was never the same again. Azeb and Oona continued to enjoy each other's company, though not as in days gone by. But that change was not the result of any hostility directed against the Hardings' daughter; it was her father who insisted that, for a while at least, she limit her activities. Werknesh was against involving the children in family squabbles. One Wednesday afternoon not long after the dreadful incident, she stopped Oona, who was about to scuttle away from the market without so much as making eye contact, saying, "Honey, what took place between the men shouldn't alienate you from us. True, when two elephants fight, it is the grass that suffers most, but we shouldn't be the silent type of grass." Oona later recalled that, following this encounter, she felt a burden lift from her shoulders.

Azeb remembered those difficult days for a different reason: they brought her news of a part of her past she had long thought would remain lost to her. Delivering the tidings was one of the policemen, who had lived in Gelemso before his transfer to the village.

"Do you have a sister who lives in Gelemso?" he began.

"No," she replied, assuming that he was referring to Genet, who lived nowhere near the big town.

"Strange," he said, "I remember her saying that she had a baby sister who roamed about the village, arms locked with a little white girl—like you two here. Is there another white girl in this wretched place?"

"No," answered Oona.

"What is your name, anyway?"

"Azeb."

"Are you sure you don't have a sister named Beletu?"

"She does," Oona replied excitedly.

"Where is she now?" Azeb asked, when she had recovered her poise.

"She's at the Memorial Hotel."

Azeb sprinted homeward without saying another word. "Get away from me," she cried when Oona began to tail her. "Stay away from me!" she repeated. Oona had heard what the policeman had said, but she couldn't figure out what was so significant, much less agitating, about the news.

Not until she had reached her godmother's home some fifteen minutes later did Azeb stop to catch her breath.

"Is Beletu a prostitute?" she barked at Etiye Hiywet.

"Hush, what a dreadful thing to say!" Etiye Hiywet scolded her. "Go inside and wash those nasty words from your mouth with tar soap and water."

"But I heard she is at your hotel!"

"That she is, and the reason I didn't tell anyone, including you, was because she didn't want me to," Etiye Hiywet explained.

"But is she a prostitute?"

"If you say that one more time, I will flog your rear end until your skin turns raw," Etiye Hiywet threatened.

Azeb had never seen her godmother so provoked before, and she calmed down at once.

Etiye Hiywet heaved a deep sigh of anguish before adding, "I can't say that she is getting any better, though."

Not until many years later, when she received a visit from the teenaged prostitute whose acquaintance she had made at the Memorial Hotel, was Azeb able to fill in the missing chapters of her sister's adventures.

According to the young woman, whose colourful account would long ring in Azeb's ears, Beletu left Mechara following a heartthrob she had met at the bus terminal. He was a hard-hitter, a go-getter, a no-nonsense entrepreneur who owed his success to nothing but his father's connections. His father was a rogue, and a crude and abrasive one at that, who had been kicked out of every police precinct in which he served, until, approximately fifteen years earlier, he was transferred to the only office that would take him in, no questions asked: the fledgling Bureau of Finance Officers, the branch of the regular police force in charge of monitoring contraband activities in areas bordering Somalia and the city state of Djibouti. Good riddance, his former colleagues said.

As a finance officer, the man found his métier. The pay of a finance officer was not remarkable, with only a nominal hardship allowance distinguishing it from a regular police wage. Worse yet, the job necessitated spending many hours, sometimes even days on end, in hostile wildernesses, away from family and friends. Unbeknownst to his former colleagues, however, the position carried with it a rare and rewarding perquisite.

Patrolling an open border measuring thousands of kilometres and traversed by nomads better armed than most police forces in the continent required battalions of well-equipped, elite soldiers. In the absence of such an army, the Emperor devised a system that would ensure the desired outcome for only a fraction of the cost to the throne. On His Highness's initiative, the finance officers were promised twenty percent of all contraband goods they confiscated, the contraband comprising rolls of imported fabrics, ready-made clothing, bottled fragrances, bags of incense, candies, and whatever else the markets seemed to demand at the moment.

This lucrative incentive proved to be the spark that lit the kindling inside the father of Beletu's friend. His patriotic drive in high gear, the man was now unstoppable. He put in hours far exceeding his mandate or the time logged by his fellow officers, and he quickly rose through the ranks. He was loathed by all who knew him. His locker at the station was vandalized more than once; twice it was smeared with human excrement. But he figured as long as he hadn't offended the All-Knowing above, which he routinely did (although not on Sundays, when he wore his imported raiment to church), and his superiors in Addis Ababa were satisfied with his records, which they were after they received the bounty he unfailingly sent them, everything else was hunky-dory.

The job of a finance officer wasn't always risk-free. Shots were sometimes fired in the cat-and-mouse game. The father of Beletu's friend recognized that, from time to time, men had to lay down their lives in the service of their beloved country. But if someone had to die for his beloved country, he decided, it might as well *not* be him.

It wasn't that he didn't cherish his motherland, or that he was a rabbit-hearted, yellow-bellied, lily-livered, no-good bastard (he was literally a bastard, though) who would scurry under the rocks, or hide under his wife's tent-sized skirt, at the first report of enemy gunfire. His reason was prosaic, it is true, but his rendition of it was poetic both in tone and in content. "Hell!" he said. "What good is love of king and country if it means the premature demise of good people like me?"

And so, on his orders, one of the other officers partaking in a raid was often dressed so as to pass for the head of the team himself, and was therefore the nomad marksmen's target of choice. Two of his impersonators had already been killed in the line of duty; another was paralyzed from the neck down. Since a hazardous job such as masquerading as head of a raiding team entitled one to more than twenty percent of the spoils, the father of Beletu's friend wrote a stinging letter to his superiors in Addis Ababa, demanding that *his* cut of the loot be upped to, at the very least, a percentage point or two above what was paid the dummies who readily acted his part. "If the job is as hazardous as you claim it is, we will find you a safe replacement elsewhere" was the answer he received from someone who had vied to give the lucrative position to his own nephew.

Beletu's new-found love couldn't have been more proud of his enterprising father. For his old man promptly figured that there was actually nothing standing between him and the entire loot. After all, the smugglers never went to the state courts, or the headquarters of the Finance Officers, to protest the seizures. As free-spirited nomads who criss-crossed the Horn of Africa at will, with no regard for political or geographic barriers, the state courts and legal apparatus held no meaning for them. They preferred dealing with their adversaries *mano-a-mano,* and if they didn't manage to reclaim their property on site, whether by the power of the gun or through wads of banknotes exchanging hands, they abandoned it altogether.

With the entire seizure at his disposal, the father of Beletu's lover was able to cultivate a world of friends. He bought his only son (his remaining four children were all girls) a Land Rover pickup truck, and sent him to find his own calling. Entrepreneurship didn't come as easily to the son as to the father. Still, with a caring sire like his, failure wasn't easy to come by. No matter how badly the young man floundered, or how spendthrift his habits became, his losses were always made good by his doting father, no questions asked.

WHAT BELETU SAW in the young man was the promise of a good life that her own small world didn't offer. She was lured by the assortment of gifts and souvenirs he brought her after each trip to his hometown: bottled fragrances, makeup kits, silk scarves, matching bras and underwear, and much, much more—stuff that, regrettably, she couldn't put to use while still under the thatched roof of her exacting father.

A visit to his family home in Harar, a four-hour drive from Mechara, only reinforced her hopes of a better life to come. His family resided in a manor the likes of which she hadn't come across even in her photo clippings. The walls of the six-bedroom residence were all covered from ceiling to floor in imported fabrics, each room with its own unique colour and design. The wood floor was checkered with Persian carpets. In two of the service rooms, which were detached from the main building, there lay rolls of fabric in their original plastic wrappings, colour-fully patterned blouses, silk scarves, bras of all sizes, underwear, slacks, and countless boxes of women's shoes. "Take whatever you like," said her friend. "I will wait for you in the living room." Beletu found herself living out a dream.

The occupants of the manor were equally refined, she noticed. The girls were the epitome of elegance and sophistication, each dressed in her individual style like the fashion models that Beletu so vividly recalled from those foreign magazines. And they spoke with a stately flair. (Their Amharic was punctuated with choice English words.) Their mother was a sight to behold. Beletu had seen some well-fed people in her time, but nothing on this scale. The woman needed two assistants to help her out of her seat. Breathing was an ordeal for her. In a region where the average person weighed no more than his or her midday shadow, the woman had earned notoriety for her bulk. Not that she was derided, mind you. On the contrary, her uncommon size and aura were a badge of honour, a ticket that opened doors for her, though she rarely needed that many doors opened.

In the late afternoon, when the heat of the day abated, the woman became a rocklike fixture under the shade of a tree outside the iron gates of her fortified compound. In her padded chair, with a tiny Oriental paper fan in her chubby fingers, she looked to passing men and women like a sovereign on a retreat. Strangers saluted her. Men tipped their hats; women lowered their *netela* and bowed their bare heads in abject humility. In a town where the streets had no names, the buildings no numbers, and the landmarks were few and far between, the mother of Beletu's friend served as a reliable benchmark. Women sending their children on an errand often said: "Turn right at the fat woman's house, then go straight to the cactus bush before making another ..."

If Beletu wondered how the woman had achieved such extraordinary girth and presence, she didn't have to wait long for an answer. That evening, at the sprawling family dinner table, her eyes beheld what she had never seen even at commemorations of the most notable members of her home village. There was enough food for a small army, dishes that Beletu couldn't make out, and cutlery that she had seen only in pictures. If, earlier in the day, she had marvelled at the number of kitchen help, which made it unnecessary for the women of the manor to do any everyday chores at all, she almost choked on her breath when a butler in uniform waited on her.

At dinnertime, all eyes were on Beletu. Her dining etiquette was under the microscope. How she handled her fork and knife was scrutinized; how she neglected to dab the corners of her mouth at periodic intervals raised eyebrows. Beletu felt itchy under her collar; sweat accumulated above her eyebrows. Without eating even half of her serving, much less satisfying her hunger, she excused herself, feigning stomach ache. In her assigned bedroom, she cried her eyes out. Not that she held her hosts responsible for her plight, mind you. No, she only had fate to blame for delivering her into a village where such basic items as knives and forks, napkins, and china plates were luxuries. Although Beletu didn't know it at the time, it wasn't *her* lifestyle that was atypical, but that of her hosts.

Beletu didn't remain a dumb country girl for long; she quickly eased herself into the lifestyle which she felt instinctively to be her own. Gone were the days when she got up at the rooster's first crow, "like a family of beggars," in her words. Now she could sleep in to her heart's content. When she finally woke up, it was to a waiting breakfast, the menu of which changed almost every day, and a glass of freshly squeezed mango juice, which the town was known for. She whiled away the balance of her mornings sifting through the mountain of confiscated merchandise. She spent the afternoons sightseeing and sampling the entertainment the town had to offer, which often included a stopover at the cinema. Life was good, and she knew it would last.

But it didn't.

Even the son of an affluent finance officer had to make a living, and the young man, finally tired of asking his father to bail him out, had put his foot down (on the gas pedal, at least) until he could balance the books. And so, a fortnight after her arrival, Beletu left Harar, following her friend, to seek their fortune as truck operators. Visiting drab little towns, the two slept in cheap, cockroach-infested, ill-lit hotel rooms. There was no butler in uniform or exotic menu in these godforsaken outposts, but good old *injera* with the traditional sauce. Her past seemed to have an unbreakable hold on Beletu.

"I hate this life," she told her friend one morning, almost two months after they had left his parents' home, while they were packing their bags for yet another leg of their endless journey. "Find me a place that I can call home," she demanded.

And so, at her insistence, the young man found her a place, but of the kind that only *he* could call home: a one-bedroom detached house. When, compounding her disappointments, he refused to hire domestic help, Beletu felt obliged to speak out.

"I didn't leave Mechara to live like this," she told him. "I will stay only if you fulfill my demands: a three-bedroom residence with a lawn the size of a soccer field, a sedan with tail fins, which I can drive around, a servant (make that two), a—"

"What is a tail fin?" he said, befuddled. "As to the servants and the three-bedroom residence, we will earn it in time."

And that was why, a mere five months after she had eloped with the young man, Beletu found herself almost back where she had started: Gelemso. She headed for the one place where she knew she would be welcomed with open arms: the Memorial Hotel, her godmother's establishment.

"I don't know what you plan to do with yourself," Etiye Hiywet said to her, "but as long as you're in this town, you don't have to worry about food and shelter." After a drawn-out, anguished sigh, the godmother added, "I have seen far too many runaways. The young women you see here all began the way you have. I don't want you to be one of them, so think long and hard about what you really want to do with your life."

Beletu thought long and hard about what she really wanted to do with her life, and she discovered, to her immense surprise and relief, that her dreams hadn't changed one bit. She still dreamt of owning a sprawling manor with a roomful of servants and a butler in uniform; a luxurious sedan with tail fins, a wardrobe full of trendy clothes, a fur coat that she would turn up at the collar (as boys did), a little tan dog that she would be able to tuck under her arm, a brown leather bag with large golden buckles, and, inside the bag, petty cash that wasn't all that petty. The Memorial Hotel appeared to her to be precisely the place to find a man who could make her dreams come true.

If Azeb thought she got off on the wrong foot with Fatima, the hotel manager, when she asked if she were an American, the lowly held caste, Beletu was unable to land on her feet at all. "It was hate at first sight," the teenaged prostitute told Azeb many years later. "Beletu reminded Fatima of her own lost youth and beauty, so she wanted her out of her sight."

Not that Beletu helped matters. The day Etiye Hiywet introduced the two, Fatima had the impertinence to ask if Beletu's hair was actually hers, and she got an equally smug answer: "No, I borrowed it." Despite Fatima's obvious hostility, Etiye Hiywet instructed her prickly godchild that, should she choose to watch the nightly scene, she should remain behind the bar in the manager's lair, lest someone mistake her for one of the working girls.

For the girls, the nightly routine hadn't changed. After the evening ceremonial coffee had been served, they assumed their seats, one at each empty table. Eyes trained on the door, they waited for that first carefree customer to walk in. The moment they spied a well-dressed patron, they beckoned him with their pleading eyes to take up the empty chair next to them, not so much for his warm company but in hopes that he would buy them a drink and, most importantly, buy *them* for the night.

Much of the evening crowd had remained the same as well. The police chief arrived, accompanied by the good governor. The director of the State Highway Authority was still preceded by a waft of imported cologne. At the predictable hour the postman walked in and handed out pieces of mail to men who repaid his unparalleled diligence with a complimentary drink or two. The manager of the state-owned electric power station ambled in, and was instantly mobbed by men who had been waiting to have an audience with him, since he was seldom available to customers at his office desk. His terrier-like secretary saw to it that he wasn't distracted from doing nothing, greeting each visitor with the unchanging line: "He is in a meeting. Come back tomorrow." The next day the visitor would receive the very same advice. Day in and day out, the unwary supplicant would be greeted with the same line, until it finally dawned on him that there was another venue available to him—the Memorial Hotel.

First to accost the manager was a man who had built a new home in the outskirts and had been waiting for a power link-up for a year and a half. The overhead distribution line had required the installation of four new timber poles, three of which the homebuilder had already secured, some said, after parting with a manager's ransom.

"Have you had another shipment of poles?" he whispered in the manager's ear after the customary greeting, his proverbial tail between his legs.

"Yes, but there are others ahead of you," the manager replied with a far-off look in his eyes.

"One more pole and I won't bother you anymore," the home-builder pleaded, tucking a padded envelope in the manager's jacket pocket.

The next in line was the flour mill owner, who had been waiting almost a year for extra power to operate an additional mill.

"My case is very simple," he reminded the manager, smiling pitifully. "I already have a power line. All I need is some more juice."

"You people don't seem to get it," barked the manager. "There is a power shortage in this country." The mill owner was a teetotaller, seldom stepping inside a pub of his own free will, but he ran the largest bar tab in town, since the manager drank only imported whiskey. "I will see what I can do," the manager finally relented, if only to get the man off his back.

The manager eventually settled in his usual seat by the bar, away from the working girls. Anticipating his wishes, Fatima fetched his favourite brand of whiskey, Black & White. She double-rinsed his drinking glass before him, raising it towards the overhead light to check for stains, before pouring his customary double shot over three ice cubes—his lucky number. While placing the bottle back on the glass shelf, she whispered in Beletu's ear the identity of the distinguished client.

"He and he alone wields the power to make or break businesses in this town," Fatima stressed, "so be extra civil to him."

"I don't care," replied Beletu.

The manager had been eyeing Beletu, intrigued, it seemed, by her air of aloofness and hint of arrogance. Only the polished wooden counter and a cloud of cigarette smoke stood between them.

"Hand me an ashtray," he said to her.

"Get it yourself," she replied.

The room fell dead quiet. No one spoke, stirred, or appeared to breathe. All eyes were trained on Beletu, some assessing her state of mind, others seeing her for the first time, wondering if she had popped out of one of the empty bottles on the glossy counter, like the genie from Aladdin's fabled lamp. The deepening silence was punctuated only by the rhythmic scratches of an old phonograph machine, which had long since finished playing James Brown's "Papa's Got a Brand New Bag."

"What did you just say?" the manager demanded when he regained his voice. The long-stifled cigarette smoke escaped from his mouth in angry spurts.

"You heard me," she told him.

The manager adjusted his necktie as though posing for a portrait. He gulped down the remaining whiskey and stubbed the barely smoked cigarette in the empty glass before getting to his feet. Finally awakened from its collective trance, the crowd swooped to his side. Men and women alike gathered around the riled manager, pleading with him not to leave, not to take the nameless young woman seriously, but he simply brushed them aside and strode into the deepening nightfall. He left behind not only a distraught crowd but also a clutter of chairs and glasses, and one shattered *portière*— which, made from beads of curled bottle caps, had been strung above the doorway as an early warning signal of arriving visitors.

The manager marched past the last of the town dwellers, a family of beggars vacating the ghostly streets, who saluted him by name but got no response. He galloped past a pack of semi-wild dogs, ignoring their angry growls, and turned left at the remotest kiosk, which was open for business even at this late hour. (The shopkeeper remembered to greet the manager, but was no luckier than the family of beggars.) The manager didn't catch his breath until he emerged from the business district and left all human contact behind.

Once outside the business district, the street lights became sparse, with only one incandescent lamp casting its dim glow from every second pole. Soon the manager was plodding along in utter darkness. The quiet was unnerving, but he remained unconcerned. Gravel rattled under his hurrying feet, and the shifting wind brought the sounds of conspiring beasts heading for the abandoned town. Lost in a haze of anger and vengeful-ness, the manager didn't pay much attention to his surroundings until he made another left turn kilometres from downtown, and after a hundred urgent strides he arrived at his ultimate destina-tion, a compound, tucked away behind a grove of wild olives, that shone blindingly bright, as though a shooting star had landed on it.

The iron gate of the compound was locked from within, and there was no sign of the guard on duty. The manager's anger finally spilled over. He yelled and shook the cast iron bars until the gate threatened to come off its hinges. When the watchman stumbled out of an abandoned warehouse, buttoning his fly and tightening his belt, there was panic written on his weathered face. Guilt was what the manager saw, however, because he knew the man's mistress was hiding behind the closed door. But as long as the watchman's wife didn't mind the illicit affair, the manager magnanimously reasoned, it was all right with him.

What wasn't all right with him was the fact that he was unable to locate his keys. He fished for them frantically, turning his pockets inside out, but his hands emerged full of crumpled banknotes, loose change, and badly mangled sticks of Wrigley's gum. The manager was about to scream his head off, giving vent to his pent-up anger, when he finally located the one key that mattered and slipped it into the grey steel door's small keyhole.

Within the concrete enclosure, the powerful motors, which from the outside seemed only to hum, were blaring thunderously. The heat was stifling. The manager stopped at a metal counter with banks of blinking instruments. Flipping a safety catch open, his sweaty fingers reached towards an array of switches. He threw one, and a motor died down with a relieved swoosh. Slowly, savouring each moment, the manager threw the remaining switches, one by one, until the town that fifteen thousand people called home was engulfed in complete darkness.

"What happened?" was the question on everybody's lips the next day.

"The generator is acting up," the manager replied listlessly.

Just how badly the generator could act up didn't become entirely apparent until the second night, when, moments after the lights came on at six o'clock, they went out again. An hour later they were back on; half an hour later, they went out. On again. Off again. On. Off. On, for about half an hour; then off, for the last time.

The manager achieved a much higher level of creativity and insight on the third night, when incandescent bulbs all over town began to expire in record numbers. The light surged powerfully, until the thin filament inside the glass bulbs sizzled like a firefly trapped in melting wax, and then rooms all over Gelemso turned pitch-dark. Riots seemed imminent. Many were seething with anger. If there were any individuals among the town's fifteen thousand captives who weren't biting their lips at the manager's excesses, they were the owners of hardware stores, who, after a brisk sale of light bulbs, candles, flashlights, kerosene, and electric fuses, were able to double prices overnight.

The good governor was hog-tied as ever, since the manager wasn't answerable to him but to the chief executive officer of the

Electric Light and Power Authority in Addis Ababa, four hundred kilometres away, who, as the manager's adoring uncle, answered all complaints with the time-worn maxim: "The manager may be a son of a gun, but he is *our* son of a gun."

With the governor impotent, it fell on the townspeople to get to the bottom of the crisis. Home renovation expenses were immediately ruled out as a possible reason, since the manager, like the rest of his good Christian neighbours, had successfully carried out the traditional Easter remodelling only weeks before. Holiday expenses were also dismissed out of hand, since the manager, like most of his fellow citizens, hadn't yet been bitten by the gift-giving bug. Not until the fourth day, when the manager lit upon his most innovative stunt yet—turning the street lights on for twenty-four hours a day while denying power to those who needed it most—did the town elders finally get wind of what had taken place at the Memorial Hotel that fateful evening. Light and power were restored after the manager was petitioned in the name of his baptismal *Tabot*—Saint Michel.

BELETU'S CIRCLE of admirers grew manyfold. Most notable among her new fans was the director of the State Highway Authority, himself a long-time member of the notoriety club by virtue of the number of women he took to bed each night. It was love at *second* sight. (Their first encounter, which took place before her run-in with the manager, had failed to register on his impaired mind.) It would have been even more unusual had it been love at third sight, or even fourth or fifth sight, for the director, who tallied his sexual conquests by the shots of gin he downed each night, seldom saw a woman twice.

"He seldom sees a woman twice," Beletu told anyone who came to warn her about him. "Doesn't that say anything to you?" she angrily demanded.

"Yes," replied the teenaged prostitute, "it means he's unstable."

"On the contrary," Beletu protested, "it means he didn't find his true love until now."

With her new-found love at the gate and her previous mistake all but forgotten, Beletu got up each morning with a song in her heart. Arms locked, the two roamed the bars and restaurants of the town, sampling the services that each establishment had to offer. The director introduced his prize catch to those who until then had known her only by reputation. Beletu was on top of the mountain, and she knew it.

The end came as quickly as it all started, when the director showed up with a new girl on his arm.

Broken-hearted for the second time, Beletu began taking careful stock of her life, and she arrived at the conclusion that Gelemso, with its raw and uncouth inhabitants, was far too small a place in which to realize her dreams. She needed to move away. Three months after she had deserted her first love, long after she had unceremoniously left behind her home, family, and friends, she found herself at the crossroads once more, although this time she was contemplating a move that no one, except perhaps Etiye Hiywet, thought she would ever make. When it finally ran its full course, her latest decision would affect many lives, but none more than her own.

Beletu decided to make herself available to paying customers.

"Fatima had a lot to do with her decision," the teenaged prostitute would tell Azeb. "She made your sister's life so unbearable that the only way out of her predicament seemed to be to leave town altogether. The easiest method of raising the necessary cash was to do what the rest of us did for a living."

Despite her reckless choice, however, Beletu had the presence of mind to realize that the shelf life of a young woman such as herself was woefully limited in the sex trade. She didn't have far to go to see those who had fallen on hard times. In the alleys and back streets of Gelemso, as indeed in much of the country, were middle-aged women who had squandered their golden years and were now providing their services to schoolboys and drifters—those who could ill afford the relatively high fees charged by the clean women in the bars. Most of them ended up as alcoholics, and if the alcohol didn't send them to an early grave, one of their sadistic clients most certainly would. In a time and place where homicides were seldom documented, much less investigated and prosecuted, the passing of such women was rarely considered a loss.

BELETU KNEW that she wouldn't end up in the back streets of Gelemso; that as soon as she saved a thousand *birr*, she would pack up and leave the cursed town for good. And with her ravishing good looks and tender youth, it didn't take her long—a mere four months, in fact—to raise the money she needed. At the last minute, however, unforeseen circumstances thwarted her plans. A routine checkup at the clinic confirmed what she had begun to suspect—that she was in the family way. Abortion may not have been illegal, but it wasn't a routine procedure either. It took Beletu two weeks of thorough canvassing before she finally located a midwife who would assist her in the hazardous task at a price she could afford.

Slight complications arose following the procedure. Two days later, Beletu was leaving a puddle of blood in her wake. Standing up made her dizzy. She took herself to bed early, giving up work altogether. At night, when the common bed at the Barn was sought by the working girls tending to paying customers, she slept under the bed, thereby avoiding the expense of renting a room for herself. (Fatima had taken away her free-room privilege in return for keeping her affairs secret from Etiye Hiywet.) Beletu's ears witnessed what went on in the bed above, but she remained unfazed. Sometimes a co-worker lingered behind, after seeing the unsuspecting man out, to check on Beletu. The teenaged prostitute always remembered to say good night before she left the compound with her man of the evening.

In those forlorn days, Beletu was assailed by childhood memories. At times she was unable to tell whether she was dreaming or if she had travelled back in time to those carefree years when the most scandalous conduct a young woman such as herself could be accused of was visiting the public teahouse or laughing aloud in public.

Family rituals, which she had sneeringly dismissed not so long ago, calling them stifling, backward, and impossible to live with, became dear to her in her solitude. Her eyes moistened at the thought of the private communions her villagers held each month, to commemorate a favoured saint, with cherished friends and neighbours, over a drink of *tella* and some ceremonial bread. Named *Maheber* and *Zikirt,* these occasions were highly anticipated in the priest's household. On St. George's day, May 1, as she reeled from another loss of blood, she asked the cook, one of the few hotel employees not involved in the sex trade, to secure her a slice of blessed bread and some homebrew.

She longed for home cooking. The *injera* she used to deride, the vegetarian dishes she hated so much—which at home she would have been served 180 days of the year, because of the ritual fasts—pervaded her thoughts. More than once she paid the same hotel cook to smuggle her food from her own kitchen. She craved the scent of the church chambers, the unique aroma associated with the church thurible. At home, if she had regularly observed Mass, it was because it was demanded of her; now she could hardly wait for Sunday to arrive, so she could make her peace with God.

As her energy continued to wane and she became increasingly bed-bound, she found solace in memories. Given her strict Christian upbringing and personal history, it is not hard to imagine what else may have gone on in her mind: she would have seen a bunch of boys harvesting brushing twigs at her command, an image of herself taking a bath in the river, savouring the attention she was drawing from the adjacent bushes.

The river was too cold. Her skin shrivelled and her teeth rattled uncontrollably. "Why can't I get out of this freezing water?" she asked herself. Scanning her surroundings, she was surprised to discover that she was in the Epiphany segment of the river. "No one is supposed to swim in the Epiphany water," she said to herself, but seeing that people had gathered on the river-banks to gaze at her in mournful silence, she sensed that it might be the yearly festival. "The *Tabot* can't be far away," she thought.

The sun was shining, but its warmth eluded her. Looking up at the bright sky, her eyes beheld, not a glaring star, but a grey-haired man with an overflowing beard. He was smiling at her benevolently. She found comfort in the fatherly countenance. She saw his arms extending towards her, but before they could reach her, the brimming sleeves of his white frock cast deep shadows around her, leaving Beletu in a theatrical spotlight.

Puzzling her still, the paternal countenance became the origin of the spotlight. Like a baby in a crib seeking its parents' reassuring cuddle, Beletu extended her arms, hoping to be plucked out of the freezing waters and into a warm, tender embrace.

"Beletu, Beletu," called out her co-workers, returning early from work. "Beletu! Beletu!"

But Beletu never spoke again.

15

SMALL CONSOLATIONS

*J*t fell to Etiye Hiywet to break the news of Beletu's
passing to the priest's family. Since tidings of death were
never delivered by a single person but by a troop of mourners, she
had to take into her confidence some of her good neighbours
before asking them to accompany her.

Tidings of death were not delivered at just any old time of the
day, either. Etiye Hiywet and her company of three men and three
women had to wait for the rooster to crow the next morning
before knocking on the priest's door, thus ensuring that members
of the household hadn't broken their night-long fast with the
curse of the Grim Reaper upon them. Werknesh was the first to
emerge. Catching sight of the venerable crowd, her experienced
eyes told her the purpose of their visit.

"Get your mourning girdle," Etiye Hiywet instructed before
the priest's wife had a chance to frame her question. Aba Yitades,
who caught a whiff of the exchange, emerged carrying his wife's
mourning waistband. Before delivering her next instruction,
Etiye Hiywet helped Werknesh fasten the piece of cloth firmly
around her waist so that she wouldn't hurt her back during the
rigours of weeping that would soon follow.

"Now go back inside," she said.

"Is it Genet?" Werknesh screamed, finally finding her voice.

"No," replied Etiye Hiywet, her long-stifled emotions uncorked
at last. "It is Beletu," she said, in between spurts of sobbing.

Werknesh and the company of women beat their chests, crying at the top of their voices, while Aba Yitades and his fellow men quietly lamented, each covering his face with the end of his *netela*. Azeb joined the clamour. And before long the priest's compound brimmed with mourners, who grew in number as they descended from their distant abodes. "We don't yet know who the deceased is," they said to one other, "but you'd better hurry up and come join the family."

Some of the men headed for the warehouse of the village *eder*—the co-operative that provided the necessary facilities for a funeral ceremony, as it did for a wedding. They brought a sprawling tent, including floor covers and dining utensils, on the backs of donkeys and mules. Removing the front fence of the family compound for better access, they pitched the tent. Then they spread the mats and mattresses along the tent's length and breadth, with pillows and headrests scattered around the perimeter. Aba Yitades and Werknesh were ushered into the tent that would be their home for the next three days.

Beletu's coffin was removed from a car that had been parked discreetly behind the compound and was carried inside the family hut, where the body would be washed and scrubbed clean before it was taken to its final resting place the very same day. Overcome with curiosity, Azeb stole towards the back of the building, where, straining over a large boulder, she watched the procedure through an open window. Preparing the bier was Etiye Hiywet, assisted by two women considered to be closest to the bereaved.

While the women removed Beletu's *netela*-wrapped body from the wooden casket and laid it on a palm mat spread over the dirt floor, Azeb saw her sister's arm sluggishly fall to the side, and she cried out loud, "They are going to bury her alive!"

All three women looked up with a start.

"Get away from there," cried Etiye Hiywet. "No child should see a mortuary rite."

But Azeb had her curiosity to satisfy, so as soon as attention was diverted from her, she went back to her post.

Although almost twelve years old and fast approaching the age of consent, Azeb couldn't yet fathom the vagaries of death. It all seemed surreal to her, rash and arbitrary, that a young and vivacious person such as Beletu should be deprived of life at such an early age. "It is a dream," she said to herself, "a very bad dream." And she remained hopeful that her rebellious sister would sit up at any moment, stretch her arms, yawn lazily, and declare what a miserable life she had, as she had done so many times before, and wistfully long for the day when she would be permitted to finish her sleep. But as she watched, Beletu's body was returned to the coffin, the coffin was nailed shut, and six men marched inside to ferry her away.

At the sight of the sealed coffin, the hullabaloo outside intensified. The women resumed their chest beating and the men hummed their lamentations together. Surrounding the closed casket, the clergy, who had arrived not long after the mourning tent was pitched, conducted Prayers of Ascension. The deacons and scribes recited their psalter. The first of the seven absolutions was carried out in the deceased's last earthly home, with the priests reading from the *Ginzet,* the Funeral Service Writings, before they all headed for the church.

"Beletu would have been most impressed by the complete attention she finally commanded," Azeb related years later to a young activist she befriended. Indeed, in Mechara's long and illustrious history, no other person had been accorded the level of service lavished on the priest's daughter. Not one of the multitudes of deacons, scribes, *dabtaras,* nuns, and monks cried off the event. More impressively perhaps, not one of the village teenagers, boy or girl, stayed at home, although by virtue of their tender age, none was expected to attend a funeral.

FIVE OF THE REMAINING SIX absolutions were conducted on the way to the church. For each one, the pallbearers lowered the bier and placed it on the ground in a symbolic reunion with mother earth. For the seventh and last absolution, by far the longest one, the casket was taken to the *Dej Selam,* a building inside the Holy Precincts that was reserved for such events.

AZEB HAD REMAINED in the shadows throughout the rituals. She was absent-mindedly wandering about the church grounds— ignored by many, shooed away by not so few, pitifully gazing at her sister's coffin from a distance—when she felt a friendly hand press lightly on her shoulder. It was Mrs. Vivian Harding, with the rest of her family not far behind her. Oona was uncharacter- istically quiet, but instinctively she took Azeb's hand. Her eyes were elsewhere. Still smarting from their recent spat with their neighbours, the Hardings gave the flood of mourners a wide berth.

The seventh absolution took longer than many had antici- pated, as the deacons and scribes recited their drawn-out psalters and the priests read extraneous chapters from the *Ginzet.* Many a censer rattled, engulfing the cloth-draped casket in aromatic fumes. Inevitably, though, the service came to an end, and the casket was taken to the waiting gravesite, where it was lowered with the head facing east. The acting head priest tossed a handful of dirt over the coffin, giving the signal to shovel the rest back in. A wooden cross was erected over the mound of earth, and the priest delivered a parting recital before the service concluded.

"May the Grim Reaper steer clear of you and your loved ones for many, many years," he said with a far-off look in his eyes.

"Amen," came the collective response.

"May the Lord grant you someone to bury you at your own ultimate departure."

"Amen."

SEVEN YEARS LATER, when Azeb learned the circumstances surrounding her sister's end, she bitterly accused her godmother of concealing the truth from her. Etiye Hiywet responded equally angrily. "Do you know where your sister would have ended up had I revealed how she met her end?" she said. "You should thank me that she received a proper burial, and all seven absolutions at that!"

Etiye Hiywet wasn't exaggerating. For not everyone was entitled to a burial in the church cemetery, much less to all seven absolutions. In fact, only the month before, Aba Yitades had sent away the coffin of a woman suspected of sorcery. She was laid to rest by a hillside, a good five kilometres away from the church proper. Also, when a mother of two drowned while attempting to cross a raging river on the back of a lame mule, the priest didn't hesitate to pronounce the incident a case of suicide, denying her burial in the church grounds altogether. "To consider the alternative would be to offend the living," Aba Yitades reasoned. Had he attributed her death to irrational thinking instead of suicide by a reckless act, it would have meant that the woman, Etiye Tsehai, wasn't in her right mind when, six months earlier, she had married her second husband—a man who was suspected of drowning his Eucharist-wedded wife in a half-filled bathtub to qualify for his second marriage. The case against Etiye Tsehai herself, which stemmed from the sudden and mysterious death of her own Eucharist-wedded husband, would also stick. "Better that she met her Maker on a lesser charge of self-endangerment than accused of taking another person's life," Aba Yitades angrily defended his ruling. Etiye Tsehai was buried by the bank of the river that had claimed her life, her sins all but forgotten.

"Your sister would have ended up right next to Tsehai," Etiye Hiywet pronounced. "Her vindictive cousins would have seen to that!"

ON THE DAY of the funeral, all this was far off. Foremost on Etiye Hiywet's mind was Genet, the priest's first-born, who had yet to receive the sad tidings. Also, the godmother had to figure out how to accommodate the multitude of mourners who would flock from all over in the days that followed to share the family's grief. Many of them would have to be provided with temporary lodging, as they might have spent a day on the road in order to get to Mechara. A mourning tent had been set up for such eventualities, it is true, but since there was no way to predict the number of visitors (the priest's family hadn't lost any kin before, so there was no guessing who might show up), Etiye Hiywet alerted her good neighbours to expect to share their homes and beds with some of the guests.

Azeb, like all children, would be kept away from the mourning tent during the three days of sorrow. Rather than send her godchild to sleep at a neighbour's home, as most people would do in her position, Etiye Hiywet chose to let her cuddle in a bed she had known, her godmother's own.

"Oona, honey," said Etiye Hiywet, taking the Hardings' daughter to one side, "would you mind keeping Azeb company for the next couple of days? I have already spoken to your mother and she says it is all right with her if you sleep over."

"I don't mind at all," Oona responded joyfully.

"That's my girl," said Etiye Hiywct, visibly relieved. "Now, there is a clean set of bedsheets in the trunk under the bed, and you can find a supply of candles and kerosene in the kitchen, although I don't think you should start the kitchen fire. The last couple of days has been *Gahad,* so I didn't prepare much of a meal, but there is some money under the mattress, close to the headboard, so the two of you can buy …"

If there was one problem that Etiye Hiywet didn't have to solve, it was how to feed the guests during the three-day-long mourning. That task fell to members of the community, who brought along ready-made food and homebrew. However, along with the abundant supply of food and drink arrived many more visitors, further taxing the godmother's schedule. Beggars set up camps all around the tent site, and the street dogs marked their territories, each with its individual scent. Storks, black kites, crows, and other winged predators carved circles above the mourning tent, while wild beasts of the four-legged variety converged on the village under cover of darkness. Mourning was truly an event that brought families together.

Genet was one family member who arrived late, as she had to cross mountains and rivers. Like all visitors, she and her husband were received with a torrent of wailing and chest beating. Since Genet was expecting, however, and the arduous journey had begun to take its toll, the village elders had to make a hasty ruling, and persuaded her to conclude her mourning rituals earlier than tradition required for a lost sibling.

Azeb and Oona came running to meet Genet the very evening they learned of her arrival. It had been a full year since any of them had seen her, and their curiosity was justified in the eyes of Etiye Hiywet, who ushered them into the mourning tent with a word of caution not to linger too long. Azeb found her eldest sister a much-changed person, not only physically but also in her attitude towards her. Genet did kiss her on both cheeks, as tradition demanded (she did likewise to Oona), but Azeb could detect no warmth or affection.

"Genet is not feeling well," Etiye Hiywet told her peeved godchild. "You know, she is due any day now. And pregnancy does change a woman's behaviour, as you may find out for yourself someday. Also, she is severely traumatized by Beletu's untimely death. I am sure her love for you hasn't changed one bit."

The day after Genet's arrival, on the third-day commemoration, the family members, friends, and relations filed to church bringing with them three baskets of bread, three pots of *tella*, three dishes of sauce, a load of firewood for the Bethlehem— which the vulgar persisted in calling the kitchen—and absolution money for the officiating priest, the acting head.

As usual, the food and drink were divided up so that the poor, the officiating priest and the chamberlain each received one-sixth and the rest went to the deacons and scribes. Rare for a third-day commemoration, a live bull was also brought along "for the drying of tears"—courtesy of Etiye Hiywet. It was slaughtered and the carcass divided up in accordance with Leviticus.

Then the mourning tent was removed.

GENET WAS UNABLE to go back home, since her labour had begun. Almost twelve years before, the midwife had made an offhand prediction, confidently declaring that the priest was about to become the proud father of a son. When his third child turned out to be another girl, Aba Yitades' disappointment was immense.

The midwife didn't venture any such forecast this time around, and Aba Yitades didn't solicit his Maker for a baby boy, having finally come to terms with the fact that he was destined to remain a man with no one to inherit his name. So, when the midwife and her company of women let out a cry of joy from the birth chamber, it wasn't Aba Yitades but his male friends who held their breath and began to count the number of ululates with mounting hope. Five intermittent ululates, it will be remembered, indicated the birth of a baby boy; three, a baby girl.

"... Four ... five! ... Six ... seven," the men counted in unison, their confusion growing, "eight ... nine ... ten!"

"What does it mean?" Aba Yitades gasped.

"Congratulations," came the answer, "for you are now the proud grandfather of twin boys!"

For years afterwards, whenever misfortune befell him or someone he knew was gravely forsaken, Aba Yitades would recall the small consolation he had found so soon after he lost his second daughter, and he would aptly remark: "ሳይደግስ አይጣላም፥"—"He [the Lord] doesn't close one door before opening another."

BOOK V

Decline of the Neck-Cord

16

THE FORSAKEN

*S*even years had passed since the Hardings moved to Mechara; five since their school was rebuilt and its doors opened. For the first two years, student enrolment was dismal, barely filling half the classrooms. Afterwards, though, the end of the waiting line was nowhere in sight. Applications arrived from near and far from parents convinced that their children, once accepted, would be destined for high places; for job placement was one thing every graduate of St. Paul's School could count on.

The advantages of modern education revealed themselves a month after the first batch of students received their General Adult Education Diploma. They all secured lucrative positions as translators, purchasers, or bookkeepers, mostly at international aid agencies operating in the region, which paid handsomely. Graduates of St. Paul's School not only could make arithmetic calculations without resorting to counting a bagful of beans, but they also spoke and wrote passable English—the unofficial second language of the business world.

Hot on the heels of their successful general education program, the Hardings introduced a juvenile curriculum, which was offered to students coming from afar with the extra incentive of free board—in addition to the tuition fee deferral that all had come to expect. Even those families who previously hadn't cared a fig about modern education couldn't pass up such largesse. Four academic years would elapse before the Hardings noticed a deceitful trend in the school's enrolment: The number of students swelled between the farming seasons, at which time a child was more of a liability than an asset to families who had on average nine mouths to feed. As soon as the skies darkened and the rains appeared imminent, the peasants removed their children from the school to assist in the fields.

Mr. Harding was deeply hurt by this treacherous practice, but if he didn't take the bull by the horns, it wasn't out of fear of the animal's formidable muscle, as many had suspected, but because confronting the abusing parents would be, in his view, more alienating than constructive. He chose to adjust the class schedules instead, so that the long semester breaks coincided with the ploughing and harvesting seasons. "That man is no bovine," was Aba Yitades' grudging compliment.

THE HARDINGS' Church of the Redeemer may not have taken off with blazing speed, but neither did it fare half as badly as many had confidently predicted. There were not many local converts, it is true, but those who paraded to the biweekly sessions were cut from a much finer fabric than Aba Yitades' traditional flock.

As wage-earning employees of the state-owned Coffee Board, the Office of Skins and Hides, and St. Paul's School, the natives who attended the Church of the Redeemer were better groomed, and they graced their Amharic with select English phrases. Reading the Holy Bible in this foreign language rather than in their mother tongue somehow made it more alive to many of them. The chronicles were more powerful, and the teachings had a ring of truth to them, truth that had escaped their attention when delivered to the accompaniment of sistrum rattles, resonating drumbeats, smoke-filled censers, a chant of anaphora, and a *Tabot* that refused to be moved at critical junctures.

The English roll call of saints and apostles differed from its Amharic counterpart in both tone and membership, and for many of the converts this cast of characters, like those on the silver screen, provided a welcome variation. Welcomed most, however, was the fact that fasts and *Gahad*, clean and unclean foods, and other time-worn rites and practices were cast aside with a careless flick of Mr. Harding's learned pen.

Even good old Leviticus, guardian and mentor of priests from time immemorial, wasn't spared Mr. Harding's exacting scalpel. Whole chapters and verses of the Book lay scattered on the editing-room floor. No more absolution fees were coming the priests' way; no fellowship or sin offerings either. No guilt or burnt offerings, nor offerings of grain, were tolerated, even as a simple act of charity. "We don't have to give the priests anything" was in fact the consensus.

"Not even a farthing?" asked Abebe the Bandit the day he learned about the reforms at the opening ceremony of Mechara's first modern pub.

The answer rang out, *"Nada!"* and it echoed through many halls.

Admittedly, a collection bowl was passed at the biweekly service of the Church of the Redeemer, but the money was for the disadvantaged elsewhere.

SOME OF THE OLD RITUALS blossomed under the new system. For instance, funeral services were given high priority at the Church of the Redeemer, and the dead were brought in a wooden box before a roomful of worshippers, who prayed and reflected for hours on end from the comfort of the shaded and polished benches. The Arab storekeeper was the first to recognize the clear advantages of this new trend, and he imported caskets that, unlike the traditional boxes made by inept hands, were skilfully put together. "If you have to be the centre of attention," he declared, "you may as well dress up accordingly." And without Aba Yitades' staying hand, he could exercise his unbridled imagination. He offered caskets in the shape of a mammoth banana, a

Coca-Cola bottle complete with its red and white logo, one that resembled a green Land Rover vehicle, and "just about anything your little heart desires." *If you can fashion it from timber and tin, we will make it for you* was his motto.

The Arab hired two part-time carpenters, in addition to the full-time employee he already had, in anticipation of the trend taking off. It seemed to him all but a foregone conclusion that the Church of the Redeemer would spread to nearby hamlets like untamed wildfire. When asked why he had become so money-oriented, the merchant gave a sage reply. "Don't blame the caterer," he said, "I only tend to their wishes. Besides," he added with a chuckle, "if I don't offer them the choice they deserve, someone else will."

Not even Abebe the Bandit, the most liberal-minded member of the old church, would take this lying down. "Did you send your father packing in a Coca-Cola casket?" he mockingly asked, the day the Arab returned home from his father's funeral in Gelemso.

"Are you out of your mind?" was the Arab's angry retort. "My faith doesn't allow such material worship." Indeed, his people buried their dead wrapped in a simple white piece of linen—much like the early Orthodox Christians.

THE ARAB MERCHANT was not immune to surprises, however. He scratched his head, as did many of the villagers, when Mr. Harding mounted the first clock Mechara had ever seen at the entrance to St. Paul's School, "as a last-ditch effort to instill the concepts of time, hours, and minutes in the students," in Mr. Harding's own words. "Something happened to that man" was the widespread belief. "Why won't his people send him to a medicine man?"

As in most villages in the country, life in Mechara ambled along a well-worn path with a predictable rhythm. The question "What time is it?" was likely to elicit an answer of, say, time for lunch, time for the second coffee break, time for prayer, time to sow or harvest—or, simply, What do you mean, time? The notion of consulting a timepiece didn't cross many minds, since no one, not even the flamboyant divorcee, Aba Yitades' Eve, whose jewellery box brimmed with an assortment of expensive trinkets, owned a wristwatch.

Granted, Etiye Hiywet did find it necessary to mark some of the hours of the day. Mid-morning, for instance, was when she burned incense at the gates of the church, and visited the tombs of her loved ones. Mid-afternoon was time to break her nine-hour *Gahad.* Noon was time for lunch, but that was easy to figure out by one's shadow, which disappeared entirely under one's feet.

Indeed, it was by the location of the shadow that Etiye Hiywet established her hours. She drove two pegs into the ground and used the shifting outline of her rooted residence to mark time. Since Mechara is so near the equator, the length of the day doesn't change from week to week, or even from month to month, so the margin of error of her time-markers was a few insignificant minutes. On those rare cloudy days when she was unable to consult her time-pegs, she erred on the generous side, prolonging her *Gahad* into late afternoon. Although Etiye Hiywet, like the infamous divorcee and other well-to-do men and women of Mechara, could afford a timepiece, she thought the idea of keeping track of the minutes and seconds of each passing hour the workings of an idle mind.

WHAT HAD DRAWN a crowd before the gate of St. Paul's School wasn't merely the fact that Mr. Harding had been idle enough to mount a timepiece for everyone's benefit, but that he got his hours, like so many other things, laughably wrong. His clock was set to register the morning shortly after midnight, which would have concluded the twelve-hour daytime at high sun! Why, even a bumbling idiot could distinguish daylight hours from hours of darkness, many argued. Even a dumb rooster could tell that morning begins at the crack of dawn, when the timepiece should have registered twelve o'clock, marking the end of twelve hours of darkness, instead of six, as Mr. Harding had it; and that the day ends with the setting of the sun—twelve o'clock, not six.

"Maybe in his country the sun rises a minute past midnight," scoffed the infamous divorcee, echoing the thoughts of many.

"No, I think he wants to be different," was Aba Yitades' observation. "The Good Lord saw fit to divide the day into twelve equal hours of sunlight and darkness, and it won't change one bit merely because Mr. Harding wants it to."

If the clock at the school gate indicated the wrong time, the calendar in Mr. Harding's office told the wrong month, even the wrong year! Just to be different, Mr. Harding had divided his year into twelve months, instead of thirteen, as it was meant to be. His months had a number of days that even Oona—the brightest one of the family, by the villagers' unqualified admission—didn't quite know by heart.

"Oona, how many days does February have, according to your father's calendar?" people asked her.

"Thirty days has September, April, June, and November ..." she hummed, circling around the answer before alighting on it: "Twenty-eight!" Only after she realized she was being teased did she laugh.

Mr. Harding's calendar was, on average, eight years ahead of the correct one. "It should make him eight years younger," Endale Fluoride noted. It was a quip that triggered an uproar.

ABA YITADES wasn't laughing when the Hardings unveiled their ecclesiastical calendar. Lo and behold, they even got the Lord's birthday wrong! Instead of January 7, which even the Muslims of Gelemso knew by heart, the Church of the Redeemer maintained that the Nativity was December 25. Perhaps worse than getting the Nativity wrong was the way they set about ushering in the occasion.

The first time Mr. Harding was seen wearing an oversized, red, and ridiculous outfit, a white fake beard, a funny-looking hat, and carrying a bagful of trinkets on his back, many people thought he had finally lost his head. "Merry Christmas," he said to each cluster of alarmed villagers, but no one answered him. He handed out toys and other things to kids, who like their counterparts of years before—those who had first met the white family—hesitated for a moment or two, and scanned their surroundings for available exits, before they snatched the plastic-wrapped gifts and dashed for safety.

"He used to be a fine man," said many of the grown-ups, shaking their heads in disbelief. "He began to lose his reason when he mounted that clock."

"How sad," observed others, "to fall apart like this in a foreign country."

"All that sunbathing must have fried his brains," speculated the infamous divorcee, whose keen eye for a man's flaws few doubted. "For the life of me, I never understood why they would toast themselves like that."

"My heart goes out to his wife and kids," said a grandmother, dabbing her tear-filled eyes with the end of her *netela*. "And he must have a mother somewhere, who really cares for him."

Other men and women wondered out loud if there was anything they could do to help. No one, not even Aba Yitades, who was still reeling from the jolt of betrayal and deception he had experienced at the revelation of the Hardings' actual mission, had an unpleasant thing to say about Mr. Harding that day, because if one can't say a good thing about the dead and the insane, then one must say nothing at all. And Mr. Harding was undoubtedly insane. He even laughed like a madman.

If Aba Yitades had misgivings about how the Hardings had inaugurated their Christmas, it didn't become entirely apparent until that first night, when Azeb came home carrying two gift boxes, one for herself, the other for Werknesh. Scarcely had she removed the colourful wrappings of her own prize, exposing its contents—beautifully patterned knitwear and an equally fine-looking head scarf—than Aba Yitades instructed his daughter to put the items back inside the box and return both packages to the gift givers.

"I am getting fed up with your father," said Oona, seeing Azeb with the boxes in hand. "No one rejects a gift."

In his own eyes, Aba Yitades had done a most noble thing by returning the goods in their original state, and resisting all urges to reach for the cleaver above the fireplace, as he had often done in the past, and chop them up into unrecognizable pieces. He explained his uncharacteristic leniency from the pulpit that very Sunday morning. "If Mr. Harding has gone stark raving mad, squandering his children's rightful inheritance as though money has gone out of style," he said, "good Christians shouldn't give in to abject temptation and be part of his wastefulness. Reason must prevail."

And it was reason that the priest had in mind when he installed a large bamboo basket at each of the three entrances to the church building, so that those parishioners who had given in to abject temptation by taking part in the feeding frenzy would be remorseful enough to return the "gifts" to their rightful owners, the Harding children. A week later, when the baskets were finally removed at his instruction, not one of the parishioners had taken this piece of advice to heart.

Blatantly working against him was the Arab shopkeeper, who hailed the gift giving not only as a most desirable boon, a welcome shot in the arm for struggling merchants such as himself, but also one that ought to be emulated on a much larger scale.

"The government has an obligation to do good for its law-abiding citizens from time to time," he declared before a rapt gathering of men, including Abebe the Bandit, "and there is no better forum in which to demonstrate that goodwill than at the cash register."

"How do you propose the goodwill should be demonstrated?" Abebe the Bandit demanded.

"My suggestion is that merchants throughout the country send wrapped gifts to their neighbours, submitting the bill directly to the government. Who better than your neighbourhood store-owner to recognize your pressing needs and wishes?"

"Who indeed," Abebe the Bandit concurred, before asking the Arab storeowner to recognize his needs and wishes, and give him a carton of Nyala brand cigarettes and a box of safety matches (make that two), settle his accumulated debt at the butcher's and the pub, and send the bill directly to the government.

"I didn't know that you smoked," was the surprised Arab's rejoinder. "In any case, you aren't that law-abiding."

Aba Yitades, however, was as law-abiding as they came, and he had come to ask the most pressing question. Rumour had it that the Arab storeowner had ordered crates of gift items from abroad. The priest wanted to know if the speculations were well founded. Well founded they were, he was told.

"This is most un-neighbourly conduct," Aba Yitades angrily declared. "You are giving children reasons to steal."

"Aba Yitades," began the Arab when he had mustered his courage, "I am a businessman. I pay rent and taxes, and I create jobs. For years now I have done your bidding, closing my shop on *your* holidays, refraining from physical work on *your* saint days. Times have changed, and they have changed fast. The village has grown many times over. The new settlers may not be all to your liking, but to me they are welcome patrons. I have to look after them, as I have been looking after your needs. In any case," he added in a conciliatory tone, "a gift does not corrupt children—people do."

Years later, when his twin grandsons, who had by then taken up residence with him, began pestering the priest for toys and trinkets and other costly material incentives to look forward to Christmas, he would lay the blame for the corrupting influence not only on the Hardings but also on the Arab storekeeper.

Indeed, in a matter of four years, the blink of an eye as tradition goes, the practice of Christmas gift giving and gift exchange grew to such a degree that even parishioners of the Church of the Redeemer, who as employees of established offices drew regular and fairly decent wages, began to fret at the arrival of the event. The payroll man assumed the traditional place of the Christ child. It was *his* advent that many anticipated with mounting hopes—not for the earned paycheque, mind you, for it had already been squandered, but for cash advances. The "Model 10 Forms" that government employees filled out to apply for an overdraft arrived by the crate. Paying the Christmas bills entailed not just a month of belt-tightening but half a year, even a full year, of arduous struggle.

Although children weren't sufficiently seduced by the glittery display of imported toys in the Arab's window to reach for their mother's money belt, as Aba Yitades had feared, their entrepreneurial instincts were honed remarkably quickly. The *chibbo,* which boys built for festival bonfires, became a lucrative source of revenue for many of them. In an oft-cited anecdote, a lone grandmother who complained that she had no one to build a *chibbo* for her was told by a caring young man that he would take care of her needs. "Etiye Zewditu," the boy was quoted as saying, "don't worry about affording a *chibbo,* I will sell you one for half the going rate. And you don't even have to pay me right away, you can take your time."

Little wonder, then, that when, in 1974, the nation was engulfed by a revolutionary movement led by a military junta promising to root out the proliferating corruption and other "insidious influences of American imperialism" and install in their place a system based on innate human equality, even some traditionalists, Aba Yitades to name one, thought it high time that some change was effected. A full seventeen years would elapse, and many people would mourn a loss or two, most of them the victims of summary execution by revolutionary cadres, before they saw the error of their ways. In 1991, another popular uprising would remove the military junta from office, but not before entrepreneurs such as the Arab storekeeper were ground to dust through nationalization and punishing taxes, and the country was thrust into spiritual and economic gloom.

GLOOM DIDN'T EVEN BEGIN to describe the mood of Mr. Harding the day he caught sight of the child born to the family housemaid, the butcher's soft-spoken daughter. The infant had emerged with golden locks and skin devoid of any earthy hues. All of a sudden the anecdote that Aba Yitades had told him many moons before, about the butcher's philandering son who had ended up losing his restless appendage when he was found in bed with someone else's woman, came back to him with full force. He dispatched his guilty son, Jeff, back to his country under cover of darkness, and paid indemnities to the butcher and his wronged daughter.

But no amount of money would remove the stain of adultery from the butcher's hapless daughter or restore her family's good name. "The Hardings came to our village when we were reeling from an epidemic that had left our sheep balding," said Endale Fluoride. "Three years later, children are balding all over."

Thankfully, not everyone was as cruel, or as insensitive. Visiting women often had kind words to say to the butcher's beleaguered daughter. "Don't worry," they counselled her, "newborns tend to have bleached skin. Come his six-month birthday, he will have acquired a human pigment."

As she waited anxiously for the six months to pass and for her child to acquire a human pigment, the butcher's daughter became a tourist attraction. Voyeurs arrived from far and wide to catch a glimpse of the curious infant. Many of them emerged from the visit utterly bewildered, as though they had witnessed an everyday mare raising a little egret, or a white-tailed mongoose. "Do you suppose she will be able to communicate with her child when he grows up?" was the question on the tip of many a tongue.

Although the butcher's daughter had by then been in the employ of the Hardings for almost three years, it didn't escape the visitors' attention that her English was most rudimentary.

"How will a good Christian woman like her raise a heathen?" was another oft-asked question.

"What bothers me is how she could cook her boy unclean food without contaminating the entire family," pondered a grandmotherly figure, an out-of-villager, who had heard that the Hardings' favourite food was pork or warthog meat.

"Is her seducer still alive?" was the most common query of visiting men, one that was uttered with a clear underlying desire for revenge.

Jeff's child was born not only in the wrong place, where few of his like were seen, but also at the most inopportune juncture in history. A decade and a half later, when the revolutionary junta, which had elbowed the feeble monarch out of office and into an unmarked grave, began meting out arbitrary arrests and physically torturing reactionary elements—the "remnants" of American imperialism and the old feudal system—Jeff's son, barely a teenager, would be subjected to more than his fair share of political persecution. According to a knowledgeable *dabtara,* the name his mother had picked out for him, Sintayehu—which means "How much have I endured [because of you]!"—was partly to blame for his plight.

In 1991, when the military junta was finally removed from power and the new administration once more opened the doors to Americans, Oona came looking for her embattled nephew. After a disappointing first marriage, which had ended in a costly divorce, she had hoped to recapture some of her fondest memories. She wasn't destined to meet her nephew, though. Like many of his peers, he had by then fled the country to escape execution.

Rumour placed Sintayehu in one neighbouring country one day, then in another the next. In the search for him, Oona left no stone unturned (although many of the stones were already spinning from frequent turns at the hands of mothers looking for their own missing children); she left no resources untapped, visiting, for instance, the regional office of the United Nations High Commissioner for Refugees, as well as other international aid agencies catering to refugees. But nowhere in their swollen files was his name to be found.

WITH HER FAMILY reduced by a quarter following Jeff's sudden enforced departure, Oona found herself leaning heavily on her childhood friend.

"You are now the only sibling I have," she said to Azeb in a moment of nostalgic reflection.

"And you are my only remaining sister," replied Azeb, giving her a tender hug.

Mrs. Vivian Harding, too, increasingly sought the company of the priest's daughter. The three of them were often seen together, not only at the Wednesday market—which, with the exception of a brief spell following the feud between the two families, they had always attended together—but also at the weekly family picnic. If Aba Yitades appeared to have mellowed with time, giving his daughter free rein, there were two good reasons: his grandsons.

As soon as the twins took up residence with him, shortly after the birth of Genet's other two children, another boy and a daughter, the priest rearranged his priorities so that he could devote every spare moment to raising them to be not only upright Christians like himself but also peerless warriors, who, unlike him, would each earn the village's respect and adulation by standing over the carcass of a warthog he had killed. And nothing demonstrated his dedication to his prized progeny more than the sheer financial burden he incurred and the distance he travelled to replace his house, which had long stood as a monument to frugality and the abhorrence of materialism.

In place of the one-room hut, there now stood a two-bedroom timber structure with a corrugated metal roof and cement floor.

Imported furniture cluttered the residence. Standing against the whitewashed wall of the family room was a towering armoire with a full-length mirror on one of the swinging doors. Instead of the traditional woven food table, the *messob,* which the family used to produce from storage as needed, there was now a real wooden table, permanently affixed in the sprawling dining room, with enough chairs for a small congregation. As the kitchen was detached from the main residence, the rooms were smokeless. And from the dining-room rafter dangled a lone incandescent bulb—a quirk, as there was still no electricity in Mechara.

"A QUIRK" was also Abebe the Bandit's impression the day he saw the priest emerge from the Arab's store with newly purchased toy handguns for his grandsons. Transformation wasn't confined to the priest, however. Abebe the Bandit himself had, at long last, changed for the better; he had secured gainful employment.

"What sort of employment?" asked Aba Yitades, pleased with the glad tidings.

"I am working for the United Nations," declared Abebe the Bandit.

Some six weeks before, two representatives of the World Health Organization (WHO), a branch of the United Nations, had visited Mechara as part of a worldwide effort to eradicate smallpox. Walking from door to door, they carried out their lofty mission, urging villagers to reveal the identity of suspected patients, promising a sum of two thousand *birr* for each confirmed case. Abebe the Bandit took them up on their offer. Having laid his hands on a small vial of the virus in the form of pus from a bedridden patient, he was looking for volunteers to inject when the priest ran into him.

"But that is worse than your banditry!" Aba Yitades barked.

"Hardly. This is a win-win and win situation, Father," replied Abebe the Bandit.

"How is that possible?"

"I'll collect the two thousand *birr*, which I am willing to split smack down the middle with the volunteer; the volunteer will receive immediate medical attention from the WHO; and the WHO won't be disappointed with the outcome, as they have been looking for ways to spend their money."

While Abebe the Bandit was assisting the World Health Organization in its grand effort to eradicate smallpox from the globe, a more deadly "disease" was making its way back to Mechara. Endale Fluoride, who had been serving time for murdering his hapless wife, had been paroled.

17

THE LOST SHEEP

*E*ndale Fluoride would have passed into history as a little-known bully, a chronically unemployed bum who had preyed on unfortunate women both for his living and to satisfy his insatiable lust, and those who came after him would have found no reason whatsoever to think of him, had it not been for the fact that he became instrumental in Azeb's eventual fall.

He was a daring man, at best. "Pushy" was how many described him, though. His childlike tantrums and his propensity for violence were cause enough for many a villager to steer clear of him. He had no male friends. His female lovers seldom saw him twice. Indeed, his private life, which came to light in all its ghastly detail during a highly publicized court trial, suggested a man who was pathologically suspicious of the world he lived in, and depressingly insecure about himself and his enviable record of amatory conquest. His live-in lady friend, the one he ended up sending to an early grave, did love him, by all accounts. Her doglike loyalty and nauseating submissiveness led many of his critics to suspect that he might have cast a spell on her. For it wasn't entirely uncommon in those days for both men and women who were insecure in their relationships to hire a *dabtara* to cast a spell on their partner, so that the individual would do their bidding, no questions asked.

"Give us an account of a typical day at Endale's home," the defence lawyer asked a woman on the witness stand. As the family's long-time domestic help, she was better placed than most to know what went on behind closed doors.

"Well, I don't know where to begin," she said, fidgeting.

"Start with the opening of your tavern on any given day. You opened for business at six o'clock, didn't you?"

"Except for Sundays and holidays, when we closed for the entire day," she replied. And the witness went on to recall in vivid detail how Endale Fluoride had come to befriend her mistress, the owner of the establishment.

"Business was brisk," she began, "when Endale began to frequent our establishment. As it was the only tavern in Mechara, men flocked there in droves each evening, and they seldom left before the *tej* had run out, or the doors closed at midnight." As one might expect, the alcohol had a liberating effect on many a man who ordinarily would have been inhibited by tradition from raising his voice, much less getting involved in a barroom brawl. Fist fights soon became commonplace, and patrons who had been denied credit sometimes made a scene.

Endale Fluoride became the self-appointed guardian of the lady of the establishment. He was a man built to command the respect of his fellow men, and those individuals who didn't bow out of his way in a timely fashion, or who were brazen enough to stand up to him, were simply trampled underfoot. Calm and peace reigned in his wake. The lady of the house was often at a loss for words when attempting to express her gratitude. Endale Fluoride dismissed her awkward thankfulness with a self-effacing maxim. "It is nothing that any man with any manhood wouldn't do," he said with disarming humility. "It so happens that in this wretched place I am the only man with any measure of manhood."

Their relationship had stalled, and seemed fated to end with no indication that the woman would ever yield to Endale's lustful gaze, when the defining moment arrived, not after a barroom brawl—when the lady of the house could have been forgiven for

being swept off her feet by Endale's manly deeds—but on a mundane Easter Saturday morning, when he was the last thing on her mind.

Like all families in Mechara, as indeed in the rest of the country, the lady of the establishment was ushering in Easter by sprinkling the blood of a sacrificial rooster at her doorstep.

"At the time, madam didn't have a steady male friend who would say the appropriate prayers over the sacrificial bird and slaughter it for us, so I was sent out to look for a man," remembered the housemaid on the witness stand. "Nothing reminded the madam of her hollow existence more than days when she couldn't find anyone to do a man's job around the house," she added, dabbing her tear-filled eyes.

No living mould of Eve would dare raise a knife to break the celebration bread, much less slaughter a sacrificial animal. (As in many other Christian churches, women were not supposed to say the paternoster required before such events.) Those families without an Adam figure at home looked towards the community when the occasion called for a man's hand. Boys made the rounds on the morning of Easter Saturday, asking if this lone grandmother or that sonless divorcee had someone to slaughter the rooster for her. If no one seemed to remember the pub owner, it wasn't a mere oversight, but a silent though forceful protest against the business she chose—which was exceptionally unpopular among upright homemakers.

Endale Fluoride, however, wasn't as discriminating. He agreed to cater to her needs, which, if it was all right with her, might extend past her bedroom door. "Anything she wants, I will do. I am her man," was the answer the witness recalled years later. "Endale was kind enough to keep us company afterwards," the housemaid added. "And, for the first time, when we closed for the night, he wasn't on the other side of the door."

Soon, Endale Fluoride settled into his new role as a lover and true lord of the den. Gone were the days when he sat in a remote corner, looking dejected and nursing a single drink until someone was kind enough to buy him another. Now, not only could he afford to drink to his heart's content (stomach's, actually), which at times meant half the profits went down the drain, but he could also indulge his refined taste buds. He demanded that his *tej* be brewed from the finest of ingredients and that the alcohol be fermented long enough that his nose could feel the buzz long before his taste buds did.

The lady of the house no longer wondered when her rowdy patron, the one who marred the evenings by instigating scuffles and breaking her costly furniture, would walk through the door, for he now lived with her. "Endale could no longer stand the sight of another man talking to his woman," noted the housemaid. "He became morosely edgy."

His fisticuffs weren't always confined to the male competition, however. His lady friend began emerging from her bedroom with a fresh set of moons around her eyes. Worse than the bruised skin, which could be dressed until it healed so that no one would suspect the nature of her behind-the-door life, was the verbal abuse he increasingly inflicted on the lady of the house before a roomful of villagers. More frightening still were the moments when he sat quietly in his corner, drink in hand, staring at her with infinite hostility.

As their relationship alternated between episodes of *blitzkrieg* and *sitzkrieg,* and with the regular patrons increasingly taking their business to new establishments, the family concern floundered into a wartime economy. Getting the business out of its *wehrwirtschaft* doldrums and putting the wind back in its sails meant, at least in the eyes of the owner, selling assets. Golden bracelets, necklaces, rings, and other valuables she had accumulated over the years found their way to the Arab's emerging pawnshop. "It was touch and go for a while," stated the housemaid, recalling those difficult days before a courtroom of people, and sounding as though she were talking about someone who was bedridden. "But nothing seemed to get us out of the muck."

It didn't take the pub owner long to realize that selling assets and infusing the proceeds into a floundering business wasn't quite award-winning economics. The *tej* house was about to close its doors for good, finally succumbing to its chronic malady, when the owner herself unceremoniously shut up shop. Recalling the closing hours of her madam, the housemaid, who had long been listening in on private conversations through the thin wall separating their bedrooms, stated that the fateful night was no different from many others. "There were cries and pleas for mercy," she said, "when, shortly before the rooster crowed at dawn, calm finally reigned."

Found guilty of a crime of passion, Endale Fluoride was sentenced to a ten-year prison term, to be served in a penal complex in Gelemso. With good behaviour, he was released a scant five years later.

AND IT WAS because of those five years, during which she did not have to look over her shoulder for him, that Azeb was unable to place her old tormentor when she ran into him at the Arab's store. He had been assessing her with an enigmatic smile, searching perhaps for a hint of recognition in her eyes, when, moments before she walked out the door with purchased candies in hand and her bubbly friend in tow, he decided to accost her.

"You're Azeb, aren't you?" he asked.

"Y-e-e-e-e-s?"

"You are quite grown up now," he said with a fiendish grin. "Had it not been for your friend here, I wouldn't have recognized you."

"My friend's name is Oona. Who are you?"

"He is Endale, of course," the storekeeper pitched in, his discomfort at the presence of his infamous visitor plainly written on his face. No other villager would have allowed the convict to darken his doorstep, much less been seen with him in public.

"He has been released, you know," the merchant added with a forced smile.

"The creep," Oona spat the moment the two of them were safely out of earshot. "I don't understand how anyone would set him free so soon after killing his wife."

"I think he would have been better off behind prison bars," said Azeb, echoing what many had been saying for years—that as soon as the convict was released, one of his victim's cousins was likely to do him in, if not to avenge her wrongful death (to tell the truth, she wasn't all that popular among her relations), then to honour her family's name. "He does look very handsome, though, don't you think?"

"Prison life must have been good to him," was Oona's angry response.

"Can i buy you some tea?" Endale Fluoride asked Azeb the next time he ran into her.

Taken aback by his uncharacteristic good manners, she blushed. "No, thanks." Azeb felt her heart flutter and her knees weaken, but she refused to believe that she was falling under his legendary spell.

"Do you want me to help you with that?" he offered the next day, materializing out of the woods. Before Azeb could form a sentence, he removed the jug of *tella* she was carrying on her head and began marching by her side. Overcome with conflicting thoughts, she heard little of what he said during the ten-minute walk to church.

"Can I wait for you?" he said at the gate, handing her back the receptacle.

"No," she curtly replied, finding her strength.

"Are you planning to go to the Epiphany festival this year?" he asked her at their next encounter—barely two days later. Azeb couldn't help but notice his propitious arrival, which coincided with a moment when she was alone.

"I never miss it," she replied coyly.

"Perhaps I can escort you back home after the event."

"I'll see."

Gone were the days when Azeb would take flight at the sight of Endale Fluoride. Now it was her heart she couldn't hold in check. Each time she ran into him, it beat so loudly she feared her rib cage might come unzipped. She finally recognized in him what other women had long seen and admired: his sexual magnetism. Not one to admit that she was falling under his spell, and yet wishing to gauge her friend's reaction, she uttered a few complimentary remarks about him.

"I like his goatee," she told Oona. Ever since his release Endale Fluoride had adopted the practice of trimming his beard to make it appear like a work of abstract art.

"He has nothing to do, so he may as well turn his face into a painter's canvas," Oona replied disdainfully.

"He has a nice behind," Azeb said one Wednesday afternoon as the two girls gazed at his retreating back.

"He needs it to warm up his seat," came the response.

"I heard he is seeing Helen, Gash Abraham's daughter."

"I don't want to talk about the creep," Oona concluded.

THE EPIPHANY FESTIVAL arrived a week after Azeb's latest encounter with Endale Fluoride. Unlike the traditional celebration of Christmas and the Feast of the Finding of the Cross, both of which had of late declined in popularity among the young crowd, mainly because of the negative perception cast by the Church of the Redeemer, the Epiphany festival never lost its appeal.

Foremost among its attractions was the rare opportunity the occasion afforded the young and the unattached to mingle freely with the opposite sex. A girl who normally had to admire the village hunk through the fence gaps of her restricted residence, or snatch a yearning glimpse of him during the Sunday Mass, would be free of all inhibitions during the festival of Epiphany. She could now dance with him, talk freely with him, and, if she was a little daring, win meaningful pinches, without drawing critical attention. Some even hugged and rubbed cheeks, if only discreetly. The most brazen stole towards the nearest woods, giggling and nervously vacillating, yet visibly excited at the prospect of being kissed and caressed.

Azeb and Oona derived pleasure from watching the sparks fly between lovers, but they were not once tempted even to hold hands with a persistent admirer. Endale Fluoride set out to change all that, and with proper timing, he knew, he would come out on top. He was, after all, the unsung hero of Sturm und Drang, the Romantic Movement; the Rembrandt van Rijn of the art of seduction, whose masterworks had not only endured the harrowing test of time but also transcended the clear divides of age and culture. "He is also a convicted murderer," said a young woman to a visiting friend who thought he was dashing.

A window of opportunity opened for Endale Fluoride when he located Azeb and Oona watching a performance from the outer rim of a swelling ring of spectators, their backs vulnerably exposed to a prowling predator. Slithering through the open window, he lodged himself right behind Azeb. Neither of the girls noticed his presence at first, their attention riveted on the performance before them. Also, the semi-darkness and the seasonal blanket of fog gave him a decisive edge, another few panes in his window of opportunity, so to speak, to bring to fruition his version of *Nacht und Nebel Erlass*—the Night and Fog Decree.

Azeb felt a hard object press between her buttocks. Startled, she turned around to investigate, only to find Endale Fluoride breathing on her back. Her heartbeat increased, her knees quivered. Her outwardly calm reaction was the signal he had been waiting for to take his audacious act to a higher level. He reached for her heaving chest. In place of the tiny buds he so vividly recalled, he now found firm, ripe bulbs.

"What do you think you are doing?" cried Oona, who had turned sideways to investigate why her friend had stopped clapping only to find her in the grasp of the village monster.

"What do you think you are doing, you creep?" Oona intoned, as she now stood facing him, both hands on her waist like a village hawker confronting a stealthy pickpocket.

"Watch your mouth," he said, taking a step back and appearing, in the dim light, meeker than an altar boy.

"Oh yeah? What will you do to me, if I don't? Kill me too?"

The crowd abandoned the dancing and singing to witness the rare spectacle of the Hardings' daughter losing her cool. Many were eager to come to her aid. Quickly realizing the predicament he was in, Endale Fluoride quietly retreated, but not before firing a venomous parting glance Oona's way.

"What happened?" was the question on everybody's tongue, and it was answered only when Oona turned on her mute friend.

"How could you let him fondle you?" she barked, running her fingers through her shoulder-length hair as she often did when agitated. Although in the twilight no one could see her face change colour, those who knew her could well imagine her glowing red. "How could you even let him near you?" she pressed.

Azeb began to cry.

"Now what did I do?" Oona was quickly deflated. "I thought he was—"

Azeb didn't wait to hear the ending of her friend's inexcusable outburst of public reproach. Chastised and embarrassed, she scuttled homeward, fighting her way through the growing crowd.

"Where are you going?" Oona yelled, unable to catch up with her. "I'm sorry, Azeb. I thought he was assaulting you."

"Get away from me," cried Azeb, sprinting ahead.

"You have to stop first. We need to talk," Oona pleaded.

"I don't want to talk to you. Get away from me."

The trails leading towards the settlement were eerily quiet. Unlike the Epiphany grounds, which was lit by campfires, the neighbourhood was pitch-black. Each time Azeb walked past a residential compound, a guard dog leapt out of the shadows and followed her, barking, though only from behind the fence. No sooner had she escaped one such angry beast than she encountered another. Even so, Azeb didn't stop running until she arrived home. She didn't pause to light the kerosene lamp before she headed for her bedroom, which she shared with the twins, who were still at the Epiphany grounds, and slumped on top of the bedspread, enveloped in the velvety darkness.

Moments later she was back at the Epiphany grounds and next to her friend. Oona seemed to have all but forgotten the incident of only an instant before. Close to midnight, the two of them spied Endale Fluoride shuffling towards the woods with two teenaged girls in his arms. Curiosity overcame their everyday caution and they proceeded to follow him.

Hiding behind an overgrown shrub, they watched, mouths gaping wide, as Endale Fluoride peeled off his trousers, shirt, and underwear and tossed them aside. He went on to undress his mute conquests as well. Lifting one of the girls by her slender midsection, he kissed her full on the lips before pinning her to his brutal extension. "Mother Mary!" cried the girl.

Oona could hardly stifle her laughter. Azeb remained dead quiet. It was a hauntingly familiar scene to her, a rerun of an earlier play, and she was desperately searching for clues in her gloomy surroundings when the girl straddling Endale Fluoride turned sideways and Azeb found herself staring at—*herself*!

She shot out of bed and sat at the edge of the four-poster holding both hands to her chest, but her attempts to steady her racing heart proved futile. She felt a lump in her throat. Breathing became an ordeal. When she finally managed to snatch some air, she choked on it. She coughed and sneezed until tears coursed down her face. Azeb didn't remember closing her eyes again, but she slept until she was awakened by a noise in the room. Werknesh had returned home at dawn and was preparing the twins for bed.

THE MORNING AIR and the friendly sun didn't mend Azeb's frayed nerves. She remained edgy for much of the day. Oona was the last person she wanted to see that day, and when the two of them eventually met, Azeb had little to say. Her eyes were restless. They looked up and down and from side to side. They looked everywhere, probed ceaselessly, but they failed to alight on the one place where they would most certainly have found comfort and sympathy: Oona's own pleading eyes.

"Azeb, I am so sorry about last night—" Oona began.

Azeb cut her short. "I don't want to talk about it. Not ever."

"Not ever" was also a refrain Azeb employed to remind herself of her resolve not to talk to Endale Fluoride again, much less find herself in the same compromising position. The very thought of the Epiphany incident gave her shudders for days. Like a sleep-walker who had found herself in a strange situation, she felt disoriented but curiously uninvolved. It was a slip-up, no doubt, but she knew it wouldn't happen again.

Endale Fluoride wasn't so easily deterred, however. Like a beast that had tasted the sweet blood of its prey, he hunted her cease-lessly. But each time he located her, she was in the company of others, in the safety of the herd, so to speak. He hovered in the distance, watching her every move, assessing her wounds, looking for signs of faltering, a buckling of her legs, perhaps, that would allow him to snatch her from the protection of the group and take her to his feasting ground.

A week passed without incident. Then another. One evening, her old routine finally restored in full, she was humming her way home after an afternoon at the Hardings' without a care in the world. In the murky distance she could make out the last of the shepherd boys bringing home the family herd from the bush. Bats whizzed by. Perched high in a *zegba* tree, a lone owl sang its solitude.

Out of the woods, Endale Fluoride materialized. Instinctively, she began to run, but he quickly caught up with her.

"Please," he said, "I just want to talk to you."

"But I don't want to."

"Please let me explain what happened last time."

"There is nothing to explain." She was adamant. "It will never happen again."

"Can't we just go to a place where no one will see us talking?" he asked, leading her by the hand towards the adjacent woods. Azeb made a half-hearted attempt to free herself from his grip and run for safety. I am overreacting, she told herself, there is no harm in simple talk. Barely had the two of them left the relative security of the open trails, however, than he planted a passionate kiss on her lips. Azeb feebly tried to fight him off, but somehow she couldn't muster much enthusiasm.

Before she knew it, Endale Fluoride had unbuttoned her blouse and his hands were exploring places where no other person had ever ventured. She felt an odd sensation well up inside her. Her knees rattled. Soon she could no longer feel the ground; she hung in mid-air. All along she had expected to find herself saying, "Mother Mary." Instead, she felt a piercing pain between her legs and let out a savage cry.

Her resolve fully restored, her inner goodness singing aloud of the redeeming forces residing within her, she fought him off with all her might. But her angry thrashing spurred Endale Fluoride on. He didn't let go of her until he had sated his lustful hunger.

"Be here the same time tomorrow," he instructed her, before disappearing into the gripping darkness.

RACKED WITH GUILT and remorse, angry with herself for faltering so soon after the Epiphany incident, Azeb began to cry. "I sinned," she said. "I have fallen." Unable to muster the courage to face her parents, she headed for the backyard garden, where she hunkered down in a fetal position, and where she would have spent the long night had it not been for Werknesh, who emerged to observe a nightly ritual of splashing water on her private parts, as many a village woman did before retiring to bed.

"Azeb, is that you?" Werknesh called, guardedly approaching the bundle in the bush.

"Yes," came a whimper.

"What are you doing here, honey?"

"I am sick."

"Sick? How?"

"I have a stomach ache."

"You almost gave me a heart attack, honey," sighed Werknesh, visibly relieved. "Come inside."

Werknesh was the first to notice the bloodstains on Azeb's skirt. "I see your menstrual period has been particularly harsh this month," she said, helping her daughter out of the tarnished clothing. She rubbed the stain marks with a bar of soap and left the skirt to soak in the water before reaching for the medicine chest. Producing an assortment of bruised herbs, she mixed them with water before administering them to her daughter. "In the morning, I want you to urinate on a warm pile of ashes," she said. "It's the only other way of checking excessive menstrual blood loss."

Two DAYS had passed and Oona hadn't seen her friend. Early on the third day, she went looking for her. "She is at the church," Werknesh told her while thrashing a dusty blanket that she had hung from the clothesline, "helping out the poor. I hope she will stay that way, because she hasn't been herself of late." She was talking as much to herself as to Oona.

"What has gotten into you?" Oona cried the moment she stepped inside the church compound and caught sight of the lone figure of her friend perched on the stone-paved stair of the church veranda.

"Nothing," Azeb replied.

"You will never guess what good news I received yesterday," Oona rambled on, settling next to Azeb and slinging her arm over her friend's shoulder. Azeb was relieved to know that *she* wasn't the news.

"Jeff sent you a letter?" she speculated.

"I wish. No, my college application has been accepted."

"Congratulations," said Azeb, equally pleased. "Does it mean you will be leaving us soon?"

"No, it will be at least another six months before I'm packed."

"How do you feel about going back home after all these years?" Azeb wondered.

"Well, I have mixed feelings."

"How is that?"

"I'm not all that pleased to leave this place," Oona admitted. "After all, for a long time now this has been the only home I have known. But I am also pragmatic. As they say, 'When a leaf dies, it goes back to the roots.' Ultimately, I have to find my roots, and my roots are in America."

"You are poetic today," observed Azeb. "Anyway, I will miss you."

"And I'll miss you," replied Oona. "But I won't be gone for good, I'll be back after each school year."

The church compound suddenly came alive. A group of deacons emerged from a nearby school and formed small clusters, debating the day's lessons. A family of *guereza* monkeys made a grating noise in a high tree, fighting off an intruder. A drunk *dabtara* staggering past the veranda they sat on gave the girls a reason to smile.

"Do you know what I will miss most when I leave this place? Next to you, of course."

"The *guereza* monkeys."

"Not just them, but this whole crazy scene," she said, making a sweeping gesture that took in her surroundings. "And do you know what I look forward to most in America?"

"Ice cream," replied Azeb, and the two roared with laughter.

Azeb never forgot her first experience of ice cream. Oona was on a three-month vacation in America at the time, and Mrs. Harding, with the approval of Werknesh, had taken her to Gelemso. After an afternoon of shopping, the two had stopped by the home of the Hardings' friends, the expatriate staff running the charity clinic in Gelemso. A rare ice-cream feast was in progress, and Azeb was served a cone. After only one giant bite of the frozen stuff, she got such a piercing headache that she decided, right there and then, that ice cream was the invention of madmen. She vowed not to touch it again. On days when Oona reminisced about the varieties of ice cream she used to enjoy in America, Azeb told her that it was the headache she was missing.

"I know that's what I told you before," admitted Oona. "The truth is, ice cream, like many other things, is a passing fling. After a while it becomes mundane. What I enjoyed most during my three-month hiatus in the States, what I never got over, was the fact that no one stared at me there. I was invisible."

"No one stares at you here," Azeb reminded her.

"Not in this village. Not anymore, at least. Anywhere else, however, I still draw lots of attention. Once, Mom and Dad took us to a village not far from Addis Ababa. It was a market day, and there were many village women with babies strapped on their backs. At the sight of us, the babies raised such a deafening racket, crying and thrashing, that you could trace our trail by the din of angry mothers and hysterical infants. Jeff and I joined the ruckus, crying and demanding to be taken home. Mom made an effort at calming us, telling us that the locals didn't mean us harm, that they hadn't seen white faces before and were startled by our unexpected presence, but it was no consolation to me or my brother.

"Even in Addis Ababa, a metropolis of sorts, children wouldn't touch me. It was as though I were a leper. I had hardly any playmates, mostly children of the embassy staff. When we first came to this village, I thought it would be even worse, given that it had just opened its doors to the outside world. When we got off at the bus terminal, I thought I was proven right when all the kids tailed us and the adults gawked. Thankfully, their curiosity didn't last long."

Azeb maintained an embarrassed silence.

"I distinctly recall the first time I met you," Oona continued, not noticing her friend's discomfort. "You were harvesting grass in this very compound—right there, in fact, where the egret is scratching the ground. When I came to talk to you, I expected the same old reaction, but you only remarked about my hair, not the colour of my skin. When you took me by the hand to show me the *guereza* monkeys, I knew then that we would become friends."

Azeb was relieved that she wasn't one of the indicted. "It *is* the colour of your mane that caught my attention," she said, playfully ruffling Oona's hair. "Come to think of it, I haven't quite got over it yet." And they both exploded in laughter.

Azeb felt obliged to explain the unseemly behaviour of her fellow citizens. "Dad said the reason we don't see that many white people is because our country has never been colonized," she offered.

"That's true," Oona readily admitted. "And that's not such a bad thing. Mind you, when I said people avoided us, I didn't mean they were hostile to us. Their reaction, I can now understand, was a simple fear of the unknown. They'd never had a colonial experience, so they couldn't possibly have a negative perception of us." Fingering the talisman that dangled from Azeb's neck, the one Azeb had received from Etiye Hiywet while still a toddler and which had intrigued Oona ever since she had cast an eye on it over a decade ago, she added, "I have to see what is inside this pouch before I leave for America."

"Then you won't be leaving after all," Azeb declared, glad that the topic had changed, "because I will never open it."

"What if there is a treasure map concealed inside, instead of the medicinal inscription you think is there?" Oona argued. Not long ago, a dead stranger who was found lying by the riverbank, victim of a botched robbery, was identified by the scroll inside the leather pouch hanging from his neck-cord. Ever since, Oona's interest in Azeb's talisman had been intense. "We will seal it again before anyone notices," she pressed.

"N-o-o-o-o-o."

"Aren't you too old now to believe that its magical power would wane if it were opened?"

"Perhaps it wouldn't. All the same, I would rather not know what is in it," Azeb insisted.

"Well, I won't leave this country before I see its contents," Oona concluded, getting up to go home. Azeb decided to stay behind and spend the balance of the morning attending to the needy.

THE NEEDY weren't confined to the church grounds; nor were they all old and frail. Endale Fluoride relentlessly pursued Azeb, asking her, sometimes with tears in his eyes, to attend to his needs as well. She snubbed him with relish. Once she even threatened to report him to the governor if he didn't cease shadowing her. The governor, who had been spending an increasing amount of time at the town hall in Mechara (at his out-of-sight retreat, actually), attending to dignitaries of both sexes—men with wads of banknotes in their hands and women in skimpy dresses—was kind enough to reveal the terms of Endale Fluoride's parole. "One more wrongdoing," he declared, "a strand of hair out of place, and I will send him back to jail to complete his sentence."

Abebe the Bandit reiterated the governor's declaration in simple-to-understand language when he said that Endale Fluoride was not unlike an Easter rooster (slated for slaughter), except that no one had yet mustered the courage to hand him over to the butcher. The butcher, meanwhile, wasn't concerned about either Easter or Endale Fluoride. "When your only grandson has resisted acquiring a human pigment," he mournfully told a gathering of men, including Abebe the Bandit, who had come to consult him about Endale Fluoride's violent ways, "when you don't know whether or not a piece of your flesh may grow up to be a loathed heathen, Endale Fluoride is an irrelevant diversion."

WHETHER IT WAS because of his relentless pursuit, or because she couldn't quite resist his animal attraction, or simply because she wanted to say "Mother Mary," Azeb couldn't remain adamant for long. Almost eight weeks after their first physical encounter, long after she had reaffirmed her vow to her Maker to remain chaste and righteous, moments after she had deposited an offering of a candle at the church door, asking the Almighty's forgiveness for her past sins, she was back at her seducer's side. She didn't meet him at some desolate bush, however, but safely behind the walls of his deserted home.

Azeb was pleasantly surprised to discover that Endale Fluoride had gone out of his way to make the reunion a merry one. Before her was an assortment of ready-made food and a bottle of authentic Greek ouzo. Candlelight flickered from all corners of the room; four candles glowed on the dining table alone, giving the scene that rare touch of romance.

Azeb had never before drunk anything stronger than a homebrew *tella,* and the ouzo went to her head immediately, even though her host had diluted it with water to dull its effects. She felt giddy. She heard something humorous in every word he spoke, found his casual touches irresistibly ticklish. Her uncontrollable giggles would have attracted all sorts of prying eyes and ears to the latched doors and windows had he not been vigilant enough to take her to the bedroom at the rear, far from the street side.

Looking back at the defining moment five months later, Azeb couldn't quite recall taking off the last of her garments that evening. She retained, however, a vivid recollection of her energy waning, of the last drop of resistance melting away from her body when the two of them, finally, became one. She didn't say "Mother Mary," as she had always thought she would when the right man came along. She remembered the words that issued spontaneously from her mouth in powerful spurts: "If—you—stop—now, you—and—I—will—be—Muslim—and—Christian!"

18

UNHOLY COMMUNION

"*I* want to marry him," Azeb told her mother a week after the tempestuous affair had really begun.

"Marry who?" Werknesh demanded.

"Endale."

"Endale *who?*"

"How many Endales do you know?" Azeb snapped back, hands defiantly on her hips, fully prepared for the inevitable tussle.

"Don't be saucy with me, young lady. Answer my question— Endale who?" As the identity of the individual in question finally dawned on her, Werknesh could no longer remain seated. "Oh, no," she cried, setting aside the cloth she was mending and rising to her full height, which no longer exceeded that of her daughter. "Oh, no," she repeated. "Not *that* Endale!"

"Yes, *that* Endale," Azeb said, as though mocking her mother.

"Over my dead body," came the rejoinder.

"If you decide to be unreasonable," Azeb threatened, "I will ask Etiye Hiywet to give me away at the altar."

"Let me tell you something, young lady," said Werknesh, her own hands on her hips, as though mocking her daughter. "I married your father because I was foolish enough to take that woman's advice."

Azeb gave a start. At no time had she thought of her parents' marriage as anything but happy, nor had she ever heard her mother refer to Etiye Hiywet as "that woman."

Werknesh wasn't finished. "Get this. If you so much as whisper your intentions to your father, he will disown you."

Disown was not the word that leapt to the priest's mind when he learned the scandalous news that evening, however. "I will not survive this one," was his initial reaction. He had emerged from one major family crisis only to be presented with a fresh one. "It is a family curse," he told his wife accusingly. "What I don't know for sure is whether it is your side of the family or my own that is the carrier of it."

The priest could never forget how, soon after Beletu ran away, a good number of his parishioners had sought to remove him from power and authority altogether. A man who can't administer a simple family precept, his critics argued, shouldn't be allowed to wield the sceptre over a respectable parish. His own assessment of the situation was apt: "It is the bloody warthog all over again." If later the villagers rallied behind him once more, it was merely because his sinful daughter had paid the ultimate price. After all, in Mechara, as in the rest of the country, death bound the living more than life ever could.

ONE COULDN'T WISH for the death of a delinquent child in order to escape blame and responsibility, however. Few avenues remained open to the besieged father to set things right. He could, for instance, send Azeb to live with Genet while he kept an eye out for an eligible young man. Alternatively, he could address the other side of the equation, inducing the good governor (with the almighty *birr* as a go-between) to revoke Endale's parole. In five years, the time it would take for the convict to complete his full sentence, Azeb would most likely have forgotten about him.

WERKNESH THOUGHT Azeb might heed her friend's advice. "Oona, honey," she said, taking the Harding daughter aside, "I need your help like I never needed it before." And she spilt out her anguish to her.

"Tell me it is not true," Oona cried the moment she saw Azeb, that same afternoon.

"It is true," came the defiant response. "I want to marry him."

"A murderer?"

"I don't care. I love him."

"Azeb, do you hear yourself? Something must have happened to you to talk like this. No woman in her right mind would want to marry Endale Fluoride."

Azeb for once wondered if indeed she was experiencing a lapse of judgment, wanting to marry a man whom no one would speak kindly of. But the longer she thought about him, the more entrenched she became in her convictions: she loved him. True, Endale Fluoride had lost some of his physical charm, she admitted to herself. His girth was expanding and his face showing the scars of alcohol abuse. But he had retained, she concluded, what no other man in her village could boast: that irresistible animal attraction.

As people clamoured to knock some sense into her, long before her beleaguered father could obtain the co-operation of the governor, and while her childhood friend was thinking she could yet devise a means to foul the fated union—Oona later said that she had hoped to bribe Endale Fluoride, whom everyone knew to be hard up, to leave her friend alone—Azeb quietly moved in with her wooer. A week and a half later, when nothing seemed capable of prying her loose from the monster's grip, Etiye Hiywet made a fateful decision: she set out to formalize the union. "I know what it is like to be tried for the unpopular choices one makes," she said, herself once ostracized for marrying a man her neighbours disapproved of, and now forced to take a stand on the same issue. With the sands of her life beginning to run out, she was in need of her neighbours' support more than ever before.

"I can't pretend to see what you see in this man," the godmother revealed with a dismissive gesture towards Endale Fluoride, who sat quietly in the dim corner of the room. "I do respect your decision, though. I will bring a priest from Gelemso to formalize your wedding. I don't want to see you living in sin."

Etiye Hiywet had this conversation with Azeb at the pub, which, in the absence of a legitimate heir to his star-crossed wife, Endale Fluoride had simply taken over. Since the death of its lawful proprietor, the *tej* house had not seen a single paying customer. If Etiye Hiywet detected any parallel between the original owner of the establishment and her own godchild, she gave no indication of it. She cast an appraising eye over the strewn furniture. Running an index finger over the dirt-encrusted table before her, she studied the exposed woodwork as though asking herself if the furniture was beyond all repair. The glass shelf behind the counter was broken, and what few bottles she saw on display were bone dry.

Endale Fluoride followed her wandering gaze from his corner, hoping, he later told Abebe the Bandit, that she would revive the business, if only for her godchild's sake. Etiye Hiywet, however, had only one thing to say to Azeb as she prepared to take her leave. "You do realize what all this means to me, don't you?"

"Yes," said Azeb in an ashamed whisper. "Dad will not forgive you."

"That is the least of my worries," the godmother replied, feigning a chuckle. "What worries me most is that in a village where I buried my umbilical cord, I may not find anyone who will inter my remains. Equally horrifying, I may end up at the riverbank, right next to Etiye Tsehai." She dabbed her tear-filled eyes with the end of her *netela* before reaching for her cane.

"I DON'T WANT YOU to set foot in this house again," Werknesh told Etiye Hiywet the day she learned that the old woman had secretly arranged her daughter's wedding. "For as long as I live, I will not forgive you."

Although Werknesh's outburst was not unexpected, Etiye Hiywet was hurt by her anger and attempted to reason with her.

"If it is any consolation, you should know that I don't approve of Azeb's choice of husband either. But as you know, I was once shunned under similar circumstances, and have since vowed to God that, as long as I live, no woman will be treated the way I was for marrying a man of her heart."

"That is no consolation at all," Werknesh retorted.

Aba Yitades was no more forgiving. "You and I are Muslim and Christian," he said. "I will see to it that you are not buried at the church cemetery."

Even her own soul-father was baffled by her conduct. "You might have consulted me before rushing into action," he mournfully told her. "Even the patriarch won't be able to mend your mistake now."

What was most surprising to Etiye Hiywet, however, was that Oona, the most liberal-minded of them all, should join the fray. "What has gotten into you?" Oona demanded, glowing red, running her fingers through her flaming mane. "If Azeb has gone stark raving mad, wanting to destroy herself, how could you, a sane and balanced person, hand her the rope to hang herself with?" Oona concluded by saying, "I will not set foot in your house again."

If there was one person among the five thousand inhabitants of the village who wasn't wagging an accusatory finger at the old woman, it was Abebe the Bandit. His own daughter had come of age and he was in the market for an eligible man (his own words). "No one will laugh at my daughter now, even if she settles for a tanner," he gleefully declared, "and I have Etiye Hiywet to thank for it."

Now seen by all as a doomed father, a man whose past seemed to have an unshakable hold on him, Aba Yitades publicly disowned Azeb as a small step towards restoring his good name and reputation. As well, he excommunicated Endale Fluoride. As in the days following the flight of Beletu, he forbade his remaining family members, his wife and grandsons, to mention his defiant daughter by name. Azeb received this piece of news with an uncommon detachment. "A drenched person," she said, "is not afraid of a light shower." She had cast her lot with the village monster, and she knew it.

And her lot, Endale Fluoride, was a man of discriminating taste. He discriminated against a badly behaved wife—a nagging, opinionated, አመለኛ, self-assured spouse who wouldn't do as she was told. He frowned upon chastity (when it involved himself, of course), humility, self-reliance, gainful employment, and a host of other virtues that the ordinary person takes as the Lord's own Word. And he was proud of his unique character. "I am a monk-in-reverse," he liked to quip.

"What is that supposed to mean?" demanded Abebe the Bandit, having heard this phrase once too often.

"What characterizes a monk?"

"You tell me."

"Okay, here is your answer: poverty, chastity, and humility. I am against all three, so I am a monk-in-reverse."

And nothing could be more taxing to the pocketbook than the tastes of a monk-in-reverse, as Azeb would soon discover. In addition to his preferred Marlboro cigarettes and authentic Greek ouzo, both of which were imported, there was the small matter of his diet to consider, which precluded fasting entirely. Her father used to say, "No better equalizer exists than a ritual fast," the logic being that with everyone forced to dine on cabbage and potatoes during fast days (or to skip meals altogether, as was the case in *Gahad*), the rich were reduced to the status of the poor.

POOR WAS NOT how Azeb characterized her marriage, though. Thanks to her doting godmother, her financial woes were removed long before they made their presence felt. Etiye Hiywet didn't revive the pub business as Endale Fluoride had hoped, but she gave the newlyweds a generous wedding present, money that would tide them over and permit them a carefree beginning. For a while at least, Azeb did not need to worry about the grocery bills or how to pay for her husband's small indulgences.

With nowhere to go and no one to visit, Azeb divided her days between exploring the switch inside her that might someday enable her to cry "Mother Mary" and making herself presentable to her husband. Fearful of running into her disquieting past, she seldom ventured outside in daylight hours. Running errands became a chore that she dreaded more than the plague. Endale Fluoride, for a change, understood her plight and hired village boys to do the everyday shopping when he himself was unable to do it.

However, if Azeb thought the passage of time would mend the rejection she had suffered following her unpopular marriage, she badly miscalculated. A month later, the mere sight of her still triggered an unseemly commotion. She would always remember the Wednesday she went to the butcher's shop to make an urgent purchase. Since many of the patrons were from outside the village, she had hoped her presence wouldn't attract undue attention and that she could slip in and out unrecognized. But it was not to be. All of a sudden, men and women, some of whom she had known all her life, began hurling insults at her.

"What is it like to share a bed with a murderer?" one of them spat.

"Is he so good in bed that you bartered your family for him?"

"Your mother made a mistake when you were born," a visiting woman observed. "She threw away the baby and kept the placenta."

Unable to leave because the mob had blocked the only exit, Azeb began to sweat. She felt disoriented. She would most certainly have passed out on the crowded floor had the butcher not plucked her from the room and shoved her through the back exit.

"For your own safety," he said before heading back inside, "I think it is best if you don't come here anymore."

Sick to her stomach, Azeb took to her bed.

TWO WEEKS LATER, Azeb was able to galvanize herself into venturing out once more, though not before she thoroughly scrutinized the road and the open-air market from the safety of her doorway, making sure that none of her family members or friends were in sight. As an extra precaution, she had wrapped her face with the end of her *netela*. Walking past the bus terminal, however, she heard a familiar voice. Her old friend had been lying in wait for her.

"How are you, Azeb?" Oona asked, her imploring eyes probing Azeb's own.

"Fine," came the unconvincing response.

"You've been avoiding me," Oona accused her.

"No, I haven't."

"Then how come we never meet?"

"I've been busy."

"Azeb, I've missed you, did you know that? We've all missed you."

Azeb felt blood gushing towards her face. Her eyes moistened. Why is she torturing me? she asked herself.

"Azeb, don't you ever think of me?" Oona pressed.

Azeb remained quiet. If she so much as opened her mouth to tell her friend how badly she had missed her, she knew she would burst into tears. She averted her eyes lest she betray her emotions.

"My birthday is fast approaching," Oona continued.

"Congratulations!"

"It is next Saturday. Would you like to come?"

"I don't know."

"What is there not to know? You've never missed my birthday!"

Another minute of this, Azeb said to herself, and I will go mad. Why won't she leave me alone? Why won't they all leave me alone? she quietly ruminated. Her wandering gaze latched onto the ground below and refused to let go, as if she hoped, against monumental odds, that the mute earth might part in two, as in some ancient drama, and suck her down to a distant safety.

"Azeb, you never missed my birthday," Oona repeated.

"I know. But I don't think I can make it this time."

Engulfed in their small talk, the two hadn't heard Endale's footsteps.

"Is there a problem?" he demanded. Although he addressed his wife, he expected an answer from her nosy friend. His eyes remained riveted on Oona. "I want you to leave my wife alone," he finally told her, "or else ..." He half expected her to finish his sentence, "Or else you'll kill me too?" But Oona had the presence of mind not to provoke him when the brunt of his anger would be borne by her hapless friend. "I saw the Devil's eyes," she later remarked, recalling the encounter.

"You come with me," said Endale Fluoride to his wife, leading her out of the marketplace by the hand as though she had suddenly turned blind.

"I have yet to do the shopping," Azeb said as a face-saving gesture.

"It can wait."

What couldn't wait was for Endale Fluoride to mend the damage that his wife's meddling friend had done. That afternoon, for the first time since her marriage almost six weeks before, Azeb saw the side of her man she had only known by reputation. Barely had the two of them stepped indoors and the door closed behind them than he began to unbuckle his belt.

As he stood over her, flexing the raw leather, Azeb instinctively sought protection. She turned sideways, hoping to find Etiye Hiywet with a billet of wood on her back, ready to intercede on her behalf. She even expected Endale Fluoride to say, "What does Hebrews chapter 12, verse 8 tell us about child discipline?" And she remembered the answer: It tells us, "If you are not disciplined, then you are an illegitimate child ... No discipline seems pleasant at the time, but painful. Later on, however, it produces a harvest of righteousness and peace for those who have been trained by it."

Amen.

"WHO DID THIS to you?" Etiye Hiywet demanded a day later, alarmed by the sight of bruise lines criss-crossing her godchild's arms, and a ghastly wound that marred her tender cheek—the latter the result of a stray belt buckle. Etiye Hiywet turned to Endale Fluoride when her godchild refused to answer. "Did you do this to her?"

"She did it to herself," he replied, contempt dripping from his face.

"How?"

"She wouldn't stay away from that friend of hers."

"I want you to hear me, and hear well, because I won't repeat what I have to say," Etiye Hiywet began. Suddenly she appeared to have regained her long-lost youth and agility, and to have grown a full metre in height. "If you as much as lay a finger on her again, or chase a fly from her face—or if you step on her mute shadow and she feels slighted—I will have you sent back to jail!"

No one had ever spoken to Endale Fluoride so violently and walked away, but he knew enough not to make an enemy of her. Although scorned by many of her neighbours for marrying off her favourite godchild to the village monster, and generally derided, the old matriarch still wielded considerable power and influence in the community. Not one person doubted that she could twist around her little finger both the police chief and the good governor, all two hundred kilograms of them, though such an impressive feat was known to be beyond all human capacity. Whereas many a villager needed to apply for an audience with the governor a week or two in advance, proponents of the "little finger" theory held that Etiye Hiywet could walk into the town hall unannounced and command his attention. Having Endale Fluoride thrown back in jail on a charge of violating the conditions of his parole would not be difficult for her; the hard part would be reconciling with her godchild after the fact.

ETIYE HIYWET summoned Azeb to her home for a little heart-to-heart. "Azeb," she said the moment they assumed their seats, "you do realize that if I blessed your wedding without so much as voicing my reservations about your choice of husband, it was simply because of the love that I have for you, and the promise that I made myself long ago that no woman should be subjected to scoff and ridicule merely because of the man she chose to marry."

"Yes," Azeb replied meekly.

"You realize, too, that I wouldn't normally meddle in your family affairs, had I not made the fateful decision of marrying you off to begin with. After all, I am only your godmother, not your soul-father."

"Yes."

"Azeb," said Etiye Hiywet, her godchild's hands firmly in her grasp and looking her intently in the eye, "Azeb, if you have second thoughts about your marriage, it is not too late to right the wrong."

"I don't understand." Azeb was clearly lost.

"Well, you are not married to him by Eucharist, so if you decide to leave him, this is probably the right time to do so. I am certain, now more than ever, that Endale is not a man who will abandon his abusive ways."

Azeb was agitated. "This is the first time he has laid a hand on me, and I have myself to blame for it, because he warned me many times to stay away from Oona."

"Honey, you are in the thick of it now, you can't tell abuse when you see it," Etiye Hiywet stressed. "Remember, he has already sent one woman to an early grave. And she wasn't such a bad person."

"But he said he didn't kill her, and I believe him." Azeb wasn't being quite forthright. Not only had she been confirmed in her suspicion that Endale Fluoride was responsible for his former wife's demise—when in his cups, he made reference to how she succumbed in his grip—but she had begun to worry that her own end might not be that far off. But she had to maintain face. She had to give the impression, even before her godmother, that marrying him hadn't been a mistake—contrary to what she told herself in private. "He said he didn't touch her," she repeated, as though to convince herself.

"Now that is silly. You don't really think she killed herself. Or do you?" Etiye Hiywet heaved a deep, helpless sigh before adding, "In any case, I didn't bring you here to make you feel depressed. I only want to tell you that should you decide to leave him, you can always come back here. If you choose not to live in this village, feeling shame, I will buy you a small house in Gelemso. You can always go to school. Did you know that there is a good typing school in Gelemso, where you can learn some skills?" the old woman added with a faint smile. "Gelemso is a big town now. There is an insatiable demand for secretaries."

IF ETIYE HIYWET HAD SOWN a seed of discord, or nurtured a seedling that had just sprouted, it didn't become apparent for a while. Azeb went back to her old routine, tending to her daily chores and looking after her man, who had become increasingly morose since his encounter with the godmother. A week later he came back from a brief visit to Gelemso with a .38-calibre revolver and a box of ammunition. "If that old witch thinks she can send me back to jail and live another day," he told Azeb after downing half a bottle of ouzo, "if she thinks that I am a sheep she can herd at will, she is totally wrong."

With his revolver next to his ouzo bottle and his legs up on the round table, Endale Fluoride became a fixture in the living room. What little social contact he had ended shortly after his clash with Etiye Hiywet became public. Even the Arab merchant, who remained impartial regarding village politics as long as his business wasn't affected by the outcome, wouldn't take the unnecessary risk of befriending Endale the Outcast. "I will sell you what you want," he told Endale Fluoride, "but I don't want you to hang around my store anymore. I have a family here, and I have to think of their welfare, of what someone might do to them as a payback for befriending you."

Abebe the Bandit knew when a man was down on his knees. Whereas a weak and cowardly person might have exacted a measure of revenge on his old adversary at such a vulnerable moment, he chose to lend a helping hand.

"Take my hand," he said to Endale Fluoride, finding him lying drunk by the roadside late one afternoon. "Take my advice too, it's free. The best way of getting over the social hurdle facing you is by embarking on a long and invigorating hiatus. And there is no better place to get that fresh start than in a virgin jungle, particularly with a .38-calibre revolver in hand. Trust me, life on the run is not half as bad as you think."

"I have not been thinking of life on the run," Endale Fluoride murmured in a drunken haze.

"That's what I have been saying all along," Abebe the Bandit cried, vindicated by Endale's rare admission of heedlessness. "If you *had* been thinking, you would have packed a small bag and headed for the jungle a long time ago. I would have done so myself had it not been for my children and the welfare of the community." Abebe the Bandit was almost in tears at the thought of the carefree life he had denied himself by staying home and looking after not only his own family (his eleventh child was on the way) but also the assets of the Coffee Board, the Office of Skins and Hides, and St. Paul's School. (His mandate with St. Paul's School had increased when he undertook to guard the clock at the gate from unidentified stone-throwers for an extra two *birr* a month.)

THE BRIEF SPAT between the godmother and the village monster transcended the bounds of verbal dispute: it hit Endale Fluoride in the pocketbook.

"It seems as though the old witch is not about to share her loot with us," became a refrain that punctuated his daily accusations.

"What do I have to show for marrying you, but an extra mouth to feed?" he asked Azeb one dreary evening when he was exceptionally drunk. "I could have gotten the wedding present the old witch gave us had I married the daughter of Abebe the Bandit or the tanner."

Azeb sat quietly in the dim corner of the living room, shifting uneasily when he called her godmother names, careful not to say a word that would provoke him into yet another assault.

"Because of you," he continued, "I've lost what few friends I had. I have been shunned even by the Arab merchant, denied service at the butcher's shop. I have been told not to set foot at the church, although I don't really care about that, and my membership of the village *eder* was revoked. Whenever I walk past your ancestors' compound, I now have to look over my shoulder lest one of them ..."

And so it became his habit, following a drunken binge, to indulge in a drawn-out nitpicking in which he reiterated all that had gone wrong with his ill-fated marriage—some of it real, most of it imagined—and recounted the sacrifices he had made on behalf of his ungrateful young wife, while Azeb kept her silence. When he finally stopped talking some four months later, Endale Fluoride had earned another dubious distinction, for having delivered the longest monologue in recorded history.

19

CROSSING A CHASM

*A*lmost three months after a similar reunion had unleashed on her the wrath of her husband, when she was beginning to feel comfortable in her self-imposed exile, Azeb once again stood facing Oona.

The moment that precipitated their awkward encounter had occurred two weeks before, when the wedding present Etiye Hiywet had given the couple finally ran out and she refused to advance them any more money. "Tell him to get off his lazy butt and find a job," Etiye Hiywet angrily told Azeb. "Or don't tell him. I am sure he will do so on his own once he learns the true meaning of hunger. As for you, my house will remain open—you won't starve." But Endale Fluoride had yet to rise above his disdain for gainful employment. So it fell to Azeb to earn their living.

No longer having the luxury of lingering at the doorway to look for signs of her friend and her family members, Azeb now left her bed and home early with her meagre merchandise piled on top of her head to stake out her lot in the open-air market, before the surrounding farmers and merchants took up the most strategic spots. Spread out before her were used claywares—a coffee kettle, a *tella* jug, and two cauldrons; but also an iron frying pan, glassware, framed pictures of saints, eight empty ouzo bottles, and a small stool with one of its four legs missing. Among her less conventional merchandise were Endale's departed wife's shoes and clothes—items that one would normally have given away to the church poor on the third-day commemoration. "She doesn't need them anymore," Endale Fluoride had callously remarked before packing them away.

The drizzle that had begun early in the morning soon turned into a tropical downpour, forcing every living soul in sight to seek shelter in nearby buildings. Huddling under the eaves of shops and teahouses that girdled the open-air market were men and women as well as the four-legged market habitués—street goats, sheep, and dogs. Only Azeb remained anchored in her stall, choosing a useless umbrella over human company.

From their doorways, shopkeepers regarded the lone figure of the priest's daughter with mixed feelings of pity and disdain. "Look where she ended up," she suspected them of saying, not unjustifiably. As the rainfall began to gather momentum and a thunderclap rumbled in the distance, a teenaged boy came running towards her, dragging behind him a large plastic sheet.

"Go inside the store until the rain lets up," he said. "I'll cover your merchandise for you."

Not knowing whether her husband would approve of her seeking shelter in someone else's doorway, she took a quick glance towards home. Endale Fluoride remained rooted where she had left him hours before, on the dry veranda of the defunct pub, smoking his imported cigarettes, but because of the heavy rainfall Azeb could make out only his distorted silhouette. As she sat undecided, the boy made up her mind for her. "Come with me," he said, dragging her by the hand.

The grocery shop had just opened for business. Besides the aging proprietors, a couple Azeb had known all her life, and their teenaged grandson—the boy who had come to her aid—there was only one other soul inside, a skinny five-year-old boy who stood clutching a paper cone of purchased sugar. Like the goats and sheep under the eaves, he was eagerly waiting for the rains to abate so that he could be on his way. Azeb had once been in his unenviable shoes. Before dispatching her on an errand, Werknesh would pretend to spit on the ground. "*Tif.* Do you see that spit?" Which of course Azeb couldn't. "I want you to come back before it evaporates. No more playing hopscotches on the way, you hear?" Memory of this everyday routine compounded the nostalgic effect of the early morning rain, and Azeb grew tearful.

The lady of the house awakened Azeb from her reverie. "Would you care for a cup of coffee?"

"Yes, thank you."

"How about a snack?"

"Yes, thank you."

Much to the shock of her hosts, Azeb scooped up a fistful of the roasted legumes and began munching with pathetic haste. (Ordinarily one only nibbled, and with a detached look that said, "If I gobble up your snack, it isn't for lack of food at home.") Azeb couldn't afford the luxury of pretense, however. Her last decent meal—a pastry she had secretly purchased from the teahouse and ate hiding behind a bush, lest her husband accuse her of squandering his drinking money—had been two days ago. The elderly couple heard her unspoken plea. The lady shuffled out of sight and moments later emerged with a plate of *injera* drenched in a spicy sauce.

"Here, honey," she said, "have something decent. I don't suppose you had time to prepare breakfast."

Before the day had mellowed, Azeb's silent cry of help reached the ears of her godmother, who came rushing to her aid. "If I refused to give you any more money," said Etiye Hiywet, taking Azeb aside for another heart-to-heart chat, "if I said, 'Let him get off his butt and find a job,' I didn't mean for you to go hungry. Frankly, I didn't quite believe it when you said the wedding money I gave you was already exhausted. After all, two thousand *birr* isn't a paltry sum. In any case," said Etiye Hiywet, rubbing a stain mark off Azeb's cheek with the end of her *netela* after dabbing it on her tongue, "in any case, my home and kitchen will remain open for you. Or if you choose not to come, for fear of village gossip, I will make arrangements for you to dine at the teahouse. Only one thing: I don't want that scumbag you call a husband to live off my money." Etiye Hiywet pressed a roll of banknotes into Azeb's hand, saying, "This should tide you over for a while. Make sure he doesn't see it."

See it Endale Fluoride did, however, the very next day, after word reached him of the godmother's secret visit. "I knew the old witch wouldn't leave you high and dry once she discovered you were hawking our cast-off wares for a living," he began his monologue that evening. Two newly purchased bottles of imported ouzo sat before him, one of them half consumed. A carton of Marlboro cigarettes, extra boxes of safety matches, a bottle of soda water, and candy wrappers littered the round table.

And so, two weeks later, Azeb was back at her trading post. That was the day she encountered Oona and relived her disquieting past. It was also the day that would bring about the inevitable rupture in her ill-fated marriage, and her ultimate downfall.

THE DAY ITSELF had begun not unlike the earlier one, with a light shower that soon turned into a downpour. And business was dismal. Azeb was packing her shabby merchandise to leave when she was interrupted by two familiar faces—Mrs. Vivian Harding and her shadow, Oona. Once past the midday mark, the Hardings' usual shopping hour, Azeb had been lulled into a belief that she wouldn't run into either of them.

"I have always wanted to be a merchant," announced Mrs. Harding, radiating her usual smile, which that day seemed somewhat forced. "You look good, sweetheart," she continued. "Oona darling, don't you think Azeb looks good?"

Oona didn't share her mother's enthusiasm and kept mournfully quiet.

"We have use for another coffee pot at home, don't we?" Mrs. Harding prattled on. "And here is what we need most," she said, picking up the broken stool. "Who wouldn't have use for a stool with one leg missing?" She chuckled at her own banter.

Azeb, like Oona, maintained a tortured silence.

Mrs. Harding finally got down to business, much to Azeb's relief. "How much for the stool, honey?"

"Three *birr*, I guess," Azeb answered in a barely audible whisper.

"That is too low, sweetheart. More like five *birr*, it seems to me. How about for the coffee pot?"

"One *birr*, I think."

"Now, that is a throwaway price. A good pot such as this would fetch twice that amount. I'll give you two *birr* for the pot and five for the stool." Mrs. Harding weighed her next words carefully before letting them drop. "How is he treating you?"

"Okay."

"He doesn't beat you or anything, does he?"

"No."

"Azeb," said Mrs. Harding, drawing a deep breath, "you should go out from time to time, you know."

"Yes."

"Oona will be leaving for America in a week. Did you know that?"

"No." Quite involuntarily Azeb looked up, and for the first time her eyes met Oona's. She would later say that in place of her childhood friend, she found an adult she didn't recognize.

"We will be giving a farewell party for her," Mrs. Harding revealed. "Would you like to come?"

"I don't know."

"You should try, sweetheart. You two are like sisters, you know." Azeb began to weep uncontrollably. "Now, now," said Mrs. Harding, suddenly deflated, "I didn't mean to make you feel sad, sweetheart, I was only trying to—"

"Is there a problem?" barked Endale Fluoride, who had been watching the goings-on from his porch. "Stop harassing my wife," he said, glowering at the Harding women. "This is my last warning! Or else …" Shifting his jacket to the side, he revealed the polished stock of his revolver.

"You refused to listen," he said to Azeb the moment the two of them were behind closed doors. Removing his revolver, he tossed it on the dining-room table. He hung his jacket on the back of a chair, rolled up his shirt sleeves, stubbed out his half-smoked cigarette between his fingers, and put it back in its box, before pulling out his belt. Whether in disbelief that he would resort to violence so soon after Etiye Hiywet's threat or because she thought he would have second thoughts, Azeb remained where she stood, by the door, her small merchandise at her feet, until he landed a shattering blow on her head.

She let out a savage cry, doubling up on the concrete floor with her head between her arms, making herself small. Although the belt continued to lash at her like a thunderstorm, her lack of physical reaction infuriated Endale Fluoride. In his twisted state, her stifled moaning sounded like mockery. He resorted to kicking her with his boot, until a well-aimed slug in the side of her rib cage finally rendered her unconscious.

For the next four days, Endale Fluoride kept a vigil over his wife as she lay sick in bed, moaning and grunting. Her bruised face ballooned like a ripe melon, and her eyes swelled shut. She spat dollops of blood. Whether it was dawning on him that he might end up with another dead woman on his hands, or whether he sensed that word of his excesses might reach her feisty godmother and that he would, in either case, be sent back to jail, he became remorseful.

But that didn't last. "Ask that witch of a godmother to advance you some money to revive the pub," he said a week later, jokingly, with a half-empty bottle of ouzo by his side.

"No, I won't."

"In that case, tell me where she stashes her money so I can go get it myself," he offered. "An old fart like her wouldn't trust the bank entirely. I am sure she has a safe somewhere inside the house or buried in her backyard, where she stashes the bulk of her loot. Find the location for me."

"No, I won't."

"Do it for her sake."

"What does she get out of it?"

"Her life."

"How is that?"

"Do you see the etching on this shell?" he said, pulling a bullet out of the six-shooter on the table. "It has your godmother's initial on it. The day I decide to go out with a bang, I will have two for company. You'll never guess who the third one is."

"You are drunk."

"I may be, but I am still in full control of my faculties. I can shoot straight as an arrow—see?" he said, spinning the chamber of his revolver and taking aim at her. "Pow!"

Not for the first time since she had married him, Azeb found herself assessing her own mental status. What did I see in this man? she wondered. He is physically repulsive, morally crippled. His face is bloated, his paunch is hanging. A murderous thug, he is not even remotely manly. Look at him, urinating right inside the house like a bratty little boy!

As though reading her mind, Endale Fluoride turned towards her, and while buttoning up his fly he said, "Yeah, I know you get a kick out of watching me piss." He peered into the chamber pot, turning it from side to side as if he were wondering if he had left more than waste fluid. The accumulated urine threatened to spill onto the floor. "This pot hasn't been washed since God knows when," he observed. "Toss out the contents and bring me back the scrubbed metal."

"Do it yourself," Azeb told him.

"Excuse me?"

"You heard me."

"You little brat. So, you are itching for a little spanking, are you?"

Azeb finally spoke the unspeakable. "You touch me again and I will have you sent back to jail."

That seemed to sober him up. He remained motionless with the chamber pot in his grasp. An awkward silence settled over the room. Slowly he bent down and deposited the pot on the floor. Reaching for his glass of ouzo, he drained its contents with one giant gulp.

"So, you think you can have me sent back to jail and live to see another day?" he demanded.

Azeb maintained her silence, sensing that she had pushed him far enough.

"I asked you a question," he shouted, whipping up a temper. "I think it's time you learned some manners." He unbuckled his belt. Azeb struggled to her feet and attempted to get out of his reach by putting the table between them. As he tried to lift the table and toss it out of his way, the handgun slid off and fell within reach of Azeb's hand.

Azeb realized the predicament she was in when Endale adjusted his grip on the belt so that instead of holding the metal buckle, as he had done in the past, he now held the belt from the other end. With the strip of leather coiled around his hand and the metal gleaming at the swinging tip, he began chasing her.

"I won't be done with you until I see what is under that pampered skin of yours," he promised.

"Get away from me. Get away from me!" She now stood with her back pressed against the hard wall, the handgun firmly in both hands.

"Well," said Endale Fluoride, pausing for a moment, "if you must shoot, at least you should know a thing or two about a gun. First, cock the hammer. You see, your finger is not even on the trigger."

Azeb did as she was told. He had just begun to take another step, the belt raised high above his head, when the gun discharged. The weapon itself flew one way, Azeb the other. Endale Fluoride fell on the floor.

Azeb darted out of the room and into the dark backyard. Hiding behind a shrub, she waited for him to get up, dust off the smoke and spilled urine, and come looking for her. An hour passed. A second hour pealed. Dogs barked. Wild beasts announced their claim to the night.

Azeb headed back to the house. Through the crack in the door, she searched for signs of movement. If she thought Endale Fluoride was playing another one of his tricks, lying where she had left him earlier, there was nothing playful about the pool of blood next to him.

Thus commenced a new chapter of her life.

BOOK VI

Revelation of the Neck-Cord

20

THE LAMB AT THE ALTAR

*A*s she was brought to the district courthouse in handcuffs, past a motley crowd of hushed strangers, Azeb wondered, for what may have been the hundredth time since her arrest the week before, when her problems had really begun, and she concluded it was the day she ate a roasted sheep's testicle despite the grim warnings of her family.

She dredged up other childhood misdeeds as well. She recalled, for instance, how, following her first attempt at baking *injera,* Werknesh tried to rein her in by force-feeding her the ruined bread mixed with ash and water, and how, when Azeb tried to avoid blame and accountability by taking refuge behind her godmother's accommodating skirt, Aba Yitades stepped in with all the might and fury of an early summer storm. Hebrews chapter 12, verses 8 to 12 had come to assume a special place in Azeb's heart following the incident.

With startling clarity, seemingly innocuous episodes came back to haunt her. She shuddered at the thought of how, not long after the *injera* incident, she had violated one of her father's most rigid tenets, slipping unseen inside the church Bethlehem to satisfy her curiosity. "No matter what you do," Aba Yitades had told his negligent daughter the first day he brought her along as his personal attendant, "no matter how itchy your legs feel, do not set foot inside the Bethlehem. If no one else sees you, remember, Saint George will, and he will come after you with the same wrath and resolve as he did after the serpent that had browbeaten Etiye Brutawit." Years too late, Saint George finally had, Azeb told herself.

When she recalled the last six months of her life with the man who had become instrumental in her downfall, Azeb asked herself, "How did I tolerate his excesses for so long? How did I fail to see what so many others saw, the telltale signs of my doomed marriage? How come I ..." What Azeb also failed to see was the possibility that her court trial would turn into a circus, drawing voyeurs from as far away as Europe.

ALREADY ON THE DAY of her arraignment, a sizable home crowd awaited her at the approach to the courthouse, thanks to the Hardings, who had gone from door to door picking up those who wished to come along: Werknesh, who reluctantly donned her *netela;* an aging *dabtara* whom Azeb had once nursed back to health; two cousins from the old colony, her father's loathed relations; and Genet's best man, who by virtue of the Oath of a Mizae had become her surrogate brother, making him duty bound (now that Genet was home bound for health reasons) to be by Azeb's side in her darkest hour.

Etiye Hiywet and her soul-father had arrived long before, prepared to call the Memorial Hotel home at least until the arraignment was concluded. Aba Yitades, true to his word that he had washed his hands of his scandalous daughter, stayed behind.

THE PRESIDING JUDGE was unique among that most singular of breeds—district judges—in that he had no formal training. But that only made him one of the people. He was a self-proclaimed reformist, a revolutionary of sorts. And that was the problem, not only according to Etiye Hiywet, who had a lot at stake in Azeb's trial, but also to many respectable members of the community.

As the son of a humble weaver and the fifth of seven children, the judge had been destined to eke out a living at a menial job.

His steely resolve and will to rise above his lowly beginnings became apparent at the tender age of ten, when he enrolled in the public school following the Emperor's initiative, which gave preferential treatment to children of ethnic minorities. And he excelled in his studies.

By the feudal standards of the day, sixth grade was considered a dizzying height of formal schooling, so as soon as he earned his certificate, the young man set out to find his calling. Entrepreneurial as few others were, he scraped together his meagre savings and purchased a folding chair and a collapsible writing desk, which could be carried home after a busy day. A fountain pen, an ink blotter, and a box of bond paper rounded out his office supplies. The office itself was an open-air corner in the court precincts, which in Gelemso, as in much of the country, brimmed with letter- and affidavit-writers.

Before long, his flair for the written language, his genius at summarizing in a few words what would have taken many paragraphs to explain in full, earned him fame and recognition, bringing him clients in droves. The nature of everyday lawsuits seldom changed, the young clerk quickly discovered. There were, for instance, abused housewives, divorcees with overdue alimony, slighted public officials, jilted mistresses, rent-increase disputes, and the occasional land-related argument.

To expedite his clerical work, the young man began composing his letters at home, at night and on weekends, so that each morning he brought with him a stack of half-finished documents, which he methodically arranged on his tiny desk, each under a prominent heading. *Alimony,* read one; *Renegade Borrower,* declared another. The moment the young clerk spied a badly dressed woman heading towards him with her young brood in tow, he would quickly pull out a half-completed form from the pile under *Alimony* and begin to fill in the blank spaces, seldom pausing to ask her for more than the bare minimum of details. The pre-drafted document read:

The Honourable Judge ___,
The Family Court of Gelemso,
The Year of Our Lord 19__,

   Your Excellency: My name is ___. I am daughter of ___
and ___, both good Christians and landowners. I am a poor
woman, Your Honour. My personal asset had been my
looks, which I no longer possess, as my lawfully wedded
husband had slowly but cruelly chipped it away over the
___ years we have been together. I have ___ children whom
I am raising to be God-fearing, elder-respecting, and law-
abiding. My children are old enough to eat, but not old
enough to work.
   I am pleading with you, My Lord, in the name of Saint
___, the *Tabot* of your birth and baptism, to rule in my
favour and grant me ___.
   Wishing you God's blessing and guidance,
      humbly yours,
         [Thumbprint here.]

A swarthy man with a bulging neckline and bouncy midsection who arrived in the company of a scrawny attendant was
treated with no less enthusiasm and efficiency by the adroit clerk,
who looked up from his busy writing only to inquire the amount
of money he was owed and the particulars of the irresponsible
borrower.

   No matter how well one performed as a letter-writer, however,
there was only so much room for career advancement. And no
one appreciated the limitations of the position more than the
enterprising young man himself, who soon began casting his eyes
on the biggest prize of all: the district magistracy. In the absence
of formal training for the bench, he undertook his education by
attending daily court sessions and committing to memory the
most significant rulings.

"I wanted to be a magistrate," he ruminated years later, at Azeb's arraignment, encouraged by a roomful of rapt listeners, among whom—most significantly to him—were the white faces he seldom saw in life. "I worked hard for this bench not because of the fame and recognition it would bring to me, but because I wanted to see justice done." And the judge had seen many injustices handed down from the very bench that he eventually inherited. Most troubling to him was the bias shown against the outcast ethnic group condescendingly labelled Americans. Himself a member of another minority, ethnic prejudice easily got under his skin.

The judge was, in fact, from the largest ethnic group in the country, which composed no less than thirty percent of the total head count. The Emperor's kinsmen, those who had hailed from the northern and central highlands, were the actual minority, numbering barely fifteen percent of the population. But since they ruled the vast country with an iron fist, systematically imposing their language, culture, values, and prejudices on the conquered multitude, the judge aptly deduced, the Emperor's kinsmen had become a visible *majority*, despite their disadvantage in numbers. By the same token, the judge's ethnic group had achieved the exact opposite.

"I tolerate no prejudice," he reiterated. "I am particularly appalled by the mountains of injustice visited on the American ethnic group each year."

Some of the judge's best friends were believed to be Americans.

"Some of my best friends are *not* Americans," the judge laid to rest the long-held rumour. "A few of the individuals I deal with on a day-to-day basis, however, *are*. I have an American laundress and an American gardener. My barber, to whom I lift up my chin in full confidence, is also an American." The judge stroked his clean-shaven chin as he made this pronouncement, as though to show how he had survived his barber's exacting razor without nicks or bruises and, most importantly, with his head firmly on his shoulders.

"As long as I am on this bench," continued the judge, "as long as I am alive and kicking, I will tolerate no derision against these hard-working people." Many in the audience appeared uneasy. A few of the men coughed loudly, as if in protest. The judge carried on, unfazed. "Of course, I tolerate no Americans on the witness stand, because people who willingly consume a roadside kill can't tell right from wrong, and I would be damned if I were to take their word to convict or acquit anyone.

"As always," the judge went on, laying out the ground rules for witness candidates, "well-diggers and loggers are exempted from testifying, because if one is reckless enough to engage in a life-threatening line of work, as these people willingly do, then one can't be taken seriously in matters involving other people's lives." One out of every three well-diggers was buried alive when a wall caved in; loggers were often found under the massive trunks of the trees they felled.

"As I said before," the judge's words flowed on, "there is not a single bone in my body that could remotely be construed as bigoted and intolerant." The audience shuffled a tad more. Some smiled contentedly. "In matters of the court, however," he ploughed ahead, paying no heed to the charged undercurrent, "when a life is in the balance, I am pragmatic. So, I don't allow on the witness stand convicted murderers, thieves, arsonists, or for that matter anyone who has spent more than a week in jail. Sorcerers, spell-casters, and other such shadowy characters better not set foot in my court unless they want to be shipped directly to jail."

He paused a moment, gathering his thoughts. A paternal smile teased his wizened face, winning him instant friends. "I see the defendant has some foreign friends here," he said, pointing at the Hardings, who were seated at the rear of the courtroom, trying desperately to be inconspicuous. Benches creaked as heads turned to view the white family. "The community knows all too well how kind they are," the judge graciously noted. "Their charitable works should put us good Christians to shame. However, I must say to the Hardings, ladies and gentleman, that none of you may bear witness either, because anyone with a suspect faith cannot possibly be sworn in."

The Hardings blushed.

BACK IN HER JAIL CELL, the lineup of potential witnesses seemed to Azeb nothing more than the memory of a distant luxury. She had a more pressing need.

"I am hungry," she had told her stick-wielding guard the day after she was brought in in handcuffs. "What time do they serve dinner?"

"What do you think this is, a hotel?"

"No, but I have to eat all the same."

"Everyone has to eat. What makes you so special?"

She attempted to reason with him. "Well, I am a prisoner. So one would think I would be served at least a meal a day. It is now past six p.m., almost thirty-six hours since they brought me here."

"Young lady, do you know what would happen if we were to cater to everyone they brought here in handcuffs?"

Azeb tried to imagine what would happen if they were to cater to everyone they brought in in handcuffs, but she couldn't come up with an answer.

"I will give you the answer," he droned. "This place would crawl with people! That's what would happen."

"I don't get it."

"What is there not to get?"

"I can't think of anyone wanting to be imprisoned for food."

"But I can." And the guard did know many people who wouldn't mind being in jail if it meant a steady supply of meals until the rains returned. In fact, his personal story was instructive. He had left his ancient village in the northern highlands to escape a recurring famine—not, as some townspeople thought, to reunite with his long-lost cousin, the governor, who secured him the job.

"Moving to this town is not half as bad as going to jail," Azeb challenged him.

"On the contrary, there is nothing worse than leaving your birthplace, a land that you are permanently bound to by your buried umbilical cord. Prison is a picnic."

"Still, I don't know who would want to be in jail for food."

"Do you know how many of the fifteen thousand men and women who call this town home go to bed hungry?" the guard asked.

"No, I don't."

"Well, I will tell you how many of them go to bed hungry: thousands. They may not admit it, because of a misplaced conceit, but half the townspeople are famished. If we were to serve food to everyone they brought here in handcuffs, half of the town would call this place home. Why shouldn't they? They get free protection thrown in. Detention is the least of their worries—they have nowhere to go."

"Surely you are not suggesting that you bring people here and starve them to death?"

"Now don't put words in my mouth." He was suddenly on the defensive. "All I am trying to say is that in order to be eligible for a steady meal, one must have committed a truly heinous crime. The harsher the crime, the merrier the treatment."

"What is more heinous than murder?"

"So, you are now bragging about your crime?"

"I didn't say that! What I was trying to—" Azeb stopped in mid-sentence. This is truly insane, she said to herself. Realizing that she wasn't getting anywhere with him, she decided to apply for an audience with the police chief. After all, her godmother could still twist the chief around her little finger, despite the extra twenty kilograms of bulk he had picked up.

"What I have been trying to tell you," the guard carried on, somewhat deflated, "is that you are in a police station, a tempo-rary detention centre, with no facility to cater to someone who stays more than twenty-four hours. As long as one is in this dungeon, the prisoner's family supplies not only the daily meal but also the mattress, pillow, and blanket. You are here only because they have no place for women at the penitentiary. Once they have found you a spot at the big house, you will qualify for two meals a day, a blanket, and a mattress. Congratulations, you have hit the jackpot."

And so the guard concluded his drawn-out banter by handing Azeb twenty-five cents of his own money to purchase a loaf of bread and a cup of tea. The next morning his charitable wife brought her a small basket of hearty home cooking.

The same afternoon, Etiye Hiywet came to visit her with Fatima, the manager. Azeb told them what the guard had said.

"He meant it as a joke," the godmother reassured her. "Even the church poor wouldn't look to prison for food and shelter. In any case, you no longer have to worry about the basic necessities. Fatima here will see to it that you get your meals on time and that your laundry is done for you. Anything else you wish, she will get it for you, as long as it is something money can buy. Just ask."

The day Etiye Hiywet left town, following the arraignment, Fatima made herself scarce. But Azeb never lacked visitors. Many of those who came to say hello were total strangers, voyeurs whom she seldom saw twice, but there were also some whose hearts and daily thoughts she eventually won. Old friendships were renewed, as well—with Oona, the day she came for a visit, and shortly afterwards with the woman who had been the teenaged prostitute Azeb had befriended during her brief stay at the Memorial Hotel.

"More than one friendship was revived," Oona told a journalist she met later, speaking of her own experience. "Etiye Hiywet and I were back on speaking terms. With the rest of Azeb's family reluctant to visit her, the two of us had to work out a plan so that each week at least one of us would be in Gelemso."

Oona recalled the conversation she had with Werknesh the day she offered her a ride to Gelemso and got no for an answer once more. "I think you and Etiye Hiywet are doing her a disservice by visiting her so often," Werknesh had said. "What Azeb needs now is solitude, so that she can make amends with her Maker, say her prayers, and show true contrition for all the wrongs she has done. With time on her hands, she might give some thought to the Commandments she has so grossly violated, as well."

Mrs. Vivian Harding was no less critical of her daughter's commitment. When Oona announced her plan to postpone her departure to America and to college, she said to her, "There is nothing you can do for her by staying here. Don't squander your scholarship. Go to school. I am sure Azeb would understand."

"There is nothing you can do for me by staying here. Don't squander your scholarship. Go to school. I understand," Azeb told Oona the next time she came to visit.

"You are such a parrot!" Oona replied, laughing. "You didn't change even one of Mom's words."

"I can think for myself." Azeb made an attempt to sound credible.

"If you can think for yourself," Oona challenged, "then tell me, what made you marry that man? Don't say you fell in love with him, because I won't accept that."

"It so happens that I have been asking myself the very same question," Azeb admitted.

"And?"

"I don't know the answer."

"That's silly. Endale was a man we both liked to hate. Something magical must have happened for you to want to marry him all of a sudden."

"Do you recall the Epiphany festival that you and I attended together the first time? It is so long ago, but I still remember it as though it were only yesterday. Endale brought those two girls to the bush. You and I followed him ..." Azeb stammered.

"Goodness!" screamed Oona.

"I had this recurring vision of him."

"Good Lord!" Oona was clearly agitated. "I am so sorry, Azeb. I was the one who insisted that we watch to the end of it. I am very, very sorry."

"All I was trying to say is—"

"Let us not talk about it anymore," Oona concluded, turning beet red.

Azeb never got to tell her how badly she had wanted to say, "Mother Mary."

TWO MONTHS AFTER Azeb's incarceration, long after Oona had become a common sight at the police station, she was suddenly denied access to the prisoner.

"What did I do?" Oona demanded, baffled.

"Not you. It is your friend," came the cryptic response from the guard on duty, a corporal of advancing years.

"What did she do?"

"Your friend now thinks she is a revolutionary as well."

"I am a revolutionary," Azeb confirmed to Oona when the two got together, following an appeal to the police chief.

"Are you out of your mind?"

"No, but this revolution thing is growing on me."

"You must have gone truly insane."

"Why don't you give me some credit?" Azeb protested, suddenly fired-up. "I am finally doing something positive, something that will ultimately benefit not just you and me, but the downtrodden masses of the world."

THE REVOLUTION Azeb spoke of with such passion and conviction was the student uprising, which, initiated at the university in the nation's capital, was gradually spreading to public schools throughout the country, including the high school in Gelemso. In less than a decade, the student unrest would mature into a popular rebellion, removing from power the "two-thousand-year-old" monarchy, as it was officially known, and ushering in a military junta that would prove to be one of the most violent regimes the volatile continent had ever seen.

Rallying the country's youth was the plight of the serfs and peasants who formed the economic backbone of the agrarian system, yet who were denied equal rights before the law. Students marched bearing placards that read, *Land to the Tiller* and *Down with the Monarch*. The demonstrators were not members of the downtrodden masses, since the country's peasants and serfs could hardly afford to send their children to high school; the rioters were members of the elite class, which they had vowed to destroy.

The government's response to the unrest had been predictable: the students were rounded up and thrown in jail for a day or so. Azeb met some of them during one such roundup. No fewer than twenty crowded her small cell.

"What brought you here?" a dashing teenaged girl had asked Azeb.

"I killed my husband."

"Wow!"

As the students peered deeper into Azeb's background, unearthing more of her story, they discovered that she was nothing less than a living symbol of the uprising—a walking, talking, gun-toting, husband-killing, and not all that bad-looking figurehead. Socialist literature wasn't readily available at the time, and few of the young people had a clear grasp of the ideology, but the consensus was that any future paperback would have Azeb's story in the opening chapter. For the time being they were willing to settle for an extra placard. *Free Azeb* soon became a stirring motto at each demonstration.

"They will probably hurt your case," Oona told Azeb.

"I don't see how."

"Well, you know how much the establishment resents their cause."

"That doesn't surprise me."

"You also know that if the authorities haven't come down hard on the rioters, it is only because many of the kids come from powerful families."

"I know that much."

"So, it seems logical to me that if the authorities can't vent their anger on their own children, they will probably do so on you. Remember, the judge is a big landowner."

The judge made his resentment felt, Oona believed, when on the day of the trial he further shortened the list of eligible witnesses. "Anyone who was seen or heard advocating the overthrow of the Emperor is barred from the witness stand," he declared with an unseemly display of bile, "because if one can't honour the living symbol of God the Almighty, then one can't possibly have any regard for truth and integrity. Disqualified also is anyone who was found defacing the likeness of His Highness, or—"

"Who is left?" cried Etiye Hiywet, standing up.

"Be quiet, and remain seated. As I said, disqualified also are pamphleteers, freethinkers, flag-burners, window-breakers, and, for that matter, anyone who had planned to commit such a seditious act. And anyone who is in the process of planning, dreamed of planning, planned of planning—"

"P-l-e-a-s-e-! Your Honour."

"Lady, I am warning you for the last time, don't test my patience." He took a sip from his glass of water before picking up where he had left off. "As I was saying, anyone who was even vaguely tempted to plan a seditious act, but chickened out at the eleventh hour, is barred from this courtroom altogether."

"Madman," mumbled Etiye Hiywet.

"Madmen and mad women, alcoholics and—"

Etiye Hiywet could stand it no more. "I beg you, My Lord, in the name of Saint Michel, the *Tabot* of your baptism, to—"

"Lady," said the judge, truly worked up, "you have either gotten up on the wrong side of your bed, or you love your godchild so much that you wish to join her in jail. God knows, if you interrupt me again, I will instruct the bailiff here to haul you away."

"All the money I spent on his cronies has been for nothing," Etiye Hiywet protested under her breath. "A lowly son of a weaver!"

The judge was indeed a lowly son of a weaver, who was ill-suited for the bench he had sworn to serve. If he had a shred of integrity, his critics argued, the judge would have done what a less qualified man would do in his shoes, and collected all the kick-backs that had blown his way, then pored over the case before him, weighing the evidence with care (using both metric and imperial scales of justice, if need be); evaluated the trustworthi-ness of parading witnesses; and in the end ruled in favour of whoever had doled out the largest sum of money. Why, even a bumbling idiot knew that evildoers were to be found only among the poor and dispossessed; that when the well-heeled found themselves in an occasional jam and justice was in the balance, the deciding factor should *not* be a simple matter of whodunit, but class background. And nothing gauged class background more accurately than good old *birr*.

The judge's lack of integrity perplexed many, most notably Abebe the Bandit, who seldom concerned himself with the law unless it came knocking on his door. "Who does he think he is?" was his initial reaction, the day he found out that Etiye Hiywet was unable to buy the judge's favour. "Bribery is as old as the motherland, as sacred as the Holy *Tabot* and the Bible," he angrily declared. "Or is the judge a subversive, attempting to conduct a revolution from the bench?"

With the judge refusing to be bribed, Etiye Hiywet set out to buy everyone who was remotely thought to have any influence over him. She paid a thousand *birr* each to his soul-father, his two cousins, the godmother of his only daughter, and the police chief. She doubled the governor's cut, although she knew that, as an appointee of the Department of Justice, the judge was no more answerable to him than the manager of the Electric Light and Power Authority had been.

"I can guarantee only an early parole for your godchild," was the governor's promise to Etiye Hiywet when he collected his sum.

"I want a promise of her acquittal," Etiye Hiywet insisted.

"In that case, I suggest you pray, and pray hard," he advised.

Etiye Hiywet was still praying when, on the eve of the ruling, she was visited by a clear premonition of doom: the town of Gelemso was engulfed in yet another power outage. (Rumour had it that the manager of the Electric Light and Power Authority had found a fly in his soup.) The next day, as the godmother quietly chanted her rosaries in the teeming courtroom, the justice reached a verdict: guilty of manslaughter.

"Son of a weaver!" Etiye Hiywet screamed.

21

PETITIONS OF A KIND

"You should now think of going to college," Mrs. Vivian Harding told her grieving daughter. "By staying here and lamenting, you will only become another casualty. There is nothing more you can do for her, so please, pack up and go. I am sure Azeb would want you to look after yourself."

"These people are warriors," said Mr. Robert Harding, reinforcing his wife's argument. "They have an acute sense of fairness. They don't kick someone who has already fallen on the ground. Take, for instance, Endale's own sentence: I can't think of many countries that would have released him a mere five years after killing his wife. The judge was undoubtedly harsher on your friend, handing her down ten years, but I am sure she stands as good a chance of being paroled after serving only half the sentence."

"She won't spend another day in jail," was Oona's response to both. "Not as long as I live." She could not imagine that she had just committed herself to a crusade that would cost her almost two years of her life, a great deal of heartache and frustration, as well as all the money she had saved since she began piggy-banking at the age of four; and that, when she finally achieved a measure of success, after criss-crossing the country many times over and petitioning every conceivable authority figure, her relationship with her own parents would be strained beyond its elastic limit.

If her parents vied to dissuade Oona from taking on Azeb's cause, Etiye Hiywet was giddy at the prospect of finding someone who would stand shoulder to shoulder with her through the arduous appeal process. "Werknesh won't have any more to do with her daughter," the godmother began, the day Oona went to apprise her of her decision to stay and fight by her side. "I can't understand how a mother could be so cruel to her own flesh and blood," the matriarch continued. "Genet, as you know, hasn't fully recovered from the birth of her last child. I don't know if she ever will. She has lost control of her bladder, so she avoids public places altogether. Aba Yitades has long written off his troubled daughter. So, you see, Azeb has no one but us two."

"That is two *plus* the One Above," Oona corrected her playfully.

"But of course. How can I forget Him?" Etiye Hiywet took the reminder to heart. Looking up at the rumbling skies, she crossed herself, mumbling a rosary. "Do you know what frightens me most?" she then asked.

"No, I truly don't."

"What frightens me most is that I may not live long enough to see the appeal through. Every day now I see those from the Other Side, you know. Only yesterday, Beletu was here with me in flesh and blood. She didn't leave until the rooster crowed at dawn."

Oona was clearly uneasy. "Beletu is in her final home, Etiye Hiywet," she intoned, "playing with little angels, so let us not talk about her."

"I see *them* too, you know."

"See who?"

"My husband and sons. Last night they were all here taking—"

"Etiye Hiywet, please! They are all dead, as we both know. Nothing can be gained by brooding over them. Worse yet, we will be distracted from the problem at hand," said Oona, sounding more mature than she felt at only eighteen. "We must now focus on Azeb, Etiye Hiywet," she stressed. "She is the one who needs our undivided attention."

Oona was struck by how quickly this once-vigorous matriarch had aged. Her eyes were droopy; her hair was completely white and was thinning at the crown; her wiry limbs trembled uncontrollably; and she was unsteady on her feet, even with a cane in hand. Oona secretly hoped that the godmother wouldn't become senile now, when she so badly needed her help.

"Promise me, Etiye Hiywet," she said, pressing a tad harder on those wiry hands, "promise me that you will stop worrying about the ones who are no longer with the living."

The whisper was laboured. "I will try."

WHAT ETIYE HIYWET HAD CONCOCTED without much effort was an appeal strategy that, at least in her muddled thinking, was dependably foolproof.

"Only the Emperor can pardon a convicted murderer," she accurately explained to Oona, "and the appeal process begins by bribing the *Afe Negus*—"

"What is *Afe Negus*?"

"Literally translated, it means 'Mouth of the Emperor.' *Afe Negus* is the man who gathers the written petitions, sorts out the ones with merit, and presents them to the Emperor. He is a gatekeeper of sorts."

"So why the bribe?"

"Well, honey, the *Afe Negus* needs convincing before he will open a file on the case. Strength of the claim alone is not enough. I would say five hundred *birr* will do the trick. Another five hundred, or perhaps a thousand more, may be required to bump the case ahead in the line. One must remember his subordinates, too. I would say another two hundred *birr* for the *Wambar* and an additional two hundred, or maybe three hundred, *birr* for—"

"What is the *Wambar*?"

EXHAUSTIVELY PRIMED on the details of the appeal process, and laden with wads of banknotes, Oona left the godmother's presence secure in the knowledge that victory was in sight. In the days that followed, she bought herself a brand new traditional dress—a *netela* with a matching skirt, both made of the finest weave and with the most elaborate trimmings. And she plaited herself a totemic neck-cord—her first ever. The godmother attempted to talk her out of wearing the neck-cord, but Oona was adamant. On the eve of her departure, Oona had her hair braided, with cowry shells fastened to the end of each plait, and she borrowed Etiye Hiywet's anklet, "to add that last bit of authenticity," in her own words.

Transport was one issue that Oona never thought she'd need to worry about, but when she asked her father if he would drive her to Addis Ababa, his response was scornful: "All five hundred kilometres and back?"

"It is the least you could do," she snapped back.

"Young lady," he said, leaning back in his reclining chair and massaging his well-trimmed beard to facilitate his thoughts, "young lady, you are now old enough to assume responsibility for the choices you make. You have decided, against our advice, to pursue this incomprehensible course, even at the price of your scholarship. But that is your problem. Our problem is the mission. It is the reason we are here. As I have told you many times before, no matter how at home we feel here, there are things we don't dare do, one of which is involving ourselves in domestic politics. Do you know what became of those foreigners who poked their noses where they didn't belong? I can think of no fewer than half a dozen of them, mostly our fellow citizens, who were given twenty-four hours' notice to leave the country. It may happen to us too, unless you abandon this insane idea of yours. Do it if only for the sake of the mission," he pleaded, adding, "I'm asking you for the last time."

"I can't see how one could remotely construe a court appeal to be political," Oona angrily replied.

"That's because you don't know what these people consider political."

"That is a racist remark," she blurted.

"Take that back!" Mr. Harding almost shot out of his seat. "I want you to take that back! How dare you accuse me of bigotry after all the hardships I have endured on behalf of these poor people, the sacrifices I made to bring them the Word. Do you know where I would be today if I had stayed home and pursued my own interest? I live with my family broken in two, my son living a thousand miles from here, only because I placed their welfare ahead of mine."

Oona shrank back in her seat, realizing she had crossed a line. If her father truly expected her to apologize, however, he was disappointed.

"Honey," Mrs. Harding chimed in at long last, "what your father said about what they consider to be meddling is right. I seem to recall that shortly after we moved here, a prominent Arab merchant in Gelemso was ordered to leave the country merely because he proposed to build a private bridge over a main road that the Emperor might someday have used."

The Arab merchant Mrs. Vivian Harding referred to had applied for a permit to link his two shops, which were on opposite sides of the main road, by an elevated walkway, when the vigilant governor asked, "How do you propose that the Emperor travel along the road?" And the heedless storeowner replied, "Like everyone else, of course—under the bridge." Found guilty of belittling the Emperor, he was ordered deported. He disposed of his merchandise at a fire sale, removed his three kids from school and the only homeland they had known, and headed for Yemen, his native soil, which he had left as a teenager.

OONA WASN'T MOVED by her parents' arguments, pleas, or threats. Two days after the memorable tussle with her father, she packed up a suitcase and put Etiye Hiywet's bills into a money belt, instead of the converted vacuum bottle that Etiye Hiywet had proposed as a safe way of transporting money over a long distance. "Even the most practised pickpocket would mistake the bottle for a brew of coffee or tea," she had said. Oona then slipped into a pair of jeans and a white T-shirt, and left home without much fanfare.

Monday was inordinately slow in Mechara, and when Oona finally arrived at the bus terminal, she found more lethargic beasts than fellow passengers. The inside of the parked bus buzzed with persistent flies; the heat was stifling. After languishing inside the reeking vehicle for two long hours, with no clear indication that it would move any time that day, she finally summoned enough courage to consult the driver. The young man sat in the shade of a tree not far away, playing a game of dominoes with an idle villager. He appeared to be in no hurry to go to anyplace.

"Excuse me," Oona interrupted him, "but what time does the bus leave?"

"What do you mean, 'time'? When it is full, of course," he snarled, angry that anyone should distract him from his game with such a stupid question.

"But of course!" she readily concurred.

With time on her hands, Oona found herself assessing her surroundings. Whether it was because she was looking for ways to vent her momentary frustration, or because she was suddenly steeped in that rare insight of one on the verge of leaving a place behind, she was critical of what she saw.

A dirt trail snaked before her, dividing the sleepy village in two. A week after the spring rains, the dark clay soil had already become desiccated, resembling the checkered back of a giant crocodile. In places the fissures yawned ominously. "It's a wonder," Oona said to herself, "that no child or animal has got trapped in the holes and broken its leg. How come no one ever thought of covering the trail with a bed of gravel?"

Without its Wednesday crowd, the open-air market at the end of the trail appeared to her dreadfully alien. More than a market-place, it was the *Meskel* Square, where all major festivals, including Christmas and the Feast of the Finding of the Cross, were celebrated. "Why don't they pave it with cut stones?" she thought. "Surely it doesn't take all that much effort to ferry some limestone from those mountains over there." The sight of the mountains themselves brought a flurry of questions into her mind. Had they always been so closely cropped? Did the soil used to be so gullied with erosion? Was the heat so stifling, and the people so ragged? Had she imagined it all, or did this place once look like the Garden of Eden?

The place had, indeed, resembled the Garden of Eden as recently as nine years ago, when her family first came to visit. Lush vegetation blanketed the landscape, including the mountain peaks. A lumbering mass of clouds shrouded the village for much of the season, and when the skies eventually cleared, the sun was mild. Oona and her family wore woollen knits in those days, like many of the villagers, and they seldom went to bed without lighting the tinder in the fireplace. True, few of the locals would have made the cut in a fashion magazine, but they weren't as ragged as they were now, either. No one, not even the church poor, had gone hungry until, following the deforestation, the rains ceased to be dependable. All it took to strip the picturesque village down to its bare bones in less than a generation was the ancient practice of slash-and-burn agriculture, coupled with the recently introduced mechanized logging.

THE BUS STARTED ROLLING. Watching the world whiz by from the comfort of a family vehicle was, Oona quickly discovered, not the same thing as experiencing it up close. Once removed from her familiar surroundings, she became what she had always dreaded being, the centre of attention; it was her early childhood all over again. But, unlike the pre-teenaged girl who had wailed her way out of the marketplace, she now knew how to deal with the locals. For, as boys and girls, these people had been raised under the strictest moral code: to respect their elders; to lend a helping hand to a stranger; to speak only when spoken to, and, when they did so, to refrain from looking the other person in the eye, as it was most disrespectful.

Except when dealing with your equals, they had been taught, take your hands out of your pockets and stand with your head slightly bowed, as a sign of deference. Extend both hands when greeting an authority figure, and tuck your hands behind you immediately after. Don't show the underside of your feet even to an outcast, they were all warned, as it is a most offensive gesture; display humility even in your crowning moments.

They would have been severely chastised if they failed to jump to their feet at the sight of an elder walking by (within reach of a cane, as a rule of thumb), or if they neglected to bow to the level of their knees when accepting a gift. In any case, don't rush to accept largesse, they were told time and again. Say no twice (but not more, otherwise you will kick yourself for passing up a freebie). Pretend you couldn't resist the arm-twisting.

And no matter what you do, they were all warned, never, that is *never*, gawk at someone, no matter how alien the individual appears.

But their ethical precepts lacked elasticity, their reach limited to their own kind. Oona managed to increase the scope of their moral grasp by demonstrating to them that, though she might appear different, she wasn't all that alien. Each time she turned around to address them in their own tongue, they were all reminded of their old good manners, and sullenly looked away.

OONA WOULD LATER RECALL her debut as a lobbyist with a sense of disbelief. A day after arriving in Addis Ababa, she called on her embassy. Donning a traditional outfit in a town where the young and trendy strove to leave their "antiquated" past behind, she drew more than curious glances. Her attire was most offensive to the native receptionist, who herself looked as though she had marched out of the glossy pages of a European fashion magazine. Her "Can I help you?" was more an affront than an offer of service.

"አምባሳደሩን ላናግራቸው እፈልጋለሁ።" Oona replied. The receptionist raised an eyebrow, as if saying, "Are you sure you want to speak Amharic?" A moment of uneasy silence elapsed before Oona was forced to rephrase her query. "አማረኛ አትናገሪም?"

"Of course I speak Amharic," came the angry answer.

"Well, in that case please connect me with the ambassador," Oona repeated.

"I will see what I can do."

Oona took offence at what the receptionist said into the mouthpiece of the telephone: "There is a character here who wants to see the ambassador."

"I do speak English, you know," Oona reminded her.

"I see."

Soon every male in the building, except the ambassador himself, was in the lobby, studying the red-haired girl, who might have marched out of some storybook. When her attempt to reach the ambassador fell on deaf ears, she settled for an audience with the cultural attaché, a sympathetic young man who solemnly told her what she had already heard, that her case was political.

"Who said anything about politics?" Oona demanded.

"The judicial practice of any country is an internal affair, which, as diplomats, we steer clear of," he explained. It was a response that Oona would hear many more times in the coming days, as she lobbied family friends at other embassies. Ten days after she left home, having exhausted her preferred options, she headed for the Emperor's palace.

LIKE PALACES the world over, the Emperor's citadel was guarded by a small army of dedicated men who seemed to have been chosen as much for their chiselled good looks as for their imposing physiques. The morning Oona stopped by, two such men watched over the front gate, one on each side, dressed alike in

khaki uniforms so stiffly starched that they appeared to be made
of a malleable alloy. The brass buttons on their jackets shimmered
in the morning sunlight, and their hands were enclosed within
white gloves. Even the wooden stocks of their vintage M1 rifles
were exceptionally well polished, Oona noticed, and the bayonets
at the tips shone menacingly.

At the sight of an official-looking black Mercedes sedan
approaching the exit from within the grounds, the guards came to
a drilled attention. Clicking the heels of their polished boots in
perfect unison, they raised their rifles chest high, slapping the
stocks twice on the ascent, before lowering them again. The cast
iron gates retreated sideways, making room for the limousine to
emerge. Although she had seen the ritual before, Oona was
mesmerized by the guards' performance. Long after the vehicle
had disappeared out of sight, she was still gawking, when a high-
ranking officer, who had been regarding her from a distance,
came to ask what she wanted.

"I want to see the *Afe Negus*," she told him.

"You do, eh? Well, you missed him by a few short moments,"
he said, assessing her from the cowry shells at the end of her
braids to the pendant on her ankle. "You missed him by one
hundred years, to be exact." Indeed, the *Afe Negus* position had
not been filled for a considerable time.

"How about the *Wambar*?" she followed up, with diminished
hope.

"How come you speak such flawless Amharic?" it was his turn
to ask. "Are you a spy or something?"

"Something," she replied angrily.

"I shot my last bolt," she muttered to herself, remembering her
American heritage on the way back to her hotel.

OONA CONCEIVED her most effective move during a forlorn
moment at the restaurant in her hotel, while watching a flickering
black-and-white picture on the only TV set in the building.

"I knew from past experience that the station had limited resources to fill up its nightly time slot," she later told a rapt home audience in Vermont. "They couldn't afford to purchase the serial rights to foreign films, and locally produced programs barely existed."

The mass media—whether TV, radio, or newspapers—were all owned and operated by the government. Competition for the limited headlines was intense. At the time of Oona's visit, for instance, a seasonal war was raging in a fringe province between nomadic herdsmen jostling for a diminishing pasture. The student rebellion was unrelenting. And a coastal region was being visited by a devastating drought. More embarrassingly for the Emperor, perhaps, a breakaway province was finally receiving international attention. The undeclared war had already cost an untold number of lives.

Newspaper editors sifted through the avalanche of reports behind closed doors, and with a keen eye on the public interest, they chose the ones that merited headlines. A GALE RAVAGED JAPAN, bellowed the daily edition in Oona's hand. The storm had left in its wake upturned fishing boats and wrecked coastal farms, the article expounded, depriving an estimated two hundred families of their source of income.

RESCUE ACCOMPLISHED, cried another front-page piece. A team of dedicated firefighters in America had rescued a puppy trapped in an abandoned water well, the solemn article unveiled. Pictures of the poodle in the hands of its valiant rescuer, a giant of a man in overalls and a crash helmet, adorned the article. A large portion of the front page was, as usual, reserved for His Highness, his daily activities, and the homage he routinely received from visiting dignitaries.

"My heart sank after leafing through the papers," Oona remembered years later. "My worst fears materialized. I knew then that no one would care to write, much less hear, about a young woman who had killed her husband." But Oona wasn't easily deterred. She headed for the television station.

Like most men and women of position, the manager of the
TV station had received his training in America, the language
and culture of which he had wholeheartedly embraced. His
English had that rarefied American inflection, and his wardrobe
was unmistakably Western. In Oona he found someone who
truly understood him, better yet a spectacle his nightly viewers
wouldn't be able to resist watching. At a time when foreigners
were a noteworthy sight even in the nation's capital, a white
woman speaking impeccable Amharic was a true draw. And so he
welcomed her with open arms, ready to put her on the show.

"How do you like life in this country?" was the opening
question Oona faced that first evening. Conscious that the show
was broadcast live, the young man didn't ask questions the
answers to which he didn't already know.

"I love it here so much that after I finish school, I intend to
move back here for good," she replied.

"Surely you aren't implying that you prefer this country to
mighty America?"

"I certainly do."

"What do you like most here?"

"Everything."

"Can you be more specific?"

"The people are mild-mannered and welcoming," Oona
rejoined, shifting slightly in her seat as she adjusted the *netela*
around her shoulders. "Mechara, the village where I live, is
everyone's image of the Garden of Eden. And the pace of life is
agreeably slow."

"I understand that your family faced a difficult time when it was
revealed that you were missionaries," he read from his cue card.

"I was too young to remember. But if there were any problems,
they must have been mere hiccups, because they exist no more."

Oona made her strongest impression on the viewing audience
that evening when she corrected her host's language. As was the

practice among educated people of the time, the young man pretended to have misplaced his Amharic, and said "progress," in English. Oona readily fetched for him the word he had been looking for, እድገት. "Exquisite," he said a moment later, and she once again handed him the Amharic equivalent, ያማረ; "fashionable": ዘመናዊ.

The next day's newspaper bore Oona's traditionally attired image against a prominent heading that read, AN AMERICAN WE ALL MUST EMULATE. The article was a scathing reproof of the trend of mixing foreign words with their three-thousand-year-old language; a language that, among other things, the Almighty in heaven had seen fit to employ as a medium of communication in His sacred domain. The newspaper, like the national TV and radio, found in Oona the perfect middle ground to the daily news, one that comfortably straddled the gap between the puppy rescued by a team of dedicated firefighters and the gale that had ravaged Japan.

And so, in addition to TV appearances, she was sought by radio and newspaper journalists. Oona delivered her views on issues ranging from childbirth and baptism to death and commemoration.

"Have you taken a crack at traditional cooking?" asked the television host on her second appearance.

Oona replied, by way of sharing her experiences, that baking *injera* could be simplified a great deal. "The use of *absit,* for instance, could be eliminated altogether," she said, "because preboiling a portion of the batter won't achieve what an extra day of fermentation couldn't."

Her host couldn't conceal his surprise. "How did you come to see what so many others haven't?"

"I suppose I have retained an outsider's nosiness," was her memorable reply.

OONA WOULD SPEND a full week in the painful glare of the media, and the journalists would run out of issues to discuss, before she could finally say what had brought her to town. Not that she had forgotten her friend at any moment. In fact, not a day had gone by that she hadn't attempted to reach Etiye Hiywet in Gelemso by phone and learn of the prisoner's status. In those days most hotel guests didn't have access to a telephone, so Oona had to go to the Telephone and Telegraph Head Office, half an hour's ride from her hotel, to dial Gelemso. Long-distance lines were often out of order, so many of her trips proved fruitless.

Azeb had finally been transferred to the penitentiary, Oona learned a week after her arrival, and was assigned to the prison kitchen detail. The judge had repeatedly refused to refer her case to the high court, the recurring student unrest having stiffened his resolve, Etiye Hiywet told Oona with a discouraged sigh. "Unless today's kids are reined in early," she quoted him as saying, "there is no telling where they will ultimately lead the country."

"The governor's hands were tied, as ever," Etiye Hiywet told Oona during a rare static-free connection. "He was unable to control even the bungling postman." When his paycheque was delayed by a fortnight once too often, the mailman affixed a permanent Closed sign to his office door and dropped out of sight. Those who were expecting a vital delivery had to go look for him at his favourite hangout, a dry goods store run by a man suffering from undiagnosed obsessive-compulsive disorder. "You might say that the mailman now works for the storekeeper," Etiye Hiywet added.

The storekeeper was in the habit of checking and rechecking things he had done, particularly at closing time, when he was known to spend upwards of three hours making sure that the shop door and windows were properly padlocked. On exceptionally difficult evenings, when the merchant's repetitive behaviour became unbearable, the postman intervened, hauling the man home in a straitjacket. Such a heroic deed earned the mailman not only the adulation of the merchant's fretful wife and two daughters, but also a tidy compensation.

"The only dependable person in this crazy town is the manager of the Electric Light and Power Authority," the godmother confessed to Oona. "For two days now he has shut down the power supply entirely, because a handyman he had hired to mend his broken fence bungled the job, and the police chief refused to arrest the inept mason for lack of sufficient evidence.

"Mechara isn't any better, either," Etiye Hiywet continued. "Sure, your parents are fine, and the school is running well even in your absence. It is my own hard luck that is never improving. Aba Yitades attempted to excommunicate me from church, even though my own ancestors helped build the edifice. Unfortunately for him, I have a few good teeth remaining in my mouth— friends who haven't abandoned me yet. Occasionally, I run into Werknesh. She either looks the other way or lifts up her *netela,* so as not to make eye contact.

"The one person who hasn't changed at all is Abebe the Bandit. Only a few days ago he concluded a gentleman's agreement with truck operators. For an undisclosed sum of money, he agreed to keep an eye out for vandals mining the highway with lethal weapons. The week before, two trucks and a loaded bus lost a tire each when they rolled on a spiked peg carefully concealed in a pothole. As you know, the cost of a replacement tire is higher than a teacher's monthly wage. Abebe is now a public safety consultant, in addition to his other job with the Coffee Board."

Almost four weeks after she came to Addis Ababa, Oona had some glad tidings to offer. "A lady lawyer came to talk to me last night after seeing me on TV and reading about the case in the newspaper," she told the godmother, her voice cracking with emotion. "She is optimistic about the appeal. Azeb is now a celebrity of sorts—did you know that, Etiye Hiywet? I myself have begun to receive personal commendations, you know. Only yesterday, a signed postcard awaited me at the reception desk, with the U.S. embassy emblem on it. The news has already reached Europe, I am told. A Dutch journalist is planning to follow up the case in person. She will be interviewing both Azeb and myself—and maybe you too! Isn't that wonderful, Etiye Hiywet?"

The lady lawyer Oona referred to was one of the recent wave of professionals who, after their training in America, came to serve emerging multinational corporations. "My practice is strictly civil litigation," the young lady told Oona before she set her hopes too high, "but I do have an adequate educational background to find my way in criminal cases as well. More importantly, however, I have a friend in Harar who is also willing to volunteer his time. The two of us have already discussed the case over the phone. Like me, he is a graduate of Cornell."

Altogether, over the next eleven months, Oona made nine trips to Addis Ababa and Harar. In that time, she would come to understand the intricacies of the legal system and the true meaning of red tape better than most people do in a lifetime. Initially, she was enraged to see that even a simple typist could delay a case by a fortnight merely to satisfy a perverse lust for power. "Look," Oona imagined the clerk saying, "I may not have a decent change of dress or be able to pay my next grocery bill, but I can make you cool your heels too."

"Oona went into the appeal process as a child," said Mrs. Vivian Harding during an interview with the ubiquitous Dutch journalist, "and she emerged a fully grown person."

"Weren't you concerned about sending your daughter, a mere teenager, so far away from home, to spend a month in a hotel by herself? In your own country, your conduct would be viewed as child neglect," the Dutch journalist observed.

"Listen," said Mrs. Harding, clearly angry, "my husband and I have an entirely different take on child rearing. We don't want our children to grow up in antiseptic settings, protected by us throughout their formative years, so that as adults they will fumble through life." She paused for a moment before adding, in a more conciliatory tone of voice, "Did you know that in this country a five-year-old boy is expected to fend for himself, sent out, for instance, to herd animals in the jungle, where wild beasts rule the roost, armed only with a flimsy twig?"

"As a matter of fact, I do."

"Well then, tell me, what is more dangerous: letting a child find her way through an asphalt jungle, or sending her into true wilderness, where nobody hears her cries for help?"

"I was only making a point."

"Well, the point is, strength of character can't be drilled in, as we have been led to believe. It can be achieved only through trial and error. I might have had some misgivings at the beginning of my daughter's campaign, but I am now proud of her achievements. And I also know that without the leeway her father and I gave her, she wouldn't have been able to do what she did."

No one, not even the critical Dutch journalist, would suggest this was a mother exaggerating her child's achievement.

22

DAY OF ATONEMENT

*H*ad it not been for the high perimeter walls and the uncommon sight of men in uniform wandering through the raucous crowd, some brandishing fearsome sticks, one could have mistaken the scene for another festive event. Visiting men and women alike mingled freely with the prisoners. Children played hide-and-seek, often tripping over lounging inmates. Now and then a guard blew a whistle to announce a visitor, and the ruckus died down by a decibel point or two. "Listen up," one such guard bellowed at the top of his voice the day Oona went for a visit. "A young lady here wants to see Azeb. Azeb, would you come forward, please."

Unlike the detention centre at the police station, Oona never felt at ease among the prison crowd, so she remained bolted to a remote corner of the compound, away from the hustle and bustle, and watched her friend emerge from the shapeless swarm. As the teeming distance between the two of them slowly diminished, she registered the physical change in Azeb. A year and a quarter of incarceration had finally taken its toll. Azeb looked gaunt, and her complexion was ashen. The dark blotches on her cheeks had deepened, and the twinkle in her eyes was visibly dimmer. Long gone was the cheerful "Good to see you." If the two of them hugged and exchanged kisses, it was more out of tradition than a genuine sentiment of joy at another reunion.

Oona had come to dread the visits, as she had only bad news to deliver of late. For weeks now she had been attempting to raise the money necessary to transport Azeb and her two guards to the town of Harar, the provincial capital, where the appellate court was located. "Do you really expect us to foot her holiday bill as well?" was the judge's angry retort when she approached him about travel arrangements. "Rent a car," he barked, "and you better reserve it for the sole purpose of transporting the inmate and her guards. Also, I need to see proof of payment of the guards' per diem before I can release her to their care. I can live with the fact that you went public with the appeal, denouncing my ruling and making me appear a fool and an incompetent before the whole world. I will be damned, however, before I let you stick it to the taxpayers."

Etiye Hiywet hadn't been her old self. Mostly bedridden, she drew comfort more from the company of her long-deceased relations than from the living. True, while still in full possession of her faculties she had assured Oona that she wouldn't be wanting for funds during the appeal process. "Whatever it is you want, ask Fatima here," she had said to her in the presence of the hotel manager. "She will give it to you."

"Fatima threw me out," Oona told the godmother a month before the court date. "She wouldn't even pay the guards' per diem."

"Fatima who?" Etiye Hiywet hazily mused.

"Fatima threw me out," Oona told Azeb after exchanging kisses.

"The witch."

"She told me not to set foot in the hotel again."

"The snake."

"I don't know how we can raise the guards' per diem."

"I do."

"Where from?"

"From the Dutch journalist."

"Whoever said crime doesn't pay hadn't killed a spouse," Abebe the Bandit wistfully noted the day he learned that the Dutch journalist had paid the guards' per diem in exchange for exclusive access to the prisoner. Oona's own assessment of the situation was more sedate. "ሳይደግስ አይጣላም።" she said, borrowing from Aba Yitades—"The Lord doesn't close one door before opening another." She was buoyed further by the good news that the town of Harar was the private backyard of the infamous finance officer, father of Beletu's first love. (His family loved Beletu and were broken-hearted when his son, rejecting all forms of assistance from his father, had, in a rare display of independence, set out to find his calling and plucked her from their midst.) His thrill-seeking daughters expressed their willingness to rally behind Azeb. With their intervention, the defence team soon found a place—the big mansion itself—that it could call home and use as an operations centre for the duration of the trial. In addition, they arranged for Azeb to be placed in a private cell.

The finance officer himself wasn't in a festive mood at the time, because his bid for a permanent seat in parliament—which he had sought in exchange for settling the national debt out of his personal savings—had fallen through and he was reeling from the sting of rejection. The secret negotiations came to a sudden halt, people in the know told Oona and the lady lawyer, after his wife gained a whopping fifty kilograms of weight in the midst of a raging famine, and a rumour quickly surfaced that she was responsible for the current food shortage. Even by the most liberal standards of national politics, such an insensitive person was deemed to be a liability. The finance officer paid for his wife's indulgence, his constituents agreed.

MANY YEARS LATER, in the safety of her Vermont home, Oona fondly recalled the three weeks she had with the finance officer, his scandalously well-fed wife, and two toffee-nosed daughters (the other two were married), but more significantly with the

superior court itself. "Coming from the ramshackle district courthouse in Gelemso," she ruminated before a rapt hometown audience, "stepping inside the superior court felt like walking into a
different world altogether." The sprawling edifice of hand-carved
limestone stood on a tree-lined boulevard. The inside walls were
inlaid, at eye level, with luxurious *ted* wood. The concrete floor
was finished with imported terrazzo tile, so thoroughly polished
that it gleamed under the morning sunlight. Three giant electric
fans wheezed from the five-metre-high ceiling.

Gazing down at the packed courtroom from their padded
chairs were three judges, two male and one female, each dressed
in a black gown. Like the lady lawyer and the state prosecutor, a
stylish young man, they had all received their training in America.
On the wall behind the judges were framed pictures of the
Emperor and his deceased wife, the Queen. "In short," Oona
concluded, "the setting was no different from what one sees in
this country. In a span of a few hundred kilometres, a mere four
hours' drive, I had witnessed the transformation of a decrepit
feudal system into the modern age. The future had arrived."

And accompanying the future were a few inconveniences. For
starters, Azeb was now in iron shackles each time she was brought
to court; her two armed guards seldom strayed far. She was
whisked away in a police van following every session. Gone were
the days when she whiled away her lunch break surrounded by a
comforting crowd. Visiting her in prison was no less of an ordeal,
as it involved passing through an array of manned gates and
filling out extensive forms. The market-like atmosphere that
Oona so vividly recalled from her visits in Gelemso was also
missing in the security-conscious penitentiary.

The highly regimented superior court didn't make allowances
for the exchange of ideas between the presiding judges and
animated members of the audience. Without the staying hand of
Etiye Hiywet, who remained bedridden, the lawyers drivelled
legal gibberish to their hearts' content. Every now and then, when

the case was mired in picky details, when all that was heard coming from the involved parties was "Objection," "Sustained," or "Overruled," Oona imagined the godmother springing to her feet to put in her two cents' worth. "Young man," she pictured the godmother saying, wagging an accusing finger at the state prosecutor, "didn't your mother teach you not to interrupt when a lady is talking?"

Etiye Hiywet would have approved of the absence of restrictions on potential witnesses, however. The first week alone, three individuals came forward who would otherwise have been censored by the highly biased district court. Mr. and Mrs. Harding made depositions on the third day; the housemaid of Endale's first wife, the day after. Etiye Hiywet would have been impressed as well by the expeditious way the witnesses were sworn in. Rather than sending them to church to make their oath before the Holy *Tabot,* as the judge did in Gelemso, the superior court demanded of the individuals only that they place their hand on their choice of Holy Book—the Bible or Koran—and repeat after the bailiff.

MRS. VIVIAN HARDING proved to be a star performer on the witness stand, to her daughter's immense surprise and relief. Sometimes dropping tears, periodically flashing a disarming smile, always steadfast and factual, she was hard for the state prosecutor to discredit. She told the enthralled courtroom how, in the months following her family's move to Mechara, Azeb had readily come to her aid, showing her the basics of village life, the pitfalls and taboos. "I owe it to Azeb that I can now recognize a tampered box of safety matches a mile away," she said in a moment of fleeting light-heartedness, and she went on to demonstrate how the trick worked. The audience were rolling in the aisles, and came to order only after the judge sounded the gavel.

"I learned from Azeb how to cook with firewood," Mrs. Harding continued, "and she showed me how to bake bread from scratch. I wasn't a good cook to begin with, and those early days were most difficult. Despite Azeb's tireless efforts, there were times when nothing seemed to work for me, and I often broke down in tears." She paused to dab her tear-filled eyes.

"'Etiye Vivian,' Azeb chimed the day I tried and failed to extract butter from a jar of milk that I had purchased with her help, 'extracting butter is not so difficult. Everyone does it, and you will too. Here is how it is done.' She wasn't even ten then, and she was telling me, a grown-up and mother of two, to stop lamenting (though not in as many words) and learn from my mistakes."

"Did you give Azeb any incentive to come to your aid?" the lady lawyer asked. "As you know, village kids are easily lured by candies."

"She didn't even drink our water," Mrs. Harding replied.

"How is that?"

"Because of her father. Aba Yitades was fearful that she would be contaminated with pork."

Some in the audience chuckled.

"So, whatever it was she did for you, it was out of the kindness of her heart?" the lady lawyer offered.

"That it was."

"You sound fond of her."

"I am. Had it been up to me," Mrs. Harding felt obliged to expound, "I would have adopted her, no questions asked." She flicked a tender smile at Azeb, who sat stiffly, hands tucked between her thighs.

"Do you think differently now that she is accused of a heinous crime?"

"Not one bit."

The young prosecutor set out to cast a shadow on the witness when he suggested it was Mrs. Harding's influence, her lax American morality, that encouraged Azeb to elope with a man her family disapproved of.

"I was as opposed to the affair as anyone," Mrs. Harding tersely replied.

"Did you tell her in as many words?"

"Yes, I did."

"And she ignored you?"

"That she did," she apologetically added.

The prosecutor concluded, "Do you see any contradiction between what you have been telling us the whole morning, the picture of a docile young woman you have carefully painted, and what you have just admitted to the court? You don't have to answer."

Mrs. Harding answered all the same. "Love does strange things to people."

ENDALE FLUORIDE'S REPUTATION suffered the most damage from the testimony of the housemaid, who had come into the service of his first wife at the age of twelve, when her tubercular mother gave away her six children shortly before her death. The maid had remained faithful to her employer until the day Endale Fluoride snuffed out her life. Now middle-aged and still unattached, she dedicated her days to serving the monks and nuns in a distant monastery. She was plucked out of her tranquil existence on the promise that, by recounting her ex-employer's final days, she would be doing her a final service, which would bring closure to both of them.

Although not yet a member of the religious order, the former maid donned a mozzetta-like cap, as a nun would, and brandished a prayer stick and the customary fly-switch of the trade. Her white habit was hand loomed, and it fell to her ankles. Shuffling into the packed courtroom, she drew curious glances. Before assuming her assigned seat, she bowed to the level of her knees, facing the presiding judges. Turning around, she extended the same level of homage to the hushed audience. When the bailiff approached her with the court bible in hand, she stopped him in his tracks.

"If you don't mind," she said, looking up at the bench, "I have brought my own bible."

Producing a leather-bound copy from under her padded waist-band, she began leafing through the worn pages. The judges exchanged puzzled glances. The audience sank into a deep silence. A dark shadow crossed the face of the young prosecutor, and he shot an accusing glance at the lady lawyer, who seemed to relish the unfolding drama.

The witness finally located verses in the Book of Ecclesiastes that suited the grave moment. "'When you make a vow to God,'" she read tentatively in her peasant drawl, "'do not delay in fulfill-ing it ... It is better not to vow than to make a vow and not fulfill it. Do not let your mouth lead you into sin.'" Her fingers located a folded corner in the pages of Exodus, from which she contin-ued to read with greater conviction. "'Do not help a wicked person by being a malicious witness. Do not follow the crowd in doing wrong. When you give testimony in a lawsuit, do not pervert justice by siding with the crowd, and do not show favouritism to a poor person in his lawsuit.'" She stopped reading and, looking intently at the three judges, recited from memory, "May God himself, the God of peace, sanctify you through and through. May your whole spirit, soul, and body be kept blameless at the coming of our Lord Jesus Christ. Amen."

The silence was powerful. What seemed like generations passed before the chief judge shattered the lingering quietude with his booming "Amen." The lady lawyer swiftly rose to her feet and, facing the audience, crossed herself and repeated after the judge, "Amen." The state prosecutor remained pinned to his seat, dejection written all over his face. The balance of the day turned out to be an endless indictment of the deceased, one that would remain seared into the memory of all those who attended the event.

The maid-turned-nun told the attentive courtroom the memorable story of how Endale Fluoride had ingratiated himself into her mistress's heart and home, and how, in a matter of months, he had metamorphosed from a protector into a raging monster, one who would fly off the handle at the slightest provocation. Her mistress's cries for help could be heard from her grave, and they brought tears to the eyes of many. "One of the reasons I have remained chaste, rejecting marriage and family life entirely, was because of those harrowing nights," the nun said. "I am still fearful of sleeping with my door unlocked—an anomaly when one lives in a convent."

OONA TOO MADE an indelible impression on the court, recounting the sexual assault she experienced at the hands of the deceased at the tender age of ten. In those days few had heard of sexual abuse of a minor, and some in the audience suspected Oona of making up the story to assist her friend. Seeing her cry her eyes out, however, few remained sceptical for long. Her revulsion was palpable.

GIVING VENT to his pent-up frustration, the young prosecutor later told the Dutch journalist that he had never known of a murder victim who had been so reviled. "I couldn't produce even a single person who would put in a word in his favour," he said. Normally at a murder trial, the courtroom swarmed with cousins and nephews of the victim. At such a trying time, many would discover relations they had never known existed. Even in death, Endale Fluoride was distinguishing himself.

When the court adjourned for the New Year holiday after two weeks of hearings, the final verdict was nowhere in sight.

OBSERVED ON SEPTEMBER 11, the Ethiopian New Year coincided with the end of the main rains, when the vast countryside turned into a verdant tapestry. The bare soil would become invisible under a carpet of wheat, barley, maize, sorghum, *teff,* and a host of legumes. Where farmland had been left fallow, wildflowers and meadow grass covered the earth. Welcoming in the New Year was, therefore, more than simply turning the page of a calendar; it was the celebration of a promising future.

In the days immediately preceding the New Year, children harvested wildflowers and cut and trimmed each one. On the morning of September 11, they left home dressed in their new outfits and with the flowers in hand to visit family friends and relations. As they handed out the bouquets, they said: "Thanks be to the Lord who let you cross from the year of John to the year of Matthew [the names changed]."

"Thanks to Him we have both survived for this," came the answer. The recipient then pressed a few pennies into the child's eager hands.

In towns and cities, where wildflowers weren't abundant, the children painted daisies on pages torn from a notebook. Those with means used imported crayons. Many mixed their own ink from the juices of plants.

"I was very creative," the lady lawyer told Oona as the two of them sat outside the gate of their hosts' compound, watching the children march by. "I discovered early on that you could produce all sorts of hues from the primary colours—red, yellow, and blue. Even with my middle-class background, I couldn't afford a complete box of crayons, you know."

Oona and the lady lawyer had got up early to watch and admire the boys and girls giddily swarming the city streets. The lady lawyer handed out pennies to those she guessed to be from the poorest families. She asked them to sing a holiday song or two in return. Oona revelled in the festive atmosphere. The lady lawyer, whether because of the colourful muumuu she wore in place of her usual business suit, or simply because she was steeped in the holiday spirit and was letting her guard down, appeared to Oona exceptionally lively that day.

"I feel s-o-o-o-o-o good," Oona confided to her. "I am s-o-o-o-o happy that I am afraid something terrible may happen any moment."

"You have been spending too much time with Etiye Hiywet," the lady lawyer told her, laughing.

Oona's premonition came to pass two days later, when, during a routine visit to the jail, she found Azeb in a straitjacket. The evening before, a merchant she knew from Gelemso had brought Azeb tidings of her godmother's death. He was surprised that she took the news so hard. "When an old person dies," he attempted to reason with her, "one must not weep as much. In fact, one must dance and sing, because once past the age of seventy (and many suspect your godmother to have been in her nineties), death is not the enemy, but a saviour of sorts."

Etiye Hiywet had passed away the week before, lying calmly in her bed—all by herself, as she had long dreaded. If there was any consolation for Azeb, it was the fact that her godmother didn't end up by the riverbank, as she had sometimes speculated, but next to her loved ones. Her soul-father, himself teetering at the edge of his grave, saw to it that she was accorded the proper pomp and ceremony and received all seven absolutions. "It was all for the better that your father refused to conduct the funeral service," the merchant told Azeb.

THE THREE-DAY MOURNING PERIOD over, Azeb was brought to court yet again, though this time for what might prove to be the defining moment. Present by her side on the historic day were, in addition to the lady lawyer and Oona, the finance officer's daughters, the affable Dutch journalist, a few local newsmen, and Mr. and Mrs. Harding, who had made the long journey for the express purpose of attending the event. Conspicuously absent were, as before, Werknesh, Aba Yitades, and Genet, though the latter merely because she was still suffering from debilitating incontinence.

Dressed in a floral skirt and a matching top, her feet in a pair of imported clogs, the fashion of the time (all donations from the finance officer's considerate daughters), Azeb looked dashing that morning. If there was any remainder of her peasant past, it was the talisman she wore on her neck-cord—a legacy of her godmother. Even the reserved Dutch journalist couldn't help but remark what an eyesore the piece of leather was, how it marred Azeb's new look. "It is supposed to contain a healing writing, which would lose its power if opened," the lady lawyer told the Dutch woman, without much conviction. Oona related the story of the stranger whose bloated corpse surfaced in Mechara, and who was later identified by the scroll in the leather pouch hanging from his neck-cord.

"It could contain other than medicinal inscriptions," the lady lawyer corrected herself. "There are much-publicized cases of adopted children who found details of their heritage—and other surprises—from the contents of their talisman. In the northern highlands, mothers routinely attach such pieces of information to a child. Many a lost child is found this way and brought home to its parents."

"I have to see its contents before I leave for America," Oona once again told Azeb as they all headed for their separate seats. "It is not open for discussion."

ALTHOUGH FEW DOUBTED the trial's favourable outcome, one could have cut the suspense in the courthouse with a knife. Adding to the tense mood were student demonstrators who shouted "Free Azeb!" from behind a police barrier, steps away from the court gates.

Reading from his prepared notes, the chief judge seemed to take pleasure in the limelight he was suddenly thrust into. Much of his rhetoric was of little relevance to the case at hand. He recounted how, in a matter of a few decades, the three-thousand-year-old feudal judicature had been taken over by a progressive system; enumerated the challenges encountered during the historic voyage; and explained how, in the end, many had benefited from the heroic transformation.

"It is not the mandate of this office to second-guess the rulings of a lower court," he said. "We are here only to see if a defendant's rights were infringed. In the case of *Azeb Yitades v. the State,* the appellate judges unanimously agree that her rights were violated when the district court censored potential witnesses." The chief judge raised his gavel to bring the excited courtroom to order. "There is more to this case, though," he continued. "There has been a wilful violation of the rules. The Codes and Procedures, which took decades to draft and introduce, were entirely ignored by the district court." Much cheering ensued. The judge didn't raise his gavel this time.

"Every good story has a villain and a hero. The hero (or heroine) in this case is Ms. Oona Harding. Like most people involved in this case, she saw the injustice done to her friend, but unlike the others, she set out to do something about it. It is an example that ought to be emulated on a much larger scale. It is unfortunate that Ms. Harding and the defendant should have spent almost two years of their young lives this way. The court can't do much about the personal sacrifices they have made. It is, however, within the mandate of this office to remedy past mistakes. The defendant is acquitted of all charges."

There was no longer any restraining the student mob; they poured inside, tearing the giant doors off their hinges. The ululates and cries of joy resonated across the seven seas. Flashbulbs went off. Strangers hugged each other. Azeb was lifted off her feet by excited young men and taken outside, where they would all view the symbol of their struggle under the bright sunlight.

"The future has arrived," the lady lawyer declared before flashing cameras. "There is no turning back to the arbitrary rules of the past."

Little did she know that what she had just witnessed was the tail end of a shooting star; that in less than a decade the entire legal system, modern or otherwise, would come undone at the seams, when the military junta that yanked the old monarch from power set out to rule the vast country with high-sounding decrees. A generation would come of age ignorant not only of the true meaning of the rule of law, but of the very existence of the written codes. Few would be able to imagine that a young murder suspect (and a female one at that) had once been represented in the nation's high court by a team of qualified lawyers, and was acquitted by an equally competent assembly of judges. Fables would be spawned surrounding the insufferable two-legged species called attorneys, whom the revolution would relegate to the swelling ranks of the dodo and the *Tyrannosaurus rex.*

The three judges and the lawyers involved in Azeb's case would all be hauled to concentration camp–like surroundings, ostensibly to receive ideological rehabilitation, but in effect to be exorcised of insidious American ideas. Following their crash indoctrination, they would be shipped to proliferating collective farms, where they would live and work beside other petits bourgeois, appreciating the privations of the peasants, who were the true champions of the revolution.

Following six months of hard labour—having weeded and ploughed lots under the watchful eyes of political cadres—the lucky ones would be assigned new jobs, mostly as enforcers of the revolutionary ideology. Many, however, would perish along the way. The lady lawyer would be executed by a firing squad on the trumped-up charge of spying for the enemy.

"She was labelled a CIA operative," a visiting aid worker told Oona in New York, where Oona was spending her long summer vacation at the United Nations, petitioning international aid agencies still operating in Ethiopia to help her locate Azeb and her own nephew, Sintayehu, Jeff's illegitimate boy. Sending a letter to the people she had left behind would have been more detrimental than constructive, since recipients of a piece of mail bearing a U.S. stamp would most likely have been labelled as traitors.

At the sad tidings of the lady lawyer's tragic end, Oona recalled the New Year of 1972, the carefree moment the two had spent together handing out pennies to gleeful children, and she broke down in tears.

"Your father was suspected of being the ringleader," the Dutch aid worker continued. "It is a good thing your family left the country early, because Mr. Harding is now believed to have been the regional recruiter for the CIA. Anyone associated with him, or for that matter with you, is labelled reactionary. Hardest hit are members of your father's parish, the Church of the Redeemer. Those few who survived the firing squad are now languishing in prisons, serving an open-ended sentence."

It was a story that was all too familiar in the restless continent.

23

A REDEEMING TOTEM

*B*arely had the priest's home seen so many august elders. They had come at the urging of Etiye Hiywet's soul-father, a saint of a man, as those who knew him would readily admit, who rarely involved himself in the affairs of others, much less became the champion of their cause. "Hiywet would have wanted me to do this favour for her," was his argument when he left his bed that breezy September morning to gather his peers and "bread companions" and head for the priest's home.

At the priest's doorstep, the intercessors formed a mournful cluster, declining, as tradition required, Werknesh's invitation to enter until the man of the house gave them some indication that he would entertain their plea.

"Please summon Aba Yitades for us," the soul-father requested. "We will enter only if he agrees to consider our petition."

"What is it you want, my brethren?" Aba Yitades queried, reluctantly emerging. The unusual presence of Etiye Hiywet's soul-father had given him a clue to the gist of their visit. He feigned ignorance all the same.

The soul-father answered at length. "We have come on behalf of your daughter Azeb, godchild of the late Hiywet, who, as this village knows all too well, had been under my spiritual tutelage for much of her adult life. The departed asked me from her grave to do this final favour for her."

"What is there to talk about?" Aba Yitades was proving more resolute than they had anticipated. "I thought I made myself clear on that issue." He hesitated a moment before adding, "Well, don't make me look an evil man, standing outside my door like this. Do come in. I may not promise to do your bidding, but grant you an audience I most certainly will."

And it was quite an audience.

The intercessors were still haggling with their host when the compound slowly began to fill. Among the curious crowd were a few new faces—journalists and gossipmongers who had arrived from yonder. There were also respectable members of St. George's parish who felt duty bound to make their voices heard, having realized at long last that Azeb had paid her dues and was therefore worthy of forgiveness. Oona and her family could be seen at the far end of the compound. Mr. and Mrs. Harding hadn't strayed this near the priest's domain, whether his residence or the church, since Beletu's funeral. Not a word had passed between the two and Aba Yitades since that fateful night, some seven years earlier, when a raging mob, feeling betrayed at the revelation of the Hardings' mission, set upon the newcomers.

The mediation appeared to be all but a lost cause when, close to midday, almost two full hours after they had entered the priest's house, one of the elders stormed angrily outside. A moment later he was back inside, carrying a billet of wood upon his shoulder, saying, in effect, "Before you say no once more, here, fashion my cross first." History was being made that day. Whispers whirled that the Holy *Tabot* would soon be fetched in a last-ditch effort to induce a positive outcome. (Only twice before was St. George's *Tabot* asked to intercede, and both times it had acted as a benign catalyst.) Finally, as the crowd outside held its collective breath, a cry of joy emanated from the conference chamber. The priest had relented.

"Hiywet can now rest in peace," the soul-father proudly announced before the gathering outside, "and Azeb will be with us in a day or two." Women ululated; the men clapped in unison. Carried away by the singing and dancing, Abebe the Bandit stood before the giddy crowd and promised to relay the good tidings to the land of the Mongols before the week was out. At the time, the land of the Mongols was believed to be a three-day journey by horse off the beaten trail.

Before the day concluded, the intercessors delivered yet another miracle.

"Aba Yitades," said Etiye Hiywet's soul-father as soon as he resumed his seat, "as we all know, none of this would have been possible without Oona's tireless effort and intervention. It is time we did right by her and mended fences with her family. The Hardings are no more a threat to us, to our faith or lifestyle, than the newly opened pub was." And thus mended was another broken fence.

Later that day, after a feast of *tella* and *arake,* Aba Yitades escorted the Hardings back home. While still reminiscing about the past two turbulent years, the trials and tribulations they had all experienced as a result of Azeb's unfortunate choice, Mr. Harding sagely noted, "ሳይደግስ አያጣላም።" Aba Yitades readily concurred. "Indeed," he said, "He doesn't close one door before opening another." Then, registering that Mr. Harding had been discoursing without his translator's aid, the priest spun around, wondering about the whereabouts of the cocky young man, who was nowhere in sight. And it finally dawned on him that Mr. Harding had crossed a pivotal threshold. For, whereas a common language brings people together, it is a shared dialect that cements a friendship, and Mr. Harding had spoken in a popular dialect.

Before turning the last corner, Aba Yitades had a difficult question to ask. "Mr. Harding," he began tentatively, massaging his greying beard, "you must have noticed how rapidly Genet's twins have grown up."

"That I have," said Mr. Harding. "It is true that time flies."

"I have been meaning to enrol them in our seminary school," Aba Yitades continued, "but, as you know, time is not on our side. I never thought I would live to see the day when modern education ruled the roost. But I have the boys' best interests at heart, so I have been thinking of—"

"Aba Yitades," Mr. Harding interrupted, "is this your way of asking me if we can accommodate your boys?"

"I suppose it is." The priest, embarrassed at having to beg for a favour, could feel blood rushing to his face.

"Well, why didn't you come right out and ask? We will always have openings for Genet's children. All you have to say is when."

"I suppose a thank you is in order," the priest grudgingly acknowledged. "Only one thing," he said, summoning his waning courage. "Their training should be confined to the academics only—none of the religious stuff."

"That goes without saying."

"WE WILL PHONE YOU at the finance officer's home and let you know when it is safe for you to come home," Mrs. Vivian Harding had told Azeb before leaving Harar. "In the meantime, sit tight and enjoy the company of your new friends."

Two nights later, Azeb packed her bag, against her host's advice and pleas, and headed for Gelemso. "I felt homesick," she would later say. The Memorial Hotel was her first stopover. Arriving at a siesta time, she didn't find any of the working girls. What awaited her was the sombre face of Fatima, the manager.

"Did you break out of jail?" she barked at the sight of her old nemesis.

"No, I have been released," Azeb replied coyly. "Acquitted, you know."

"Do they now release a confirmed murderer?"

"In my case, they did."

"Well, someone must have gone stark raving mad, unleashing upon the world a confirmed murderer. In any case, I won't have you anywhere near my establishment. Go away! Now! Or I will call the police and have you arrested for trespassing."

"Trespassing?" Azeb found herself dicing the word, as though it were an alien language. Trespassing! Since when has she become the proprietor of the establishment? Azeb asked herself. Or is there something I don't know, some sort of will Etiye Hiywet signed in her dotage, leaving her property to someone she wasn't related to in any shape or form?

No matter how well disposed Etiye Hiywet may have been towards the hotel manager, Azeb couldn't imagine her godmother leaving her property to someone who didn't share her faith. The church and the monastery were the obvious beneficiaries.

"Can I at least spend the night?" Azeb heard herself begging. "I have nowhere to go, you know."

"Okay, you can spend *one* night," Fatima relented, her eyes dancing with delight, feeling avenged at last now that the girl who had once ruffled her feathers by calling her American, if only unknowingly, was now crawling under her feet. "Only *one* night, you hear!"

"Yes, thank you."

"You can sleep in the kitchen, but not before the restaurant closes at ten o'clock. Also, I want you to do the dishes and wipe the floor before retiring. When I get up in the morning, I expect you to be gone," Fatima rattled on.

"Yes, thank you."

Upset and humiliated, Azeb retreated towards the remote corner of the compound, where she sought shelter under the eaves of a service room. Lost in a daydream, she found herself tugging at the talisman that dangled from her neck-cord. "Maybe," she said to herself, "my hard luck is written inside this pouch." She gave the worn stitch that held the leather case together a heavy yank, and a folded piece of sheepskin came tumbling down. Hands trembling, eyes darting from side to side looking for an accusing stare, she laid the document on her bent knees. With mounting excitement, she read through the lines again and again—four times altogether. Sweat crested on her eyebrows and upper lip. When she raised a clenched fist to wipe off the sweat, she noticed her knuckles had turned a ghostly white from the strain placed on them. She stretched her fingers and sat holding the piece of parchment tightly to her chest.

She opened the parchment once more and read its contents out loud:

> *Will and Testament:* I, Hiywet——, the sole child of Ato——and his adoring wife Weizero——, hereby make this will while in full possession of my faculties, in the presence of my soul-father, Aba——, and two witnesses, whose signatures are affixed below.
>
> Upon my death, my youngest godchild, Azeb Yitades, shall inherit the Memorial Hotel and my liquid assets in the state bank and the village *kub*. The remainder of my property is to be divided up into four equal parts, and one each shall go to my other two godchildren, my soul-father, and the church poor. In the unfortunate instance of the death of any of the aforementioned beneficiaries, the money goes towards the church poor.

Lost in a reverie, Azeb hadn't heard Fatima's footsteps or her persistent calls. "Have you turned deaf or what?" the manager demanded, tugging at Azeb's hair. "Don't test my patience or I will have you thrown out. Now, here is what I want you to do: take this bucket and box of detergent and scrub the latrine, and ..."

Azeb looked up at her, and smiled.

AFTERWORD

*A*s a boy, Emperor Menelik II wore a talisman much like those worn by the characters in this work (and, indeed, by the author). His leather pouch was thought to contain the *Scroll of Righteousness,* until he was captured by a rival king, Theodore. "Where is the treasure your late father left you?" King Theodore was believed to have said to his young captive, who answered, "All that I inherited from my father, what he told me to guard with my life, is what I have on my neck-cord." Opening up the pouch, Theodore found what he had been looking for: a treasure map. Nowadays, leather-enclosed talismans, like the neck-cords themselves, are largely confined to the countryside among the peasantry.

THIS BOOK DRAWS HEAVILY on existing beliefs and practices. As with many works of fiction rooted in reality, there has been some dramatization. The game of *Gena* as it is played by two of the protagonists in this narrative seems to be a form of bloodletting. Nothing could be further from the truth. Everyday soccer leaves more bruised ribs and bloody noses than either *Gena* or the game accompanying the Festival of Epiphany, *Guks.* It is true, however, that on the off chance that such mishaps do happen, there are rules in place, unwritten but no less binding, stating, "There is no compensation for life or limb lost, as a result of *Gena* gone wrong. Nor shall one contemplate vengeance."

The communal bonfire adorning the Christmas scene in this work is usually seen during the Feast of the Finding of the Cross. It is not, however, unusual to see *chibbo* during other festivities as well.

In one of the scenes, during the yearly Festival of Epiphany, a procession comes to a sudden and unscheduled halt because the Holy *Tabot,* resting on the head of one of the priests, "resists" moving. Although not a common occurrence, such an event has come to pass, and its effect is as dramatic as suggested in the narrative. In my own home, the incident was received with grave solemnity. In the days and weeks immediately after the Holy *Tabot* "resisted" moving, my mother became exceptionally pious. She remembered to say her daily prayers, added a few more fast diets to our menu, and skipped some more meals herself (observing extra days of *Gahad*); and she dutifully set aside alms for the troop of beggars who made their rounds each morning. Inevitably, the inspiration wore off in time and she reverted to her old ways, looking after her own family's daily needs.

In another scene, Aba Yitades, the vigilant shepherd, oversees group penitence in a specially erected tent. He doles out numbers of prostrations depending not only on the gravity of the sin but also on his personal feelings towards the individual. Parishioners who felt unduly targeted by the priest, it will be remembered, secretly assigned someone else to do the penance for them. In real life too, members of the upper crust were known to hand over their extra prostrations to the domestic help.

The outcast ethnic group flatteringly labelled Americans do roam the land, but not in the region where this work is set. The treatment meted out to them takes place in real life as well.

The drama played out in the district courthouse is familiar to many Ethiopians. And the prevalence of corruption among former public officials is no secret, though not to the degree depicted in this narrative.

ACKNOWLEDGMENTS

I would like to thank Jennifer Glossop, a freelance editor living in Toronto, for editing the early drafts of the manuscript. My thanks are also owed to editor Helen Reeves and publisher David Davidar at Penguin Canada for their editorial contributions. Freelance editor John Sweet has done a wonderful job of copy editing the text. I would also like to thank Eliza Marciniak, my production editor at Penguin, for her role in the creation of the book. As usual, my deepest gratitude is reserved for my literary agent, Jacqueline Kaiser of Westwood Creative Artists in Toronto.